"Classic Hoffman: a bewitching world of time and place (in this case, Coney Island and its boardwalk freak show in the early 1900s) suffused with magical moments, a mysterious disappearance and romance."

—Darcy Jacobs, *Family Circle*

"One thing's for sure. Alice Hoffman knows how to tell a story. . . . [She] gives us extraordinary things and extraordinary times. And more."

—Ed Siegel, The ARTery, WBUR

"Hoffman breathes fiery life into an enrapturing fairy tale and historical fiction mash-up. . . . Ravishing . . . Dramatic . . . Hoffman unveils both horror and magic in this transfixing tale of liberation and love in a metropolis of lies, yearning, and metamorphosis."

—*Booklist* (starred review)

"Mesmerizing . . . Hoffman evokes all the glory and grit of 1911 New York City in her tale of two young lovers."

—*Publishers Weekly*

— Praise for —

The MUSEUM of EXTRAORDINARY THINGS

"In *The Museum of Extraordinary Things*, Alice Hoffman mounts an arresting display: a New York City tale rich with literary inspiration, history, and urban legend. Readers often talk about being immersed in novels; this is a satisfying swim in tidal waters. Take the plunge."

—Gregory Maguire, author of *Wicked* and *Out of Oz*

"Alice Hoffman understands and delivers the ordinary and the extraordinary in this contemporary novel of the past. As always, her powerful, elegant prose embraces tremendous passion with constant, clear-eyed compassion."

— Amy Bloom, author of *Away*

"As always, Alice Hoffman amazes me with her ability to use words the way other master artists use watercolors, painting the dreamlike world of a girl who grows up in a hall of wonders only to learn that something as ordinary as love is the greatest marvel of all. Many novels these days are called 'stunning,' but this one truly is: part love story, part mystery, part history, and all beauty."

—Jodi Picoult, author of *The Storyteller* and *Lone Wolf*

THE MUSEUM

OF

EXTRAORDINARY

THINGS

A NOVEL

ALICE HOFFMAN

SCRIBNER

NEW YORK · LONDON · TORONTO · SYDNEY · NEW DELHI

Scribner
A Division of Simon & Schuster, Inc.
1230 Avenue of the Americas
New York, NY 10020

First Scribner trade paperback edition October 2014

SCRIBNER and design are registered trademarks of The Gale Group, Inc.,
used under license by Simon & Schuster, Inc., the publisher of this work.

For information about special discounts for bulk purchases,
please contact Simon & Schuster Special Sales at 1-866-506-1949 or
business@simonandschuster.com.

The Simon & Schuster Speakers Bureau can bring authors to your
live event. For more information or to book an event, contact the
Simon & Schuster Speakers Bureau at 1-866-248-3049 or
visit our website at www.simonspeakers.com.

Book design by Ellen R. Sasahara
Cover design by Emily Mahon
Cover photograph by Joyce Tenneson, www.tenneson.com

Manufactured in the United States of America

1   3   5   7   9   10   8   6   4   2

Library of Congress Control Number: 2013036572

ISBN 978-1-4516-9356-0
ISBN 978-1-4516-9357-7 (pbk)
ISBN 978-1-4516-9358-4 (ebook)

I have heard what the talkers were talking, the talk of the beginning and the end.
But I do not talk of the beginning or the end.

—Walt Whitman, *Song of Myself*

Contents

The Museum
of
Extraordinary
Things

ONE

THE WORLD

IN A GLOBE

****

Y OU WOULD THINK *it would be impossible to find anything new in the world, creatures no man has ever seen before, one-of-a-kind oddities in which nature has taken a backseat to the coursing pulse of the fantastical and the marvelous. I can tell you with certainty that such things exist, for beneath the water there are beasts as huge as elephants with hundreds of legs, and in the skies, rocks thrown alit from the heavens burn through the bright air and fall to earth. There are men with such odd characteristics they must hide their faces in order to pass through the streets unmolested, and women who have such peculiar features they live in rooms without mirrors. My father kept me away from such anomalies when I was young, though I lived above the exhibition that he owned in Coney Island, the Museum of Extraordinary Things. Our house was divided into two distinct sections; half we lived in, the other half housed the exhibitions. In this way, my father never had to leave what he loved best in the world. He had added on to the original house, built in 1862, the year the Coney Island and Brooklyn Railroad began the first horse-*

drawn carriage line to our city. My father created the large hall in which
to display the living wonders he employed, all of whom performed unusual
acts or were born with curious attributes that made others willing to pay
to see them.

⁓

My father was both a scientist and a magician, but he declared that it
was in literature wherein we discovered our truest natures. When I was
only a child he gave me the poet Whitman to read, along with the plays
of Shakespeare. In such great works I found enlightenment and came to
understand that everything God creates is a miracle, individually and
unto itself. A rose is the pinnacle of beauty, but no more so than the exhibits in my father's museum, each artfully arranged in a wash of formaldehyde inside a large glass container. The displays my father presented were
unique in all the world: the preserved body of a perfectly formed infant
without eyes, unborn monkey twins holding hands, a tiny snow-white
alligator with enormous jaws. I often sat upon the stairs and strained
to catch a glimpse of such marvels through the dark. I believed that each
remarkable creature had been touched by God's hand, and that anything
singular was an amazement to humankind, a hymn to our maker.

When I needed to go through the museum to the small wood-paneled
room where my father kept his library, so that he might read to me, he
would blindfold me so I wouldn't be shocked by the shelves of curiosities
that brought throngs of customers through the doors, especially in the summertime, when the beaches and the grander parks were filled with crowds
from Manhattan, who came by carriage and ferry, day-trip steamship
or streetcar. But the blindfold my father used was made of thin muslin,
and I could see through the fabric if I kept my eyes wide. There before me
were the many treasures my father had collected over the years: the hand
with eight fingers, the human skull with horns, the preserved remains of

a scarlet-colored long-legged bird called a spoonbill, rocks veined with luminous markings that glowed yellow in the dark, as if stars themselves had been trapped inside stone. I was fascinated by all that was strange: the jaw of an ancient elephant called a mastodon and the shoes of a giant found in the mountains of Switzerland. Though these exhibits made my skin prickle with fear, I felt at home among such things. Yet I knew that a life spent inside a museum is not a life like any other. Sometimes I had dreams in which the jars broke and the floor was awash with a murky green mixture of water and salt and formaldehyde. When I woke from such nightmares, the hem of my nightgown would be soaking wet. It made me wonder how far the waking world was from the world of dreams.

My mother died of influenza when I was only an infant, and although I never knew her, whenever I dreamed of terrible, monstrous creatures and awoke shivering and crying in my bed, I wished I had a mother who loved me. I always hoped my father would sing me to sleep, and treat me as if I were a treasure, as valued as the museum exhibits he often paid huge sums to buy, but he was too busy and preoccupied, and I understood his life's work was what mattered most. I was a dutiful daughter, at least until I reached a certain age. I was not allowed to play with other children, who would not have understood where I lived or how I'd been raised, nor could I go upon the streets of Brooklyn on my own, where there were men who were waiting to molest innocent girls like me.

Long ago what the Indians called Narrioch was a deserted land, used in winter for grazing cattle and horses and oxen. The Dutch referred to it as Konijn Eylandt, Rabbit Island, and had little interest in its sandy shores. Now there were those who said Coney Island had become a vile

place, much like Sodom, where people thought only of pleasure. Some communities, like Brighton Beach and Manhattan Beach, where the millionaires built their estates, had their own trains with paid conductors to keep out the riffraff. Trains for the masses left from the Brooklyn Bridge Terminal and took little more than half an hour to reach the beachfront communities. The subway was being built, to begin running beneath the East River in 1908, so that more and more throngs would be able to leave the brutal heat of Manhattan in the summertime. The island was a place of contradiction, stretching from the wicked areas where men were alternately entertained and cheated in houses of ill repute and saloons, to the iron pavilions and piers where the great John Philip Sousa had brought his orchestra to play beneath the stars in the year I was born. Coney Island was, above all else, a place of dreams, with amusements like no others, rides that defied the rules of gravity, concerts and games of chance, ballrooms with so many electric lights they glowed as if on fire. It was here that there had once been a hotel in the shape of an elephant, which proudly stood 162 feet high until it burned to the ground, here the world's first roller coaster, the Switchback Railway, gave birth to more and more elaborate and wilder rides.

The great parks were the Steeplechase and Luna Park, whose star attraction, the famous horse King, dove from a high platform into a pool of water. On Surf Avenue was the aptly named Dreamland, which was being built and would soon rise across the street, so that we could see its towers from our garden path. There were hundreds of other attractions along Surf Avenue, up to Ocean Parkway, so many entertainments I didn't know how people chose. For me the most beautiful constructions were the carousels, with their magical bejeweled carved animals, many created by Jewish craftsmen from the Ukraine. The El Dorado, which was being installed at the foot of Dreamland Park, was a true amazement, three-tiered and teeming with animals of every sort. My favorites were the tigers, so fierce their green eyes sparked with an inner light, and, of course, the horses with their manes flying out behind them, so real I imagined that if I were ever allowed onto one, I might ride away and never return.

Electricity was everywhere, snaking through Brooklyn, turning night into day. Its power was evident in a showing made by electrocuting a poor elephant named Topsy, who had turned on a cruel, abusive trainer. I was not yet ten when Edison planned to prove that his form of electricity was safe, while declaring that his rival, Westinghouse, had produced something that was a danger to the world. If Westinghouse's method could kill a pachyderm, what might it do to the common man? I happened to be there on that day, walking home from the market with our housekeeper, Maureen. There was a huge, feverish crowd gathered, all waiting to see the execution, though it was January and the chill was everywhere.

"Keep walking," Maureen said, not breaking her stride, pulling me along by my arm. She had on a wool coat and a green felt hat, her most prized possession, bought from a famed milliner on Twenty-third Street in Manhattan. She was clearly disgusted by the bloodthirsty atmosphere. "People will disappoint you with their cruelty every time."

I wasn't so sure Maureen was right, for there was compassion to be found among the crowd as well. I had spied a girl on a bench with her mother. She was staring at poor Topsy and crying. She appeared to be keeping a vigil, a soulful little angel with a fierce expression. I, myself, did not dare to show my fury or indulge in my true emotions. I wished I might have sat beside this other girl, and held her hand, and had her as my friend, but I was forced away from the dreadful scene. In truth, I never had a friend of my own age, though I longed for one.

All the same, I loved Brooklyn and the magic it contained. The city was my school, for although compulsory education laws had gone into effect in 1894, no one enforced them, and it was easy enough to escape public education. My father, for instance, sent a note to the local school board stating I was disabled, and this was accepted without requirement of any further proof. Coney Island then was my classroom, and it was a wondrous one. The parks were made of papier-mâché, steel, and electricity, and their glow could be seen for miles, as though our city was a fairyland. Another girl in my constrained circumstances might have made a ladder out of strips torn from a quilt, or formed a rope fashioned of her own braided hair so she might let herself out the window and experience the enchantment of the shore. But whenever I had such disobedient thoughts, I would close my eyes and tell myself I was ungrateful. I was convinced that my mother, were she still alive, would be disappointed in me if I failed to do as I was told.

❧

My father's museum employed a dozen or more living players during the season. Each summer the acts of wonder performed in the exhibition hall several times a day, in the afternoon and in the evenings, each displaying his or her own rare qualities. I was not allowed to speak to them, though I longed to hear the stories of their lives and learn how they came to be in Brooklyn. I was too young, my father said. Children under the age of ten were not allowed inside the museum, owing to their impressionable natures. My father included me in this delicate group. If one of the wonders was to pass I was to lower my eyes, count to fifty, and pretend that person didn't exist. They came and went over the years, some returning for more seasons, others vanishing without a word. I never got to know the Siamese twins who were mirror images of each other, their complexions veined with pallor, or the man with a pointed head, who drowsed between his performances, or the woman who grew her hair so long she could step on it. They all left before I could speak my first words. My memories were of glances, for such people were never gruesome to me, they were unique and fascinating, and terribly brave in the ways they revealed their most secret selves.

Despite my father's rules, as I grew older I would peer down from my window in the early mornings, when the employees arrived in the summer light, many wearing cloaks despite the mild weather, to ensure they would not be gawked at, perhaps even beaten, on their way to their employment. My father called them wonders, but to the world they were freaks. They hid their features so that there would be no stones flung, no sheriff's men called in, no children crying out in terror and surprise. In the streets of New York they were considered abominations, and because there were no laws to protect them, they were often ill used. I hoped that on our porch, beneath the shade of the pear tree, they would find some peace.

My father had come to this country from France. He called himself Professor Sardie, though that was not in fact his name. When I asked what his given name had been, he said it was nobody's business. We all have secrets, he'd told me often enough, nodding at my gloved hands.

I believed my father to be a wise and brilliant man, as I believed Brooklyn to be a place not unlike heaven, where miracles were wrought. The Professor had principles that others might easily call strange, his own personal philosophy of health and well-being. He had been pulled away from magic by science, which he considered far more wondrous than card tricks and sleight of hand. This was why he had become a collector of the rare and unusual, and why he so strictly oversaw the personal details of our lives. Fish was a part of our daily nourishment, for my father believed that we took on the attributes of our diet, and he made certain I ate a meal of fish every day so my constitution might echo the abilities of these creatures. We bathed in ice water, good for the skin and inner organs. My father had a breathing tube constructed so that I could remain soaking underwater in the claw-foot tub, and soon my baths lasted an hour or more. I had only to take a puff of air in order to remain beneath the surface. I felt comfortable in this element, a sort of girlfish, and soon I didn't feel the cold as others did, becoming more and more accustomed to temperatures that would chill others to the bone.

In the summer my father and I swam in the sea together each night, braving the waves until November, when the tides became too frigid. Several times we nearly reached Dead Horse Bay, more than five miles away, a far journey for even the most experienced swimmer. We continued an exercise routine all through the winter so that we might increase our breathing capacity, sprinting along the shore. "Superior health calls for superior action," my father assured me. He believed running would maintain our health and vigor when it was too cold to swim. We trotted along the shore in the evenings, our skins shimmering with sweat, ignoring people in hats and overcoats who laughed at us and shouted out the same half-baked joke over and over again: What are you running from? You, my father would mutter. Fools not worth listening to, he told me.

Sometimes it would snow, but we would run despite the weather, for our regimen was strict. All the same, on snowy nights I would lag behind so I might appreciate the beauty of the beach. I would reach into the snow-dotted water. The frozen shore made me think of diamonds. I was enchanted by these evenings. The ebb and flow at the shore was bone white, asparkle. My breath came out in a fog and rose into the milky sky. Snow fell on my eyelashes, and all of Brooklyn turned white, a world in a globe. Every snowflake that I caught was a miracle unlike any other.

I had long black hair that I wore braided, and I possessed a serious and quiet demeanor. I understood my place in the world and was grateful to be in Brooklyn, my home and the city that Whitman himself had loved so well. I was well spoken and looked older than my age. Because of my serious nature, few would guess I was not yet ten. My father preferred that I wear black, even in the summertime. He told me that in the village in France where he'd grown up, all the girls did so. I suppose my mother, long gone, had dressed in this fashion as a young girl, when my father had first fallen in love with her. Perhaps he was reminded of her when I donned a black dress that resembled the one she wore. I was nothing like my mother, however. I'd been told she was a great beauty, with pale honey-colored hair and a calm disposition. I was dark and plain. When I looked at the ugly twisted cactus my father kept in our parlor, I thought I more likely resembled this plant, with its gray ropy stems. My father swore it bloomed once a year with one glorious blossom, but I was always asleep on those occasions, and I didn't quite believe him.

Although I was shy, I did have a curious side, even though I had been told a dozen times over that curiosity could be a girl's ruination. I wondered if I had inherited this single trait from my mother. Our housekeeper, Maureen Higgins, who had all but raised me, had warned me often enough that I should keep my thoughts simple and not ask too many questions or allow my mind to wander. And yet Maureen herself had a dreamy look when she instructed me, which led me to presume that she didn't follow her own dictates. When Maureen began to allow me to run errands and help with the shopping, I meandered through Brooklyn, as far as Brighton Beach, little over a mile away. I liked to sit by the docks and listen to the fishermen, despite the rough language they used, for they spoke of their travels across the world when I had never even been as far as Manhattan, though it was easy enough to walk across the Brooklyn Bridge or the newer, gleaming Williamsburg Bridge.

Though I had an inquisitive soul, I was always obedient when it came to the Professor's rules. My father insisted I wear white cotton gloves in the summer and a creamy kid leather pair when the chill set in. I tolerated this rule and did as I was told, even though the gloves felt scratchy on summer days and in winter chafed and left red marks on my skin. My hands had suffered a deformity at birth, and I understood that my father did not wish me to be thought of with the disdain that greeted the living wonders he employed.

Our housekeeper was my only connection to the outside world. An Irish woman of no more than thirty, Maureen had once had a boyfriend who had burned her face with sulfuric acid in a fit of jealous rage. I didn't care that she was marked by scars. Maureen had seen to my upbringing ever since I was an infant. She'd been my only company, and I adored her, even though I knew my father thought her to be uneducated and not worth speaking to about issues of the mind. He preferred her to wear a gray dress and a white apron, a proper maid's uniform. My father paid Maureen's rent in a rooming house near the docks, a cheap and unpleasant place, she always said, that was not for the likes of me. I never knew where she went after washing up our dinner plates, for she was quick to reach for her coat and slip out the door, and I hadn't the courage to run after her.

Maureen was smart and able, despite my father's opinion, and she often treated me as an equal. I liked to sit on the back steps beside her as we took our lunch together. She fixed lettuce and butter sandwiches to share with me. I thought she was quite beautiful, despite her scars.

She was the one person other than my father who knew of my deformity, and she concocted a mixture of aloe and mint to rub between my fingers. I was grateful for both her kindness and her matter-of-fact air. "It fixes most things," she said knowingly of the salve. "Except for my face."

Unfortunately, the elixir did nothing for me either, yet I grew accustomed to its scent and used it nightly. Maureen smoked cigarettes in the backyard although my father had expressly forbidden her to do so. Only whores had such habits, he said, and besides, he had a tremendous dread of fire, for a single spark could ignite the entire museum and we would lose everything. He stood on the roof with buckets of water during summer storms, keeping a close watch on the movement of the lightning when it split through the sky. His collection was irreplaceable. In the off months, when the museum was shuttered, he covered the glass cases with white linen, as if putting the mummified creatures on display to bed for a long winter's rest. He was surprisingly gentle at these times. "I'll sneak you into the exhibits if you want," Maureen offered every now and then, though she was well aware that children under the age of ten were banned from entrance.

"I think I'll wait," I remarked when Maureen suggested I break my father's rules and enter the museum. I was not the rebel I later came to be. I was nine and three quarters at the time and hadn't much longer to wait before I was old enough to gain entrance to the museum. I wore my black dress and buttoned leather boots. My black stockings were made of wool, but I never complained when they itched. If anyone had asked what was the first word I would use to describe myself, I would have immediately answered well behaved. But of course, few people know their true natures at such a tender age.

"Waiters wait and doers don't." Maureen's skin was mottled as if she were half in shadow, half in sunlight. At certain hours of the day, noon, for instance, when the sun broke through, she looked illuminated, as if the beauty inside her was rising up through her ravaged complexion. She gazed at me with sympathy. "Afraid your daddy will make you pay if you misbehave?"

I was, of course. I'd seen my father enraged when a player came to work late or broke one of his rules, smoking cigars in public, for instance, or forming a romantic entanglement with a member of the audience.

He'd taken his cane to a fellow from England who called himself the King of the Ducks, for this gentleman had flesh in the shape of wings instead of arms. My father told the King never to return, all because he suspected him of sipping from a flask of whiskey during museum hours. It was unfair, of course, considering how much my father liked his rum.

I didn't need to explain my hesitation to our housekeeper.

"I don't blame you." Maureen sighed. Her breath smelled like mint and rosemary, her favorite kitchen seasonings. "He'd probably have you running up and down the beach for a whole night without a bit of rest to punish you. You'd be limping at the end of it, panting for water, and he might not forgive you even then. He's a serious man, and serious men have serious rules. If you defy them, there will be consequences."

"Was your boyfriend serious?" I dared to ask. It was a topic Maureen usually did not speak of.

"Hell, yes," she said.

I loved the way she used the word hell; *it came naturally to her, the way it did to the men who worked on the docks loading herring and blue-fish.*

"What was his name?"

"Son of shit," Maureen said evenly.

She always made me laugh.

"Son of a dog's mother," she went on, and I laughed again, which egged her on. "Son of Satan." I loved it when she grinned. "Son of hell."

We both stopped laughing then. I understood what she meant. He'd been a bad man. I'd seen such men on Surf Avenue and along the pier. Con artists and thieves, the sort a girl learned to stay away from early on. Coney Island was full of them, and everyone knew the police often looked the other way when paid off by these crooks. A fiver would get you pretty much anything you wanted on the streets of Brooklyn, and there were girls my age who were bought and sold for much less. Some bad fellows looked friendly, others looked like demons. Maureen always told me you couldn't judge a book by its cover, but if anyone should ever call me into an alleyway, I was to run, no matter what gifts I might be offered. If the need arose, I could kick a fellow in his knees or in his private parts, and that would most likely force such an individual to keep his distance.

"You know what love is?" Maureen said to me that day. Usually she went about her work and was somewhat tight-lipped regarding the larger issues of life. Now she became more open than usual, perhaps more like the person she'd been before she'd been scarred.

I swung my legs and shrugged. I didn't know if I was old enough to discuss such matters. Maureen tenderly ran a hand through my long hair as she dropped her hard veneer.

"It's what you least expect."

WHEN I TURNED ten my father called me to him. My birthday was in March, and I never knew what to expect from that month. Sometimes it snowed on my birthday, other times there'd be the green haze of spring. I don't remember the weather on this particular occasion, during the year of 1903. I was too excited at having my father focus on me, a circumstance that was rare due to the hold his work had over him. Sometimes he labored in the cellar all night long and didn't get to his bed until dawn. And so it was a special event for him to turn his attentions to me. When I approached him shyly, he told me that in good time every secret must be shared and every miracle called into question. He made a grand event of my entrance into the museum. We went onto the path outside so we might go through the front door, as customers did. My father wore a black coat with tails, very formal, and a top hat he'd brought from France. He had sharp all-seeing blue eyes and white hair and he spoke with an accent. He had set globes of electric lights outside the entranceway to the museum.

Sphinx moths floated near, drawn to the bright flares, and I ignored an urge to catch one in my cupped hands. I was wearing my black dress and a strand of pearls my mother had left me. I treasured them, but now my father told me to remove the necklace. He said I should leave off my gloves as well, which surprised me. I didn't like to look at my hands.

It was midnight, an hour when the neighborhood was quiet, as it was the off-season. In the summers there were crowds all night long, and great waves of excitement and noise in the air. But those hordes of pleasure seekers would not arrive until the end of May and would continue on until the new Mardi Gras celebration to be held in September, a wild gathering that would become a yearly event where those celebrating lost all control, and the police Strong-arm Squad would have to be called out to beat them back to their senses. The construction in Dreamland was going ahead full steam as the owners built more and more rides and exhibitions that would rival any entertainment palace in the world and be even more impressive than Luna Park. Unlike the other amusement parks, which some of the wealthier residents of the island called vulgar and pandering, this one would be as splendid as any entertainment found in the capitals of Europe, the buildings all starkly white, as if made for the angels. Because it would be west of us on Surf Avenue, my father feared it would put us out of business. At night we could hear the roaring of the lions and tigers in their cages, attractions being trained to be more like dogs or house cats than wild beasts. In this quiet time of the year, seagulls and terns gathered at twilight in huge calling flocks above the park. The steel skeletons of the rides still being constructed were silver in the dark. I imagined they shivered in anticipation of all they would become.

My father opened the curtains made of heavy plum-colored damask that hung across the entranceway to the Museum of Extraordinary Things.

He said I was the evening's only guest, then bowed and gestured for me to step over the threshold. I went inside for the first time. Though I had managed to spy a few rows of the exhibits from occasionally sneaking a look, the contents of most had been a bit cloudy from my vantage point and I could never distinguish a green viper from a poisonous tree frog. Tonight the glass jars glittered. There was the sweet scent of camphor. I had looked forward to this day for so long, but now I was faint with nerves and could hardly take it all in.

There was a hired man who often came to care for the living beasts. I'd observed him arriving in a horse-drawn hansom carriage delivering crates of food for the mysterious inhabitants of the museum. A whirl of incredible creatures was before me as I stood there: a dragon lizard who flared his scarlet throat, an enormous tortoise who seemed like a monster of the deep, red-throated hummingbirds that were let out of their cages on leashes made of string. When I looked past this dizzying array, I spied my father's birthday surprise decorated with blue silk ribbons and garlands of paper stars. It stood in a place of honor: a large tank of water. On the bottom there were shells gathered from all over the world, from the Indian Ocean to the China Sea. I did not need my father to tell me what would be displayed, for there was the sign he'd commissioned an expert craftsman to fashion out of chestnut wood and hand-paint in gold leaf.

THE HUMAN MERMAID

Beneath that title was carved one word alone, my name, Coralie.

I did not need further instructions. I understood that all of my life had been mere practice for this very moment. Without being asked, I slipped off my shoes.

I knew how to swim.

MARCH 1911

IF CORALIE SARDIE had lived another life, in another time and place, she might have become a champion swimmer, a lauded athlete with garlands crowning her head, surrounded by crowds who pleaded for her autograph after she crossed the Channel from England to France or circled Manhattan Island. Instead, she swam in the Hudson as dusk crossed the horizon, making certain to keep to the shadows. If she were a fish, she would have been an eel, a dark flash secreted within the even darker water, a lone creature set on a journey northward, unable to stop or rest until her destination had been reached. On this raw night, she stepped out of the river when she could swim no more, shaking from exertion. The relay swimming title had just been granted to a fellow from the New York Athletic Club who'd been dubbed the Human Fish, but Coralie could have beat his time with ease. She climbed onto a deserted bank under a sky swirling with stars and stood ankle deep in the mud. She wrung out her hair, a smile playing at her blue lips. This had been her longest swim thus far. She'd lasted ninety minutes in the frigid river, a personal record. A wind had picked up and the weather was raw; few swimmers would have been able to tolerate the cold rushing water. All the same, Coralie was no champion; she had no clock and no admirers. She wore men's clothes, which made her movements easier, fitted trousers and a white shirt tucked into her waistband. Before dressing she coated her limbs with bear grease mixed with digitalis, a concoction meant to act as a stimulant and keep her warm. Still, despite this elixir and her training to withstand inhuman circumstances, she shuddered with the cold.

As she forged her way through a tangle of reeds, Coralie realized the rising spring tide had carried her off course. She was much farther north than she'd anticipated and had arrived in the no-man's-land of upper Manhattan, where the Dutch had once farmed enormous tracts in the wetlands. Not far to the east, there were still small villages along the Harlem River, inhabited by communities of black Americans and Irish immigrants who had settled on that river's sandy coves, their houses hidden from view by enormous beech and tulip trees that were more than three hundred years old.

Unlike most rivers, the current in the Hudson ran in two directions, pushed north by the Atlantic Ocean, turning into rivulets and streams and meeting with the Harlem River before the combined waterways receded south to the harbor. After a winter of heavy squalls and snowfalls, the Hudson was moving much faster than expected. Coralie's father's calculations had therefore proved wrong. The Professor was waiting nearly three miles to the south, alongside the liveryman and his carriage, ready to greet Coralie with a wool blanket and the flask of whiskey he vowed would keep her from catching a chill in her lungs.

After eight years of performances, Coralie's fame had waned. The public's hunger was for curiosities that had never been seen before, not for creatures they'd become accustomed to. Barnum and Bailey's circus was opening in Madison Square Garden. It was the same location where Barnum had first exhibited his spectacles when the area was occupied by the Great Roman Hippodrome, an arena without a roof or heat. People were entranced by the prancing steeds, the spectacle and wonder of acrobats and trained seals, the thundering Roman chariot race that drove dust into the air. Barnum had begun his career with a museum in lower Manhattan, showing off taxidermy and fossils, along with questionable exhibits such as the Feejee Mermaid, a monkey's torso with a fish tail attached. It was that swindler Barnum whom Professor Sardie wished to surpass, for he felt himself to be a true man of science, whereas Barnum was nothing more than a charlatan. Yet Barnum was an American hero, and the Professor's fortunes were failing.

Coralie had been a star attraction as a child in Coney Island, but she was a child no more. The tail she wore was made of thin strips of bamboo that were flexible, covered by silk that had been treated with paraffin and copper sulfate so they would be waterproof. The breathing tube attached to the side of the tank could not be seen by onlookers. When she turned to flash her blue tail, she gulped in air from the tube. Her father suspected that the crowds had caught on to their tricks and asked that she use the tube as infrequently as possible. Her childhood training of remaining underwater in a tub had increased her breathing capacity far beyond the abilities of a normal woman. Sometimes she felt she barely needed air. At night she slipped into the tub in the washroom for comfort, settling beneath the warm, soapy water, a balm to her cold flesh and pale hands, which were dipped into blue dye every morning.

Between her fingers there was a birth defect, a thin webbing that the indigo tint emphasized. This was the reason she wore gloves in public, though her abnormality rarely hindered her in practical matters. Still, she despised herself because of this single flaw. She had often imagined taking a pair of scissors to her flesh so she might snip through the pale skin. The one time she'd attempted to rid herself of the webbing with a sharp knife used for coring apples, beads of blood began to fall onto her lap after she nicked the first bit of skin. Each drop was so brightly crimson, she had startled and quickly dropped the knife.

Even when the crowds faded, there were still a handful of faithful admirers who continued to gather beside Coralie's tank, men whose sexual interest was evident in every fevered glance. No man had ever possessed her, although several had offered the Professor extravagant sums in exchange for her virginity, one going so far as to include a proposal of marriage. All advances were denied with an edge of fury from her father. Coralie was certain these same suitors would have not even glanced at her in her daily life, when she was nothing more than her father's pale, ungainly daughter dressed in black, stopping at the market stalls on Neptune Avenue to choose turnips and spinach and fish. The men who were her greatest admirers were looking for the depraved and wicked thrill of possessing a freak of nature. They would be shocked to discover how ordinary she was, for her greatest pleasure was to read one of the novels she found in her father's library, or to sit with Maureen on the back steps to plan a spring garden. She was no man's dark dream, only a girl forced to swim half-clothed.

This past January, when Coney Island had been dotted with snow and the waves in the murky Atlantic had kept even the most experienced fishermen at home, Coralie had entered the museum to discover that her tank was no longer in the center of the exhibition hall. It had been lifted onto rollers by the liveryman and hauled to a corner, then covered with a tarp. Coralie had always imagined she would be grateful to be released from her obligations, but suddenly she was nothing, not even a fictitious mermaid. Who was she then? A quiet girl no one noticed, invisible to most men's eyes. She realized that she had formed an attachment to her false persona, for a mermaid was a one-of-a-kind creature that commanded attention, whereas she was nothing of any worth.

Her father, however, was a man of the future. He had no difficulty moving on. He was quick to dismiss employees who no longer drew a crowd; tears and pleading were insufficient once a curiosity was of no further interest to the paying public. Many of the living wonders Coralie had known since childhood had been let go as soon as their popularity began to diminish, never to be spoken of again. The woman covered by bees had refused to change her act to include wasps, for their stings could be deadly. After a heated conversation with the Professor, she was forced to go. Her employer would not even allow her the time to collect her hive of bees, which were left in the garden in a wooden box. Later in the season, when Coralie tried to set them free, it did no good. The bees huddled together in the only home they had known, where they sickened as the weather grew raw, and soon enough died.

There were other wonders who disappeared without a good-bye. The crowds quickly tired of the goat boy with hooves instead of feet and the bird woman who dressed all in feathers and could whistle any song, from an oriole's trill to a magpie's fierce cry. The tiny lady who could fit into a set of child's clothes, Marie de Montague, alternately drank from a baby's bottle (filled not with milk but with weak Red Rose Ceylon tea laced with gin) and smoked a cigar. But she was soon viewed as old hat, for there were wonders many inches smaller than she. In the end she was employed by a second-rate theater on Neptune Avenue, where the raucous crowd called out insulting names, tossing pennies at her as they urged her to show her small bottom or breasts, which she was known to do on wicked nights when there were no ladies in attendance.

If Coralie had been anyone else, a hired act like any other, she would have already been turned out of her father's house. She wondered if she might have preferred a life as a housemaid or as a clerk in a nearby shop, but her father drew her close and told her he would never let her go.

"What we do not have, we will create," he assured her.

He had already fashioned his clever plan. The new creature might be an alligator or a snake, or some strange combination of the two, wrought by thread and nails and ingenuity, a being far superior to Barnum's Feejee Mermaid. There was a workshop in the cellar, a space Coralie had never been allowed to enter, not even after she'd passed the age of ten. Two locks bolted upon the door, one made of iron, the other of brass. The keys were kept on the Professor's watch chain.

"Our creature will be whatever people imagine it to be," he'd confided to Coralie. "For what men believe in, they will pay to see."

The Professor brought her with him in his search. He often struck a more satisfying deal when he presented himself as a family man. He had a scant few weeks before the season began in which to find a wonder that would satisfy not only his customers but also the press. They went first to the docks in Red Hook, but there were no giant squids or whales as large as leviathans, no albino sea lions or jellyfish of enormous proportions. On the far west side of Manhattan they went to the meat markets, where the cobbled streets ran with blood from the many slaughterhouses nearby. Among the carnage there might be skulls and bones that could be sewn to the pelts of living creatures. While the Professor went through the markets, the liveryman stayed to guard their cart, for a ragtag gang of men scrutinized the rig. They eyed Coralie, calling out rude remarks. She often carried a knife in the pocket of her dress when she was out in public, and was glad to have it in her grasp now. It was the same knife she had used to draw blood when she cut through the webbing on her hands.

The street was desolate, and the gang edged closer. Coralie felt her heart grow heavy, but, as it turned out, the liveryman chased off the mob with a few well-aimed rocks. He was a burly, silent man who had spent hard time in Sing Sing for crimes he wouldn't disclose. After the mob dispersed, he came to check on Coralie. She said she'd like some air and leapt from the carriage so that she might stand beside him, though she knew her father would have disapproved of her doing so. The soles of her boots were soon dyed red with butchers' blood, which ran between the paving stones.

"I'd never eat a living creature," the carriage man said, surprising Coralie with his ease of conversation, for he'd never spoken to her before this day. "They've got as much soul as we do. More if the truth be told." A sparrow perched above them in a leafless plane tree and sang boldly. "See there." The hired man pointed with his thumb. "That's heart and soul."

When the Professor returned empty-handed they continued on to the morgue at Bellevue, a dim and wretched place that the liveryman referred to as the bone house when he was instructed to set off in the hospital's direction. To gain entrance, Sardie would state that they were looking for his poor daughter's beloved mother, who had disappeared. They had done so before, much to Coralie's shame. If they were at first turned away, Coralie would weep and appear distraught; the guards would then pity her and allow them to view the unclaimed dead. This time, however, as they walked up the granite steps, Coralie found she could not cry. She had begun to fear they would be punished for their conniving ways if indeed God saw and knew all of mankind's deeds. Perhaps there was a hell below this earth, and they would burn in it for all the lies they'd told.

The Professor took Coralie aside when he saw her difficulty. "If you cannot cry, then I can see to it that you're able," he said. He caught her arm and squeezed it affectionately. "Not that I would ever have cause to do so."

Coralie then understood what she must do. She pinched her own arm, hard, bringing bright tears to her eyes.

Once allowed in, they searched the morgue, though the smell was overpowering, and the contents horrifying. The Professor gave Coralie his linen handkerchief to place over her nose and mouth. There were several women laid upon the marble slabs, one so covered with blue-tinged bruises Coralie quickly turned from the sight. Another section was filled with children, unclaimed and unknown, their still, pale forms veined with cold, but, like ice, they appeared to be melting, their features pulled into expressions of sorrow. "None of these will do," her father muttered. Back in the street, Coralie felt faint. She no longer thought she would have to pinch herself if she were again commanded to cry today.

They went on to an area called Frenchtown, where women and children were sold by the hour for sexual use and pleasure. There were evenings when only clients in formal evening clothes were allowed in and the whores were trained to speak with men of the upper classes and wore the most elegant and revealing gowns. Some of the houses were fitted with velvet couches and beds covered with silk duvets; others were filthy, dimly lit, tragic storehouses of sorrow and flesh. Within such places, some of those on sale were considered more desirable if they possessed abnormalities, exactly what the Professor wished to find. Coralie waited in the carriage while her father visited two of these wretched houses, one where boys were clothed in dresses, wearing rouge and color on their lips, the other a grim tenement filled with girls dolled up in oversized gowns, costumes that only served to show how very young they were. Neither house was the least bit interesting to the Professor, and he left both quickly enough. But at the second house he was followed by a heavyset man who had with him a child no older than six. The man did his best to get the Professor's attention as he toted the girl in a rope sling, for she had neither arms nor legs.

"Here's what you're looking for," the man shouted. "She'll be to your liking. You can have her for a fair price."

The child had begun to wail, but one smack from her caretaker and she hushed quickly enough. She appeared too stunned to cry any more. The Professor shook his head and stalked away. Still, the brutal man called after him. "You said you wanted a monster. She's right here! Look no further."

"What will happen to the child?" Coralie asked after they had climbed into the carriage, escaping the stranger's escalating rage.

"Go on," the Professor told the liveryman.

Coralie cast a swift backward glance to watch the child dragged away to what was surely a dreadful fate. The Society for the Prevention of Cruelty to Children had tried to stop children from being allowed to beg, or solicit alms, or be in shows of acrobatics or be included in any immoral or indecent exhibition, especially those presenting an unnatural physical formation. But, in truth, such laws were rarely enforced. Children were not recognized as having rights.

"It's not our business," the Professor remarked, sure of himself. "We are here on behalf of science."

"Perhaps it should be," Coralie protested. "I could take care of her. It would be no trouble." The tears that had refused to fall before came freely to her now, though she was quick to wipe them away.

"If you tried to right all the wrongs in the world you'd exhaust yourself in under an hour. This is God's business."

"Is it?" Coralie wondered aloud. "Is it not our business to help in God's work?"

"Our business is to acquire a creature that will draw a crowd, and thereby pay for food and coal and the shoes upon your feet."

When Coralie strained to see behind them now, the street was empty. The man and his charge had vanished, engulfed by the darkness. It seemed as though they had left God's sight in this part of the city where human beings were bought and sold as if they were sheep ready for market. "It should be against the law for men to be so cruel," Coralie pronounced.

"That man is her father." The Professor turned to his daughter, so that he would not be misunderstood. "And to all the world, he's well within his rights."

The Professor had already set in motion his plan for their renewed success. In the first months of 1911 a rumor had begun, one that had been formed inside the Professor's mind. A monster had settled in the Hudson River, and if a man stood on the banks he might spy it swimming in the dark. Or perhaps it could be sighted at the first light of daybreak, when the water was silver and still. The first to take up the story were two boys fishing for their families' suppers. They vowed a strange river creature had stolen the catch from their lines; when questioned by the police, each swore it wasn't a shark, which were abundant in New York Harbor, some reaching fourteen feet long. True, they'd seen a flash of scales set upon the creature's spine, but it was something entirely different, a being that was dark and unfathomable, almost human in its countenance, with fleet, watery movements. A panic went up. Constables in rowboats patrolled the shores, from the docks downtown all the way up to the Bronx. Several men on the ferries on the four lines which ran from Twenty-third Street to New Jersey leapt into the frigid depths as if they could walk on water, insisting they had heard a woman's voice call to them, convinced someone had been drowning.

Coralie was the monster that had been sighted from the shoreline, the mysterious creature men wished to either rescue or trap. All she had done was show a glimpse of what might be possible, a water-logged and furtive river-fiend that had drifted out of nightmares and into the waterways of the city of New York. Seventeen sightings had been recorded in the papers. Each one corresponded to a time when Coralie swam farther north in the cold, gray river, drifting among the eels, just now arising from the sediment after a winter's sleep, and keeping pace alongside the striped bass that spawned upriver, certain of herself even in uncertain tides. In the mornings she would sit in a pool of sunlight on the back porch so she might read about herself in the *Sun* or the *Times,* a huge beast with teeth not unlike a shark's and green scales, who was in reality nothing more than a hundred-and-twenty-pound girl who favored simple black dresses and leather-buttoned shoes and was never seen without her gloves.

Coralie knew her father was in desperate need of an exhibit that would compete with Dreamland and Luna Park and the other grand amusements in Coney Island. Two years earlier the famous Sigmund Freud had come to Brooklyn, to try to understand the American point of view; among the few things that were said to have impressed him were the magnificent amusement parks. Imagination was all in Brooklyn, and this was what Sardie had to sell; it was his gift, one he thanked his maker for each and every day. He always insisted that his establishment was not a freak show, like the well-known Huber's Dime Museum on Fourteenth Street in Manhattan, which had been a purveyor of the strange and unique for many years until *finis* was posted on its door in 1910, or the dozens of dreadful little entertainments that lined lower Surf Avenue, exhibitions that debased and degraded their human skeletons and amputees, their conjoined twins and the men who allowed fleas to suck the blood from their bodies, along with the wrestling rings and vaudeville halls, the worst and most exploitive of them having moved northward, to an area known as the Gut. The Museum of Extraordinary Things was a true museum, a place of edification, wherein natural curiosities were displayed along with human marvels. Now, however, they needed more, and, when more could not be found, it must be invented. If there was anyone who might be able to succeed in such an act of trickery, it was the Professor, who had been a magician in France, quite famous in his time, known for acts of wonder so astounding they had made people doubt their own eyes. He understood that not only could a man's eyes mislead him but his mind could deceive him as well.

Coralie followed her father's instructions, as she had all her life, though her heart sank at the nature of her obligation, a trick to be played upon all of New York. The headlines called her the Hudson Mystery, for no one had managed to spy her features. Two fellows in a canoe had caught sight of her tonight as she'd raced past so these witnesses wouldn't be able to make out her womanly form. Instead they saw only what they imagined, exactly as the Professor had predicted, and men's imaginings were dark in these dark times. It was a season of great and terrible clashes in the streets, of bosses and politicians and police pitting themselves against working men and women. Debates became free-for-alls, with arrests of workers wanting nothing more than their fair share. The gap between the immigrant populations relegated to the overcrowded tenements of the Lower East Side and those who lived in brownstone mansions surrounding Madison Park had created a tinderbox of hatred.

And yet despite the news of labor troubles—strikes of ship workers on the docks of Brooklyn and garment workers in Manhattan gathering in near riots—there was always a story in the *Sun* and in the *Times* on the day following a swim, for the Hudson Mystery had caught their readers' attention. The creature of the deep had become a riddle discussed on street corners and in shops. In the morning, the eighteenth news story would appear, a fortuitous number, as it was Coralie's age, her birthday having been celebrated two days earlier with a ginger-apple cake Maureen had baked, rich with sugar icing and dotted with candles that sparked when Coralie tried to blow them out.

Once she'd left the river, Coralie walked through the newly unfolding swamp cabbages and fiddlehead ferns that grew in wild profusion in the boggy woods. Freedom was a treasure, even for a scant few hours. The chance to become a heedless wraith wandering through the chill landscape was a gift. No one could command her here. She might easily be a water nymph who had clambered onto the shore of a new and tender land. The world looked aglow, as if a door had opened and there, on the other side, was a vivid haze. She imagined it was the future that awaited, the unexpected life she might lay claim to if she never again returned home. Shadows threaded through the locust trees. The night's dark color washed over the landscape in a mist of blue. She removed the mask she wore to make her seem inhuman, one fashioned by the same woodworker who made the museum signs.

Coralie gazed across the river at a shore she did not recognize, unaware that the white cliffs shining in the dark were called the Palisades. She was not far from the last wild land to the north, but she had no idea of where north was, as she had no idea that the Bronx itself was being remade after the building of the Grand Concourse, modeled on Paris's Champs-Élysées. Monsters did not carry maps, and when they were lost they had no recourse but to rely on human kindness. Coralie peered through the thickets before her. In secluded patches of Manhattan that had once belonged to the original Dutch landowners, the acreage was still overgrown with ancient stands of hickory, chestnut trees, and black-green elms. Through the shadows, she caught sight of a curl of smoke rising into the dark. She followed it as if it were a beacon, hoping for a hot cup of coffee and a blanket to throw around her shivering body.

Her clothes clung to her as she went on; but even when she was weighed down by her sopping trousers and shirt, she had a swimmer's easy gait. She swiftly made her way up the slippery bank. Brambles clung to her, but she managed to untangle herself from the stickers. The silence of the night was intoxicating. There were no crickets yet, for the season was still too cold, no peepers, and no birds sang at night. The swamp cabbage that was everywhere had a pungent stink, green and sharp. Just then a dog barked, the sound echoing. All at once Coralie had a rush of panic. What had she been thinking to look for company? What questions might be asked of a young woman swimming in the river in this harsh season? And who was to say there were not criminals camping in these woods, homeless men who would think nothing of attacking her?

Coralie crouched down and narrowed her eyes, peering past the shadows. Through the locust trees she spied the form of a young man at a bonfire, fixing a late supper over the flames. She darted behind the nearly heart-shaped leaves of a linden tree, the better to see who she had come upon. She thought of Whitman. *Stranger! if you, passing, meet me, and desire to speak to me, why should you not speak to me? And why should I not speak to you?* And yet, as she watched this stranger, she was mute. He was dark, with handsome features, rangy and more than six feet tall. He was sunburnt from his day at the river, and he whistled to himself as he cleaned the fish he'd caught. Something about him moved Coralie in a way she didn't understand, an almost magnetic pull. She felt alarmed by the thrum of her own pulse. The dog beside the young man was the sort used for fighting. It spied her in the woods and began to bark in earnest.

"Quiet, Mitts," she heard the man say.

The pit bull terrier looked at his master and considered, but was clearly too high-spirited to obey. The creature bounded into the woods, in her direction. The man let out a shout, but the dog continued on.

Coralie took off running, her breath coming in bursts. She felt a sharp pain below her breastbone as her heart thudded against her ribs. Her father had kept her separate from the public, except for those hours when she was on exhibit. He believed that living wonders could be made common by their association with outsiders, who could not possibly understand them and would most likely take advantage of them and ruin them. "Once you are ruined," her father had warned, "there's no way back."

The dog crashed through the underbrush. Coralie could hear him racing behind her. She did her best to outpace him as she tore through the brambles, but in no time the creature was at her heels. She turned, afraid she might be attacked from behind. Her blood felt hot within her chilled flesh as she steeled herself, ready to be bitten. She knew how red her blood was, how on fire despite how waterlogged she was. The pit bull's ears and tail were cut to nubs, and he had a compact, muscular body. Coralie expected him to leap at her, foaming at the mouth; instead he wagged his rear end and gazed up at her, utterly foolish and friendly. This was no vicious beast, only man's best friend.

"Go away," Coralie whispered.

"Mitts!" the man shouted through the woods. "Damn it! Get back here!"

The dog panted and wagged, sniffing around his quarry, ignoring Coralie's attempts to urge him away. She waved at him and hissed beneath her breath.

"Mitts, you idiot!" the young man called.

The dog was torn between his great find and his loyalty to his master. In the end he turned and crashed back into the underbrush. Through the fluttering leaves, Coralie could now fully see the man. His face was all angles, with a worried expression and broad, sensitive features. His wide mouth broke into a grin as soon as he spied his dog. "There you are." He sank down to pet the dog with tenderness, and the beast responded by leaping and licking his master's face. "Are you aiming to get yourself lost?"

Coralie felt something pierce through her, as if she were a fish on a hook, unable to break free. She felt a tie to the stranger, drawn to his every movement. Without thinking of the consequences, she shadowed him when he returned to his camp. Despite the dog, she crept closer. The young man had been cooking two striped bass over the smoky fire, one for himself and another for his dog, whom he fed before taking his own dinner. He called the dog an imbecile, but he set out a bowl of fresh water and petted the pit bull's wide head again. "Dummy." He laughed. "Are you looking to be a bear's dinner?"

A large camera had been placed atop a folded overcoat so that it might be sheltered from the wet ferns and damp soil. He was a photographer as well as a fisherman. Then what would he see if he looked at her through the lens? Gray eyes, long glossy hair falling down her back, the scales of a sea monster painted upon her skin. A liar, a cheat, and a fraud. He would see that and only that, for, as the Professor had warned her, what men imagined, they most assuredly found. Coralie wished she were nothing more than a lost woman, someone he could share his supper with, but she was something more. She was her father's daughter, a living wonder, an oddity no common man could ever understand.

Navigating through the brambles, shielding her face from the thorns, she found her way back to the river. She heard footsteps following her. For an instant she felt a sort of thrill, as if she wished to be discovered. But when she turned it wasn't the man from the campfire. Her heart sank, for there in the undergrowth was the shadowy form of a large, gray beast. For an instant, Coralie thought it was a wolf. In the fairy tales she had loved as a child, the villain was always punished, granted the fate he or she deserved. She flushed to think of the evil she had done in the world, the trickery and masquerades. She had seen to her father's bidding without question or remorse. Perhaps this was her rightful fate, to be eaten alive by a fierce beast, a proper penance for her crimes. She closed her eyes and tried to still her heart. If her life was over, so be it. She would be nothing but glimmering bones scattered beneath the brambles, and the strands of her hair would be taken up by sparrows to use in their nests.

The wolf stood in a hollow, eyeing her, but she must have appeared worthless, for it shifted back into the woods.

A mist was fluttering through the trees when she at last reached the appointed meeting place. Coralie was stone-cold, and yet she was possessed by a rising tide of emotion that coursed through her with its own brand of heat. She realized there was only one explanation for what she'd felt as she'd hidden behind the tree in her sopping clothes, watching the young man, her heart pounding. Maureen had told her that love was what a person least expected. It was not an appointment to keep or a trick or a plan. It was what she had stumbled upon on this dark night, without any warning.

When Coralie saw her father pacing beside the carriage, she felt the sting of resentment. The Professor had never raised a hand to her, but his disapproval was wounding and he would not be happy to have been kept waiting till dawn. Starlings were waking in the bushes even though the last of the stars were still strewn across the sky. Coralie often wondered if her father truly cared for her, or if perhaps another girl in her place would have suited him just as well.

"There you are!" the Professor shouted when Coralie appeared. He rushed forth with a blanket to quickly wrap around her shoulders. "I thought you had drowned."

The Professor hurried her into the carriage. The liveryman, who was often overpaid to buy his silence, would likely demand double for this journey, for it would be bright morning by the time they reached Brooklyn. There would already be crowds on the Williamsburg Bridge, men and women walking to work on this blue March day, unaware that a monster passed by them, and that she wept as she gazed out the window of the carriage, wishing that she might be among them and that her fate might at last be her own.

TWO

THE MAN WHO

COULDN'T SLEEP

****

I REMEMBER *my other life, the one in which I loved my father and knew what was expected of me. I had been named Ezekiel, after the great prophet of our people, a name that means God strengthens. Quite possibly it was a fitting name for me at some point, but, just as strength can be given, it can also be taken away. Mine was a path of duty and faith set out before me in a straight line, and yet, without asking anyone or even discussing my plan, if that is what it was, I changed my life and walked away from the person I might have been and, most certainly in my father's opinion, the man I should have been. There have been times when the decision I made resembles a dream, as if I went to sleep one person and awoke as someone else, a cynical individual I myself did not know or understand, changed by magic, overnight. There are those who believe that evil spirits can imbue mud and straw with life, breathing wretched souls into inanimate objects to create living beings, and that these dybbuks walk among us, leading us to temptation and ruin. But what is made of water and fire—for isn't that what a man whose nature opposes his responsibilities can be said to be? Does one quench the other, or do they combine to ignite the depths of the soul? I have wondered all my life what I am made of, if there is straw inside of me, or a beating heart, or if I simply burned for all I did not have.*

My father brought me to this country from the Ukraine, where our people were murdered merely because of our faith, our blood marking the snow. All across the countryside there were pogroms, which in our language means devastation, a storm that devours everything in its path. When the horsemen came, they left nothing behind, not breath or life or hope. My mother died in that far-off place. She was alone in our small wooden house when the wild men on horseback came to burn our village to ashes. There was no one to bury and no body to mourn. My father and I did not acknowledge what we had lost or speak my mother's name. When we traveled we kept to ourselves, trusting no one. I do not remember the ship or the sea, only the taste of the bitter, rusty water we had to drink, and the bread we brought with us from the Ukraine, the last taste of our past life falling to pieces in our hands. But I do remember the forest in Russia. For the rest of my life I carried that with me.

Our first residence was shared with twenty men and boys in a tenement building on Ludlow Street. The toilet was in an alleyway. There was no heat, only a stove that burned whatever coal and wood we could gather from the streets. There was very little light and the rain came pouring in through the roof. Out in the alleys people kept pens of geese, as they did back in their homelands; often the geese would break free and could be found wandering along the streets. Lice were everywhere, and it was impossible to get a good night's sleep, for the bedbugs drove people crazy with itching as they spread from mattress to mattress, a plague we couldn't purge.

Other men from our village who had also escaped the pogroms of the wild Russian horsemen soon befriended my father. In our homeland we called a village a shtetl, and each one was a world unto its own. The men, brothers. The women, sisters. Our brothers took pity on us and helped us find better living quarters, where we might, once again, be on our own. Farther down Ludlow Street we found a kind of salvation. A single room, but ours. My father had a bed, and I slept on the floor atop the feather quilt we had brought with us, sewn by hand by my mother. It was the only thing of any worth that we owned.

Every morning we recited the same prayers, swaying back and forth in meditation. We dressed in black coats and black hats. We were Orthodox in our practices and beliefs, as our grandfathers and great-grandfathers had been. In the Ukraine I would have been a scholar, but in New York I followed my father to work, as I followed him in all things. His name was Joseph Cohen, known in our village as Yoysef, and he took pride even in the lowliest tasks, as if he were still a scholar reading God's commands. If he'd had a wife and daughters, they would have been employed, and, like many other Orthodox men, he would have spent twelve hours a day in study and prayer, but that was not meant to be. In the factory I sat on the floor watching his nimble fingers turn rolls of fabric into dresses and coats. In this way I learned the tailor's trade. I was proud to bring my father needles and spools of thread. Other men murmured they wished they had a son as smart as I was, as promising and as studious. I was a worker from the time I was eight years old, and I had a gift for creating well-made clothes out of plain cloth. That was the way my fate unfolded. And yet, despite the harshness of our lives, I did not question my faith. I still carried a prayer book in my coat pocket.

We knew we were lucky to have employment. Bands of day laborers waited for work in Seward Park on the corner of Hester and Essex; when we passed by we shook our heads and said they were like pigs at the market.

I was alongside my father and his friends when the bosses came unexpect-
edly to the factory one day and fired everyone without warning. This was
the day my life changed, when I lost my soul, or found it, depending on
what you believe. As garment workers, we had no rights, but at least
we earned enough to survive, until the bosses decided otherwise. They'd
brought in new workers, cheaper labor, men just arrived from Russia and
Italy who would toil eighteen hours a day for pennies and never complain
when they were locked into workrooms to ensure they didn't take time
to eat or drink or even to rest for a few moments. These newly arrived
men asked for even less then we did, and the Jews, desperate for the pen-
nies we would earn, agreed to be at their sewing machines on Saturdays,
the holy day for our people, when as Orthodox Jews we could not work.
It seemed we were no longer needed, and no objections would be toler-
ated. Men who looked like gangsters stood at the door; should anyone dare
to complain, they wouldn't hesitate to beat down the agitators. On that
afternoon some of those who had been dismissed went home and cried,
some looked for work, but my father went to the river.

I was tall for my age, as quiet as I was studious. My life was in the shul
and in the factory, but on the day we were let go I followed my father to
the docks of Chelsea, and because of this I became someone else. Something
inside me grew hardened, or was it that something inside me was freed, a
bird that flew from its cage? I trailed after my father, though he told me to
hurry back to Ludlow Street. The docks were crowded with men in black
coats, some who were clearly of our faith, friends of my father's, but oppos-
ing them were a gang of thugs cut from the rough cloth of the docks, men
who carried brass knuckles and were good and ready for a fight. I could
think only of keeping up with my father. When he noticed me, he shouted
that I must go home. I ducked behind some barrels, hoping he'd assume
I'd done as I was told. That was when it happened. My father seemed to
leap all at once, like a strange unwieldy bird he rose into the air and flew

away from the pier. There was the slapping sound of flesh into water that I still hear.

Dockworkers nearby were unloading a ship of its cargo, huge steel beams, each of which took a dozen men to handle. When they heard the splash they all came running. My father floated, his heavy coat spilling out around him like a black water lily. I feared this was to be our last good-bye, and I would now be on my own. I sprinted back to the dock, sweating and in a panic. My feet were on the railing and I was about to jump in to rescue him. I didn't know how to swim, but that was not the reason I did not leap in. It had often seemed possible that he might take his life when we wandered through the forest. Once I had discovered him with his belt made of rope looped in his hands. He was staring into the branches of a tree filled with black birds. I grabbed his arm and told him there was a path only yards away, and then, as we wandered forward, I found it.

We had come this far together, and I was stunned that he was now willing to leave me behind in this world of grief. But hadn't he been looking for a way to rejoin my mother? Wasn't his love for her more compelling than his concern for me? Now the cage had opened; the bird had flown. In that instant, my responsibility to my father vanished. It was then I decided the person I would save was myself. I owed nothing to my father, nor to anyone else in this world.

The dockworkers pulled my father from the river and wrapped woolen blankets around him, but I walked away. That night, when my father came home, he acted as if nothing had happened, and so did I.

But it had.

After that I avoided people in our neighborhood. I no longer considered myself Orthodox, and I left my hat under the bed whenever I went out

alone. I was drawn to the river, and began fishing. I went farther and farther on my expeditions, away from the harbor where blue crabs ate the bait off my line and the fish tasted of petroleum. The very act of angling calmed me and allowed me to think. I studied what other men did and thereby learned where to search for night crawlers and how to spy a run of shad in the darkening waters. I went ever farther uptown, looking for solitary places, and finding them.

In those days I was walking through a dream rather than living my life. I had become someone else, but who was that someone? The watcher at prayer meetings, the false son who sat in silence at our meager dinner table, the boy who had failed to rescue his father. He had finally found employment again, sewing women's blouses, and I worked beside him once more. Here the conditions were even worse than in the first factory. We were not allowed to speak or open any of the windows, most of which were nailed shut. There were no fire escapes where we might sit and catch a breeze from the west. In the summer it was sweltering; in winter we wore gloves with the fingers cut off so that we might still sew. Rats ran inside the walls, and I sometimes put my ear up so I could hear them. The truth is, I envied them their freedom, and longed to be among them, darting into the alleys, living out of sight, doing as they pleased.

There were several other boys there, and I was befriended by one, Isaac Rosenfeld. We did the pressing of finished clothes with gas-fueled irons, in which a flame burned so hotly we needed to take care to ensure that we didn't burn ourselves or drop sparks onto the piles of lace and muslin spread around. We shared whatever food we had—an apple or some raisins that we stole from the pushcarts on the streets when no one was looking. We did not speak much, but we usually worked side by side. When the supervisor walked through, Isaac always made an obscene gesture behind his back and we had a few laughs. We shared our contempt for the rich and well fed, and that bound us together.

By then I was eleven years old. I had swallowed my share of bitterness, but a portion had stuck in my throat and turned to rage. That rage was there night and day, looming at all hours. Sometimes I would see the owner's children come to visit their father in a horse-drawn carriage, a boy my age and a younger girl. I felt a hatred inside me that seemed too large for me to carry. My father's fingers bled every night, and he soaked them in a glass of warm water to soften the calluses. One day I was sent to the storeroom for thread. As I walked along the corridor, I heard the owner's children laughing and playing in their father's office.

I crept nearby to spy on them. They were seated behind a large, handsome oak desk playing cards, using real pennies to bet. The girl was wearing a rabbit coat over a ruffled dress, and the boy was saying, "That's not fair, Juliet, you're cheating. You have to play by the rules." Perhaps my stomach rumbled, or I breathed out my hatred in a foul gasp. They looked up to see me in the doorway, dressed in my father's old black trousers, a scowl on my face. From their expressions I could tell they saw me as menacing. Immediately, the boy held out his watch. I didn't think twice. If they expected me to be a robber, then I would accommodate them. I grabbed the watch from the owner's son and stuffed it in my pocket. Luckily, I no longer carried my prayer book.

My victim was also eleven years old. For some reason he told me his age, and I looked at him as if he were mad. Why would he think I cared? Did he expect me to treat him more tenderly because of it? The little girl was crying. Her face was pinched and I saw she wasn't pretty at all. I wished I could take her coat to give to someone who deserved it, but I didn't have the nerve. I thought she might start screaming and alert the supervisors and I'd wind up in the Tombs prison.

"Keep quiet," I demanded, and miraculously she obeyed and held a hand over her mouth. Her eyes, now rimmed with terror, were a dark blue that made me think of the sky in the forest. I felt a surge of pity for

her, and because of this I almost returned the watch, but I could hear the sewing machines rattling away in the workroom. The sound made my hatred burn brighter.

"Are you a kidnapper?" the boss's son asked. He had a matter-of-fact tone, as though he'd been expecting such an encounter and had, in fact, been warned about people like me.

"I wouldn't want you on a silver platter," I informed him. I would never want to be a boss and be at fault for the cruelty put upon workers. "But if you ever tell anyone about this I'll kill you. Understand?" I could feel a poisonous meanness pooling inside me. In a matter of instants my conduct had led me to a viciousness I hadn't known I was capable of. "I'll find you wherever you are. Even if they lock me in the Tombs for fifty years, I'll come after you and slit your throat. Understood?"

"Understood." The owner's son's voice was surprisingly deep, as if he were a man masquerading as a boy, but one who was easily coerced into giving something precious away.

I carried his watch in my coat pocket from that day on. I have it still, nearly fifteen years later. It is the most precious thing I have ever owned. On the back there remains an inscription. "To my dear son."

The night I stole the watch I came home late. My father was eating soup at our table. We had soup when there was nothing but potatoes and onions in our measly larder. My father shivered and wore a blanket around him. When I put the watch down in front of him, he raised his eyes, as if I was a stranger. And in fact, I was.

At night, I began to do as I pleased. If my father knew, he said nothing. Most likely he already understood that my path led away from him. I slinked out of our room, down five flights of stairs, into the dark streets, drawn to the roughest riverside areas as if I were a fish myself. I had

stopped saying prayers with my father. He was an educated man who would have been a teacher if he'd stayed in our village. He still maintained his studies at a scholar's level. I felt his disappointment in me on a daily basis. I often stood outside the shul and watched him gathering with the other men for the evening prayers. These men were overwhelmed by the huge, magnificent Eldridge Street Synagogue, reminiscent of a cathedral with its extraordinary rose window. They preferred their own place of worship, a small red-brick building in the shadow of the Williamsburg Bridge with a congregation made up of men from our town in the Ukraine. People called it the Tailors' Shul. I never went inside, though I was supposed to be studying with the rabbi's assistant. I slipped off my skullcap and kept it in my pocket. My father had begun to turn away when he saw me on the corner.

I had a secret life, one that earned me cash enough for us to live more comfortably. I wanted more than soup. That was why I began to work for Abraham Hochman, known as the Seer of Rivington Street, the author of such pamphlets as "Fortune Teller" and "The Key to Prophecy," which sold for ten cents a copy. Hochman lived not far from us, in a large apartment with indoor plumbing. It was said he was fearless, hired to tell which horses would win at several racetracks by the mighty Sullivan mob, run by Big Tim, a kingpin of the Tammany political machine, the corrupt arm of the Democratic Party. His main business, however, consisted of mind reading, the interpretation of dreams, and, most important, finding the lost. Perhaps it was fate that he should become my employer. I had often seen him, overweight but stylish at all times, surrounded by his devoted followers, mostly adoring women who needed his help, many of whom got down on their knees before him, begging for his wisdom. Hochman owned the Hall of Love, one of the many wedding chapels on Sheriff Street, where he drew up ketubahs, Jewish wedding contracts that had been beautifully illustrated, often by Jewish-Italian artists. Here he presided over marriage ceremonies, though he was neither a rabbi nor a judge. He was considered to be a wizard and was, in my estimation, long before I met him, a fake. He was best known for tracking down missing persons, most often husbands and fiancés, men who had left behind their girlfriends or wives and families in Russia or Poland to come work in New York. Such men promised to send for their loved ones once they were settled, but instead disappeared into their new lives, pulling their bowler hats over their brows, and the wool over their wives' eyes. There were so many of these devious individuals that the Daily Forward, the Jewish newspaper, had taken to printing a gallery of missing men. Women who had been deserted sold their wedding rings at Fass's jewelry store on Clinton Street, right around the corner from Rivington, so they might pay for the Wizard's services. It made it all the more difficult that they had to walk past H. Goldstein's shop, which was famous for fashionable wedding dresses and silk hats made to order, on their way to sell what little they had remaining from their own failing marriages. Once they were in New York, these women could not return to their old lives—for even American Jews with passports were not allowed to pass over the border into Russia—not that they would have wished to do so. They wanted what they'd been promised, though they'd been cheated by those they loved best.

Hochman vowed that the angels led him to these lost husbands and fathers and fiancés, but in truth he employed dozens of boys as runners, young spies who tracked down those wretched individuals who had deserted their families. He taught his boys the tools of discovery for seeking out lowlifes: interview the owners of taverns, whorehouses, flophouses, hunt the alleys and tenement buildings, hang around the liquor store on Delancey Street that sold Vishniak whiskey, favored by men who'd come to New York from the Ukraine. We asked the right questions because Hochman taught us what they were. If we had a photograph we'd show

it around, even if it was an old daguerreotype and the image was fad-
ing around its silvered edges. Do you know this man? we'd demand of
as many people as we could find who would listen to our pleas. It will be
worth your while to tell us, we went on. He's won a contest, an award,
a free meal, and there may be a reward in it for you as well if you take
me to him. Did he grow up in your village back home, do you have pity
for his family, are you sure you yourself aren't running from something?
We were posted in the places where men who disappeared were known
to gather, whether they were drowning their sorrows or creating new
identities. Once a boy had done his dirty work and the good-for-nothing
individual had been located, Hochman claimed to have found the missing
person with his psychic skills.

The Wizard didn't seem to think much of me when I met him on the
street and asked for work. As always he was fashionably dressed despite
his girth. He wore a blue serge suit and a top hat. His secretary was with
him, a thin bad-tempered man named Solomon, whose duty it was to
keep the Wizard's many admirers away. I pushed past the secretary and
walked beside Hochman as if I had a right to accost him. He eyed me
coolly, and yet a smile played at his lips. He liked people with spirit. He
said he had never employed an Orthodox Jew, though he himself was a
pious man. He feared my father would make trouble if I worked for him.
He suggested that I should go back to my studies and leave the wicked
world to men who knew how to deal with such matters.

"My father has no say in my life," I told Hochman. In the newspapers
the Wizard was referred to as Doctor or Professor, but I was fairly certain
he had no degree. He took out a cigar and offered me one, but I refused. I
didn't want him to catch me choking on the smoke.

"Why is that?" he asked. "A father is a father, Orthodox or not."

"You're so smart, you tell me."

I had nerve, but my matter-of-fact retort did the trick. Hochman all-

out grinned as he hired me, thinking an Orthodox boy dressed in black with long hair would have a special sort of access, and that people would confide in me. As it turned out, he was right. Men told me their loathsome tales, how they'd run away from their nagging wives or fallen in love with a Christian woman, how they had a right to their freedom. I was a good listener, and I didn't make pronouncements. I was so accomplished at what I did that Hochman soon paid me double what I earned at the factory. Much to my father's distress, I quit my job as a tailor. I spent my mornings sleeping, and my nights on the streets. Hochman was quite famous, and even the Times went to him when children were missing or when there was a crime the police could not solve. My status in the neighborhood either ascended or was deeply tarnished by my new occupation depending on who you were and what you believed.

That winter I found one of the missing children who had been written up in all the papers. It was front-page news for a time. An Orthodox boy of seven was missing. It was thought he'd been kidnapped, perhaps by an employee of one of those houses on Third Avenue where sex was cheaply bought. I questioned several of his friends on the street where he lived, and they all told me the same thing—this boy was a wanderer. He often climbed down the fire escape in the middle of the night. He liked to ramble along the East River, where he dreamed of running away to sea. I began to search the pathways that ran along the river. Every now and then I came upon a group of displaced individuals, lost men with no homes and no goal other than to stay alive. These poor souls lived on the edge of the city, scavenging what they could. I knew enough to stay away from these men, who would bash in a fellow's head in order to steal his boots. Because I was tall I seemed older than my age, and I cursed a blue streak if anyone approached, therefore no one accosted me. I had taken to carrying a knife for my protection, and once or twice I showed it when someone began to follow me.

I discovered the missing boy beneath the Brooklyn Bridge, a feat of construction considered to be one of the wonders of the world. The boy lay in a pipe that allowed water to rush from the streets into the river. I guessed he had sneaked out, then gone too far. It was likely that he'd become exhausted and had curled up to sleep, freezing to death as the snow fell. I understood what it was like to want to run away from home, and maybe that was why I felt so disturbed. I shook his shoulder, but he didn't respond. I pulled him out of the pipe and sat beside him for a long time. The truth was, for all my bravado, I had never seen a dead body before. Though many in our village had been killed, they had become cinders that rose up with the wind. I could not look into this boy's face. I thought I would be haunted if I did, and he would then follow me from that place. I kept my eyes averted as I covered him with a blanket I found nearby. I was naïve; I thought the dead could still feel cold. I folded my coat into a pillow, for I was convinced that the dead wished for comfort as well. As I left, snow began to fall again, and I was grateful, hoping when the police brought the boy's mother here, she would be spared the aura of death that clung to this miserable place, and would instead see something that might resemble heaven, a bank of white, a boy who slept peacefully, his head resting on my coat.

There was a huge funeral, paid for by Hochman. The dead child's mother clung to the Wizard's arm as if he were her savior. There were photographs on the front page of every newspaper. I knew Hochman's business would double and because of this my pay would increase. At the age of twelve I earned enough to buy myself a new coat, and I bought one for my father as well, but he never wore it. It stayed in a box, kept beneath the bed. From then on, I spent the money on myself.

I soon became the boy Hochman turned to with his difficult cases. I had a sense of where the lost might go, since I was, in my own way, one among them. Still, I was not prepared for the degradation that I saw. I was a

*harsh judge of the men who left the families they'd once claimed to love,
but I didn't set myself above them. I judged myself as well. That is why I
knew how to find them, and why I was Hochman's best boy. I knew what
it was like to fail someone.*

*I saw the alleyways and tenements of the Lower East Side as a place
where good people could not win out against the devil. There was an
underworld that decent men like my father knew nothing about. It could
pull a person down into it when he least expected it to, and it tugged at
me. I did things I was not proud of, mostly behind the alehouses where
women all but gave themselves away. Still, I excelled as a finder of lost
men, my habits of insomnia and mistrust benefiting me in this work. I
was such an asset to Hochman that he told me he wished he had a son as
bright as I. I'd heard that before, from my father's friends.*

I could not think of anything I would have wanted less.

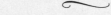

*The streets that I knew made me sick at heart, and, though I provided
my father with a better life, with food we could have not afforded on his
factory salary, when he looked at me I felt he despised me. I still had the
urge to be alone.*

*One night I found myself walking to the hills of upper Manhattan,
farther north than I'd ever been before. The city fell away beyond Morn-
ingside Heights. Between the residential areas there were patches of dark
greenery, and then, at last, the woods that were filled with a weave of
birdsong. There were still a few farmhouses on the cliffs of hard, white
marble, and I heard cowbells ringing, as if I had stumbled upon a world
of pastures. I passed the flooded juncture where the Hudson ran into
the Harlem River in the area the Dutch called Spuyten Duyvil. Here
there were oysters as large as a man's hand, and herons lingered over the*

marshes, building nests out of sticks in the tall locust and sycamore trees. Fishermen stood on the bridges angling for striped bass, bluefish, porgy, and flounder, as well as the mysterious hard-to-catch eels. Skiffs floated near the best fishing holes. I imagined I might never go home; I could live in the woods, feed myself with oysters and rabbits, foods that were denied to me because our people kept kosher and were forbidden from eating such creatures.

It was November, and frost was forming in patches on the grass. I would soon be turning thirteen, but I knew I wouldn't be standing with the men in the shul to recite the bar mitzvah prayers, though my reading of Hebrew was perfect, taught to me in the years when I was still my father's obedient son. The leaves were brown and the river ran darkly, but the moon was full and it was nearly as bright as day. I had no home, other than the city of New York. I had no people, for I had forsaken them. And yet on this night it seemed I had walked into the dream I had longed for ever since I'd lost my faith, as if I had discovered a world apart and separate from all those who had been in my life, the men in black hats loyal to a path that was no longer mine, although there were times when I wished that it were. If I were still an obedient son, I might be able to sleep at night, and not wander through the streets, into taverns and trouble, into the sorrows of lost men, into the arms of women who would do anything for a few pennies, into the woods where the herons stalked through the tall grass.

I saw a flash of light and followed it up a bluff. Perhaps God was calling to me as he had called to Moses in the wilderness, perhaps he would punish me and berate me for my fall from grace. I had spied on men. I'd followed them like a shadow. I wrote down their trespasses and their sins. I made no sacrifices and held nothing dear, and in doing so I became one of those creatures I'd heard about, a dybbuk made of straw, with nothing inside.

Pheasants were flushed from the underbrush as I walked along. It was hard to believe that the teeming streets of lower Manhattan were less than a day's walk from what was still a sort of wilderness. The wild tulip trees were two hundred feet tall. There were said to be bear here, come down from the Palisades in the winter, crossing the Hudson when it froze, along with wild turkeys, fox, muskrats, and deer. I thought of the forests of the Ukraine, where cuckoos sung in the trees and owls glided through the dark. My father and I had stopped to make camp for several nights on our travels. I was only a small child, but it was there, listening to the voice of the forest, that I had lost the ability to sleep.

I wondered if there was a reason for my insomnia and if, indeed, it was God's plan. Had I been able to sleep I would never have ventured out to stand before a grove of twisted locust trees on this particular date. My cold breath rose into the chilly air. Before me stood a man in a white shirt and black trousers. His head was covered by a piece of burlap, which served as a makeshift dark tent. Beside him there was a large wooden trunk filled with chemicals and solutions, funnels, a pail for rinsing water, and several glass plates on which the images would be captured. The stranger peered into a large camera he had arranged on a stand in the grass. He was photographing trees in the moonlight, his attention riveted. When he heard the game birds in flight, he withdrew his head from the burlap and turned, quite annoyed to spy me there. He had a long beard, and long gray hair held back with a strand of leather. He raised his arms and gestured, to shoo me away. "Go on," he shouted. "Leave me in peace."

But it was too late. I had already seen the light spilling down around me. The night was aglow. I wanted to look through the lens of his camera. I wanted it so badly I felt an ache in my chest. There was another world I had never known, one of great beauty that could make me forget what I had seen in my short time on earth.

I LEFT HOME a few weeks later. I had very little to take with me. My new coat, a pair of boots I'd bought for myself, the watch that had once belonged to the factory owner's son. That was something I would never give away, for it reminded me why I'd made the decision to go my own way. I left a packet of cash underneath my father's prayer book; whether or not he used it was his decision. I took up the feather quilt from the floor and folded it, knowing I'd never sleep on it again. I thought of my mother's hands at work. Then I stopped thinking about her. It was not possible to hold on to ashes. In my dreams I had always walked out of the past, and it shut behind me, a door I couldn't unlock. Now I intended to do the same in my waking life. At the factory, other boys my age were working for the labor movement, trying to change the world, but I couldn't even see their world; it seemed a prison to me. Hochman had treated me fairly, and I knew he had high hopes for me, but I never told him I was leaving. I didn't feel the need. If he were as adept at locating the missing as he claimed, he would know where I had gone.

The photographer's name had been printed on the wooden chest that held his equipment: Moses Levy. He was one of us, from the Ukraine, and our world was small enough for me to track him down. Finding people was what I did, after all. As it turned out, Hochman's secretary, Solomon, was the one who led me to Levy. In his files I found the address of Levy's studio. The photographer's services were often used when there was a wedding. Thinking back, I believed I had seen him at the Hall of Love, a stooped, elegant figure setting up his camera. Levy had been considered to

be a great artist in Russia but was now forced to take marriage portraits simply to make a living.

I found my way to Chelsea, heading toward the river, for it was here that the great man lived and worked, in a workshop loft above a livery stable. I climbed the stairs, but when I knocked on the studio door there was no answer. I'd never found the lost by giving up, so I knocked harder. I was already impulsive, not easily dissuaded or turned away, and my methods for getting what I wanted could be considered obnoxious. I knew how to rattle people, how to make them respond when all they wanted was to slip away from my prodding. I kept rapping at the door. After a while it opened a crack and the old man peered out with his fierce eye. Perhaps he recognized me, or perhaps I was simply an annoyance like any other.

"Get out," he growled. "I didn't ask you here!"

But I felt he had, for he had shown me the light. In doing so he had opened another world for me, one beyond the darkness I had found on Ludlow Street and in all of my wanderings. Ever since that night upriver I had been able to catch a few restful hours of sleep, something that had always been so difficult for me. I now dreamed of photography, and because of this I looked forward to sleep for the first time.

In my dreams the world was mine to create, something brand new.

I bunked in the livery below the photographer's rooms at first, paying off the stable owner so that I might stretch out in the straw beside the horses. "You'd better not make me regret this," the landlord said to me, clearly concerned for his horses, for there were more horse thieves in New York City than there were in all of the western territories. I promised I wouldn't, and luckily he believed me. It was the dead of winter by now and exceptionally cold. I had developed a hacking cough. At thirteen I appeared disheveled, maybe even dangerous. I had recently reached my full height of six foot two inches, and was so thin my wrist bones were *knobby. I was made of sinew and muscle, even though I was starving, thinner than ever. My dark hair reached to my shoulders, as was our people's practice, but on my first night in the stable I cut it off with a pair of shears, so short my scalp showed through. I did this to seal my commitment to my new life. I now looked nothing like my own people, who grew their hair and beards to show their faith and their obedience to God. I drank from the horses' trough, and when I was hungry enough, I tramped down to the Twenty-third Street dock and caught oil-laden fish that I cooked over an open fire in the alleyway behind the stable. I suppose I could be heard hacking in the night. Most likely I kept the photographer awake. Snow fell and dusted the cobblestones on the streets, and in their sleep the horses groaned and I groaned along with them, miserable, nearly desperate.*

Then one morning the great man himself, Moses Levy, came down with a cup of tea and some bread and cheese. Even before I thanked him, I begged to be his apprentice.

"You don't think your father will miss you?" he asked when I told him of how we had left the Ukraine, a village not far from his own, and how we had worked at factories until our fingers bled, and how I had left without saying good-bye. I omitted the more questionable section of my life as one of Hochman's boys, for in that profession I felt less like a detective than a rat and a snitch.

"He doesn't know me, how can he miss me? I have my own life," I insisted, exactly as I'd insisted to Hochman when I first stepped away from my original life and changed my fate. I wolfed down the food that had been offered me. "I make my own decisions," I assured Levy.

Although I had not said the bar mitzvah prayers that brought a boy into his adult life, I thought of myself as a man. I had worked as a man, and I'd lived as one, too, outside my father's view. The direction of my life would have shocked my father had he known anything of my actions on those nights when I slipped out of our room. I'd done as I pleased when working for Hochman. That was what I'd thought I wanted, a sinful and thoughtless existence. After the day when my father leapt from the dock, as if his life was so worthless he was willing to cast it away, I made a vow to look for pleasure in my own life. But despite the rules I broke, the women who'd raised their skirts for me, the money I'd made working for Hochman, nothing had made me happy until I'd stood in the locust grove and watched Levy with his camera. I couldn't see the beauty of the world until I saw the trees looming in the moonlight.

MARCH 1911

THE AIR was pale, as gray as smoke. March meant good fishing in the Hudson, with schools of shad running beneath the silver mist that settled over the water in the early hours of the day. Eddie Cohen could see the river from the domed window in his studio, and in his opinion it was one of the wonders of the world. Light moved through the water in bands, changing the color of the depths from violet to pewter to copper, and then, as spring approached, a heavenly blue. Eddie had inherited his quarters in a shabby neighborhood of storehouses and stables near the docks. The loft where he lived had been used for storing hay in a previous incarnation, and the stink of horse-flesh still arose from the stable below, where a liveryman quartered a team of old nags. Eddie's mentor had bequeathed his student all his worldly goods. Upon his death, everything the photographer Moses Levy had once owned, every cooking pot and blanket, every camera and print, came to belong to his protégé. Eddie was tall and often awkward, unaware of his good looks. He was agitated, a hothead with too much of a temper to enter into the conversations of most civilized men. Women were drawn to him, but he rarely noticed their attraction, not unless light fell upon their faces to illuminate their features. Then he did approach, his camera ready for use. These women might hope for his interest, but all he wanted was their image. The women he'd known sexually, he'd felt nothing for other than lust. He had never believed in a world where love was possible.

His address was in the westernmost point of the city, beyond
Tenth Avenue, the gritty edge of an outer sphere that became more
and more fashionable as one headed eastward, reaching a glamorous
zenith at Fifth Avenue. All of the land in the area had once belonged
to Clement Moore, the author of *The Night Before Christmas,* a scholar
of Hebrew and Greek who had called his estate Chelsea after the
district in London known for its opulent Georgian town houses.
When the grid of Manhattan streets was created, in 1811, a grand
project that would forever change the city, filling in streams, ridding the map of meandering roads, Ninth Avenue cut through the
center of Moore's estate. The scholar was so appalled at the way the
future had swooped in to claim the farm he so loved that he donated
much of his land to the General Theological Seminary and St. Peter's
Church. He left open sixty lots of orchards, assuming this gift would
ensure that Chelsea would never be completely overtaken by mortar
and stone. But after Moore's death the lots were sold, with most of
the trees hurriedly chopped down. Only the churchyard and garden
remained the same, and there it was still possible to find remnants
of the old orchard. Neighborhood women often stood near the walls
of the churchyard, holding out their skirts to form baskets into which
the apples might drop. Seeds scattered, and stray saplings appeared in
yards and beside shops and warehouses, flowering pink in the summer, reminding residents that the fruit that had tempted Adam and
Eve, which many believed had not stood a chance against the builders
of Manhattan, could still bloom within the confines of the city.

Eddie had set out to photograph every one of these apple trees,
some little more than twigs, others quite massive, with thick trunks
and twisted limbs. He used the dry-plate process, which included
an emulsion of gelatin and silver bromide on a glass plate that gave
images a heightened depth, along with an inner light that gleamed.

Each tree was an individual, a soldier in the fight against pavement and bricks. In the boughs of one tree a raven had been perched, one Eddie hadn't noticed until the print was in the developing bin. In another, the wind had come up so unnoticed that he was stunned to see that outside his vision, blossoms had been shivering down to earth as a rain of white flowers, a visual snowstorm in August. Eddie had come to understand that what a man saw and what actually existed in the natural world often were contradictory. The human eye was not capable of true sight, for it was constrained by its own humanness, clouded by regret, and opinion, and faith. Whatever was witnessed in the real world was unknowable in real time. It was the eye of the camera that captured the world as it truly was. For this reason photography was not only Eddie's profession, it was his calling.

The photographer Alfred Stieglitz had headed a conference in New York so that the business of photography might be elevated and seen as an art form, no longer considered a hodgepodge, half science half magic, but rather as elements that, when sifted together into a photographic image, yielded truth, beauty, and a measure of real life that was often more miraculous than the original miracle of flower or fish, woman or tree. Stieglitz had opened Gallery 291, on Fifth Avenue, which showed photography alongside drawings and paintings, promoting the most avant-garde artists. On that fateful day when photography was seen in the true light of its worth, Eddie had stood among the crowd who'd come to hear Stieglitz, brought there by his mentor, though he was nothing more than an apprentice at the time. He was transfixed by all he witnessed. More than ever, he was converted to his art in some deep, immutable way that struck his spirit, as it had on the night he saw the locust trees in the woods of upper Manhattan. It was there, for the very first time, that he had felt truly awake.

⌒

Still, every man had to make a living so that he might afford bread
and beer and cheese. Every man was human, moved by human desires
and needs. Eddie was too hotheaded to photograph weddings, as
Moses Levy had. He could never tolerate clients who shouted out
instructions and demanded certain poses, especially those who gave
orders to an artist as noble as Levy. As an apprentice, Eddie had often
been forcibly removed from a wedding hall when he'd faced off with
the father of a bride or a groom. "How dare you tell him what to do!"
he would say in defense of his mentor, even as he was being escorted
to the street by a group of burly guests. "You're dealing with one of the
greatest photographers of our time!"

On these occasions Levy would have to make apologies for Eddie,
then finish the work without an assistant. "Are you such a fool that
you don't understand? You must see what others cannot," Levy told
his wayward helper once they were on their way back to the studio in
Chelsea. "In our world of shadows, there is no black and white but
a thousand different strokes of light. A wedding is a joyous event.
There's no shame in catching those moments for all time."

When Levy lay dying, the result of childhood pneumonia that had
weakened his lungs, Eddie had wept at his bedside. He was a man of
twenty by then, but his emotions got the best of him, and made him
critical of his shortcomings. He wished he had been a better man and
a better protégé, for he feared that his art failed both his mentor and
himself. He yearned for the ability to see into the world of shadows, as
Levy and Stieglitz did, for he saw only the light or the darkness, black
or white, and all that lay in between was invisible to his eyes.

In the five years he'd been on his own since Levy's death, Eddie
had focused on crime scenes and disasters. He gravitated to street

life, perhaps because he'd known this world so well as a boy. He soon had contacts with editors at most of the newspapers in town, though he was certain his mentor would have disapproved of the sheer commonness of his employment, which, by its very nature, focused on the degradation of mankind. Levy wouldn't hear of it when Eddie had once suggested they might work for the papers.

"We don't need to make a living off of other people's pain," the older man had insisted. "A portrait is one thing. We can celebrate the great occasions in our subjects' lives and not veer so far from our true calling that we become traitors to our art. But the newspapers want violence, retribution, crime, sin. In short, it's hell they're asking for. Is this a place you'd like to enter?"

All the same, the work suited Eddie. He was detached and professional in the face of tragedy. It was possible that his training with the wizard Hochman had caused him to become immune to other people's sorrows. He'd been raised in the world of sin, after all, inured to the grim reality of the evil people were capable of. He'd had his time in hell and knew its corners and alleyways. The runaway husbands and philandering fiancés, the whores willing to divulge secrets for the price of a drink, all had prepared him for the cruel visions he faced in his current work. Death did not faze him; a body was not a human being in his eyes, merely skin and bone. As for blood, it showed as black when caught on film. He had built up connections at police stations in the downtown wards and was able to gain information regarding crimes or disasters in exchange for small bribes. Because of this he had photographed thieves at the moment of their arrest, con artists shackled and wobbly with regret, denying their guilt at all cost. He would get down on the ground beside a corpse to obtain the best angle. Once, quite memorably, he'd taken a formal portrait of a man who had dispatched his entire family with a carving knife. There was not a glimmer of emotion on the murderer's face. The subject had stared directly into the camera with pale, heavily lidded eyes without a flutter of remorse. Even Eddie had been rattled by the murderer's unearthly calm. He knew evil when he saw it. The *Sun* ran the photograph on its front page, the perfect image of a cold-blooded killer.

Recently Eddie had begun to wonder if Moses Levy's work had been so imbued with greatness not merely because of his technical skill but because of his compassion, something Eddie did not feel for his subjects. In Levy's photographs each tree possessed a soul, each field a beating heart. As for Eddie, he remained unmoved by the plights of both criminal and victim. He kept his opinions to himself, but his judgments were brutal. He'd always believed there were some who belonged in the hell of their own making, and so it came to be that they were his subject matter.

The newspaper editors knew him as Ed Cohen, unaware that his given name was Ezekiel. This was the way he preferred it, with the past left as far behind as possible. He'd heard rumors that his father had long ago said the prayers for the dead for him, tearing his clothing as he recited the Kaddish. It seemed especially fitting that he'd been named after the prophet whose wanderings and visions had given the mourning prayers their first words to God, for it was the Book of Ezekiel from which the words were drawn. *May His great name be exalted and sanctified in the world which He has created according to His will.*

In truth, the boy who'd been unable to sleep in the forest, and who'd led his father out of the woods by the hand, had vanished many years earlier. Perhaps that was best. Eddie wanted to escape the burden of his identity. In his current life he was a twenty-five-year-old man with no family and no history and no allegiance to anything other than New York. A motherless boy is hardened in many ways yet will often search for a place to deposit his loyalty and devotion. Eddie had found this in the city he saw as a great and tormented beauty, one ready to embrace him when all others turned away.

One remnant from his past clung to him. He was still an insomniac, unable to sleep for more than a few hours at a time unless he drank himself into a stupor. The night continued to call to him. Something was waiting for him in the darkness, a part of himself he couldn't deny. Instead of returning to the taverns he'd frequented while working for Hochman, he now made his way to upper Manhattan when he felt the darkness inside. In those craggy acres where the city fell away, there was a still sense of the wilderness that had once been everywhere on this island. When he was beside the quiet inlets where streams crisscrossed through the marshland, he found himself uplifted, as if he were a believer and the wretchedness of his childhood had never happened, for at one time he had possessed a certain purity of spirit, though it had drifted away from him.

Eddie was not entirely alone on these outings, for he had the best of company; he had become the owner of a dog, an arrangement he'd never intended. Beside him trotted a broad-chested pit bull, as loyal as they come. A year earlier, Eddie had spotted a bundle of rags tied with rope floating near the pier at Twenty-third Street. When he noticed movement inside, he latched on to it with the hook of his fishing rod, pulling the bundle close to shore. He discovered a waterlogged pup wrapped up inside, ears cut into stubs. The animal was meant for fighting but had clearly been too good-natured for the terrible business that went on in cellars all over lower Manhattan where dogs were set against rats, and raccoons, and each other. Eddie called him Mitts, for although the pup's body was brindle, all four feet were white. Loyalty bred loyalty, and from the time of his rescue, Mitts refused to leave his master's side. When Eddie went out alone, the dog needed to be locked in a stall in the stables below the studio to ensure he wouldn't leap out the window to chase his beloved rescuer into the chaotic onslaught of automobiles and trolleys and carriages that caused many to refer to Tenth Avenue as Death Avenue. On several occasions, Mitts had managed to leap over the stable wall, leaving a frantic Eddie to grab him by his collar to pull him back from the street. The leather collar had been specially made by a cobbler, with the dog's name burned into the leather. Eddie imagined he was overly attached to the dog because the pup had been too young to be taken from his mother and had slept in his owner's bed for the first few nights, a practice Mitts reverted to whenever his master wasn't at home.

Eddie went fishing on Saturdays, the day he would have been at prayer had he lived the life that had been intended for him. It was easy enough to avoid civilization; he simply skirted the river. Central Park, once a boggy area good only for goats and piggeries, and later populated by squatters, along with a town called Seneca Village, home to African American and Irish immigrants and destroyed thirty years earlier, had been remade into an opulent playground for the residents of the luxurious town houses of the East Side. Those wealthy New Yorkers preferred their experiences with nature to consist of clipped green meadows and waterfalls that were turned on and off with spigots. The Citizens Union had filed complaints with the parks department to stop Central Park from being popularized, which, if it was allowed to be used for sports and ball games, would ruin the greenery by giving it over to the immigrant masses. Though Riverside Park ran alongside the Hudson for several blocks, the land along the uppermost West Side was still wild, though for how long, no one dared to guess.

There was the fresh green scent of early spring. Mourning cloaks and cabbage white butterflies filled the air. Eddie had occasionally seen the prints of fisher-cats and fox tracked through the mud. It was not far from here that he had recently imagined someone had been watching him. His dog was a gleeful hunter of moles and mice, but, on this particular evening, there seemed bigger game at stake. The hair on Mitts's back had gone up, and he'd taken off like a shot. The pit bull may have spied a deer in the undergrowth, or perhaps it was the old hermit Jacob Van der Beck, a Dutchman who lived in a rough-hewn cabin. Here was an individual so bitter toward his fellow men, so sure that the building boom in Manhattan would overtake his slice of the world, it was said he had a wolf tied up on his porch to keep interlopers at bay. His family had owned a large tract of land from the time of the Dutch settlers, with ties to the founding families, such as the Dyckmans. He still referred to the Hudson as the North River, as the original settlers had.

Eddie had once persuaded the old man to sit for a portrait in exchange for a bottle of rye. Beck had been a grumpy and withholding model; he'd crouched upon a moss-covered log and hadn't batted an eye, vanishing back into the woods as soon as Eddie took his photograph.

On the evening Mitts ran away, galumphing through the woods, dead set on chasing after some sort of prey, Eddie had eventually found the dog in a clearing. There'd been no sign of Beck and no deer tracks, yet there was a presence. The ground was damp, as if the river had washed up into the meadow grass, leaving a soft path beaten down in the patches of trillium and bloodroot. There was no one in sight, but all the same, when Eddie returned to his campsite, he couldn't shake the notion that he'd been followed.

Now, here it was, the last Saturday in March, and Eddie settled down with his rod. He'd left his studio in the dark, and it was hardly daybreak when he began to fish. On both sides of the Hudson the sky was struck with a hazy pink glow. He'd brought along night crawlers and crusts of bread in an old tin pail. Eddie avoided the Harlem River—it was overcrowded and overfished, even more so than the Hudson, littered with oystering boats. Several bridges had recently been built across the waters, disturbing the marsh birds. He knew it wouldn't be long before the countryside disappeared, as it had in Chelsea, where there was pavement everywhere.

Through the new leaves of the locust trees, Eddie spied Beck fishing farther down along the bank. An encounter with the old man appeared unavoidable, for the hermit gazed over and nodded. Eddie returned the greeting, considering how to best keep his distance. Beck was known to chase off intruders with a rifle, and there were those who said he vowed to kill any man who hunted the wildlife that was rapidly becoming rare, coyotes and fox and the huge, cantankerous wild turkeys. Past the area of Washington Heights was Hudson Heights, the highest altitude in Manhattan, at 265 feet above sea level. There was the pastoral village of Inwood, and although the subway ran this far, this section of north Manhattan was still dotted with small farms, including a house once owned by the Audubon family. Eddie joined the hermit in his agitation over the constant building in Manhattan. Apartment buildings were rising everywhere. City officials had begun to shore up the ravines that led to Spuyten Duyvil Creek, an offshoot of the Harlem River, where peregrine falcons nested in the trees. The very banks of the Hudson were being fortified against the tides with rock and cement toted by gangs of city workers. The shore of the river had become cluttered with pockets of houseboats in the calm inlets, and their inhabitants washed their clothes and pots and pans with lye soap in the shallows, leaving a yellow scrim of grease at the shoreline.

Eddie looped a rope around Mitts's neck to make certain the pit bull wouldn't charge off and annoy the Dutchman. A fisherman, especially one such as Beck who despised company, was meant to be alone at his task. The river was choppy, because of the rising wind, so Eddie made his way to a small, clear stream that filtered into the Hudson. He hunkered down, his collar raised. Soon enough he found success, a trout that fought valiantly, until it had exhausted itself. When reeled in, the trout was such a lovely specimen Eddie hadn't the heart to let it gasp its last on the grass. He sloshed some water into his tin pail, then slid the fish inside. The trout, frenzied to find itself captured, leapt up, banging itself against the side of the pail before at last settling to the bottom, spent, a slash of living light.

Eddie set his camera on its wooden trilegged stand. After all the hackwork he did for the papers, he wondered if he had lost the ability to take an honest photograph. If this was so, he alone was to blame. He was reminded of the Yiddish oath union workers took when setting out on strike lines. *If I turn traitor to the cause I now pledge, may this hand wither from this arm I now raise.* Perhaps he had become a traitor to his art and to the man Moses Levy thought he might become. The photograph of the fish would be dependent upon skill, and Eddie worried over his talent. Without shadows the image would appear to be nothing more than a bucket of murky water. Without compassion, nothing but a fish, trapped and defeated.

The hermit, who wrapped his own day's catch in newspaper, had begun to climb up the bank toward the little stream. Eddie muttered to himself, wishing to be left alone. But Beck was headed straight for him, ferns flattening under his heavy, laced boots. Eddie regretted having given the Dutchman a bottle of rye, for such kindness led to intimacy and confidences, neither of which he wanted.

The hermit stood nearby to watch as the fish was photographed. When Eddie had finished, Beck peered into the bucket. His beard was long, unkempt, his expression concerned.

"You should let that fellow go. For his own good and yours." The hermit was wise to wear a heavy coat. In town, the day was warm, but here beside the river the pale rays of sun did little to warm the chill that drifted off the water.

"Why's that?" Eddie did not raise his eyes, so as to keep his distance. He continued to busy himself with packing up his camera. He'd dealt with madmen before. Best not to meet their glance or learn too much about their wretched histories.

"You took his photograph," Beck said solemnly. "Now you're responsible for his soul. You should give him back to the river. Otherwise he'll take you somewhere you may not want to go."

Eddie did his best not to laugh. "It doesn't work that way." Only a fool would believe that a soul could be stolen on film, or that a fish was no different than a man and had a soul of equal worth. "If a camera interfered with souls, I'd be equally responsible for yours, since you sat for a portrait."

"Maybe that's why I let you trespass on such a regular basis." Beck's expression was thoughtful. "This river used to have schools of shad so thick you could walk across the river on their backs and your boots would stay dry. But then the boats came, and the nets, and now we're lucky to have what little we've got. That's why I run people off. I'd be within my rights to kill you, but now we're in this together, like it or not."

"Surely we're not in anything together," Eddie was quick to respond. As far as he was concerned the only thing they were in together was the boggy, green woods. He might have argued further, but he quickly bit his tongue when he noticed a rifle under the hermit's coat. At crime scenes Eddie paid attention only to the limp forms, the black blood, a collection of images that formed his photograph. He was there to observe and report, nothing more. He'd never wondered if the victims' throats were dry at the time of their demise, if their hands had been clammy, if they'd gotten down on their knees to beg for their lives. Now his own hands were themselves quite clammy, his throat nearly too dry to speak, though he managed as best he could. "Although I must say I'm glad I'm not another man."

Before Beck could respond, Mitts wrenched forward, pulling free from the rope so that he might trot over to the hermit. He cheerfully knocked his stocky body against Beck's legs.

"What's this supposed to be?" the old man asked, surprised by the dog's good nature.

"He was supposed to be a fighting dog. Then he was supposed to be dinner for the fish." Eddie lifted his rod over his shoulder. If need be, he could use it to protect himself if the hermit's suspicious side took over. "Now he's supposed to be my dog."

"He looks more like a rabbit. My dog would eat him in one bite."

"Then I'm glad your dog's not here."

"You should be. He's a wolf."

To appease the old man, Eddie offered up the trout in the pail. "Consider this my gift to you."

Beck shook the rolled wet newspaper he carried, filled with his catch. He'd clearly done far better than his younger compatriot. "I've got my own. I've got my own whiskey, too." He showed off a battered flask tucked in his waistband. There was a glimmer of metal as the rifle shone.

Eddie was suddenly aware that if he should die here, on this riverbank, on this day, only his dog would mourn him, for there was no one else who knew or cared he was alive. Perhaps that meant he'd led a worthless life, yet alive was what he wished to be. He knew this from his pounding heart, which hit against his ribs as the Dutchman shifted his rifle away from that fragile, beating target. He knew it from the greenness of the trees surrounding him, from the rushing of the river, a wonder and a miracle he could not bear to lose. He gazed at the hermit directly. "I thank you, sir, for the use of your river, but the fish and I are going home."

Beck stepped in still closer, squinting, a thoughtful, unreadable expression crossing his weathered face. He stunk of liquor and fish. For a moment the tension was high, then the old man grinned. "Before you go, answer this. What sort of fish walks on two legs?"

Relieved, Eddie grinned in turn. Riddles didn't intimidate him. He was quick-witted from his days of working for Hochman. He'd learned that what men most often wished to hear were their own thoughts repeated back to them.

"The kind that will take me where I might not want to go?" Eddie ventured to say.

The Dutchman laughed and jabbed his finger into the younger man's arm. "Exactly." Cheerful then, he stooped to pet Mitts. "Goodbye, rabbit."

The dog slobbered gratefully at the stranger's attentions, then bounded off when Eddie whistled to call him away. When Eddie glanced over his shoulder, Beck had already disappeared. Eddie broke into a sweat as he climbed down the hillock. The Hudson was churning as the spring melt from upstate washed into the waters, but there was great relief in walking beside it, free and alive on this green day.

It was a long way to Chelsea, and when Eddie reached home that afternoon, he realized it would have been wiser to have allowed the fish to perish on the riverbank. After more than a hundred blocks, Eddie was tired and not the least bit hungry, though he fed the dog some scraps. After setting the pail on his table, Eddie lay down in his narrow bed for a nap, still wearing his coat and his boots. He hadn't slept for more than twenty-four hours. Soon enough he dove into sleep the way a drowning man might, headfirst, unaware of the rest of the world, dreaming that the fish he'd caught had turned into a woman whose long dark hair fell down her back. Her feet were bare and cold as she climbed into bed beside him.

IT HAD BEEN a beautiful springlike day, but at a quarter to five in the afternoon on that same Saturday the sky turned a deep, oily gray and the air was suddenly heavy, the pressure sinking quickly, as it does before a storm. There seemed an instant of clarity and quiet, and then all at once, without warning, the silence of the city was shattered by a wave of noise. Eddie awoke streaming with sweat, his pulse hammering away, his dream disappearing before he could hold on to it. He could hear fire bells and a roar echoing from downtown. He leapt from bed and hurried to shift a wooden chair beneath the skylight in order to climb up and push open the glass to look outside. A cloud of black smoke was spreading above the rooftops. Sparks flew in red bursts, and then, from the east, a great torrent of flame swirled into the sky. It was the way some people said the world would end, in a fire that would engulf both the wicked and the innocent.

Eddie was thankful he'd slept in his coat and boots. All he needed to do was to grab his camera and lock up his dog before heading downtown. His heart was still pounding, as it had been in his dreams. He couldn't shake his terror. He took the stairs two at a time; once outside, he quickly headed east on Twenty-third Street. Behind him, the river had turned black with ashes. Fifteen blocks downtown, a fire blazed out of control.

Despite the protests of the past years, workers were treated no better than they had been when Eddie had first learned the tailoring trade alongside his father. In the fall of 1909, a strike had led to the Uprising of the 20,000, and in the great hall of Cooper Union, where Abraham Lincoln had once spoken, workers took an oath to be loyal to their cause: the humane treatment of every man and woman who worked in the city of New York. There had been so many strikes that the past twelve months had been dubbed the year of the Great Revolt. But most agreed, workers still had no rights. Protesters were beaten and arrested on the barricades, then brought to night court at the Jefferson Market Courthouse, the men immediately jailed, the women sent to a grim prison workhouse called Blackwell's Island. Manhattan Fire Chief Edward Croker had warned it was only a matter of time before a tragedy would occur due to the wretched unsafe conditions in the factories of lower New York. If nothing changed, every working man and woman knew there would be a terrible price to pay. Now, on this bitter afternoon, the time for that payment had come.

Huge crowds had gathered outside the Asch Building, just off Washington Square. Nearly ten thousand people would rush to this address before the day was through, though the police quickly set to holding them back, forming a human chain so that the public might be kept away from the blasts of heat and the danger of falling sparks. Because it was Saturday, the stores on Fifth Avenue were all open—Marshall Field's on Fifteenth Street and Lord & Taylor on Nineteenth Street, and all the dozens of small shops that lined the

Avenue, from corset shops to perfumeries, to Charles Scribner's Sons publishers, which had offices on Twentieth Street and Twenty-third Street where Fifth Avenue met Madison Park, a location where there was always a line of horse-drawn cabs waiting to bring shoppers back uptown. On the east side of Washington Square there were factories and tenements, but on the west side stood some of the most fashionable addresses. Here, where the grid of Manhattan began, there were dozens of brownstone town houses and the most exclusive stores in the city.

The streets were crowded with shoppers, and many among them rushed to the site where garment workers, mostly women and girls, had been trapped inside a sewing loft at the end of the workday. Fire ladders reached only to the sixth floor of the building that contained the Triangle Shirtwaist Factory, where workers as young as twelve were employed. Seamstresses on the eighth and tenth floors had been alerted that a fire had begun by the switchboard operator via telephone, but by the time Eddie arrived at the scene, the entire ninth floor of the factory was in flames.

The streets were teeming and the air had become a cauldron of heat and ash. The wind carried bits of cotton and wool cloth aflame above them, as if the sky was raining down fire. Photographers were being turned away. Eddie, however, spied Matt Harris, a reporter from the *Times* who usually had no problem with the police; he quickly attached himself to the newsman. Harris held a handkerchief over his mouth to filter out the ashes, but he could be heard plainly enough.

"I guess you're with me," he remarked drily when he noticed Eddie beside him.

"I am. If you'll allow it."

"Only the devil would want to keep this to himself," Harris muttered.

When the police let Harris through, Eddie slipped past the barricades unnoticed. He thanked the newsman, insisting he would return the favor sometime, but the reporter shrugged off his gratitude. "You won't be grateful soon enough. We're about to see a horror. Trust me, you won't thank me for this."

Like most news photographers, Eddie had the ability to vanish. He'd trained himself to fade into the background, aware that it was best to be ignored by the players in a scene so that they might, in being unaware of him, be their truest selves. He set up his camera where there was less chaos, on the Washington Place side of the building, then quickly got to photographing two elevator operators as the police interviewed them. These men had rescued as many girls as possible, nearly 150 by now, but were now themselves overcome by smoke, unable to go back up the burning elevator chutes. "What will the ones we left behind do now?" one of them cried. Eddie turned his camera to the building. Girls who could find no way out gathered on the windowsills, clustered together in frightened groups, their cries taken to heaven by the updraft the fire had created.

The stairway from the ninth floor had ended with no exit to the roof. There was only a shaky fire escape, which had melted in the heat. Those trying to make their escape via that exit, twenty-five in all, had fallen to their deaths in the alley below. Scores more followed, but found no way out. When they were unable to get through the flames, the only choice before them was the open air of the windowsills. The horse-drawn fire engines, with rolls of newly invented fire hoses onboard, had arrived, and firemen were unwinding their hoses, stretching them out on Greene Street. But it was too late for many as the fire billowed in cascades of flames. Girls had begun to leap from the windows of the ninth floor, some embracing so they might spend their last moments on earth in each other's arms rather than face their fates alone. Some jumped with their eyes closed, others with their hair and clothes already burning.

At first, the falling girls had seemed like birds. Bright cardinals, bone-white doves, swooping blackbirds in velvet-collared coats. But when they hit the cement, the terrible truth of the matter was revealed. Their bodies were broken, dashed to their deaths right before those who stood by helpless. A police officer near Eddie groaned and turned away, his head in his hands, for there was no way to save those who were already falling and no way to come to terms with the reality before them. The life nets being held out were worthless; bodies soared right through the netting. Many of the desperate leapers barreled onward, through the glass cellar lights embedded in the sidewalk, to the basements below.

The firemen from Company 20 did their best to soak the building, so that the gutters along the street turned to rivers. Charred belongings were scattered everywhere, and flames continued to burst through the air like stinging bees. Those workers who had survived, from the eighth and the tenth floors, huddled together, stunned. Eddie held a hand over his eyes so that his vision wouldn't be blurred by heat waves. He couldn't take in even a small portion of the destruction he saw. He turned back to his camera, the truer vision, the eye not tainted by human fear and regret. But the horror of the disaster was the only thing in sight, and the lens found the same anguish Eddie viewed. It was an even worse sight to behold through the eye of the camera, for its focus was sharper and more defined.

Girls and a few young men continued to gather on the windowsills, gazing out over the scene before closing their eyes and leaping. It seemed an endless stream of beautiful young people would continue to fly above them. The twisted fire escape still popped and shot off sulfurous bits of metal into the sky, the echo resembling gunfire. The only other sound was that of the water hitting the building, then running into the streets, a tragic waterfall. Before long Eddie was standing in a black pool up to his ankles.

It was then he spied the owners being ushered away in chauffeur-driven cars, behind them a carriage drawn by two fine black horses. The bosses and their associates had all managed to escape by climbing onto the roof, then making their way to the rooftop of the next factory. Eddie turned his camera, catching the moment when one of the owners gazed at the burning factory before a younger dark-haired man drew him back inside the curtains of the carriage. For an instant Eddie thought he knew this young man, though it was impossible; he wasn't acquainted with anyone of this ilk. No one he crossed paths with would wear a beaver coat and ride in a coach with velvet curtains while girls leapt into the air with no net to catch them, and no salvation, and no carriages to carry them away.

By then there were scores of bodies on the sidewalk. Even those hardened men who saw death every day, firemen and police officers, were crying as they worked. Eddie did his job, but as he photographed the fallen he had the sense that he was standing at the end of creation. If the ground split open beneath the Asch Building and took them all into the fires of hell, this day could not have seemed any more horrifying. The heat of the Asch Building could be felt two blocks away, though the flames were now smoldering. The crowd was hushed, even as more and more people were drawn to the scene, witness to the worst workplace disaster in the history of the city. Eddie took one photograph after the other. He could not stop, his angry heart convinced that he needed to document every inch of the catastrophe. In those hours on Washington Place, as he stood in the water and ashes, he lost the ability to be detached. All of those times when he hadn't felt another man's losses now came back to haunt him. He saw not only in black and white but also in every shade in between. The effect was humbling. The pools that bloomed red on the concrete were indeed blood, the white shards flung upon the cobblestones, bone. The bodies of the girls and a few strong young men were illuminated; each shone with light, the silver-edged sorrow of the recently deceased. Many were so wounded from their falls that the policemen who'd been sent to move them and tag the bodies so they might later be claimed, were doubled over in shock, the toughest among them gasping for strength and breath.

It was then a wind seemed to arise suddenly, for there was all at once a roar cutting through what had been silence. But in fact what they heard was the sound of sobbing, for those who had managed to survive were already searching for sisters and friends, and what they discovered was devastating. As the families of the dead arrived, many had to be restrained. Eddie himself felt maddened as he wandered among those who'd been lost, documenting as many as he could. He let the camera make his choices, for his eyes were burning with soot and his head spun. He continued to photograph the scene until a company man came over, there on behalf of the bosses, the very ones who had refused to install sprinklers, who some were saying were known to burn down their buildings for the sake of insurance money.

"That's enough," the company man said flatly. He was wearing an overcoat, though the air was stifling. He carried a thick wooden club he seemed more than ready to use. "Get going now."

Eddie hoisted his camera stand over his shoulder. "No problem. On my way." He muttered a few ripe curses under his breath, but he let it go at that, though he was steaming. He would have liked to have it out with the stooge, but this wasn't the moment to create an incident. Instead, Eddie went along Washington Place onto Waverly, but, as soon as the company man had moved on, he continued to work, despite the warning he'd been given. The air was cold and damp in the oncoming dusk, but his skin was burning. He was in a fever, and sweat washed down his back and chest. He couldn't help but wonder if Moses Levy had experienced this same heat, if true images burned their maker. He wondered, too, if the hermit at the riverside was right, if there wasn't some element of capturing a soul in each photograph, if he wasn't responsible for those whose images he caught, whether they be a bird in a cage, a fish in a pail, or a girl on a windowsill.

Eddie wiped his lens clean of soot. He tried to disappear from view as he photographed families desperate to find a sister or daughter, and girls crying in the gutter, arms around each other, clothes covered with ashes, the hems of their skirts singed black. In deference to their grief, he turned to photographing a clutter of personal trinkets, hair ribbons, purses, love letters, combs, all floating like debris in the drenched gutters, scattered over the cement like confetti. But every object seemed to have a soul as well, a throbbing heart, a remembrance of small pleasures and true love. There would be sixteen engagement rings found on the pavement by morning.

When darkness fell the police chased everyone away so they might cordon off the street to bring in the wooden coffins for the dead. So many were needed they could not gather enough in all of Manhattan. Carpenters came to fashion dozens more from floorboards and doors. Eddie huddled in a doorway so that he could continue on. His skin was aflame, and a cough had settled in his chest. He was still positioned on the soaked pavement when the firemen went into the building to retrieve the dead who'd been trapped in the charred rooms. They wrapped the bodies in sheets of oilcloth, and when those ran out they turned to using burlap, though the fabric quickly became damp and some of the sodden threads unraveled as corpses were lowered to the street on heavy ropes. The last image Eddie photographed belonged to one such terrible bundle, the pale feet of a lifeless young girl as she was delivered through the air.

That night Eddie went to the covered pier at East Twenty-sixth Street. The city morgue was too small for the sheer number of the dead, 147 in total, and so a makeshift morgue had been set up along the East River. The water was black as oil, and the night was black as well, illuminated by the lanterns the police held as they patrolled the pier. Eddie saw a cop he knew from the Tenth Precinct. For a fiver the officer let him past the barriers, but he told Eddie to hurry, for the families would be allowed in soon enough. One hundred thousand people would line up to view the dead before the night was through, families alongside gawkers who simply wanted to see the tragedy for themselves. The police would work through the day and night, holding up lanterns in the murky air so that the dead might be identified. Some of the bodies were so charred they were unrecognizable; others were oddly preserved, with so little damage Eddie half-expected them to rise from their coffins. Moses Levy had told him that, in Russia, children who had died were photographed in their finest clothes in the instants after death, propped up on velvet couches, to ensure that their images would be captured before their souls had flown. Perhaps it was true and a soul lingered close by after a person had passed on, for Eddie had found some of Levy's one-of-a-kind hand-tinted ambrotype prints tucked away in a drawer after his mentor's death. The technique, using nitric acid or bichloride of mercury, was so difficult and time-consuming it was rarely employed anymore. Some photographers considered it a cheap substitute for the more well-made daguerreotypes, but, in Levy's hands, these prints were magic. Silvery beads appeared upon the heads and clothing of the departed, as if they had been touched by something far greater than any human form. Looking at the serene faces of the two boys in one photograph, Eddie realized they must have been Moses's sons, children he'd never spoken of but whose images he'd managed to preserve for all eternity. And so it seemed, a soul could be captured after all.

IN THE DAYS that followed the Triangle Fire a dark lens was placed over Manhattan. The sorrow did not ease with time but instead seemed to multiply. There was a rising indignation over what had befallen the victims of the fire. Meetings at Cooper Union saw thousands attending, reminiscent of the protests of 1909 and 1910, when the city was forewarned that the conditions of the garment workers would lead to tragedy. Now the bloody portents had come to pass.

More workers gathered in the streets, their confusion turning to pure rage when it was discovered that the doors of the factory sewing loft had been locked, making it impossible for the girls to escape. A bolted doorknob had been found by investigators, there among the debris on the ninth floor, but because the door it had been attached to was nothing more than a few black planks, it could not be used as proof in a court of law. Still, every working man and woman knew what it meant. The dead had been locked into their death chamber, like common beasts, sheep penned up and forsaken. Eddie found a dark doorway from which to watch the mayhem. He bowed his head and let the words of the workers wash over him, a river of anger he understood all too well. In truth, he had been outraged all of his life.

When his insomnia gave way in the early morning hours and he at last found sleep, Eddie dreamed of the river and of his father's black coat. In his dream he was thirteen again, sleeping beside the horses, as he had when he first came to beg Moses Levy to take him on as his apprentice. He heard a knock on the stable doors and awoke within his dream. Inside his dream life, his father was waiting on the rough cobblestones. The elder Cohen had the suitcase that he kept beneath the bed. In real life, Eddie had once opened it, though he knew it was breaking a trust to do so. Inside there was a change of clothing for both Eddie and his father, along with a prayer book and a photograph of Eddie's mother.

In his dream he went to his father and stood beside him, a dutiful son once more.

"Are we going somewhere?" his dream self asked.

"No. But if we have to, we're ready," his father said reasonably.

Eddie pinned the images of the dead to the wall of his loft. He studied their faces, committing them to memory. There was a girl with freckles on her cheeks, her complexion turned chalky in death. Another donned a hat decorated with white silk daisies. Eddie thought it odd that the hat had stayed on her head despite a sheer fall of nine stories. Upon close inspection with a magnifying glass, he spied the reason for this: a hatpin in the shape of a bee. There were two sisters, neither one more than sixteen, each with lovely arched eyebrows and coils of auburn hair. At night, when he tried to sleep, he saw their faces. He listened to the fish swimming in the pail. The trout had grown larger, and it bumped against the bucket with every turn. By now there was an attachment. Eddie knew he couldn't bring himself to eat his catch. Instead, he fed it bread crumbs and worms dug from beneath the stable floor, caring for it as though it were a pet. He took photographs of his new companion at the end of each day. After so much death, there was a real pleasure in recording the image of a living creature. Still, he wished the day he'd caught it had never happened, and that he'd never gone down to Washington Place to watch those girls fly from the windowsills.

One night there was a knocking at the stable door. Eddie was deeply asleep, helped along by gin, in the thick black fog that is every insomniac's eventual fate if he stays awake long enough. He assumed it was his dream again, his father once more arriving with their suitcase. When at last he rallied long enough to realize the knocking was real, he guessed the caller wanted the fellow who had taken over the rent of the stable for the past few years, letting out his carriage and raising birds in large cages kept in the tack room. He pulled the blanket over his head and sank back into his pillow. But the banging on his door continued, and through the fog of sleep Eddie heard someone shout out for him. It was the wrong name, but he was too groggy to realize that, and, in all honesty, it was the only name he would have answered to, for in his darkest dreams he was always called Ezekiel.

He crawled out of bed, pulled on his trousers, then took the stairs two at a time. As he opened the door there was a moment when he thought his father was before him. If this was a dream in which Joseph Cohen had come to bring him home, Eddie might have agreed. On this night, he might have given up his new life in exchange for erasing the vision of the bodies of the young girls at the morgue. But it was another man at the door. The visitor was Orthodox and wore a black coat and hat. His stooped posture made Eddie yearn for his father, for this stranger was clearly a tailor who had hunched over a sewing machine for many years.

"If you're here to lease a carriage, I'm not your man," Eddie remarked groggily. "There's no one here till six."

"I don't want a carriage," the caller said. "I'm looking for my daughter."

The hour was so early that the horses were still asleep on their feet, their breath turning to clouds in the chilly predawn air.

"I can't help you with that." The only women Eddie knew were ones from the taverns, and he never brought them home. "You'll have to leave."

The older man squinted, his expression grave. Beneath his glasses he had pale rheumy eyes, hazed over with cataracts. "You're the photographer?"

"Yes."

"Then you're who I want to see."

When the visitor started upstairs without an invitation, Eddie had little choice but to follow at his heels, doing his best to persuade his unwanted guest a mistake had been made. "I don't have any women here. But look if you want. See for yourself. Then you can go."

The visitor plainly intended to do so. He entered the loft and peered through the chaos. Eddie had been working nonstop, and the pitted wooden table was littered with prints, including the shining image of the trout. It had turned out better than he had expected. Enough to give him a glimmer of hope that he might one day be good enough to call himself a student of Moses Levy.

The visitor bumped into the bucket where the fish swam in a forlorn circle. "You sell fish?"

At this point all Eddie knew was that he kept the fish because he was alive and had as much right to a life as any other creature. He shrugged and felt a fool. "He's a guest."

"He's a guest, but you didn't want to let me inside?"

"Because you're at the wrong address. Listen, there's no one here you'd know or want." It then struck Eddie that his caller might have another photographer in mind. "If you're a friend of Moses Levy, you're too late. He died five years ago."

The visitor removed his wire-rimmed glasses and cleaned the

lenses with a pocket handkerchief. "I'm a friend of your father's. He sent me. That's how I came to have your address."

Eddie took a step back, confused. "That's impossible. My father doesn't know where I live."

"He gave me your address. Therefore he knows something." The visitor spied the photographs of the dead girls tacked to the wall. "Yes. I'm in the right place. You were there." The older man crossed the room, his steps echoing on the wide-planked wooden floor. He wore heavy shoes, one heel built up with wooden filler to even out his gait, for his legs were mismatched in length. "You're going to find my daughter."

Eddie's visitor was Samuel Weiss, a tailor and the father of two daughters, Ella and Hannah, both employed by the Triangle Shirtwaist Company. Ella was safely at home, but Hannah could not be found. Weiss had been to St. Vincent's Hospital, established by the Sisters of Charity in 1849, then he'd gone on to Bellevue, and finally to the morgue on the pier. His beautiful daughter with the white-blond hair had not been among the wounded or the dead. No one in the neighborhood had seen her since Saturday, not even her closest friends. Now Weiss searched the images on Eddie's wall, but again, Hannah could not be found. When he had gone through every photograph, he sat in a wooden chair, overwhelmed, his face streaming with tears, his eyes rimmed red. The light filtering through the skylight was a pale, creamy yellow. Between Weiss's sobs Eddie could hear the horses in the stable below, restless in their stalls now that morning had risen, waiting for the liveryman and their breakfast of oats.

"Hannah worked on the ninth floor. Do you know what that means? No survivors. Or so they say. How do you believe a pack of liars? I for one don't trust anything we're told."

"Mr. Weiss, I'm sorry. I truly am. There were no survivors."

"I don't need you to be sorry! Help me! That's what I need. Your father said you could find her."

His father, whom he had not seen or spoken to in twelve years, almost as much time as they had lived together, who knew nothing about what his son was capable of. Eddie often wondered if they would recognize each other if they passed on the street, or if they had become such strangers to one another they would merely keep on walking, having no idea that they shared the same flesh and blood, that they had once slept together under the same black overcoat in the forest, in shock and mourning.

"How is it possible that there's no sign of her?" Weiss went on. "How many girls have hair so pale it's the color of snow? How many come home every night right on time and are never late?" His voice was raspy. He had been searching through the debris on Greene Street and had breathed in cinders. "They found not a scrap of clothing, not her purse, not a bit of jewelry, nothing. She wore a gold locket that belonged to her mother. I gave it to her on her last birthday. She wept with tears of gratitude and swore she would never take it off. Gold does not burn, I know that much. It melts, but it doesn't disappear. None of her friends saw her that morning. What do you think of that? I questioned everyone who survived, even her best friend, Rose, who's still in St. Vincent's Hospital, with both of her legs burned." He glared at Eddie. "Don't tell me nothing remains of a human being."

Eddie went to the bureau for some whiskey and glasses. Before the fire he would have merely insisted his visitor leave, now he felt the thorn of compassion. He put down a glass in front of Weiss and asked, "Have you been to the precinct? Spoken with the police?"

"The police?" Weiss's face furrowed with distrust. "No." He gulped the whiskey and tapped his glass on the table for more. "I wanted someone I can trust. That's why I came to you."

"Me? Why would you trust me?"

Weiss shook his head, amazed by how dense the younger man was. "Because you are one of us, Ezekiel."

"I'm not! Look at me."

Eddie wore a blue shirt and black trousers. He had no tallit around his shoulders, a garment that showed a covenant with God, and no remnants of his Orthodox upbringing. His hair was cropped short, and he'd long ago forsaken the practice of wearing a skullcap. His large, pale feet were bare, allowing a glimpse of a tattoo of a trident he'd had inked on his ankle, a true embarrassment, even to him. He'd gone to the infamous Samuel O'Reilly's shop one drunken evening, where the owner used Edison's newly invented electric tattoo machine. Eddie had immediately regretted his choice when he awoke the next morning with a throbbing headache. Tattoos were strictly forbidden for his people, and men of his faith so marked could not be buried in a religious cemetery. Eddie's regret, however, had less to do with faith than with the fact that the tattoo was so crudely drawn.

Weiss eyed the younger man sadly. "You think your father would send me to the wrong man? You think he doesn't know his own son? You're the one who can find people."

"Mr. Weiss, please." Eddie downed his whiskey and began a second glass. He wouldn't mind getting drunk.

"He said you worked for Hochman."

"He knew that?"

"A father knows his son."

Eddie shook his head. "No." He would get drunk, he had decided, without a doubt.

"He told me it was you, not that fake wizard, who discovered the boy under the bridge. The shyster took the credit, but you were the one who found him. Your father said you always had this talent. You guided him through the forest when you were a little boy. He said he would have been dead without you, or wandering there still."

Eddie was stunned. He'd never thought he'd been the one to lead them out of the woods. And surely he'd never told his father how he earned his money. He knew that his father would have disapproved of Hochman and his methods. Now it seemed the elder Cohen had known precisely what Eddie was doing on the nights he'd sneaked out. He wondered if his father had lain in bed, eyes open, as Eddie let himself out the door. Perhaps he'd gone so far as to rise from the thin mattress, slip his coat over his pajamas, and track Eddie to the Hall of Love so he might stand in the dark on Sheriff Street and mourn what his son had become. Perhaps he'd had their suitcase in hand.

"You shouldn't go around trusting people you don't even know," Eddie advised his visitor. "You'll get into trouble that way."

"I know your father, and that's enough for me." Weiss narrowed his eyes. "Do you want money? Because I have it." The older man reached into the pocket of his overcoat, but Eddie stopped him.

"No. No money." Eddie sat back in his chair and rubbed at his temples. His head was throbbing. "Even if I could do what you want, there's no guarantee you would like what I found."

Weiss shook his head, disagreeing. "If you find the truth, then you've found what I want."

"What if Hannah is dead? You want to know that?"

"If she is, show me the locket. That's when I'll believe it. That's when I'll say the Kaddish and lay her to rest."

Weiss reached for a photograph in his vest pocket. It was a poor example of the craft, snapped in one of those new ten-cent machines so popular at photo galleries at Coney Island and on Fourteenth Street. The image was already fading, turning milky, but the beauty of Weiss's daughter was unmistakable. She had long, pale hair and delicate features.

"Your father said you would find her," Weiss said, his voice seized by emotion. "Don't make him into a liar."

After Weiss's visit, Eddie slept, awaking in the morning on the floor. He'd finished the whiskey after Weiss had gone, and added a good measure of gin, a lethal combination. Apparently he'd fallen asleep beside the dog. Now his back and legs ached. He had a cough and the room felt damp. If he wasn't careful, he would find himself coming down with pneumonia, as Moses Levy had.

Eddie went to retrieve a tin box stowed beneath the floorboards. There was cash inside, his savings. He had hoped to buy a camera that would allow him to use flexible film, a new style in the art that made the development process faster and easier, but he could forgo such things. He'd gotten in the habit of hiding his earnings when he was a boy, choosing a clever spot, just beneath the table where he and his father took their meager supper each evening. In his loft he kept his savings in the same place. Eddie folded the bills into an envelope.

As he grabbed his coat to go out, Eddie spied a flash of silver light in the pail beside the sink, as if a star had fallen through the skylight. It was the trout, motionless at the bottom of the pail. He felt a rush of regret. He should have taken it back to the river, for a fish was born to be a fish, whether or not he'd been caught. He quickly folded the trout into a sheaf of newspaper, for he couldn't leave it to stink, nor had he the heart to toss it into the trash pile in the alley. He whistled for Mitts and, with the wrapped fish resting in the crook of his arm, set out.

The liveryman had recently arrived to divvy out oats and hay. The stable tenant was a short individual, with broad ugly features, his face pocked with scars. Several of his teeth were capped with gold, and he often made reference to the fact that he'd given up his wild ways, not caring to elaborate further.

Sometimes the liveryman called himself Joe, sometimes it was Johnny. He started out as what was called a sheriff at various saloons, a bouncer who kept the peace while enjoying the violence of the job. At one time, he'd risen as high as a man could in the criminal world, working for Tammany Hall and the politicians who ran the city. But a long term in prison had taken his wildness out of him, and he'd sunk to working in the stable, renting out a carriage. He had a love of animals and birds, especially the pigeons he raised in the tack room, for they sat on his shoulders as he went about his chores. He'd begun his days in a pet store, and he often told Eddie he should have stayed with that. The horses ran to him now, and he treated them kindly, greeting each by name. Sally, Spot, Little Girl, Jackson. He lived round the corner, at a flophouse on Twenty-second Street where shared rooms could be had for the night, but should one of the horses take ill, he brought over his cot and slept in the stable. He could frequently be found smoking a foul mixture in the alley, bowls full of opium, but he never did so inside the stable, to ensure his creatures would be safe and no sparks would fall into the bales of hay. Eddie had chosen to ignore the stink of opium. In his opinion, there were far worse neighbors to have. There were thousands of men who visited the opium houses of the Lower East Side. Most of them couldn't get a job, let alone keep one, but the liveryman managed well enough.

"You're keeping early hours," the fellow called as he tossed Mitts a biscuit. "Or is it that you never sleep?" He'd heard Eddie pacing at odd hours, seen him come in or leave when most men were safe in bed.

Eddie grinned and stretched his aching back. "I slept on the floor like a dog."

"Then you must have dreamed, for dogs do so nightly. Don't let anyone tell you otherwise. Isn't that right?" the carriage man said to Mitts, who had offered his paw before following his master out the heavy stable door.

Eddie loved the city when it was first waking. Energy surged through the concrete and cobblestones the way mist rises in the woods. In fact, his sleep had been deep and empty. If the liveryman was right and his dog dreamed, then Eddie envied him, for there had been no sign of the dark-haired woman who sometimes came to his bed in his dreams. Now Mitts trotted briskly along beside him on their journey downtown, clearly happy to be alive, with no thought to the future or the past. For this, Eddie envied Mitts as well, how light his burden was, how clear his purpose. He was to be his master's companion, and in doing so he became himself, the essence of a dog. When all was said and done, it was conceivable that a being's purpose remained the same throughout his life, and Eddie's purpose was exactly what it had been when he was a boy, to pursue the light and find what was lost.

His destination was little more than twenty blocks downtown. He crouched on a stoop across from the building where he had lived with his father, pulling up his long legs, leaning against the ironwork railing. It was drizzling and the sky hung down. The gutters were wet and filthy. A boy came out of the house across the street. It was Eddie's good luck that when he signaled the boy approached. He was six or seven years old, shy, Orthodox, hanging back when he reached the stoop. Clearly, he'd crossed the street because of his interest in the dog. He could barely take his eyes off Mitts, who cheerfully slobbered and returned the boy's gaze.

"You know Joseph Cohen?" Eddie asked the child.

"No." The boy most certainly had been told not to talk to strangers. He didn't raise his eyes. To gain the boy's trust, Eddie switched over to Yiddish.

"Mr. Cohen, the tailor. You know him?"

The boy glanced up, surprised that this lanky, gruff young man spoke his language. He didn't look like one of them, but the boy accepted Eddie now that he knew they were of the same faith. It was obvious that the boy was more impressed by the dog than by anything Eddie had to say. He tentatively held out his hand, and Mitts sniffed it. Startled by the dog's wet nose, the boy drew his hand back. He shifted from foot to foot, nervous but more interested than ever.

"Go ahead," Eddie suggested, recognizing a fellow dog lover. "You can pet him. He won't bite."

The boy remained suspicious. It was likely that his mother had warned him not only to stay away from strange men but to avoid strange dogs as well.

"Go on," Eddie said. "He's friendly."

The boy's curiosity got the better of him. He edged nearer, grinning when Mitts sat before him.

"Someone I met said he's a rabbit, and maybe that's what he thinks he is. A big rabbit with white feet."

When the boy petted the pit bull's broad head, a smile of delight crossed his face. "He's like silk." Mitts licked his face, and the boy laughed and wiped his cheek. "He is a big rabbit."

Eddie returned to his initial questioning. "You know the man who lives on the fifth floor? The tailor. The one that doesn't like noise and doesn't talk to anyone? He has a long, dark beard."

The boy nodded, but he corrected Eddie. "His beard is gray."

That piece of information made Eddie's throat grow tight. He held out a dime. "For you," he said, to the boy's great surprise. He then handed the boy the envelope he'd brought along. "Bring this up to him and you can have the dime." There wasn't much cash in the envelope, but it was enough to purchase new boots, a few bags of potatoes and turnips, a scarf, even a new coat, for the one Eddie had bought his father long ago must certainly be threadbare by now. "Don't open it. Understand?"

The boy accepted the dime and the envelope. Before he went on, Eddie grabbed him. "My dog can judge who's trustworthy and who's not, that's why I'm giving this job to you. He trusts you."

The boy nodded, his eyes on the dog. After Eddie let go of him, the young messenger patted Mitts one last time. "Good boy," he said in English before he ran across the street.

The Cohen apartment was at the front of the building, its single window overlooking the street. Eddie had often sat there, watching the dusk sift past the glass, waiting for the time when he could sneak away. Now he wondered if his father had been aware each time he opened the door, just wide enough to make his escape.

After several minutes, Eddie looked up to see the curtains move. He lifted his hand to wave before the curtain closed. He had no idea if his father would keep the envelope that had been delivered, or if he would burn it in one of the two soup bowls he owned, or perhaps donate it to the poor box in the shul. Eddie wondered if he'd even recognized the man across the street as his only son.

Being back in the neighborhood gave Eddie the jitters, and his skin prickled. He considered stopping at the druggist's shop on Grand Street where the pharmacist was said not to have left his store for more than twenty years, a self-imposed prisoner, the victim of love gone wrong. But the shop was often closed, and there was no cure for Eddie's ailment. He wandered, so deep in thought he didn't notice that the streets where he'd grown up had melted away. He found himself at the river. Water slapped at the row of wooden docks on stilts. He still had the trout, which he now unwrapped from its casing of damp newspaper. The silvery scales were cold and wet. The trout belonged to the river, and that was where Eddie would dispose of it. Rain had begun in earnest, a cold spring shower that left a haze of blue over the mirrored surface. Eddie could barely see New Jersey or make out the ferries that cut through the water. He leaned down, holding the trout in both hands. When he let go he expected it to sink. The rain was falling too hard to see clearly, yet he could spy a trail of light, as if the trout was racing through the water, headed for the depths, his freedom restored.

Eddie sat back on his heels, stunned. He did not believe in life everlasting, or in the prayers of his forefathers, or in miracles of any kind. The movement of the fish was most likely a trick of light, but light was something he did indeed believe in. He had the urge to leap in himself so that he might discover whether or not it was alive, and whether, if he followed the trout, he would find what he had lost when he left his father's house, when he shut the door and found himself on the dark streets of New York.

THREE

THE DREAMER

FROM THE DREAM

****

F ROM THE TIME *I began my career at the museum, my father told me I was a wonder of the world. Yet when I held up my hand mirror to study my face, it did not seem wondrous to me. My features—gray eyes, black eyebrows, high cheekbones, pale complexion—added up to a plain person, a simple individual no one would look at twice. I considered myself to be nothing special, a dull creature who could not compare to those God had made to be unique in all the world, for the living wonders my father employed were as marvelous as they were strange. There were those who could eat fire, making sure to coat their throats before each performance with a thick syrup made in the Indies, and those with limbs so flexible they could flip upside down, standing on their hands for hours at a time. There was a girl not much older than I named Malia, whose arms resembled a butterfly's wings. Her mother accompanied her to the museum every morning and made up her extraordinarily beautiful face with rouge and black kohl, so that her daughter resembled a monarch butterfly. I tried to befriend Malia, but she spoke only Portuguese, and my*

*father did not wish for me to interact with those he employed. He handed
me a book from his library and told me I would be better off befriending
the works of Shakespeare.*

~

*Of all the living wonders, I was most curious about the Wolfman. He was
so thoroughly covered with hair that when he crouched down he appeared
to be an animal, albeit one who dressed in pleated trousers, a woolen
overcoat, and handcrafted boots. He combed his hair neatly parted down
his face so that his eyes might be seen. They were deep set and luminous,
a rich brown color, so human it was impossible to judge him as anything
other than a man once he gazed at you. The Wolfman's name was Raymond Morris, and he came from a good family in Richmond, Virginia,
who had kept him in the attic to protect him, and also to ensure there'd be
no damage to the family's reputation. He'd been hidden away from the
time he was born.*

*Mr. Morris once confided in me that for most of his life he'd truly
believed he had all he would ever need, despite being raised behind locked
doors. There was a nursemaid to care for him, and later a manservant
brought whatever he wished. He had fine clothes, and any food he desired,
for a cook had been hired from Atlanta to see to his whims. As he grew
older his greatest joy was reading. Because of this passion, his library
surpassed those of many colleges. The life he led was enriched immeasur-
ably by the many novels in his collection, all of which he had read more
than once. Although he'd never felt the rain, he knew what it was like
from his readings, just as he knew about the limitless sea, and the golden
prairie, and the pleasures of love. He was convinced that his world was
enough, he told me, until he read Jane Eyre. Then his opinion changed.
He could feel the world shifting as he devoured the story. He suddenly
understood how a person could go mad if locked away from all others, and*

he found himself half in love with the first Mrs. Rochester, the character other readers might consider the villainess of the book. He climbed out his window the same night he finished the novel. For the very first time he felt the rain splash against his skin.

He came to New York because during his self-education he had studied Walt Whitman and had idolized him, as I did. Due to his reading, Mr. Morris was certain that it was only in the city of New York, so abundant with energy and life, that he would be accepted, able to exist as any other man, despite his differences. He would make his way along the great avenues and the rivers pulsing with commerce; he would walk among the shipbuilders and the workers. Instead, he was locked up on his second day in the city, arrested for creating a nuisance. It was there in jail that my father found him, huddled in a cell, blood streaking his hair. Mr. Morris had been beaten nearly senseless on Broadway in front of a massive crowd, his abusers cheered on by those who were convinced he was a monster. The constables had been of the same opinion, and had kept him cuffed and chained.

I was in the back of the carriage on the day my father went to the holding cell known as the cage in the Tenth Precinct on Twentieth Street in Manhattan. I was nearly twelve by then and nearly a woman, and I already had begun to accompany my father on business forays. Maureen said my presence gave my father credibility, a word I'm sure he never imagined she knew. I think Maureen hid how bright she was because of her position in life; a housemaid had no right to address a learned man. She had no rights at all.

My father had informants in police stations and hospitals who, for a small fee, would contact him when a particularly interesting specimen was found. Raymond Morris was brought out to our carriage, confused and covered with welts. I lowered my eyes, so as not to gawk, which would have been unseemly, especially when I considered my own abnormalities.

Mr. Morris was unique, however, and I couldn't help but peek at him. I suppose he got into our carriage because it was the only option. The Professor rolled a cigarette, which he offered to his new companion as he discussed terms of employment. Oddities profited here in our city, my father said. Raymond Morris laughed, just like any man. I was sitting behind them, even more silent than usual. I admit my first reaction upon seeing this wonder was sheer terror. To my surprise Morris had a deep, resonant voice as he answered my father's statement with a recitation.

> *"Now I see it is true, what I guess'd at,*
> *What I guess'd when I loaf'd on the grass,*
> *What I guess'd while I lay alone in my bed,*
> *And again as I walk'd the beach under the paling stars*
> *of the morning."*

In response, my father snapped, "Don't speak in riddles, speak plainly."

But I knew those words to be Whitman's and I could only imagine what Raymond Morris had guessed at before he'd come to our city and seen firsthand what cruelty could be. Perhaps I took a step away from my father on that day, and began to side with the wonders he employed.

"Do you want the work or not?" my father said coldly. "I don't wish to waste my time."

"Frankly, sir," Morris said of the employment he'd been offered, "I have no other choice."

We traveled back to Brooklyn without any further conversation, though there were dozens of questions I might have asked. Raymond Morris was left at a boardinghouse where many of the living wonders resided, along Sheridan's Walk, a stretch that ran from Surf Avenue to the ocean, and would in a few years be totally in the shadow of the Giant Racer Roller Coaster. The Professor paid a full month's rent. "I'm trusting you," he told Morris, making it clear that as an employee Morris was expected to report to the museum the following day and each day after that. "I don't expect you to let me down," my father advised. Indeed, he seemed quite convinced the new man would not run away. Morris knew what awaited him on the beach and on the avenues, a crowd of abusers, nothing more. As we drove off my father was whistling. "That's money in the bank," he said. "A true one of a kind."

I looked behind us and watched the figure of Raymond Morris on the steps of the boardinghouse, a stranger to Brooklyn and to our world. I prayed that he might indeed run away, and that he might find some empty stretch of marsh or woods where he would be allowed to be a man.

THE FOLLOWING WEEK the season began. From my window, I could see the human curiosities gathering in the yard, served coffee and tea by Maureen. There were old standbys who returned year after year, as well as fly-by-night acts, some of whom barely lasted a season. We'd had several pairs of Siamese twins, as well as an alligator man, whose skin was covered with bumps he tinted green. There'd been dwarfs and giants, fat women as well as women so thin one could nearly see through their pale flesh. I was interested in every one, for each had a story, a mother and father, a dream for the future.

On this opening day, as the wonders gathered, the hood of a man's cloak fell from his head while he waited his turn for tea. The cloak was made of fine wool and cashmere, but it was no gentleman I saw. I blinked and imagined I'd spied a wolf, then realized it was my father's new discovery. Mr. Morris gazed up, and I shied away from the window, thinking he might howl and bare his teeth. Instead he bowed and said, "Hello, little girl," in his deep, musical voice. I was so mortified at having been caught staring that I quickly slipped the curtain closed. But I went on looking at him through the muslin, and I saw him wave to me. After that I had a different feeling about what a wolf might be.

I had grown to appreciate the people who gathered in the yard and to consider them a sort of family. Still, I kept to myself, following my father's instructions. Yet with every day that passed I was more certain I was meant to be among them.

My father was the one who named Mr. Morris the Wolfman, an appellation that came to him in a dream. My father's dreams and whims were law. He commissioned a sign to be made with Morris's portrait; the painter was directed to add fangs and a long tail. People screamed when they saw the new living wonder, and he became immensely popular, with lines forming down Surf Avenue, even though some of the women in the crowd had to be revived with vinegar and smelling salts after they saw him. He was, without a doubt, our star attraction, though he never grew conceited. Maureen whispered that the crowd's reaction was not because he was so fierce—although he'd been taught to shake the bars of the cage in which he was exhibited and to grunt rather than speak. It was when they looked in his eyes and saw how human he was that he terrified them.

~

My father's new employee liked his tea with milk and sugar, and he always asked for seconds when I baked a pear cobbler made with the fruit from our tree. We had begun to use the new tea bags made of muslin and sold prepackaged, and he laughed at their silly hat-like shape. He was great company, and was always a gracious teacher when discussing Whitman, who he felt was the greatest American poet, the Shakespeare of our times, a voice that spoke for all mankind and certainly for those of us who lived in Brooklyn. Mr. Morris worried for me, insisting so much time spent in water, a good eight hours a day, was unhealthy for a girl my age. True enough, my confinement in the tank had turned my skin pale as parchment. I had grown so accustomed to the cold that the rising heat of the warm June days brought out a red rash on my arms and legs. I itched and scratched at my clothes, yet I continued to wear my gloves, as proper French schoolgirls did, for I knew my father was particular in all matters of dress. I didn't mind this fashion, for I was deeply embarrassed by my hands, which seemed less a wonder than a mistake. I did not consider myself a "one of a kinder," only an accident of the flesh. I needed the false tail and blue dye to seem truly wondrous. As far as I was concerned, what was exceptional about me was simply a form of trickery.

Raymond Morris said that if he were as free as he imagined I would become when I legally came of age, on my eighteenth birthday, he would choose to roam the globe and see the true wonders of the world. He spoke of Paris and Egypt and Siam. He told me all he knew of what he'd read of these places, and his stories kept me enraptured. I heard about the French painters Cézanne and Pissarro and of the old masters at the Louvre. I was amazed by descriptions of the tombs in the Valley of the Kings and of silkworms that ate the leaves of white mulberry trees and spun a thread so fine it couldn't be seen by the naked eye.

Maureen took to sitting with us in the yard, enthralled as I was, drawn in by Mr. Morris's deep, measured voice. He was by far the most well-read man either of us had ever met. He knew the work of the great poets by heart, and had memorized whole passages of Jane Eyre, the book he always claimed had set him free after he'd read of the first Mrs. Rochester's choice to burn down the house rather than remain imprisoned in her misery. He was also a great fan of Poe, a native of his home city, and swore the writer had died more of harassment and misunderstanding than of alcohol. He often read this author's stories as we ate our lunch. We shivered at these tales of woe and tragedy, and still we begged for more. Although Maureen said she'd never been so frightened in all her life as *when we listened to Poe's tales, I noticed she edged closer to Mr. Morris at these times. I came to understand he was not a monster in her eyes.*

Mr. Morris was with us for three years, and during that time the Museum of Extraordinary Things prospered. Unlike the other wonders, who vanished during the off-season, to carnivals in Florida and throughout the South, Mr. Morris remained in Brooklyn. He had been led here by literature, and so he remained close to Whitman's world. He was befriended by a bookseller from Scribner's Publishers who had rooms at the Brighton Beach Hotel for the season. This kind man brought him whatever volumes he wished, including modern novels such as Call of the Wild, by Jack London, which must have brought to mind the relationship between wolves and men, as well as The Jungle, by Upton Sinclair, considered radical for its exposure of the wretched conditions of the meat-packing industry.

Mr. Morris's disappearance from our midst was not sudden, though it may have appeared that way to others, for one day at the height of the season he simply did not arrive. It was apparent that my father had been watching Mr. Morris for quite some time, with disapproval and distaste. The two rarely spoke. The Professor often saw what escaped others' eyes and had a particular knack for spying people's weaknesses. He preferred flaws that he could exploit and was therefore uncomfortable with an employee who was so intelligent and learned, a man who, had he not been born as he was, would have easily been my father's equal or better. I'd overheard him say to Mr. Morris, "I hope you haven't forgotten that I rescued you. Think of where you'd be if not for me. No one else would have you. They'd run from you, stone you, cry out for your captivity. Remember at all times, you are a freak of nature, and that alone is your distinction."

It was a demeaning thing to say. I understood the sting of such a comment, for my father had often told me that after my mother's passing another man might have left me in an orphanage, particularly in light of my deformity. But he had been loyal to me, and therefore he expected my loyalty in return. Such a debt of gratitude made me feel as if I had no choices in this world, as if my future lay in only one direction, a path decided upon by my father.

Raymond Morris bowed his head when he was reminded of his time in prison, and quickly offered his thanks for his rescue, but there was a glint of mistrust in his eyes. He was a man of great dignity, and surely this was the reason Maureen was attracted to him. They often sat together, speaking in confidence. She had let slip that she visited him during the off-season and had mentioned that upon one or more occasions she'd brought him a leek and onion pie, one of her specialties. When I questioned her about how frequently she spent time with him, she informed me that polite girls didn't ask questions about a person's private life. Once, when they didn't know I was nearby, I had seen Mr. Morris take her hand. I was not the only one who noticed their closeness. Soon enough Maureen was found in his room by the landlord of the boardinghouse, who then demanded a fee from my father, insisting that a room in which two people cohabited should have the charges doubled.

If Maureen was in love with the Wolfman, she never discussed it with me. I only knew that my father dismissed Raymond Morris, though he was our most popular attraction and made the museum more prosperous than it had ever been. I was surprised at the depth of my father's fury. Morris was asked to leave the boardinghouse where he'd been deposited after his release from jail. I don't know where he went, but I do know he left Maureen a token on the day he vanished: a worn copy of Jane Eyre, set out on the kitchen counter, wrapped in brown paper and twine, with her name written upon the wrapping in his graceful script.

I heard Maureen arguing with my father in the parlor afterward. The Professor said she was a whore, so low she would get on her back for a vile *dog. That was what he called the Wolfman, Satan's dog. I thought I heard a slap, but I wasn't sure. I put my hands over my ears, but I still heard Maureen crying. After that she said no more of Mr. Morris, and although her eyes were often red and inflamed, she didn't dare to go against my father. She was his employee after all, and jobs were not so easy to come by. If she left she would likely be fit only for factory work, grueling and low paying, and she might even be turned away from that because of the burn marks on her face.*

No one mentioned the Wolfman in the days that followed, and a new exhibit soon enough took his place, a young man named Horace, whose older brother brought him from Sunnyside, Queens, in the mornings and picked him up in the evenings. Horace had only half a jaw and could neither speak nor hear, but he had been taught to growl in a menacing manner, as the Wolfman had. My father named him the Jungle Boy and employed the sign maker once more. Horace never complained and he did as he was told. As far as I knew, he couldn't read.

ONE MORNING, not long after Mr. Morris's departure, as Maureen and I sat on the back porch peeling potatoes for a stew, I found myself thinking about "The Tell-Tale Heart," a story of Poe's that Mr. Morris had read to us in which a murderer cannot escape his own guilt. I was thirteen at this time, and I was especially interested in the ways in which some men felt guilt, while others seemed free to hurt those closest to them without remorse. The protagonist in Poe's story is certain he continues to hear the heart of his victim beating beneath the floorboards, but it is the pulse of his own guilt that resounds. I wondered if all men's deeds came back to haunt them and proposed an idea to Maureen: if the Wolfman were to become famous at some other exhibition, perhaps my father would regret his decision and want to hire him again and then all would be well.

"Oh, I doubt that," Maureen said coldly. "Your father has no regrets."

"He must. All good men do, and he must have been that for my mother to have loved and married him."

Maureen studied me, and I felt pity in her gaze. Of course she thought I was naïve, and I suppose I was. I'd been kept away from the world, and what I knew of it were bits and pieces that didn't add up.

"Love is odder than anything you might find here," Maureen instructed. Her voice was kind, yet I felt she was delivering a warning. She sometimes carried Mr. Morris's edition of Jane Eyre with her, for it was pocket size and she was very attached to it. I wasn't certain if it was the story she was faithful to, or if her loyalty belonged to the man who had given her the book.

"Did you love Mr. Morris?" I asked. It was bold of me to question her so, for I'd been warned by my father never to bring up his name. But I was truly interested in Maureen's welfare, and I think she softened when she saw my earnest expression.

"He read to me when I was with him in his room, and I went there willingly. All I can tell you is that when it was dark, he was like any other man. Better," she told me. "Far better than anyone who's passed through this yard."

THERE CAME an evening when I was reading in my father's library, as was my habit when he was out and I had my pick of what was on the shelf. When I grew drowsy, I started for bed, going first to the kitchen to make sure the back door was locked. I happened to glimpse a bit of light as I passed by the stairs to the cellar. When I peered down I noticed the door to the workroom had been left ajar. I went down the steps, drawn by my curiosity before I could think things through. The door to this room was always locked and bolted twice, but somehow the Professor had forgotten

to do so on this occasion. As usual, he hadn't informed me where he was going or when he would return, but he was often gone past midnight. I wondered if the open door was a sign sent to me from above suggesting I should look inside, or if it was a simple act of forgetfulness.

It was in this cellar room that my father maintained scientific experiments, dissecting and studying some of the strange creatures he had discovered in morgues and hospitals, and in the back rooms along the docks. No one was to disturb him when he was locked away, not even if he missed his dinner. There were times when the liveryman he employed dragged a bundle down the stairs and the two men would then stand together and argue over a price in low tones. I had heard them raise their voices more than once, and I hadn't known whether I should fear for my father's safety or for the safety of the liveryman.

I made my way to the threshold of the workshop. I pushed open the door so that I might peer through the darkening shadows. Jars of specimens gleamed and dust motes hung in the unmoving air. From the corridor where I stood I could see that there were canisters of salt and formaldehyde set upon the shelves, all in readiness for any new specimens. I spied the skull of a leopard that was being fitted with a third set of teeth so that it might appear more ferocious and strange. There were fingernails that had grown ten feet long before they'd been cut and were now soaking in bleach, and a box of the bodies of bright birds captured in New Guinea, their feathers tinted even brighter shades with red and orange dye. On a white metal table there was a selection of knives and surgery tools. My father, it seemed, did not shy away from helping nature create miracles. In this way he was a tailor of the marvelous, a creator of dreams.

Although I was well behaved on most occasions, I still possessed my natural curiosity, an urge I tried my best to ignore. Perhaps my rebel's soul had been inflamed by the Wolfman's tales of wandering the world.

Surely something had ignited my disobedience, which flared with every passing day. I slipped into the workshop, closing the door behind me. The decision was quick, like diving into the sea. One step, and I was inside. The scent of amber and incense lingered, and the room felt close, for the single window in the cellar had been boarded over and no natural light entered the room other than a few pale rays of renegade moonlight that filtered around the nailed planks. No one came to clean here; Maureen was not allowed to pass through with a mop or a broom, and nothing had been tidied or organized for many years. Papers were everywhere, letters and graphs of all sorts left in a jumble. I went to my father's desk, and there I saw the bones of a baby's skeleton set out upon the blotter, like a puzzle. The bones were so tiny I could have picked up the entire spine and rested it in my palm. I, who was rarely cold, felt a chill as I stood there.

I had once asked Raymond Morris why he thought God had made him the way he was, and he'd laughed and said he did not think God had a hand in every error that humans made. He shocked me when he admitted there were times when he did not think there was a God at all, for when he looked into a mirror he believed only the devil had been at work in his creation. I disagreed with him. I thought that God had blessed Mr. Morris in some way, and that was why he was so knowledgeable and so kind. I was convinced that God had a hand in everything we did on earth, though we might never understand his ways, but I did not say so, for I was a girl at the time, and didn't believe I had the right to speak my thoughts aloud.

I don't know what made me open the top desk drawer in my father's workshop; perhaps it was God's intention or perhaps it was entirely due to my own inquisitive nature. There were papers, and contracts, and tallies of figures, along with photographs of a sexual nature I could not bring myself to look at. I may have gazed upon them for a moment, but

I quickly put these things aside. What interested me most was a leather-bound journal fashioned in Morocco, a handbook of my father's studies. I took it from the drawer, although as I did, my heart hit against my chest.

The handbook was clearly a private document, and some of it seemed to be written in code, with numbers and drawings replacing the letters. Still I could make out certain sections. My father's handwriting was elegant, a script of flourishes that created large, perfect lettering. I began with the first few pages, a remembrance of a time when my father had been one of the greatest magicians in France. I hadn't realized how famous he had been until I spied the articles about him, with photographs of the Professor as a younger man.

My father had written accounts of his card tricks and illuminations, some sketched out, lavishly illustrated. Soon I came upon his most famous trick of all, one so astounding people who witnessed it firsthand swore it was a miracle worthy of a saint. There was a drawing of a woman who was brought onto the stage in a steamer trunk, rolled out on a platform that had been fitted with wooden wheels. The woman's head and legs emerged from either side of the box. Before the eyes of the audience my father sawed through the wood; as he did, the woman was cut in half. The crowd was silent, in shock, on the edge of their seats, revolted, yet straining to see more.

My father recorded how vividly the woman screamed when the sword went through her. But when the trunk was opened, the victim leapt up, half a woman with no legs at all, able to maneuver with the use of her hands as she swung herself across the stage. The audience gasped in astonishment. They had no idea of the truth of the matter: the woman was my father's assistant, a living wonder who had been born that way. The sword's blade was dull and had done no damage whatsoever, for it had only cut through the trunk, which was already scored. The legs that remained in the trunk had been fashioned by a sculptor, carefully painted to appear real. When the living wonder was inserted back into the steamer trunk, she was made whole again, for the legs were secretly fitted into a corset that was attached with a belt and cables. Therefore she was able to walk the length of a stage with the height of a fully grown woman.

My father left France when the half woman accused him of all manner of vile deeds, which included enslavement and defilement. A yellowing newspaper article that had been slipped between the pages stated that he had promised to marry her but instead had beaten her and forced her to perform. He had abused her and degraded her in ways that I passed over, for I thought it was improper for me to read these claims. I did notice that she'd sworn she'd been treated like a common prostitute. Enough to say she told the magistrates what my father had done, and in each instance he denied any wrongdoing. He said he was a professor, and had nothing but respect for his employee. Still, his illustrations of her in the handbook after she had made her accusations were nothing less than monstrous; scorpions and frogs leapt from her mouth and from her private areas, which should not have been drawn at all, for modesty's sake, but were sketched in great detail.

The date when all this happened was ten years before my birth. Although my French was far from perfect, when I studied the article I understood that a court had ordered my father's arrest on charges of fraud and abuse. The woman in the trunk would testify against him, and a trial date was set; they expected ten thousand or more onlookers, for the case had attracted the attention of the public. But like any magician worth his salt, my father vanished before the date of his trial. The newspaper report said they found his cloak and his shoes and the key to his rooms. Nothing more.

Because my father was particular, he wrote down small details another man might have overlooked. Not only the hour when he took the train to Marseilles, a city of docks where he would find his passage to America, but also what he ate for his lunch on that train—sharp cheese, white wine, olives. He wrote down the name of the ship he took, the *Allemande*, which sailed for New York Harbor, leaving France on a bright May day. He described the sleeping berths, the lack of fresh vegetables, the swells of the ocean as the ship pushed out to sea. He had always told me that my mother was his childhood sweetheart, and that her name was Maria Louisa, and that they had sailed from France together. But there was no mention of her in the handbook, though he'd written that he'd been forced to sleep with his overcoat as his blanket at night. Still the journey made quite an impression. The stars were so bright above the water he became mesmerized, and he saw all manner of creatures below the waves, beings so fantastic that he felt his life begin anew. Because of his experience at sea, and perhaps because of the trouble he'd been in with the law, he vowed to give up magic and study science from that day forth.

He'd always told me that my mother had cried when she saw the outline of Manhattan. She'd fallen in love with the city at first sight, as my father had fallen in love with her when she was a schoolgirl dressed in black, wearing white gloves and flat black shoes, her pale hair braided down her back. His employees might disparage him, my father had often confided, for they saw him as a harsh master, a difficult, uncompromising man who thought too highly of himself. But say what they might, he was faithful, and in time I would learn that a faithful man was as much a wonder of the world as the stars in the sky.

As I was reading, I heard my father's unmistakable gait upstairs when he came into the kitchen to wash his hands for his dinner, which Maureen had left on the table. She had prepared a cod stew and a dessert of gingered apples and cream. I wondered if my father would mark down the components of his dinner later that evening in this same book I now held in my hands. I had no choice but to close the journal and replace it in the drawer, *making certain it was in the exact position where I'd found it. I went out then, carefully clasping both locks. I was a mouse, silent as I came upstairs unnoticed, but a mouse that would not forget where the trap baited with cheese had been. I never told my father what I'd done, nor did I mention the handbook in the drawer.*

But after that I knew the first part of the truth about my family.

When my father came to this city, he came alone.

MARCH 1911

IN THE LAST DAYS of March the windy month turned mild, but despite the approach of springtime, the Professor's mood was even more foul. Ashes had swept across the East River, depositing cinders throughout the gardens of Brooklyn, smoldering among the onions and the peas with a bright yellow glow. Everyone's attention had been riveted by the Triangle Fire, the greatest workplace disaster to occur in the history of New York. A wave of sorrow stretched out, and the world in which they lived seemed a much more perilous place. The dangers of ordinary life left the population dazed. The newspapers were filled with reports of worker unrest. Vigils of inconsolable mourners who had lost beloved family members went on throughout the city. The days were already lengthening, yet a darkness held fast. Even at dawn the light was a cold, bitter shade.

In Brooklyn, the Museum of Extraordinary Things was shuttered. A gloom had descended as the Professor's plans began to unspool. He'd been unable to locate a creature he might put forth as the Hudson Mystery. Soon the public would forget the sightings in the river, and the men and boys who'd vowed they'd seen a monster would be considered nothing more than fools. Readers of the *Sun* and the *Times* and the *Tribune* were gripped not by notions of magical creatures but by the politics of the city. A war of sorts had broken out between workers and business owners. Even Governor Dix, a Democrat himself, had called for an investigation of the Tammany leaders, whose pockets were lined at the expense of the working people of New York.

It was all Commissioner Waldo and Chief Croker could do to keep a rough sort of peace, one that seemed ready to explode on a daily basis. The fire was the only topic people could talk about, and there was little room for other news. If anything, the monster they were interested in was the city itself, torn apart by rage. Soon enough bloody riots erupted on the avenues and outraged workers gathered in meeting halls. The streets near the disaster had been washed with buckets of soapy water, yet no matter how often city workers might clean the pavements, there were red stains marking the cement. In between the paving stones, it was still possible to spy shimmering shards of bone.

An investigation had begun, but the owners of the factory, who'd fled before the mourners could identify their dead, had yet to be arrested. The curtain that split the city in two, separating those who could escape to the rooftops from those who could not, had been torn open to reveal inequities long kept in the dark. People were furious to find that life was considered a treasure for some but worth so little for others. A huge gathering of garment workers was arranged to take place at the Metropolitan Opera House on Thirty-fourth Street, with hundreds of women taking the stage, insisting on better conditions for the half of the city that worked for the benefit of the half that could calmly gaze at the damage around them through their windows, safe and protected from the mayhem on the streets and from the despair of those who tailored the clothes they wore.

It might have been best to let go of the idea of creating a monster, but the Professor was single-minded, convinced that, in brutal times, people longed more than ever for an escape from the harsh realities of their daily lives. Why else would the construction to spruce up Dreamland continue at such a fast pace? The renovation of the park would cost close to a million dollars. The buildings, once starkly white, had been repainted in a riot of color, and a thrilling concession named Hell

Gate was being prepared, a wild boat ride over rushing water through a covered tunnel in which an individual might become drenched and terrified as he progressed through man-made rapids and whirlpools while having the time of his life. The greatest animal trainer in the world, the one-armed Captain Jack Bonavita, would have a show of lions. And Colonel Joseph Ferrari, a genius with animals, had gathered leopards, pumas, bears, and hyenas. One of the most beloved creatures in Coney Island, Little Hip, an elephant so attached to his trainer they slept in the same room, would lead a parade circling the park each morning. Coralie had gawked through the fence at the huge ballroom overlooking the sea, now being revamped on Dreamland's Pier. A thousand electric lights would glow in tints of rose and green. She wondered how it might feel to dance in the arms of the young man from the woods. He might whisper *The whole world is ours if we make it so.*

There had been a recent announcement declaring that Dreamland would venture into the world of science, for what was more miraculous than the future men made for themselves? There was already a village built in 1904 called Lilliputia, where three hundred little people resided in a world of their own, with their own fire department and parliament, so that they might be studied by the crowds. There were exotic human beings who startled New Yorkers with their differences: Algerian horsemen, Somali warriors, Bantu women who stretched their necks and lips with brass rings. The Dreamland sideshow featured oddities and curiosities the Professor referred to as freaks rather than wonders: Ursa, the bear girl. Rob Roy, the albino. A human salamander named Schrief, who could catch flies with a flick of his tongue. There was an exhibition to display the tiniest babies in the state, each cared for by a nurse in a starched white uniform, each babe placed in a new contraption called an incubator, a machine not yet used in hospitals.

This devotion to science infuriated the Professor, for it was a realm he considered to be his own. He could never afford the huge exhibitions Dreamland would offer, and yet he felt that grand park stole from him. The Wolfman, the very act Sardie had created, was said to be one of the acts planned for display in the sideshow just outside Dreamland's gates, steps away from the Museum of Extraordinary Things. The beaten-down creature rescued from a jail cell would now be known as Professor Morris. He would wear a tuxedo and glasses and smoke a pipe as he read Shakespeare's sonnets and the poetry of that great local hero, Whitman, in a voice that was as heavenly as his countenance was beastly.

"Do you think it's true that he'll work for Father's enemy?" Coralie asked Maureen as they cleared the overgrown area that would soon be the vegetable garden. Coralie had always wished Mr. Morris had left them to travel from one wonder of the world to another, from Paris to Cairo to the Victoria Falls.

The two women tended their garden each spring, wearing muslin aprons and heavy boots as they cleared out mud. Coney Island, once pastureland for cows, flooded each winter, which was why there was a need for raised, slatted sidewalks and why the iron pier was so very popular. This year the women raked cinders and their eyes teared as they labored. These were the ashes of the dead that had drifted across the East River. By June there would be all manner of herbs in this garden, rosemary and sorrel and parsley, along with mustard, which was said to cast off gloom, and madder root, which was used for a dye. There would be bulbs of garlic that would appear burnt when peeled and tomatoes with bloody, black hearts, formed, perhaps, from their bed of embers. Coralie and Maureen did not speak of the tragedy. They usually did not discuss disturbing issues, which was why Mr. Morris was not often a topic of conversation. The museum employees likely had been directed not to ruminate over his fate, for whenever Coralie had brought up the Wolfman, the living wonders had gazed away. It had been several years since Professor Sardie had let him go. Now, as they worked side by side, Maureen paused upon hearing Mr. Morris's name, but she quickly resumed ridding the garden of stickers and weeds. "How would I know what's become of him?" she huffed. "I'm employed as a maid, not a mind reader."

Yet a distracted smile played upon her usually stern mouth. Coralie had always guessed that the housekeeper knew far more than she dared to say.

"Fine, don't tell me. Keep your secrets."

Coralie had her own secrets, the nighttime swims in the Hudson, of which Maureen would have never approved. All the same, she was hurt by this turn of events, for she'd mourned Raymond Morris after his disappearance, and had feared for his welfare. She used her spade to make neat furrows for a row of peas, turning away to ensure that Maureen wouldn't notice the tears flooding her eyes. The sun was so bright that the dim light that had been drifting over to Brooklyn ever since the Triangle Fire was finally burning up.

When Maureen came up beside her, Coralie pretended to be squinting in the haze. "It's not you I'm keeping things from." Maureen slipped an arm around her charge's waist. "Trust me when I say, it's best for both of us to keep our thoughts to ourselves."

PROFESSOR SARDIE was more desperate every day, frantic in his quest to find a wonder that would match the ones soon to be on display at Dreamland. He arranged for Coralie to make one final swim. She had always considered herself to be fearless in the water, but now she felt a wave of anxiety. For the past few nights she'd experienced a recurring dream in which she remained underwater for so long she grew gills and fins. It was a painful, bloody process. In every dream, when she attempted to climb from the river to its banks, she found she could not walk across the grass but instead slipped back into the watery depths, gasping for breath, confused as to what sort of creature she had come to be.

"Perhaps it doesn't make sense to excite people for something that doesn't yet exist," she dared to say to her father as they waited for the carriage. She felt the base of her throat, for her dream had seemed so real she imagined she'd find a line of gills, as if she were becoming what she pretended to be.

The Professor laughed at Coralie's fears, insisting a real showman could present his audience with a snapping turtle, call it a leviathan, and be believed if the story of its capture was told with enough drama and excitement. Blood helped such stories along, and for this reason he handed Coralie a small, sharp knife, the very one she'd used upon herself.

"This blade will do in lieu of fangs. If the hand of a fisherman is trailing in the water, take up the knife. Let there be blood in the water. That's how the Hudson Mystery will find its way onto the front page, despite the struggles on the street."

The liveryman brought them across the Brooklyn Bridge in the fading light of the day. The city was aglow, especially along Broadway, where the electric streetlights came on all at once, brilliant in the pale twilight. It had rained earlier, and when they reached the West Side, a single line of pink hung like a ribbon above the New Jersey shore. As they traveled west and then north, Coralie thought of the young man she had come across in the woods, and once again she was filled with a nameless longing. She had gone to Maureen for advice that very afternoon. How did she stop the attraction to this man?

"Is this someone you've given yourself to?" Maureen's expression had been worried.

"Of course not! But I hear him call to me when no one is there." Coralie had not mentioned that on these occasions her heart was in her throat.

"If you don't want to think of a man, say his name backward three times. If that doesn't work, write his name on paper, burn it, then bury it in the garden."

Coralie had laughed. "What will that accomplish?"

"We all burn for what is bad for us," Maureen had assured her. "Burn him in return. Maybe then the bastard won't have such a hold over you."

"Did Raymond Morris have a hold over you?"

"That was something entirely different." Maureen had spoken in a voice so quiet she didn't sound like herself. "You are young, Cora. So here's my advice, should you see him again, all you can do is close your eyes."

"And then?"

"Then pray he disappears, for you cannot change the way you feel. There is no spell or magic to work for that. Just be smart. Look at him clearly. See who he is."

Coralie practiced Maureen's suggestion as the carriage continued uptown through the dark streets. She closed her eyes and did not think of him. Instead, she imagined their garden; she thought of the runner beans she would plant, and the heat of the sunlight when the tomato plants began to flower. It did no good. When she opened her eyes all she could think of was the man in the woods. He was like a fever; she could feel him all over her. She was somewhat dazed, as she had been when she'd fallen ill as a child and Maureen feared she'd contracted the Spanish flu.

"What will you say to the authorities if you're caught?" the Professor asked as they neared their destination. Coralie had no choice but to pull herself together. They had rehearsed her response several times. The Professor did not believe in chance or luck but in being fully prepared. That was virtue in his eyes.

"I decided to take on the Hudson River as a challenge to my skill as a swimmer," Coralie responded by rote. She felt like a puppet on a string, but one whose heart was beating too fast, whose thoughts strayed dangerously far. If this was what love was like, it was disconcerting, something over which she indeed had no control.

The Professor nodded, satisfied.

There was to be a full moon, perfect conditions for his plan, although the river was running quite high. At this time of year, the murky spring currents carried roots and fallen trees and all manner of man-made items that had been frozen into the ice upstate and had recently been freed in the thaw. As the Professor prepared the monster's mask, Coralie went to the grassy bank to remove her coat and her shoes. The chill of the air felt like pinpricks. She stretched, as she always did before a long swim, then practiced her breathing technique. The liveryman was nearby, letting the carriage horse graze. Coralie stole a glance and noticed he was staring into the woods. When she followed his gaze, she spied a large gathering of blackbirds, a hundred or more fluttering through the trees. She wondered if this was an omen, and if she should fear its meaning or be relieved.

"So many," she said, marveling at the birds, forgetting she was not allowed to address the hired man. "I wonder if they speak to each other, like men and women, or if their calling goes unanswered."

The hired man buttoned his jacket, as if this might make their conversation more acceptable. "Men and women rarely speak to each other, though they often talk."

They were out of the Professor's hearing and sight, so Coralie continued. "People might speak freely if they didn't fear one another's judgments."

"Then let me speak freely," the liveryman said. There were scars on his face and neck, hastily sewn by a surgeon who certainly couldn't be called a credit to his profession. "I don't think you should swim tonight."

Coralie found she wasn't the least bit uncomfortable conversing with this man, even though Maureen had confided he'd once been the boss of one of the toughest gangs in lower Manhattan, willing to go up against some of the established Italian gangsters of the Cosa Nostra and the Black Hand, who were so numerous Prince Street was called Black Hand Street. The liveryman had been to prison before coming to work as the Professor's driver, a humbled man who'd done far too much damage when he was young, to others and to himself.

"Blackbirds can sense danger," the hired man went on. "You'll never see one in a storm. They take flight long before the first raindrops fall." He whistled a trilling call. Soon enough one of the blackbirds came to perch on the branch of a nearby sycamore tree.

"You can speak to him!" Coralie was charmed.

The hired man admitted that he'd kept pet birds for a good part of his life, mostly bright parakeets and parrots from South America, along with his beloved pigeons. "A bird will never lie, just as a man will rarely tell the truth. That's been my experience and no one will convince me otherwise. So I'll speak as the birds do, with honest intent. The river looks rough, miss. It's running wildly and it's dangerous. An experienced sailor could drown in such conditions. I wouldn't send my daughter into it, if I were lucky enough to have one."

The Professor was approaching, and the two who had been speaking in confidence stepped away from one another. Not quickly enough, however. Sardie had taken note of their conversation, and he threw his employee a dark look. He then drew Coralie aside. "Did I tell you not to speak to him? He's a criminal, Cora. I'm giving him a second chance, but be warned. He has killed more men than you will ever meet in your lifetime."

Coralie gazed at the hired man, who held his horse's reins as he whispered in the beast's ear. She had a surge of trust in his judgment.

"The water's so wild, Father. I wonder if we should put off this swim."

"Is that what that fool told you? He has absolutely no idea of who you are and what your training has been. I'm not the least bit worried. This is your farewell to the Hudson River. Once it's over and done, I swear I'll find a creature worthy of the news you create." He kissed her on both cheeks. "You're not a coward, are you? Tell me I didn't waste all this time on you?"

Convinced she had no choice, Coralie went to the water line and waded out. When she was to her waist, she dove in, grateful for the silence of the river, which was broken only by the slap of the waves as she cut through the water. She felt herself taken up by the north-flowing current, which was indeed moving quickly, but she enjoyed the effortlessness of her swim and went where the river led her. The moon had slipped behind clouds, and Coralie came up beside a row-boat, unnoticed in the dark. As she paddled beside the skiff, she heard two men speak of their wives and of the fish they meant to bring home to them for supper. She wondered what it might be like to have a husband who spoke of you so tenderly.

She'd been instructed to draw blood as any true beast would, but Coralie had forgotten her orders. It seemed as if she had entered into a dream, spellbound by her own thoughts. Mist rose from the water in bursts of cloudy air. There was a run of sturgeon, large fish known to bite, but they ignored Coralie and swam along beside her. It was possible that they thought she was one of their own kind, as much a fish as she was a woman. As she was carried upstream, she imagined the young man, though Maureen had warned against this. She might have gone on floating for hours more, but all at once she hit something straight on. She was suddenly and achingly present. She wondered if she had collided with a sturgeon, for the thing she'd been driven into was large, yet more pliable than a log. When she gathered her wits, she spied what she believed to be a fish nearly her own size floating before her, pale blue in the muddy water. Both Coralie and this creature had become enmeshed in a soup of floating debris.

She had already passed the cliffs of the Palisades, which she recognized from her previous swim. She'd entered into the dangerous flux where the Harlem River was aswirl with eddies as the north and south currents met, and had been caught up in waterweeds, long wavering plants whose roots reached hundreds of feet below the surface. The tendrils held fast, pulling her down so that she took in mouthfuls of water. The fish trapped with her was immobilized, not able to struggle for its life as Coralie did. Without thinking, she grabbed on to the fish and tried to pull herself up so that she wouldn't be dragged into the center of the whirlpool. She had expected cool, slippery scales; instead there was the woolly nub of sopping fabric. All at once she realized she was holding on to a drenched coat. In her arms was the body of a young woman, facedown, long pale hair flowing, arms and legs entangled in the ropes of waterweeds.

In a panic, Coralie reached for the knife in her pocket and set to work frantically chopping at the dark, slimy tendrils that had wound around them, freeing herself first. She continued to hack through the weeds, managing to tug the other girl from the grip of the twisted greenery. The two slipped underwater for one terrifying moment.

Coralie could see her companion's pale hair drifting out. When she realized that she was being pulled down by the weight of the unconscious girl, she began to kick furiously, releasing them from the whirlpool, swimming against the currents, hauling the other woman along. Once she reached the shore, Coralie couldn't catch her breath, which rasped inside her. She forced herself to crawl over the grass and the stalks of milkweed, the roots of which the Lenape Indians used to cure fever but which now tore at her hands as she pulled the other woman through the weeds. When she could go no farther, she let go of the stranger she'd rescued and lay beside her on the ground, exhausted. Her lungs hurt from the effort. She shivered uncontrollably, and yet, she had never felt as alive. Above them the sky was endless, flecked with bright stars.

"We're safe," she said.

The young woman beside Coralie was unresponsive. It was possible that she had hit her head or swallowed too much water. The enormity of Coralie's responsibility burst upon her.

"Hello!" she shouted into the woods. "Can anyone hear me?"

She prayed the young man would be nearby and hear, but her own voice echoed back and no response came, aside from the fluttering of birds in the thornbushes, awakened from sleep by her frightened cries. The birds rose like a plume of smoke, disappearing into the blueblack sky.

The rescued woman was the same age as Coralie, or a little younger. Peering through the dark, Coralie saw that she was quite beautiful. She also noticed a widening splash of blood upon the stranger's chest. She gasped, thinking her charge had been seriously wounded, then realized it was she herself who bled. She had caught her wrist on something sharp, perhaps a rock, or her own knife as she hacked through the weeds.

Coralie drew herself up to kneel beside the other girl. All she could hear was her own ragged breathing. There was a fluttering inside her, a wild emotion she couldn't temper. She leaned over the girl, placing her ear to the sopping coat. The fabric had once been sky blue, but soaking wet it had turned the color of ink. Coralie had no idea how a heart was supposed to sound; all she could hear was the deafening thrum of her own heart in her ears. But she knew that flesh should not be blue and arms and legs should not be rigid. The girl's head had fallen to the side, as if she were a doll. Coralie reached to take the drowned girl's hand, but it was tightly clenched. She held a finger to the girl's mouth to test for breath. There was none; the girl's lips were blue, her mouth clamped shut.

At last, Coralie wrenched to her feet, knees shaking. She felt the other girl's death inside her own body, a stone of grief in her throat. Acting on instinct, she ran. She blindly went toward the river. In the woods there were flashes of what appeared to be bright globes of light: migrating yellow warblers flinging themselves through the gloom. Coralie raced on, past some fishermen in a skiff, who spied her and called out. She continued through the brambles. She was too removed from the world of the living to communicate with human beings. Yet she could feel her heart banging against her ribs as she ran, letting her know that she was still alive.

She came upon the carriage in the dark. The wound on her hand was deep enough so that blood continued to rush forth, staining her white blouse. Perhaps she appeared to be a monster when she approached her father, for he backed away and did not take her in his arms. Coralie stood there, wringing wet, shivering, her complexion starkly white beneath the streaks of green paint that had washed onto her cheeks.

The liveryman came to her with a blanket. "Miss, this was a bad night for the river. I told you that."

Coralie's father now approached, concerned for their plan. "Have you been found out?"

She shook her head. When she tried to speak, no words were heard, only a croak, as if she had lost her voice in the river. Her face smarted with the cold. The silence of the girl in the blue coat had affected her, chilled her to the core.

The Professor took her arm, demanding to know what had caused her such distress. "This is not a game." He saw her silence as disobedience. "You'll tell me directly, or you'll regret it."

Coralie's pale face flushed. "I found a body in the river." Her voice sounded strangely flat. "I left her in the woods. She drowned."

Coralie expected her father to berate her, for the dead were not their concern any more than the living were. She presumed he would contend that a corpse in the grass was no different than a child offered for a good price. And yet a strange look began to play upon the Professor's face, his interest piqued. He asked Coralie to lead them to the place where she'd left the body. The liveryman took them along the road by carriage. Coralie continued to shiver. "The road ends nearby," she warned. "It's best we avoid this situation and let the authorities find her." Once, at the funeral of a living wonder, an old man with warts like a bullfrog's who had died in his own bed of old age, Maureen had cautioned her that if she should look upon a dead man twice, she would carry him forever. They'd hurried away from the funeral home, but Maureen's warning had stayed with her. "We should turn back," Coralie recommended now.

"We'll go when I say," her father told her. "Have faith in me."

At the road's end, the liveryman tied his horse to the branch of a chestnut tree and they continued on by foot. A few birds sang in the dark, but the quiet was so deep that each branch breaking under the men's boots echoed as if a rifle had been shot. A thicker mist began to rise off the water, turning the distant shore silver. The air was warmer than the cold, hard ground. The trees were pewter, the ferns black as coal. Confused, Coralie led them in the wrong direction, and then had to backtrack. The Professor grumbled, annoyed to realize she'd taken them in a circle. But Coralie wondered anew whether it might be best if they failed to reach their destination. Possibly she had been wrong and had mistaken exhaustion for death. There might well be nothing for her father to see. Surely it was within the realm of reason to think that the girl had slept for a while in the tall grass after Coralie had run off, then had awoken refreshed. She may have smoothed down her hair, buttoned her blue coat, and arisen from the meadow to walk barefoot through the woods. *You will never believe my dream,* she may have told her parents, waiting at the door, relieved beyond words by her return. *I dreamed I drowned and a girl who was half fish discovered me and brought me to the shore, intent on rescuing me so that I might live and walk on land like any other young woman and be your daughter once again.*

Their journey continued blindly, for it now seemed apparent that Coralie couldn't find her way. How mortified she would be if she discovered that she'd dreamed the encounter and they found nothing more than a great blue fish in the grass. But then the liveryman called out. "I see something in the hollow."

They followed him now, the Professor rushing through the bushes, Coralie trailing behind, for she not only dreaded what they would find, she feared the reason her father had insisted they come here. Perhaps the time had come for her to defy him. If only she could find the strength to hurl herself into her own destiny, running there head-on, resolved to find her freedom. She gazed at leaves, imagining Egypt and Paris and all the wonders of the world that awaited her.

"There she is!" the liveryman shouted.

A sheaf of blue in the dark ferns and brambles.

When they came upon the body, Coralie felt something sharp run through her. She knew Maureen was right. She would indeed carry the dead with her. Coralie had the urge to turn away, but she could not. She had already seen what was before them.

The Professor shrugged off his black overcoat and threw it over the young woman. "Take her back to the wagon," he told the liveryman. "Our treasure."

"This isn't what I do," the liveryman replied, bristling. "I've been to jail for too many years. Now that I'm a free man, I'm not about to go back."

"You'll do it, or you'll find yourself in jail for worse offenses," the Professor told him. When he saw the grim expression on the liveryman's face, the Professor tried another tactic. "There's double what I usually pay in it. That should make the deed easier for you to complete."

Coralie now noticed that the drowned girl's head rested on weeds that had been arranged to form a pillow; her hands were crossed one upon the other on her chest. Coralie had not left the young woman in this tender position, as if waiting for the world to come. She gazed into the woods to try to spy whoever might have tended to the drowned girl, but she saw nothing but locust trees and reeds that stood nearly ten feet tall along the bank. The liveryman lifted the body over his shoulder. As he did so, the girl's clutched hands were jostled, and what appeared to be two black stones fell from her grasp. Coralie bent to retrieve them. Once in her hands she realized these weren't stones at all but buttons, cold as water, made of black glass.

They went back the way they had come, only now rays of sunlight glinted through the leaves and the waking songbirds trilled. They tramped along for a time, wordless, until they came upon the carriage. The Professor embraced Coralie in a rare show of affection. "You found the Hudson Mystery," he informed her.

"Father." Coralie paled. "How is that possible? She's only a woman."

"She's that now. But when I'm finished with her, she'll be far more."

Coralie thought of the baby's skeleton she'd once found upon his desk and the surgery tools set out on the white table. She thought, too, of the specimens in the glass bottles, creatures not made by God but sewn and hammered together.

"We have no choice but to create what we need," her father assured her when he spied her worried expression. "There was a mermaid in the Hudson River who died in the cold currents, the Mystery that has haunted New York. It is our duty to preserve her so that she might remain intact for all eternity."

The liveryman had carried the body up to the carriage; he stored the drowned girl beneath the bench. Water pooled on the floor, and there was a wet, green odor that was impossible to ignore. When she took her seat, Coralie did not look at her father but instead gazed out the window as he came to sit beside her. The horse began its easy pace through the woods.

"We have our miracle," the Professor said, satisfied.

An outrage arose within Coralie, a distaste for her father's business so strong it felt like a flicker of hatred. She would never again listen to his words as if they were gospel. No matter what he intended to do in the future or what deeds he had committed in the past, Coralie was certain that in good time every secret would be shared. Every miracle would be called into question.

FOUR

THE MAN WHO
FELT NO PAIN

****

I PLANNED to sell the watch I'd stolen as a boy to pay for Moses Levy's funeral, but, as if it knew of my intent, it broke that very day. I wound the crown, and still it would not tell time. And so I kept it and instead sold the camera I had learned my craft upon, an American Optical. Moses had left me several other cameras, including his own ancient large-format wooden bellows camera whose images were developed as eighteen-by-twenty-four glass dry plates, and a Leica held together with tape that had an exquisite Petzval lens. From then on, I used these as my own. Moses's favorite camera was the old battered one, oversized and heavy to carry around town. Someone else might have thought the camera I sold was the best of the bunch, but it wasn't. A camera has its own eye, my mentor had told me. He insisted his could see the truth even when he'd begun to grow blind. I hoped it would do the same for me, for I was blind to much in this world.

Certainly I'd been blind when it came to Levy's poor health and age. He'd told me of his bouts with pneumonia, which had weakened him, but *he had such passion for his work I forgot how ill he was and ignored his labored breathing. I often accompanied him to meetings at 291, the gallery where Stieglitz showed photographs alongside paintings that seemed to come from a far-off universe, each unique and haunting. I stood in the back, an awkward apprentice, listening to the real photographers argue and talk. Once Moses went to shake Stieglitz's hand and introduce himself. Stieglitz of course knew of him, although the rumors were that Moses Levy was dead. He had disappeared from the art world and from his compatriots. Perhaps he preferred these stories to the truth, and wished to keep secret the fact he made a living photographing brides and grooms at the marriage halls of the Lower East Side. His great work had been destroyed by officials in the Ukraine, who felt that Jewish artists were dangerous, rebels by nature, untrustworthy at best, demons at worst. He could not bring himself to think, let alone speak, about his lifetime's lost work.*

"Here's one of the originals," Stieglitz called out to those in the gallery. "One of our forefathers!"

Few paid attention. The mantle of genius had already been handed to younger men, such as Stieglitz himself, who quickly moved on to speak to his own admirers. Now Levy's great work had been burned and forgotten, and there was little interest in him, even though many of his techniques had been taken up by these same young men. He was a master of the ambrotype print, in which the photographer is the conduit to the photograph, so that each is as individual as a painting, and later his use of silver nitrate or potassium cyanide to illuminate his landscapes had led the way for those who wished to take photography into the world of art. He had a unique toning technique that tinged some of his prints a golden color. Many of the younger men who gathered to speak of themselves and their work had no idea Levy had invented some of the processes they now used on a daily basis, nor did they care. I saw this was the way of the future, to leave the past behind as if it were a dream.

⌒

On the wall of Levy's studio were the two remaining prints taken in the forests of the Ukraine. Trees so tall and wide they were true giants, their limbs saddened by the sorrows of the world, filled with the sepia shades of songbirds. It was much like the place where my father and I had camped when our village was destroyed. I had led him by the hand through the tall grass and the wild asters so that he would not lose himself and give up the life he no longer valued now that my mother was gone. We did not speak to each other in the forest, for fear of what we would say. We mourned in silence so that we would not curse the world we walked through. I saw owls in the locust trees and wondered if these creatures were the spirits of the dead, for there were so many murdered in our homeland there was not room enough for all of their ghosts. I half-believed they had turned into birds instead.

Moses Levy left me his lustrous silver nitrate prints. I had them on the wall of the studio, in frames I'd built myself of plain pine, for this cheap wood was the best I could afford. But the photographs hadn't been treated properly in Moses's travels across the continents, and they faded more each day. To avoid the ravaging effects of direct sunlight, I took to covering them with a white sheet, as people of the faith I'd left covered mirrors after a death in the family. I once believed this practice had arisen to make certain there was no vanity in a time of sorrow, but now I think it was so a man could not see his own hopelessness reflected in the glass.

Sometimes as darkness fell, I tore off the sheets so I could study the gift Moses had left me. The trees became illuminated in the fading light, struck by shades of yellow on some days, and at other times enveloped by the red glow that pours over Manhattan after sunset. When I stood there before the greatness of my teacher's vision, I was reminded of the day I found my second life. I thought perhaps I did indeed have a purpose, and that purpose was to see the true beauty of the world and, like my teacher, to capture a single moment of that beauty.

And yet I was blinded to so much around me, stubborn and arrogant in the way many young men are. Could a blind man know beauty? I hadn't noticed the milky film over my teacher's eyes, nor had I realized the difficulty he had in taking the stairs in his last months on earth. To me he was indomitable, an icon who was more than human in both talent and virtue. I toted his equipment, as any apprentice would, but soon I was developing his negatives as well. He said it was so I could learn the skill of this process, but it was most likely he had me do this work because he could not stand steadily for more than a brief time. There were a few occasions when he was too tired to leave his bed, and I was forced to take wedding photographs alone. I'm sure the bridal parties were not pleased by my sour demeanor, but I did the job and learned to keep my mouth shut. I did not tell anyone to smile or to embrace—I photographed them as they were, delighted or terrified, brides who seemed too young to be married, and those who were grandmothers, grooms who shook with fear and those who rode triumphantly into the hall on the shoulders of their brothers and friends. There were occasions when my photographs were rejected by an angry bride or mother of the groom. I didn't blame them. I showed them what I saw, and what I saw was not always pretty.

I did not realize that Moses's death was coming until my teacher could no longer stand or speak. On the day of his passing, I was the one who found him. I slept in a storeroom then, and he in the bed that later became mine. Everything in the loft changed when his spirit left him, as if a whirlpool had drawn the light from the room. I sat beside his body and wept, not only for the loss of this great man but also for the darkness that settled upon me once more.

I was the only one at the funeral at the Mt. Zion Cemetery in Maspeth, Queens. I hired a rabbi who went from cemetery to cemetery for a fee. He was an old man from Russia, who owned a single suit that he wore every day. There was sorrow in the seams of his clothes, but he was used to death. It seemed that life was a bolt of cloth to him, and he was there to fold it and set it in a drawer. He said the prayers over the open grave, then, after being paid, quickly went on to his next appointment. I shoveled the dirt onto the coffin, as was the custom of our people, while the gravediggers looked on, arms folded across their chests. In our faith we are instructed to bury our own, and in doing so grant them that last favor.

I could not completely rid myself of my first life, though I tried my best. On several occasions I went to photograph rallies and strikes, sent there by the editors I sometimes worked for. This was not by choice. I gave excuses, and I often managed to get other assignments. But occasionally I was forced to go to events I dreaded. Though I looked nothing like the boy I'd been, there were times when I was spotted by ghosts from my past. Once I'd gone to photograph a meeting of hundreds of shirtwaist strikers in Washington Square. This park had once been a public gallows, with bodies still buried beneath what were now paved paths; it seemed as good a place to be haunted as any. Just as I turned onto Great Jones Street, I found I could go no farther. I felt a chill spreading through my chest. There, among the strikers who held up signs in Yiddish and Italian, I thought I saw my father. I dodged into a doorway, as if I were a common thief, and from those shadows I peered out at the crowd. Upon closer study, the person in question was revealed to be someone else entirely, a much younger man than I'd initially imagined, perhaps the age my father had been when I first began to work for Hochman. I felt an odd mixture of relief and disappointment, for in all honesty, I wanted to see for myself that he was alive and well. In a haze of emotion, I realized that my resentment as a boy had arisen not only from the idea that he was willing to end his life

and leave me when he leapt from the dock but from the fact that I felt, from that moment on, responsible for him. I was too young, or foolish, or headstrong to meet that responsibility. I did not want it, and I paid for my choice dearly simply by knowing the sort of man I'd become.

I went back into the crowd and set up my camera stand. When I scanned the mob, I noticed several young men shouting and glaring in my direction. I heard the name I never used, and then I knew their taunts were directed at me. I turned and slinked away, convinced I had been marked. Those who'd known me in my other life saw me for who I truly was, Ezekiel Cohen, traitor, the boy who had not leapt into the river to rescue his own father.

Soon after that I was sent by the Tribune to photograph a rally at Cooper Union on Third Avenue. I was young, little more than twenty-one, and I thought I could express an opinion in such matters when working for the papers. I said I preferred crime scenes, which was true enough. I went so far as to declare I had a fever and might be ill, hardly the truth at all. But no one else was available, so I had no choice but to go, even though my guts churned. I knew it would be bad for me, and it was. I came upon several leaders of the Workmen's Circle, an organization for the betterment of the workingman that was concerned with community and social justice, serving as a welfare agency, especially in times of tragedy. There among them, I spied my childhood companion, Isaac Rosenfeld. Unfortunately he spied me as well as I set up my camera.

"Here he is. The anti-Jew," Rosenfeld called out, nodding to me. "I hear you're Ed now. To some people at least."

"I'm here to do a job," I told him.

"To watch us? To stand outside of us? Maybe to judge us? You're very good at that it seems. You don't care what happens to anyone else, even your own people. What would your father think?"

"I don't know what other men think," I said. "That's God's business, not mine."

Rosenfeld spat upon the ground. I didn't react, though I suppose he wanted me to. He was a decent man and would not strike me first, but I didn't give him the pleasure of hitting him. I merely took a photograph of the crowd that had gathered, Jews and Italians who worked in factories and wanted more for themselves and their families, basic rights at the very least. Rosenfeld's father had worked with mine in the second factory where we'd found employment, and Rosenfeld and I had spent a portion of our boyhood together. We had once been friends, when such things were possible for me. I didn't react when he shoved his hand in front of my camera's lens. "Well at least you know what this man thinks," he said. And yes, I knew. He despised me.

I kept the photograph of his hand and have it still. The lines of his palm are like a map to a country I cannot name. I kept the broken watch as well, stored in my pocket after Moses's death. Soon after my run-in with Rosenfeld, I happened to pass a watchmaker's shop on Houston Street. The sign proclaimed the shopowner could repair any timepiece. If stumped he would present a customer with a new gold watch at no cost whatsoever. The proposition sounded fishy, but I could hardly afford to have the watch fixed, so I went in to see what he could do. The watchmaker was working when I entered. He was an elderly fellow, and a sign informed me that his name was Harold Kelly. It was likely clear to him that I was a young man with a chip on my shoulder. I cared little about my appearance and wore a frayed blue jacket, baggy trousers, boots, a black cap with a brim. I kept my hair clipped to my scalp, as a convict newly released from prison might have. I suppose I looked ragged in every way, lanky and dark, headed for trouble. I had spent so much time photographing criminals, I may have taken on some of their airs. I assume Kelly thought

I wasn't a customer worth the bother. He ignored me until I placed the watch on his counter. He glanced at it, and as soon as he did, he stopped working so he could peer over his glasses at me.

"Yours?"

"Inherited," I told him. I suppose that's the way I thought of the watch, not as a stolen object but as a reward I deserved. From the skeptical look on the watchmaker's face I could tell he thought it was much too good for the likes of me.

He picked it up, turned it over in his hand, and read the inscription. "'To my dear son.'"

"I have a father," I said, embarrassed by the sort of son I'd become, for I was dear to no one. I thought of Isaac spitting on the ground so he could let me know what he thought of me. The day after I'd stolen the watch I'd gone to sit beside him under a long table, where we did piecework, stitching pockets onto women's shirts. We were only boys, but boys who knew too much of the world. When I opened my hand to reveal my take, his eyes had widened. "The owner's son," I'd whispered, not needing to say more. "Good," Isaac had whispered back. "It's what he deserves."

The watchmaker removed his glasses and used an eyepiece to examine the watch further. "Made in London." He showed me a hallmark I hadn't noticed before, a leopard's head. "That marks the city of origin." Then beneath that mark, a crown with the number 22. "Pure gold. Excellent quality. Your father gave this to you? He must be quite wealthy."

"You don't need wealth to appreciate something beautiful." I now feared this fellow Kelly might call the police on me, and therefore manage to keep the watch for himself. Over the years I had grown attached to it, as men grow attached to their miseries and their burdens.

The repairman took a tiny set of tweezers and opened the back of the watch, then went deeper into the cogs, fishing around. He came upon a cog that was stuck in place, which he removed and cleaned, then reinserted.

Immediately the works began again. The sudden sound startled me, and I took a step away from the counter. Kelly nodded, fully understanding my reaction. "It's alive," he said. "A watch is like a man. You have to know how to approach it, and each one is unique. This one, for instance, has its own fingerprint." Kelly tapped upon the back with just the right amount of pressure. A small circular panel slipped up to reveal a single blue stone. "Sapphire," he informed me. "Your father truly does appreciate beauty. And of course there is your name in print for all eternity," he said with a mocking tone.

A hidden inscription had been revealed, there below the stone.

"To Harry Block, on the occasion of his eleventh birthday."

"It's a fine watch, Harry." The watchmaker smirked as he congratulated me. He had already guessed that wasn't my name. In truth, I startled at the sound of it. "If you ever want to sell this watch, I'm an interested party. Or any other watch your father presents to you. Just bring it here and I'll give you a fair price."

I paid the fee for the repair with all the money I had at the time, and slipped the watch inside my pocket. Walking down Houston Street I remembered that Harry Block had told me his age, the same as mine, as if that had mattered and had somehow made us colleagues. He'd only had the watch for a brief time before I'd relieved him of it. At that point I had already been in possession of the timepiece for so long perhaps it did belong to me.

All the same, I began to look for the original owner. I did so without thinking, since finding people came easily to me. It was what I'd been trained for, and searching for the lost had become part of my soul. I couldn't let things go, even when I should. I did as Hochman had always instructed, looked into my subject's past. He insisted to the press that he used numerology and herbs to divine a man's future and his dreams, but he told me that a man always revealed his own inner story in his actions and expressions. A man's past deeds foretold his future, and allowed any-one with half a brain to divine the path he would take.

I discovered which factories Block's family owned and made a list that I carried with me. I stood outside each one, including the loft where my father and Isaac Rosenfeld's father had worked years ago. For several years Block disappeared. I found out later he had gone to Harvard College, then to law school. When he moved back into his family's house after his residence in Cambridge, Massachusetts, I was still around. Sometimes I stationed myself across from his family's home. In the half-light I gazed through the tall arched windows. It was a brownstone mansion on Sixty-second Street, built by the architects Hunt and Hunt with beautiful cornice pieces and elaborate stone carvings. Surely, it could not compare to Mrs. Vanderbilt's block-long monstrosity of red bricks and limestone, built in 1882 across from the Plaza Hotel, inspired by a chateau in the Loire Valley. All the same, the Block mansion was grand enough. I felt even more like a criminal when I lurked there. I felt trouble course through me. I had photographed some gang members in the Tombs prison before their hangings, moments before they crossed from the courthouse to their incarceration and death over a connecting bridge that prisoners called the Bridge of Sighs. I'd wondered if these men had always known they would murder and rob and that their fates would lead them to ruin. As for me, I had no idea what I was capable of. Was the future set, or could a man change his destiny and make his own decisions as to what came next? Perhaps it was as Hochman had once said to me, that a man had many lives. Each day we chose the path we would take by our own actions.

And yet I did not feel that way whenever I turned onto Sixty-second Street. I felt pulled there by something far beyond my control.

I was jumpy and unpredictable as I stationed myself outside the mansion, like the arrested men I photographed. They often hung their heads and would not look full face into the camera. It was difficult to get a decent portrait of a criminal. Surely the same could have been said of me had my photograph ever been taken, not that it ever had been. I did not wish to be anyone's subject, or to expose what the lens might reveal.

I took to the shadows when I was positioned outside the Blocks' mansion, and in doing so became a shadow of myself. I became acquainted with the people who lived in the house by merely observing them. The scullery maids and the liveryman I knew by name. There was a maid called Agnes, and another called Sarah. Several workingmen who were in charge of the upkeep of the mansion cleared the grounds, among them a fellow they called Stick, who seemed to be their boss and who occasionally threw me a look. I slinked down the street at such times, but soon enough I was back, reckless in my need to stalk the family. I knew the schedules of the well-dressed women, Block's grandmother and mother, and an attractive younger woman with a serious expression who went in and out with her friends, all wearing large, extravagant feathered hats and silk cloaks. She was the girl I'd frightened long ago, the one with the rabbit coat. My timing was always off, and I never caught a glimpse of Block himself. Then at last I saw him headed for the doorway, Harry Block, the boy who'd handed over his watch without a fight, now a gentleman of means and responsibilities. He exited a carriage, wearing a fur-collared coat and a silk bowler. He thanked the liveryman, whom I knew to be named Marcus, clapping him on the back good-naturedly before he took the steps two at a time. Block was handsome and well mannered, at ease in the world, as rich men often were. My rage was white-hot. I felt it in my blood. It was as if the day when my father stepped off the dock had happened only hours before. Hochman had been right, the past was what we carried with us, threaded to the future, and we decided whether to keep it close or let it go. Fate was both what we were given and what we made for ourselves.

I hadn't given up the hatred I carried.

I took to following Block, and soon enough knew his routine. Once I leapt unnoticed and caught onto the rear of his carriage. I hung on as it made its way down Broadway, only inches away from him. My heart pounded as the wooden wheels hit ruts in the street, but my hands clenched the brass railings. I stepped off before the carriage stopped, leaving to ensure I didn't assault him. He oversaw the factories that belonged to his father, and also had a legal practice in which he served as the attorney for many other factory owners. He was on the boards of several charities, well known for his fund-raising abilities.

I positioned myself outside his family's mansion on the night an event was held to celebrate the new library that was being built in the Beaux Arts style between Fortieth and Forty-second Street. The building would stand in the place where there had been a man-made four-acre lake with water from the Croton Reservoir, surrounded by a twenty-five-foot Egyptian-style wall. Now a new, larger reservoir had been built in Westchester County, and the library would be considered a true wonder of the city, elegant, enormous, a free education for the people of New York. The party was to raise funds, but it was a gathering outside the usual social hierarchy, for it was unlikely that these donors would ever be invited into the parlor of the Astors, who had given the bulk of the funds. These were Jews, after all, wealthy, but still separate.

I slipped inside by assuring the doorman—whom I recognized as an elderly fellow called Barker—that I'd been sent by the Tribune to take photographs of the event. I had my camera with me, and I showed my press pass, which didn't mean much but seemed to satisfy the servant. I felt a thief simply walking over the plush carpeting. It was blue and red, a grand Chinese tapestry, and the floors of the entranceway were polished slabs of black and white marble. Another servant of some sort, one who must have been hired for the evening, for I failed to recognize him, led me past a telephone room fashioned of golden oak into the great hall, where there was a hanging Tiffany lamp of enormous proportions that cast a warm glow. The woodwork gleamed, and there were angels carved into the wooden cornices. The family was gathered here, including the father, my own father's old employer. The senior Mr. Block seemed to have some illness, as he was unable to leave his chair. I took my time in setting up my camera. I was not the only photographer. The family had hired a society fellow I knew, Jack Hailey, who had access to Manhattan's elite, and acted as if he wasn't a lowly newsman. He was annoyed by my presence and told me in no uncertain terms he planned to sell photographs to the papers so I shouldn't bother trying to sell mine.

"Fuck you, Hailey," I said. "Kiss their asses if you want. I'll do as I please."

The young woman who was Harry's sister happened to overhear. She was tall and refined with a solemn demeanor. She gazed at me, concerned, then turned to whisper something in her brother's ear. He patted her arm in a comforting but somewhat condescending manner. Harry's sister had turned out to be attractive though she hadn't been a pretty girl. When she wasn't surrounded by her silly friends, her expression was thoughtful, her eyes bright with intelligence. I'd seen her turn down glasses of champagne, and I noticed she kept to herself. Her personality seemed rather serious, and I imagined that she would have chosen to walk away from the festivities and have a moment to herself, preferring to sit on a park bench under an elm tree, for instance, watching the dark filter through the branches like any common woman. But she wore so many diamonds she would have been robbed in an instant.

I took two "official" photographs, then managed to take another when the family wasn't posed and were moving apart from one another. Juliet seemed in a hurry to be gone from that setting. In that photograph, Harry Block is the only one staring directly into the camera. When I look at that image now, I think he understood that he had been seen in some deep way, and that everything he was at his core had been caught on film. I did have a moment where I wondered if I'd stolen not only his watch but his soul.

I quickly packed up and made my way through the crowd. My hatred of those in attendance was simmering, and I suppose I was a thug if thugs are those who come uninvited to a party with murderous intentions in their hearts, acted upon or not. How was it that a terrible son such as I was able to feel such vengeance for what this class of people had done to my father? I detested how they'd caused his fingers to bleed and how they'd stripped him of his pride.

Harry Block stopped me in the hallway. The room was shaped like a teardrop, the plaster walls painted a glossy peacock blue. We stood on the enormous Oriental rug, stitched by laborers for pennies, causing some of the workmen to go blind from the smallness of their stitches and the closeness of their work. It was a beautiful creation, one I despised.

"You! Wait a moment."

The camera stand was over my shoulder. If I hoisted it, it could be used as a weapon. Moses Levy would have despaired had he known of my willingness to consider a piece of equipment meant to illuminate beauty to be equally useful in an act of brutality.

"Did you hear me?" Block called.

I turned and gazed at him directly, my enemy.

"Did I get your name?" he asked. "I was told you work for the papers."

"I've got your name," I answered. I barely recognized my own voice, for it carried a flat, dangerous tone. "Harry."

My companion was accustomed to being called Mr. Block, particularly by servants, which he clearly considered me to be. He narrowed his eyes and gazed fully into my face to see if he could conjure up some remembrance of who I might be. I could tell he saw an utter stranger. I was nothing to him after all.

I reached into my pocket and pulled out the watch. I quickly flipped it open to check the hour. "Time for me to go," I informed him.

He hadn't recognized me, but he knew the timepiece well enough. He looked at me again, even more puzzled. All the same, he didn't try to stop me as I made my way out of the mansion. I went through the darkened streets, my anger burning through me. But after twenty blocks, it was gone. It vanished and left me hollow. I thought of the grave expression on my father's face when I'd tossed the stolen watch on the table. He hadn't known me any more than Harry Block did now. From that time on I was a stranger to my father and to myself. I wished I'd never taken the thing in the first place. I wished I could have returned it. But like it or not, the watch belonged to me now, and every day I carried it, it served to remind me of who I had become.

ONE FUNERAL after another was held, at Mt. Zion and Baron Hirsch and Evergreens Cemeteries. Rain and drizzle dashed the hallowed ground at many of the private funerals, held one after the other. When Mayor Gaynor and Governor Dix both refused to take responsibility for the fire, neither one visiting the site of the disaster, it seemed no official was willing to stand up for those who had been so terribly wronged. The families of the dead were aided by the Red Cross and the Hebrew Burial Association to ensure that burial plots could be purchased for the girls whose families could not afford plots in the muddy cemeteries of Staten Island and Brooklyn and Queens and horse-drawn hearses hired. The girls themselves, having been paid only six or seven dollars for a workweek of sixty hours or more, had earned too little to pay for their own funerals. The corrupt politicians still ran the town, despite the work of Franklin Delano Roosevelt, who as a New York legislator had done his best to bring the Democratic Party back to reason.

A sea of black umbrellas preceded waves of endless sorrow. Eddie positioned himself at the edges of such gatherings, his cap pulled down, his camera slung over one shoulder. He photographed the funerals from a distance, stationing himself behind a stone wall or under a wide-limbed copper beech, doing his best not to bring attention to himself while keeping his lens free from raindrops with a soft rag. The world carried the scent of lilacs and damp earth, and the sky was a dove-colored, so laden with clouds it seemed that heaven touched the ground.

Eddie waited for the end of each service before showing the dime-store photograph of Hannah Weiss to mourners who filed by. Most of those he approached were mistrustful of his presence, so far inside their own grief he often had to repeat himself to be understood. He spoke in English and Yiddish, as well as the broken Russian he remembered from his boyhood. *Please excuse the interruption, but this girl is still missing. Perhaps you knew her? Did you see her on the day of the fire? Or the day before? Maybe recently?* One young woman who was lamenting her own losses had sputtered, "Who do you think you are asking questions here?" before stalking off. Another time Eddie had been chased off the premises when relatives of the deceased noticed his camera and charged after him, fiercely protective of their grieving family's privacy. They had thrown rocks and called him a ghoul. Perhaps he was, but the photographs of the distraught, raging mourners were among the best he'd ever taken. He added the prints to his wall of sorrow, which now ran the length of his loft, ravaged souls scattered in black and white, the exalted and the earnest, the mourners and the mourned side by side.

On the fifth of the month, New York City held a mass funeral for the unidentified victims of the fire, a procession that would take six hours to complete. The morning's drizzle would become a driving rain, but a sea of more than three hundred thousand mourners holding black umbrellas lined the street to pay their respects to those who had lost their lives. Guards had been stationed around the homes of the owners of the factory, for there was talk of retaliation. The survivors murmured to each other in remembrance of those they had lost, girls who had jumped holding hands, lovers who had kissed before the flames engulfed them, lives burning up like cinders as the owners and supervisors were skulking over the melting tar of the roof, making their way onto a neighboring rooftop. The deceased were put to rest in black coffins covered with shrouds—each had a silver plate upon it, stating that they were the unidentified departed.

The International Ladies' Garment Workers' Union, begun in 1900 to protect working people from seventy-hour workweeks and wretched conditions, had met in long sessions, swelling the halls at Cooper Union, petitioning President Taft and the governor, John Dix, only in office since January of that year, for workers' rights. The parade of mourners was more than just a funeral; it was a river of outrage. Carts transporting the dead were laden with flowers, pulled by huge draft horses draped with black netting. Thousands of mourners in black coats, the men in bowler hats, the women draped in black wool and velvet, followed the carts, including the members of the Ladies' Waist and Dress Makers' Union, Local 25, the union that had tried and failed to have sprinklers installed in the Triangle factory. The mourners carried black banners and garlands of roses. Signs carried by women's union groups called out, AN END TO GRIEF. The city still smelled of smoke, and a gray film hung above them. It was April, yet it seemed another month entirely, more somber November in mood.

As Eddie made his way through the crowd, he was looking for one person, a young woman with pale hair, the color of snow. Snow melted, Eddie knew that much. It disappeared if you tried to hold on to it. He had posted himself in the doorway of a pet shop. From this position he could see the swelling throngs. The gathering was not unruly, but the quiet was worse than any mayhem, a pulsing wave of sorrow. Soon enough, the owner of the shop came out with a broom.

There was to be no loitering, he declared, for he feared his plate-glass windows would be shattered should tempers rise.

As Eddie moved on, he thought he spotted Weiss's daughter. It was what he had come to do, yet at the sight of this girl, he grew light-headed. He shifted his camera stand over his shoulder, then folded himself into the crowd. He made his way through the mass of people on the street, trailing her, holding his breath, like a man about to jump from a bridge. She wore a camel-colored coat over blue skirts and high-buttoned boots, her pale hair falling down her back, proceeding so quickly Eddie wondered if she was a ghost, for ghosts are said to move in the corners of human sight. She disappeared in a mob on Fourteenth Street, but after a few moments Eddie spied her again. Her hair was indeed a beacon. If she chose to slip a shawl or scarf over her head, he would certainly lose her in the crowd. He pushed his way through the throngs with greater haste.

She came to a stop on a corner, and Eddie could see her well enough to tell she was no ghost, only flesh and blood. He readied his camera. Just as he took her photograph, she lifted her eyes, and stared directly into the lens. Later he would see that her eyes were dark, ember-colored, and he would recall that the eyes of the girl in Weiss's dime-store photograph were pale, clearly blue. But at that moment all he could focus on was that she had begun to approach him. He had no idea what to expect, certainly he never imagined she would strike him on the chest with open palms. He reeled backward, even though he was so tall, astonished by her fury.

"You think you can come here like a jackal and take photographs while we drown in our grief?"

"You didn't have to hit me." He was thankful she hadn't damaged the camera.

"We have some rights, you know," she remarked coldly.

When she started away, Eddie took her arm. "You're Miss Weiss?" Several young women on the corner were watching, clearly disturbed, but Eddie wasn't concerned. It was unlikely they would signal one of the many policemen stationed nearby. None of them wanted the authorities involved in their affairs.

Eddie showed off the dime-store photograph. "Is this you?"

The young woman flushed. "What are you doing with this? Are you a thief? Did you rob my father?"

"Your father came to me. He thought you were lost and asked for my help. But clearly you don't want him to know where you are."

"My father knows exactly where I am." The girl raised her chin and nodded to the photograph. "This is my sister," she said of the image.

They stood together as the crowds pushed past, an odd intimacy between them. "You're twins?"

"A year apart. Not that it's your business."

"I just want to speak to you about her."

"For all I know you could work for the insurance company, or for the police. If you follow me, I'll hit you harder. And next time I'll scream." Hannah's sister backed away, slipping into the crowd.

Eddie might have followed her, but he had learned early on that it wasn't possible to force out information; evidence gathered in that manner would be unreliable at best, threaded with half truths and assumptions. The Wizard of the Lower East Side always instructed the boys he employed that, when one was searching for a person's whereabouts, the individual's entire history must be considered. With every case, the investigator must look backward in time. Who was the woman who had set off on March 25 wearing a blue coat, a treasured gold locket at her throat? It was the path of that soul he must set out to discover. To find someone, it was necessary to follow in the way that the angels who follow men's lives on earth are said to do, charting each trespass without judgment, for judgment is never ours to give.

THE RAIN was a familiar, bleak curtain when Eddie decided to return to the territory of his youth. After weeks of searching, he knew little more about Hannah Weiss than he had on the night when her father had first come to his studio. She seemed to have vanished completely, as though she'd fallen through the sidewalk and continued her fiery descent into the deepest recesses of the earth. He couldn't help but wonder if he'd lost the knack for finding people, if his talent hadn't come so easily to him that he hadn't appreciated his own abilities.

Eddie sought out Sheriff Street. The weather was so raw he found himself shivering, and he kept his collar up, hands in his pockets. For a while he felt disoriented when confronted by the turmoil of the crowded markets, the steamy scent of vegetables and meat from the vendors, the men in wide black hats who gazed at him with contempt. The gutters in the old neighborhood ran with filth, for many tenement buildings were still without toilets, and the outhouses in the bare dirt yards drained sewage directly into the streets. The buildings were so close any bit of light would have been hard-pressed to break through even if the day hadn't been so dreary. After a while, the streets seemed familiar once more. When he let his instincts take over, he still knew the route by heart. The Hall of Love looked the same. The large wooden doors, the carved balustrades, the tiled mosaic floor in the entranceway. He entered, clapping the rain from his jacket. Several women were gathered in the unheated corridor, anxiously waiting, hoping to be granted a meeting with the renowned man whose reputation had only continued to grow in the past few years. In Russia they called him an angel, a messenger from God who tended to the forsaken and the betrayed. A few of the women in the hallway held handkerchiefs, on the verge of tears. One young mother tried to hush her baby with a lullaby, but the infant continued to wail sharp, mournful cries. The air was thick with the odor of wet wool and human despair.

Two insolent boys of ten or eleven slouched around in a corner nook, caps pulled down, joking with each other as they amused themselves with a pair of dice. They were little ruffians hired to attend to Hochman's legwork, as Eddie had once been, spending too much time in brothels and taverns. The boys lounging in the Hall of Love were most assuredly practiced in the art of eavesdropping and had learned to peer through keyholes. Those who were literate were instructed to jot down notes to bring back to their employer. Most became caught up in the tawdry life of debauchery they were only meant to report upon. The corruption was like quicksand; one step and it pulled you down.

Eddie approached the boys straightaway. *Start at the beginning, and here is mine.*

"Is the old man in?"

Eddie could feel the world he'd once known coming back to him. He may have lost his faith in taverns and whorehouses, but he'd been granted an odd variety of strength from being pitiless. His detachment had helped him survive.

The boys glared rudely and leaned closer to one another. Both had dark, rabbity faces. They'd probably been starving when Hochman offered them work.

"What's it to you?" said the one with more nerve, clearly the leader of the pair.

"I know your game, so don't think you're fooling me. You work for Mr. H or you wouldn't be here. Is he in his office?"

"You don't know shit," the leader responded. He squinted to make himself look tough. He was older than he'd first appeared, maybe fourteen, nearly a man, but the scruffy clothes he wore were small on him, giving him the air of a boyhood that was already something of the past. Eddie recalled Hochman recommending that his boys try to appear childish. No one paid attention to children, and guilty men were much more likely to admit their transgressions when they thought no one of any worth would overhear.

The door to Hochman's private office opened before the conversation grew more heated. Though he had an office on Rivington Street, it was here in his private chambers that Hochman performed marriage ceremonies and took the time to comfort those loveless women who had been abandoned by husbands and fiancés. A hush fell over the corridor as he entered. Hochman wore a velvet waistcoat and a tweed jacket, as dapper as ever. Ladies were drawn to him, and he did his best to encourage their devotion by paying attention to his appearance, even as he aged.

The rude boys shrank away, careful to mind their manners in the presence of their employer. A group of women were quick to surround the Wizard. They clasped at his arms, their emotions heightened by his presence, but Hochman excused himself. "Ladies, all good things take time, and in all good time I'll hear every one of your stories." He strode forward, pleased, for not much escaped his eye. He'd taken note of the tall young man dripping with rain and had immediately recognized his protégé. "Ezekiel," he called fondly, signaling for Eddie to approach. "I knew you weren't lost just because everyone's written you off."

Eddie winced. It was just like Hochman to wrap an insult inside a veneer of good cheer. The Wizard slapped him on the back, a little too heartily, for the welcome stung. "I know you, my boy. You're here for something. Let's not waste time. I have people waiting."

Eddie followed Hochman into his office. It was lavishly furnished, with large leather chairs and a huge, ornate mahogany desk. The carpet was an Oriental, expensive and a bit garish, in bright tints of orange and blue. The walls had been covered with sheaths of blue silk wallpaper fashioned in China, purchased at a shop on Mulberry Street. Blue was said to be the color of trust and loyalty and wisdom, all of the attributes Hochman wanted his clients to associate with him.

Eddie sat in one of the leather chairs, made of deep maroon calfskin that was well worn and studded with brass buttons. He knew the Wizard avoided shaking hands, for he had a fear of contagious diseases, quite rational considering that many of the immigrants he dealt with were in poor health; tuberculosis and measles ran rampant in the tenement houses.

There were piles of official Jewish wedding contracts stacked on a long oak table. These ketubahs were beautifully made, decorated with gold leaf, each one printed individually, many with biblical scenes painted in watercolors. The marriage contracts would bear Hochman's graceful signature after he had completed the ceremony, which he was legally entitled to perform, though he was neither a rabbi nor a city official. He charged no fee, but the larger the donation to the Hall of Love, the more fortunate the wedding couple would be.

Hochman eased himself into the chair behind his desk and offered Eddie a cigar. "No more wedding photographs? I heard you were a troublemaker and nobody wanted to hire you. You made scenes."

"I was no good at it, so I gave it up."

"You gave up quite a lot of things from what I hear."

Eddie shrugged. His defection and his loss of faith were common knowledge in the neighborhood. On the way to Sheriff Street, a bearded old man in a broad-brimmed black hat, perhaps a member of

his father's shul, had spat on the ground when he passed by. Among
the elder Cohen's circle, a son who didn't know enough to respect his
father wasn't worth much. One who didn't respect his own people was
beneath contempt.

"I was sorry to hear about Levy." Hochman pushed a silver lighter
across the desk. "He was a good photographer. A good man."

Eddie lit the cigar and choked, humbled to have the exact same
response he'd had when he finally accepted his first stogie from his
employer. He'd done a particularly good job of tracking down a missing fiancé and Hochman had invited him into his office, an invitation he could brag about to the other boys. Eddie remembered being
surprised by the conversation on that day. Hochman had asked what
he thought of love, now that he was in the business. *Nothing much,*
Eddie had replied. *You don't see how powerful a force it is?* Hochman
had asked. *How it rules men's lives?*

I see misery. Nothing more.

If that's true, son, Hochman had said, *maybe you're not as smart as I
thought you were.*

Hochman grinned when Eddie coughed. "Still not a smoker."
Clearly, he liked to get the better of people and show them their own
failings. It made for easier negotiations.

"I suppose not." Eddie propped up the cigar in a bronze ashtray, a
beautiful piece, most likely a gift from a satisfied customer.

"Tiffany," Hochman informed him.

"I suppose that means something to some people." Eddie shrugged.
"To me, it's an ashtray."

The older man leaned back in his chair. As a boy Eddie hadn't
noticed that his boss's chair was larger by half than the chair that
faced it, perhaps to ensure that a visitor would feel himself diminished
in the presence of a superior man.

"You didn't give notice when you left. I expected more from you."

"I'm sure it was easy enough for you to find my replacement. We were all the same to you, weren't we? Good little spies."

"I gave you an opportunity. Working for me you ate better, you dressed better. You can't deny you had a better life. Just as important— you learned valuable lessons. All my boys do."

"I learned that people betrayed each other, that they fled from their responsibilities and treated each other like shit. Was that the lesson you wanted for us?"

"Not at all." Hochman had aged since Eddie had last seen him, yet was still imposing with his large, leonine head and a mane of white hair which people said he powdered each morning. "It might have been shit to you, but the *Times* and the *Herald* and the *Tribune* still turn to me when they have a case they can't solve. They still write about the boy I discovered under the Brooklyn Bridge when the police force couldn't find a trace of him."

Eddie's hackles were raised. "I solved that case."

"You found him, Ezekiel, but you solved nothing. Did you know he was murdered?"

Eddie tilted his chair forward, a strange heat rising in his face. He didn't like to think about that night, even now. Still, he knew what he'd seen. "He'd frozen to death. Everyone I spoke to said he had the habit of wandering around the city at night. He died of exposure to the cold."

"You didn't grasp why he would do such a thing in such brutal weather. Was he a fool, or was he something else? You would have needed to possess empathy for another person in order to see what was in front of you. You would have had to cast off your own skin, and slip into his. In the case of Louis—if you remember, that was his name—his mother had a boarder, a Russian who drank and had a temper. He had begun beating the boy, who was certainly too afraid to tell his mother the truth about his situation. They needed the money, and I'm sure Louis thought they would starve without the income. I imagine the Russian threatened him with what he might do to the mother if he were exposed. One night, things went too far. The Russian wrapped Louis in a blanket and carried him to the embankment, leaving him beneath the bridge. The mother recognized the blanket as one she owned. She assumed her son had taken it with him, which I knew was highly unlikely. A wandering boy does not clutch a blanket when he climbs out the window. He wants to be free, not dragged down. I suppose you failed to notice the bruises around his throat. These marks led me to the truth."

Eddie felt a bit dazed. He hadn't been aware of any of this. Of course, the night had been dark, and cold. He'd been young and very sure of his opinions.

"You were with me when I called on the mother," Hochman went on. "I assume you remember?"

It had been an honor to be allowed to accompany the Wizard, yet all Eddie recalled of the incident was the inconsolable mother, who sank into a chair to sob. He remembered shifting from foot to foot, uncomfortable in the presence of such sorrow, wishing he hadn't been granted the privilege of coming along.

"There were other things to consider. The stains on the floor I knew to be blood. The mother told me the boarder had also disappeared. When I opened the door to the corridor where the boarder's cot was kept, I could feel evil. Say what you will, but evil is real. It's a living, breathing thing."

Eddie felt shamed by how much he had missed.

"There was no reason for the mother to think her son's death was anything but peaceful, so I paid the medical examiner for his silence."

"And allowed the man who killed him to go free? What kind of justice is that?"

"Justice is God's to give, not mine. All the same, I kept track of the boarder. He wound up in the Tombs prison and was murdered in a fight the following year. I still see the mother every now and then. She always comes to embrace me."

"You should have told the police."

"Exactly why I didn't go after you when you left, Ezekiel. You were talented, but talent isn't enough." Hochman leaned in and lowered his voice, so as to continue in the greatest confidence. "Would you like to know your fatal flaw?"

Eddie flushed with annoyance. He could have easily made a list of Hochman's flaws, enough to fill several pages. Still, he was curious. "Please do tell."

"You judge what you don't understand." Hochman pulled out an engraved flask, took a sip, then offered it to Eddie, who waved it away. "You want my advice? I'll give it to you for free, for old times' sake."

"I didn't think you did anything for free."

"Maybe this is a first. So pay attention. It's not finding what's lost, it's understanding what you've found." Hochman cleared space on his desktop, moving the gold pen set he used to sign his bold signature onto marriage contracts. "Let's see what you're looking for now. Put your hands on the desk."

Eddie threw the older man a look of mistrust. He knew Hochman's fortunes were often tricks, guesswork at best.

"You tell yourself I'm a sham, Ezekiel, yet you're here. That just goes to show what a man thinks and what he feels are not necessarily one and the same. Considering you don't believe in my talents, I would hate to imagine you're too afraid to hear what I have to say."

Eddie placed his hands on the desk, palms facing upward. He felt obligated to go along with Hochman. "By all means."

Hochman grasped a wooden pointer and traced the life line crossing from right to left. "It seems you will have time enough to figure out your mistakes. You'll live to be old."

"Does that prediction deserve thanks?" Eddie mocked.

"Does life deserve gratitude? If so, thank your maker, not me." Eddie noticed there was a white film over the Wizard's once burning eyes. "This is unusual," Hochman went on. "In the center is a line, as if there was a river inside you. But there's an X across the river line, an opposition. So you haven't changed as much as you think you have. You're looking for the same thing now as you were when I first met you." Hochman stared directly into Eddie's eyes; despite his failing vision, his gaze was mesmerizing. "The only way to understand a river is to jump into it."

Eddie withdrew his hand. "I don't need a reading for myself." He brought out Hannah Weiss's photograph. "I'm looking for this girl. She went to work at the Triangle Shirtwaist Factory on the morning of the fire, and there's been no sign of her since."

"I'm honored that you would come to me for advice. If you're looking for her I can tell you only what I told you long ago. Go back in time as far as you must. Speak to everyone who knew her. If you don't find her, then in all likelihood she will find you. But you know what to do. Despite your flaws, you were my finest student. So ask yourself this—did you really come to me to find this girl, or are you looking for something else entirely?"

"You have nothing that I want," Eddie said dismissively.

Hochman pushed his chair away from the desk and bowed formally, his signal, Eddie knew, to dismiss a client whose time was up. But perhaps he was more than a client, for Hochman unexpectedly reached to shake his hand, an intimacy that surprised Eddie. He recalled when they were visiting the mother of the boy who'd gone missing, after Hochman had opened the door to the boarder's sleeping area, he had made an excuse to send Eddie away. *Go get me a glass of water. Make sure it's a clean glass. Wash it yourself.* But Eddie hadn't done as he'd been instructed. Instead, he'd stood in the corridor. He'd heard Hochman recite the mourning prayer. At that moment Eddie had known his employer was trying to protect him. He'd known there was evil in the world.

It was almost Passover, the time of year when Eddie made certain to avoid his past, yet whenever he took Mitts for a walk, he found himself drawn downtown. He made his way to the address Weiss had given him. The apartment was the sixth-floor railroad flat of a tenement building on Thompson Street. The stairs were steep and worn, and through the flimsy walls it was possible to hear half a dozen conversations in Yiddish and Russian and English, some in all three languages combined. Eddie was reminded of the room where he'd lived with his father, the lingering odor of cooked cabbage and of stews, the dim hallways, the damp clinging to the walls. All he'd wanted was to escape.

He knocked at the Weisses' door, expecting to be greeted by the old man, but it was the sister, Ella, who appeared. Their first meeting had been unfortunate, and now the girl glared when she saw Eddie, instantly suspicious. Before she could turn him away, Mitts barked cheerfully and stepped forward. "Oh," Ella said, delighted. "I didn't expect you!"

Eddie grinned. More than once, the dog had been his best representative, more lovable and social than he was. Ella turned to him after greeting the dog, less than charmed by his master. "I'm not sure I should speak to someone who accosted me on the street."

"Your father came to me for help. If you don't believe me, ask him."

"I told him there was a man inquiring about Hannah and he asked me for a description. I said tall and obnoxious. Right away he knew it was you."

Eddie winced, and his discomfort lightened Ella's expression for a moment. Still, she was wary.

"He told me you have a gift, a special knowledge that will allow you to find my sister. He sits here waiting to hear from you. He has faith in you. So tell me, Mr. Detective, did you find her with your special powers?"

"I'm not a detective. I'm a photographer. He came to look at the prints I'd taken on the day of the fire. I never told him that I had the power to find your sister."

"What good are you then?" There were spots of color on Ella's cheeks. "Why did you let him think you could? Do you mean to say you can't close your eyes and see her in the great beyond?"

"Is that where you think she is?"

Ella looked away, but a sob escaped from her throat.

Eddie reached to pull her into the hallway. At last he was getting somewhere. "A sister is something special. Maybe she told you secrets she might have kept from your father. A boyfriend? A problem?"

"Hannah didn't keep secrets. She was the kindest, most open person. I don't think she ever told a lie in her life. You can't imagine how good she was. If something had been wrong I would have known.

We knew everything about each other." Ella slipped a hand over her mouth, shocked by her own words, almost unable to take in any air. "I'm speaking of her in the past, as though she's gone."

"Let's look at the facts," Eddie suggested. "You worked together?"

"The supervisor thought we talked too much when we worked side by side, so he separated us. Hannah had me go upstairs because the room was supposed to be better, not as cold. That was the way she was. Never thinking of herself. When the fire began I tried to find her, but the stairwells were filled with smoke. The door to the ninth floor was locked. No one could budge it—several of the men tried. I was pulled along with the crowd, but I should have been beside her."

"Be thankful you weren't. It was luck that you were on the tenth floor."

"It wasn't luck! It was Hannah who saved me. She sent me to the room she should have gone to. The supervisor was looking at me when he said only one of us could stay on the ninth floor." Ella fretfully plucked at her own skin. Eddie noticed a dozen self-inflicted marks on her arms. "I should have been in that fire. That's the reason I can see the other side."

Eddie wrinkled his brow, confused.

"I should be dead. That's why I see her ghost."

"That's not the way it works," Eddie assured her.

Ella managed a laugh despite her sorrow. "You know how it works? God discussed it with you?"

"Let's discuss your sister, and leave God to other business. Did you see her that morning?"

They had walked to Greene Street arm in arm, as they did each day.

"And she seemed the same as always? No worries?"

"The same."

"You went in the building together, and up the stairs?"

Ella's expression darkened. "She told me to go on, she would follow. Some mornings she ran and bought an apple from a cart in Washington Square Park. She would sneak it in, even though we weren't allowed to eat while we worked. She said otherwise her stomach would growl."

"Did she buy an apple?"

"I don't know. I went inside the doorway and never saw her again. Only her ghost."

Eddie gazed at the girl, pity shining in his eyes.

"I can tell you think I'm foolish. But I know she's gone. I dream of water, not of fire. She's trying to tell me something." Ella gazed straight at him, defiant. "Maybe you think I'm a lunatic."

Eddie understood it was possible to dream so deeply you saw what you wished to believe. His own father had searched out his beloved wife in his dreams and had spoken to her on a nightly basis, conversations so intimate Eddie always turned to the wall so he wouldn't overhear.

"I think you worry for your sister, as I'm sure she would have worried for you."

"We both know what you'll find. She's gone. Please, don't tell my father. The least we can do is let him dream awhile longer."

On his way up toward Cooper Square in the falling dusk, Eddie realized he was being followed. It was Mitts who alerted him, for the dog seemed uneasy, glancing behind them, a worried expression crossing his usually easygoing countenance. Eddie took a moment to pause in a doorway. There he feigned gazing at his watch, all the while scanning the street with a sidelong glance. Indeed there was a large man dressed in a heavy black overcoat stopping nearby so that he might study Eddie from beneath the brim of his bowler hat. Eddie set his watch back into his pocket and moved on, but so did the burly stranger, lumbering after him. This was why Hochman preferred to hire boys who were light on their feet and could easily go unnoticed in a crowd. Eddie looked over his shoulder to steal another look. For an instant his eyes locked with his pursuer's. He observed something dark peering back at him, the sort of malevolent spark he often captured on film when recording criminal subjects.

Eddie whistled for Mitts to stay close, then headed off briskly. The stranger continued to gain on them, his strut more focused now. He carried a roughly made club Eddie didn't like the looks of. The hair on the back of Eddie's neck rose in pinpricks, and he noticed that the hair on Mitts's back bristled as well.

Eddie turned down Seventh Street, hoping to lose his shadow, but the street was nearly deserted in the dusk, and it appeared he'd chosen a perfect place for an assault. Without thinking, he slipped into the first doorway he came upon, McSorley's Ale House, an establishment that had opened nearly sixty years earlier. This Irish tavern, where only men were allowed, was known for its workingman clientele. Mitts followed Eddie inside, treading softly over the sawdust scattered on the floor to mop up spilled drinks. The pit bull made for a good companion in taverns, for his breed was known for rat fighting, a form of amusement that often took place in the cellars below the alehouses and sporting houses throughout the city. In dogfights, pit bulls were champions, so ferocious many were unwilling to let go of an opponent they were pitted against. Their jaws occasionally had to be pried open with a metal bar before they would release the loser, if the other dog were still alive. Due to Mitts, space was made at the bar when Eddie approached. He asked for dark ale, keeping his eye on the door. He waited for his fare, but the fellow tending bar continued to clean glasses with a rag rather than see to his order.

"Is there a problem?" Eddie wished to know.

"No dogs," he was told.

Two tabby cats lay beside a table in the back room where several men played cards.

"He won't bother a cat. He's well behaved." In fact, Mitts had curled up on the floor at Eddie's feet, his nose in the sawdust.

"But how do I know you are?" was the response. "Maybe you're looking for trouble." The barkeep was broadly built and heavily muscled, his strength put to use if there were unruly customers. His pale eyes were difficult to read, but he pointed out a sign that declared BE GOOD OR BE GONE. Eddie realized that his ragged appearance and dark expression might have led this fellow to believe he had criminal intentions.

"I'm here to have a drink," Eddie assured him. "Whiskey is fine. I prefer to avoid trouble. My dog's the same as me."

"Are you saying I should serve him as well?" the barkeep inquired drily, but Eddie's attentions had already shifted. The man in the black coat had entered the alehouse, situating himself near the window. Eddie reached for a dime, which he tossed on the counter. He moved off the barstool and whistled low, between his teeth. Mitts rose to follow. As they headed for the double door, Eddie could sense his stalker behind him. The stranger's shadow fell forward, blurring the edges between them. As soon as they were on the street, the stalker leaned forward to grab Eddie.

Eddie turned, quick to push him away. "I've got nothing for you! Back off, man!"

His stalker said nothing in response, but a grim smile crossed his face. It was a bad moment that promised to worsen. No words were said, but the tension grew. The dog planted himself in front of his master, as though he'd been trained in the art of protection. In response the stranger lifted up his club. Eddie grabbed Mitts by the collar and drew him away.

"If you follow me again, I'll let my dog on you. Understand?"

There was no reply, just that menacing smile. When the stranger came no closer, Eddie took the opportunity to walk away, though a chill ran down his spine. He was suspicious, and rightfully so. After only a few steps, his pursuer came at him again, this time with a sudden and vicious attack. He struck at the back of Eddie's head with his club. Stunned, Eddie fell to the gutter. As the world went black, he thought himself a fool for not being more watchful. Hadn't that been one of Hochman's first lessons? Never take your eyes off a man you can't trust. He could feel the thief going through his pockets and heard him muttering while he grabbed what little Eddie carried with him.

Though Eddie was rising from the blackness, he could barely gather his thoughts. He heard Mitts barking like mad and imagined he would be hit again before he could rise. He gritted his teeth, but there wasn't a second attack. He heard shouts. Dazed, he forced himself to his feet. He could feel the heat of his own blood as it matted in his hair and dripped into his collar. His vision was blurry, but when he squinted he could make out the figures of two men fighting. The barman from McSorley's had sensed trouble and followed them. He wrestled with Eddie's attacker while Mitts lunged at the man, latching on to his leg. The thief went at the dog with his club but was unable to drive him off.

Eddie ran and took hold of Mitts. "Enough," he said, but the tendencies of the dog's fierce breed had risen, and Mitts refused to let go of his quarry. Eddie shook him, then drew his jaws apart. The stranger scrambled to his feet, a stream of blood sopping through his torn pants leg. He grabbed his bully stick and took off toward Second

Avenue, though he did so with a limp. Eddie and the barman watched the attacker vanish into the crowd.

"You said you don't like trouble," the barman remarked. "But is it possible it likes you?"

Whatever the thief had stolen had been flung to the ground in his attempt to make his getaway. Eddie collected his change and his watch. He held it up to find that the glass face had cracked. When he listened he discovered it was still keeping time.

The barman from McSorley's came to inspect the damage. "That was what he was after. Without a doubt. That's what you get for owning a rich man's watch."

That night Eddie slept upright in a chair, still in his clothes, his head throbbing. He dreamed a woman was making her way down Twenty-third Street, soaking wet. She was naked and beautiful. He had yearned for certain women, but the way he wanted this one was something more. He began to follow her. The entire street was awash in water, as if the river had flooded Tenth Avenue. Just as he was about to rush over to the woman he so desired, someone came up behind him and stopped him. *You can't have what doesn't belong to you,* a voice said.

Mitts put his head on his master's knee. Eddie rubbed the dog's skull, discovering that the dog had a lump similar to the one that had risen on his own head.

"He got you as well," he murmured to Mitts.

It was early, and the light in the room was dim. The building hadn't been wired for electricity. No one in city government thought this address was worth the bother, so Eddie lit a candle. He took his watch from his jacket to study it. He'd have to return to the watchmaker's and have the cracked glass replaced. He thought of Harry Block, and the expression of outrage on his face when he saw what had once belonged to him in another man's possession. Eddie then had a strange sensation, a bit of memory floating up like a firefly. He had seen the man who had attacked him before. Quickly, he sifted through the pile of photographs from the library gala until he found the one he wanted. There he was, the man in the black coat, a faithful employee who stood behind Harry Block only minutes before Eddie had revealed the stolen watch to his old enemy. The man in the heavy coat gazed away from the camera, as criminals often did, for none wished to divulge too much about themselves, or to have their features caught and recorded, so that they might later be identified. This man, however, was not a common thief at all but one of Block's trusted employees, clearly sent to the Lower East Side for the watch.

Eddie felt himself flush with anger. How dare Block come after him, and think himself above the law? He had half a mind to go down to the Chelsea police station and report the incident, and he might have done exactly that, but he thought of the watchmaker's suspicions that the watch was not his. He had allowed his outrage to obscure the truth. All at once, it struck Eddie that he himself was the thief. He was the one in possession of stolen property.

He wondered if every criminal saw himself as the hero of his own story, and if every thankless son was convinced he'd been mistreated by his father. Nothing was constant, he understood that now. Even Moses Levy's photographs of the trees in the forest were shifting, fading from the very light that had created them. And in that hour of dim morning light, Eddie admitted that he no longer understood who he was, a hero, a nobody, a thief, a son who'd been mistreated, or one who had wronged his father so profoundly he might never be forgiven.

FIVE

THE ORIGINAL LIAR

* * * * * * * * * *

I BEGAN to defy my father the year I turned fifteen. They were minor infractions to begin with, secret transgressions no one would notice. But each time I broke the smallest rule, I felt I had committed a crime. In truth, nothing much had changed except the way I felt, but in time I have come to wonder if that isn't everything after all. Perhaps my conversion from dutiful daughter had begun on the night I went into my father's workroom and read the first few pages of his handbook. Often I wished I had continued reading, but I'd been too frightened to go on. Was it because I feared being caught red-handed? Or was it that I dreaded what I might find in those pages? At those times when I worked up the courage to go down the cellar steps, the locks were always bolted. I put my ear to the heavy wooden door but heard nothing, only the beating of my own pulse at the base of my throat.

I passed a locksmith's shop on my route to the fish market, and one day I veered from my usual path and stepped inside. I said I had lost a key to a cellar storeroom where jars of jams and jellies were kept cool. I thought I must certainly look like a liar—my cheeks were flushed and hot, and

I stammered over my words. I wondered if the sheriff's office would be called and I would be arrested on the spot, but the locksmith treated me as if I were any other customer. When I said I could not afford to have him come to change the bolts, he assured me he had a skeleton key that would work on any lock. He took my money, but as it turned out what he gave me was a worthless loop of metal. When I reached home I slipped the skeleton key into the first lock, where it twisted and stuck fast. For a few panicky moments I feared I wouldn't be able to remove it, and would be found out when my father returned to his workroom. At last I managed to retrieve the key, pulling it out with all my might. I then ran to toss it into the heap at the rear of our yard, where we burned our trash once a week.

That experience didn't stop me from puzzling over my father's past. My curiosity became a stone in my shoe. Whenever I had the house to myself I examined the volumes in my father's library as if they might reveal his secrets. I read all manner of medical texts and books about the natural world. I went through the cabinet where he stored whiskey and aperitifs, and tasted a green liquid that reminded me of the mint that grew in our garden. I took a spade so I might dig in the earth beside the back door, where the liveryman dragged specimens through the weeds. There I searched for bones or pieces of gold but discovered nothing more than a hill of stinging ants. And then, one evening, I found the keys. My father had gone out and forgotten his waistcoat jacket. I randomly searched the pockets. There were some coins and hard candy in one pocket. In the other, the keys.

They were small, one fashioned of iron, the other of brass. They burned in my hand. I stood at the cellar stairs thinking over what to do next. I admit I was afraid. I wasn't prepared to go against my father's wishes to this extent. But perhaps there was more. Perhaps I knew if I opened the door and discovered the truth, I would have to flee. I had no idea where I could go if I left my father. Another museum or theater, if they would have me. I understood why Maureen reported in for work each day. We did not have many choices.

I returned the keys to their rightful place.

And hated myself for doing so.

⌒

Still, I could not go back to being the good girl I'd been before. When I was on display in my tank, my quiet defiance rose up more frequently. I sometimes made faces at those in the audience who came too close, pressing their noses to the glass. Once I showed my teeth as if I were a dog, and two young women fainted and had to be revived with smelling salts. Few noticed my small rebellions, not even Maureen, for I practiced humility on a daily basis. I washed dishes and helped to hang laundry on the line. I brushed my hair a hundred strokes a day and faithfully bleached my nails with a mixture of soap and lye to dissolve the blue dye from the tank that stained my fingers. In the evenings I didn't stray from the routine my father set forth for me. I read the great classics he chose and went to bed early. But with each year that passed, I found that my curious nature had a stronger hold. It rattled around inside me even when I tried my best to be good. Each time I opened the window in my bedroom I smelled salt and fish and human desire. I knew what I wanted: my own place in the world, not a path I took because I was under my father's command but one I had chosen for myself. I wanted to know how other girls my age wore their hair, for mine was still in braids as if I were a child. How had they learned to dance, choose silk dresses from the shops, form friendships? I was jealous of the girls I saw on the streets; they seemed to know so much about the world and I'd had access to only odd bits and pieces. Was anyone else in Brooklyn aware that a hummingbird's heart beat so quickly all you could hear was a dizzying whir when it perched on your finger to drink sugar water from a dropper? Did anyone care that a tortoise needed to have its shell rubbed with olive oil in cold winter months to prevent cracks from forming, or that when the creature slept it pulled in its limbs and head and rocked back and forth for comfort, like a baby in his cradle?

What I wanted to know had both nothing and everything to do with the natural world.

I wished to know love.

———

I began to sneak off to Dreamland in the summer months, though my father had told me often enough that the owners of that park were our enemies. He said we were like nations at war. All wars must be won or lost, he told me, and in time we would go to battle. I didn't want battle, however, just lovely summer nights. I knew Coney Island could be dangerous, and it was definitely changing. There was the Brighton Beach Racetrack near an area called the Gut and two others in Sheepshead Bay and Gravesend. The sport had begun on Coney Island, with the Brighton Beach Fairgrounds and the Brooklyn Jockey Club. But racetracks brought in a criminal element, and the clientele that frequented them could be rowdy. That thuggish group of horsemen and gamblers mixed with men and women looking for a good time at Dreamland and Luna Park in a world made of steel and papier-mâché. I began to climb out my window after I had finished my chores and bade my father good night. The evenings were inky, with banks of clouds and a pink-tinted fog that rolled in from the Atlantic. At first I merely sat on the roof gazing down at the rush of life on Surf Avenue, but I soon wanted more. My father had always told me that my heart and lungs were larger than an average person's, and this was the reason I could remain underwater for so long without air. Perhaps my desires were larger as well. What I wanted haunted me and wouldn't let me go. At night I tossed and turned, and usually rose from my bed without the benefit of sleep. I yearned for a different life.

I always made certain to pile clothes beneath my quilt in the form of a sleeping body when I crept out of our house, so that my absence wouldn't be noticed if my father decided to check on me. Not that he ever would. He was busy in his workroom after supper, and when he was done he went out on his own to the taverns of Brooklyn, of which there were more than a dozen on Surf Avenue alone. I was not uppermost in his mind.

"Men will be men," Maureen told me when I wondered aloud where my father went in the evenings. "Don't complain," she advised. "That's how women find their freedom. When there's no one else at home."

Maureen's words rang true enough. With my father gone I could read whatever I wanted, making myself comfortable in the overstuffed horsehair chair he most preferred. The cereus plant loomed on the oak side table, but I ignored it. I didn't believe that it would ever bloom, and that on some magical night it would change before my eyes. To me, it was a malevolent specimen, more likely to swallow spiders and flies than to flower miraculously. I immersed myself in Poe's chilling tales, though my father had often called Poe a perverted individual, a drunkard and a deviant. I dared to look through volumes from the East in which men and women performed sexual acts I tried my best to understand. I ate buttered toast and rice pudding for dinner rather than the daily routine of fish my father insisted upon, and tasted red wine for the first time. I unbraided my hair and stared at myself in the mirror so that I could consider who I might be when I became a woman. Someone with long dark hair who possessed a pale complexion and a quiet nature, who let no emotion show, yet was inwardly excited by the idea of the future, whose eyes burned with desire.

Before long, I was so sure of myself I stopped climbing out the window and simply walked out the front door. As soon as I left the museum, I felt myself become another person. If anyone had asked my name, I would have called myself Jane, the name of the character in the novel Raymond Morris had always spoken of with such reverence, the book that had set him free. It was a common enough name, yet somehow stately and independent. I was impressed by the character's statement: I am not an angel, and I will not be one till I die. Those words made me feel I was not the only one who was at odds with who I was expected to be, and that angels were meant for another world, not for ours.

The night watchman at the park's gate grew to know me so well he allowed me to sneak in without payment. The watchman seemed kindly, and he always told me to enjoy myself and stay out of trouble, but he once asked for a kiss in exchange for this favor.

"Come on, Jane," he urged, for that was the name I'd given him. His job was not to be the guardian of wayward girls but to ensure that the crowds did not get too unruly. At night, after the gates were locked, he circled the eastern arena, where the animals were kept, watching over the leopards and tigers, alongside the horses and Shetland ponies children paid to ride, keeping a special eye on the pride of lions, which included a great creature called Black Prince, who was said to behave like a dog when around his trainer and like a beast from hell should anyone else dare to approach his cage. "I've got to have my fair share," the watchman told me. When I grew flustered and tears sprung to my eyes, he waved me on. I thought it over, then went back to him. Perhaps there was a part of me that still felt I had to do as I was told, or perhaps I wanted to test myself and see what I was worth. I stood on tiptoes and pecked the watchman's cheek. In that instant I knew the power a young girl can have over a man, although I did not yet know that ability could also be a curse. The watchman always let me into the park after that. Sometimes he gave me a few dimes to spend on myself. All for the sake of a kiss.

This was before Dreamland was closed for renovations last year, in the autumn of 1910. All the same, the park was astounding even before the new attractions were added and all of the elegant icy white buildings were painted. I remember passing through the massive gate for the first time, stunned to see the gigantic biblical sculpture called Creation, an enormous winged angel. I couldn't take my eyes from her. It was as if a goddess had fallen from the sky onto the shores of Brooklyn. Though I knew it was a betrayal to be so in awe of our competitor, I had never seen anything so beautiful.

There was a tower in which thousands of lightbulbs had been installed, and the night above the park was so lit up that I sometimes feared my father would be coming home from his evening out and spy me walking along. I took to wearing a black shawl to cover my head so I might fade into the dark. But underneath the shawl my hair was unbraided, and I let it fall down my back.

Our museum was tiny and old-fashioned, a minor diversion, not a grand, heart-stopping display. I awoke each day to the scent of formaldehyde and mothballs and a schedule of dull housework as I helped Maureen with the ironing and cooking before the museum opened for business. I helped to feed the birds and watered the neglected cereus plant.

My hours in the tank had become a chore. I often curled up at the bottom dozing until my father rapped on the glass. I knew I was meant to turn this way and that, posing, and to smile through the waves I created when I splashed my tail. I was not to show my teeth or make rude faces. Each morning I coated myself with olive oil as Maureen suggested, so that my skin would not dry out and crack, as if I were another tortoise kept in the hall of science. Each night I dreamed I wandered the streets of our neighborhood until I found myself at the fish market. I was there buying haddock and clams when I realized people were laughing at me. I looked down to find I had no legs. I had not forgotten the entertainment *my father had been most famous for before he came to this country, the display of cutting a woman in half. The trick haunted me. I knew I would be a far better fish if I didn't have legs. Then I would be caught in the net of my life, unable to climb out the window at night, unable ever to run away, fated never to see the true wonders of the world.*

～

There were such huge crowds on summer evenings in the streets of Coney Island that no one noticed me, a plain girl in a black dress and gloves, my hair the color of ink. I visited Luna Park and the other, smaller entertainments. But I preferred Dreamland, perhaps because I could see its brilliant tower from my bedroom window. The park had become a part of my dreams before I ever walked through the gate. I went to every attraction and still couldn't get enough. The one entertainment I avoided was the sideshow that fronted the park, for it reminded me too greatly of my father's museum, though he called our human oddities scientific entertainments and living wonders and the sideshow's term was freaks of nature. The Queen of Fatland was one of the star acts at the Dreamland sideshow, and was said to weight 685 pounds though her height was not more than five foot two. I had seen the Queen off-season, shopping at the same fish market I frequented on Neptune Avenue. Her real name was Josephine, and she once gave me a recipe for bluefish fillet boiled with rosemary and sliced potatoes. The Queen was originally from Minnesota and now lived with two sisters in Brighton Beach, a very respectable neighborhood. She told me that my father had once offered her a position at the museum, but she was paid far more by the owners of Dreamland and, more important, she was treated with respect.

"We would have done so as well," I assured her.

The Queen laughed and patted my head, as if I were truly still a child.

She wore enormous felted hats decorated lavishly with ostrich feathers. The bodices of her gigantic silk dresses were encrusted with rhinestones and pearls.

"Honey, do you know your father's reputation? He's as cheap as they come." She might have said more, but she backed off with a sigh, perhaps because I was a young, impressionable girl. "However, he's your father, so you think whatever you'd like."

The Queen sang opera in the sideshow, favoring exquisite Italian arias. She told me there were men who fell in love with her at the moment they first heard her voice. I waved when I saw her on the evenings I passed by, but I had no interest in attending her performances. I wanted nothing more than to watch the crowds of everyday people, who seemed far more interesting and unpredictable than the living wonders I knew. The human curiosities who took their breakfasts of apple fritters and doughnuts on our back porch had come to seem no more mysterious to me than the moths that hovered over the cabbages in our garden. The men who ate fire and contorted their arms and legs into rubbery shapes spent their downtime playing cards at a table under the pear tree, like ordinary workmen. The women with too much hair or too little flesh changed into their costumes in the kitchen, revealing their frayed undergarments, asking me to fix cups of milky tea.

At Dreamland my favorite pastime was to stand in the shadows of the huge ballroom built above the iron pier and watch the lovers dance. They were so beautiful, each one unique. The music was the latest Enrico Caruso, so romantic and lovely, and Frank Stanley's popular song "I Want What I Want When I Want It." The ocean glowed in the light of the stars, so many hanging above us in the dark that no human being could ever count them all. The everyday people who attended the park screamed in metal carts that were flung down the Chute the Chutes. They kissed in dark corners. Many of them lived as if the world was coming to an end that very night, raising their skirts, making love to strangers, begging to be scared out of their wits and thrilled to their very core.

The season I haunted Dreamland was the same summer I borrowed Maureen's copy of Jane Eyre. I wanted to read it for myself so that I might understand the depth of Mr. Morris's passion for this tale. Maureen said I could only have access to the volume when I was with her, for she was so protective of the book she kept it wrapped in brown paper to shield its cover. Just as well. My father didn't approve of women authors, and he most assuredly would not have approved of Miss Brontë. I had to admit, the novel confused me. I knew I was supposed to have sympathy for the main character, the orphaned Jane, who was near my age and all but friendless and whose name I took for myself on the nights I wandered off on my own. Yet it was the madwoman locked in the attic who held my interest and compassion. I could understand how Mr. Morris might have been so radically affected by the madwoman's story he had run away the very night he finished the book. I thought if I ever fell in love, I would want my beloved to wish what I had come to wish, that the book had ended differently, so that the first Mrs. Rochester might have made her escape.

"Is your heart broken?" I asked Maureen the day I returned the book to her. The Wolfman had been gone for more than two years. After his departure, Maureen had suffered from bouts of melancholy. Her eyes had been watery and red, but she blamed her reaction on the tang of the spring onions that grew wild in our yard and all over Brooklyn. I had no idea that Mr. Morris had recently found his way back to Brooklyn, and was secretly living only a few miles away.

"Do you think I have a heart to break?" she said quite seriously.

"I know you do," I responded without hesitation. "Surely, you must worry over Mr. Morris?"

Maureen came to sit beside me. I had never understood why people on the street smirked and stared with disgust when they saw her. Birds were many colored and they were still considered beautiful, why shouldn't the same be true of Maureen? Her scars and splotches seemed another part of her, a feature no more or less important than her red hair or hazel eyes. Sometimes I imagined the burns on her face and throat had been formed from handfuls of light thrown upon her, and that same glorious light radiated back from her soul.

"Mr. Morris is a man who knows how to take care of himself." Maureen seemed convinced this was true, but I still cried a little over his fate.

"I wish he had taken me with him," I said.

Maureen took my hand in hers. Looking back on this, I suppose she felt bad not to be truthful with me, but she had spent her life protecting me and was not about to tell me any secret my father might wring out of me.

I was not wearing gloves, and my first impulse was to pull my hand away and hide my abnormality, but she held fast. "I think I failed you," she said to me in a mournful tone.

I assured her she hadn't. She alone had cared for me for as long as I could remember. It was Maureen who taught me to walk. It was she who sat at my bedside when I had childhood fevers, holding a cold cloth to my forehead, spooning chamomile tea between my lips when I was too ill to drink from a cup. She encouraged me to teach myself to read, though my father said I was too clumsy to learn to write my letters, due to my defect. Maureen could not write either, but I later taught her to read well enough so that she could decipher recipes and letters, which she said was a great gift. I told her everything, every nightmare and fear. Or at least I had. It was only lately that I had begun keeping my thoughts and deeds private. It pained me to conceal anything from Maureen—she had always been so good to me. As we sat together I gathered up my courage and confessed my secret life at Dreamland. I told her that I went along the avenue to watch the couples dance, losing myself in the crowds. I admitted that I called myself Jane if anyone questioned me, and that when I walked through the gates beneath the statute of Creation I felt I had become someone brand new.

I expected Maureen to laugh, for she was a rebel and abhorred rules and regulations. She often groused and complained about my father when we were alone, making jokes about his stern manner and his attention to detail, especially when it came to his clothes. In fact he was a dandy and preferred cashmere and silk. Maureen could imitate him perfectly, mimicking his accent and his harsh way of speaking. She could give such a good impression of the cold, chalky glare of his anger it seemed she was possessed by his spirit. I thought she might give a performance now, copying the way he bowed formally when he greeted an audience. Instead, she was angry. She told me in no uncertain terms I was never to sneak out to Dreamland again.

"You don't know the sort of trouble you can get into. You take a step too far, and you'll find there's no coming back. Promise me you'll stop sneaking around."

I was surprised by the worry in Maureen's expression. We could hear my father in the museum, making the last announcements before he closed the doors for the day. There were very few people in attendance. The crowds were already waning, and evening shows had been canceled. We knew autumn not from the change of color in the foliage but by the empty streets and the thinning crowds, who would not return until the following season.

"All right," I agreed. "I'll stop."

Maureen did not appear convinced. "I'll be the one keeping a watch on you now." She studied me carefully, lifting my chin so she could stare into my eyes. "Have you had your monthly bleeding?"

I admitted I had.

"I thought as much! And you never said a word." She was clearly disappointed to find I hadn't confided in her. "Then you're a woman and must act like one." Our heads were close together, but she lowered her voice further due to the intimate nature of our discussion. "When you leave here against the Professor's wishes, you'd better do so with no thought of returning. We're not like other people, Cora. They would never understand us."

As evening fell I sat alone in my room, gazing out my window, thinking over Maureen's advice. I saw Malia the Butterfly Girl making her way down Surf Avenue, her mother's arm drawn protectively around her. They passed by the tintype photo gallery on the corner, where an individual could be photographed against cardboard cutouts of the seashore. Malia had left behind her orange costume. Her face was no longer decorated with makeup. The kohl eyeliner and rouge painted into the pattern of a monarch's wing had been washed off at the pump in our yard, and her face was pretty and plump. She wore a plaid cloak that hid the fact that she'd been born without arms. From my vantage point, both mother and daughter looked ordinary as they disappeared into the crowd.

I could not have been more envious.

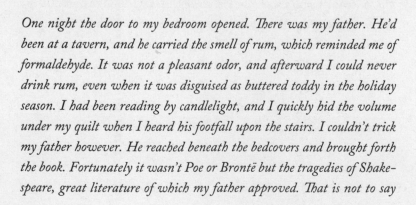

One night the door to my bedroom opened. There was my father. He'd been at a tavern, and he carried the smell of rum, which reminded me of formaldehyde. It was not a pleasant odor, and afterward I could never drink rum, even when it was disguised as buttered toddy in the holiday season. I had been reading by candlelight, and I quickly hid the volume under my quilt when I heard his footfall upon the stairs. I couldn't trick my father however. He reached beneath the bedcovers and brought forth the book. Fortunately it wasn't Poe or Brontë but the tragedies of Shakespeare, great literature of which my father approved. That is not to say

he wasn't angry with me. He told me he had been walking down the street and had seen a light in my room. He'd run the rest of the way. He quickly snuffed out the flame of the candle between his fingers. When he told me I must never burn a candle while in bed, I thought and hoped his speed in coming home was because he feared for my safety. But that wasn't his worry. He scolded me terribly, telling me I would burn down the museum if I weren't careful. I could destroy everything just by being a selfish, thoughtless girl. I needed to pull my weight, to work harder, otherwise the museum would not survive the onslaught of newer, more modern entertainments. He took my wrists in his hands as he berated me. I couldn't help but think of the trick for which he was most famous. In my thoughts I gave thanks to Maureen for her warning to stay at home. I was grateful it was not a bundle of clothes my father had discovered in my bed. As it was, there were bruises on my wrists the next morning.

I stopped going to Dreamland. It was the end of the season anyway, and the crowds at the hotels and the parks were beginning to disappear, leaving behind the local residents to get through the dreary autumn and the winter, isolated from the rest of the world. But at night I still dreamed I was walking along Surf Avenue. I walked through the gate of that wondrous park my father feared would make us poor, and once I did the whole world was before me, strung with a thousand lights. In my dreams I took off my black shawl and my gloves. I stood in the center of the ballroom and listened to music. There was no one to tell me everything I did was wrong. When I woke from these dreams I lay in bed in the dark. I told myself only foolish girls cried. Sometimes I crept downstairs, hoping to catch the night-blooming cactus in our parlor in flower. I thought I would then believe in miracles and find some sort of faith. I sat in the dark in an overstuffed chair, but nothing marvelous happened. There was nothing but sticks before me.

I had already begun to doubt the truth of my father's tales.

OUR FORTUNES *continued to fade. Last summer was the worst any of us could remember. Some days we had only eight or ten customers, some days no one appeared at the museum. My father had not yet come up with his plan for a monster that would galvanize New York, but he was planning all the same. That fall was cold and dark. The leaves in November clung to the trees, then shivered into the streets. One evening after supper, after Maureen had left for the day, everything changed. Perhaps I lost my faith that night. Certainly I lost my innocence. The Professor told me to bathe, not in the tub upstairs where I usually took my baths, but in my tank.*

We were forced to close two weeks early, for we couldn't afford to pay the living wonders. They needed to retreat to their off-season lives. Some would travel with circuses in Florida, others moved in with family members in Queens County or New Jersey, some remained in their cramped quarters in Coney Island, where they did their best to survive the winter. Once the season was officially over and our windows were shuttered, we only went past the velvet curtains that divided our home from the museum in order to feed the animals and birds in their cages. At the time we had a small baby goat with two faces that was billed as the Devil's Pet. We kept him outside tied with a rope to the pear tree until there was ice on his hooves. Then we brought him inside, tied to the kitchen sink during the day, in the cellar in the evenings. But he lasted only a few weeks, and the liveryman buried him out in the yard.

My father's demand on this evening was so strange that I faced him, and, with all the courage I had, I asked why he wanted me to go to my tank. He ignored me and told me to hurry. As always, I did as he requested. That is not to say I did not hesitate. When the museum was closed to the public, there was an eerie cast to the rooms. I made my way through the curtains into the chilly exhibition hall. The tank where I was displayed had been uncovered, and in the gloom the water appeared murky. When my father came to check on me, I was standing in my long muslin undergarments, shivering, so puzzled by his request I had not yet obeyed. I could hear the tortoise slowly pacing in its pen, as well as the chatter of parrots and cooing doves. There was the soft fluttering sound of the wings of the many tropical birds we kept. Some would die of the cold in the winter months, and the most delicate ones would be taken into the parlor, their cages set near the fireplace so that they might manage to survive. Maureen always complained there were too many feathers to sweep up, but when no one was looking she fed the birds nuts and seeds that she bought at the market with her own shopping money.

My father told me I must quickly remove every stitch and get into the tank. I noticed he had recently poured a few thimbles of India ink into the water so that it might look fresh, and that my breathing tube, usually packed in cotton batting for the winter, had been reinserted.

"Do you understand all we do is theater?" he said. "What is real to our audience is mere show for us, and what is done here is no different than what actors do upon a stage. Remember that tonight."

When he left the room, I did as I was told, dropping into the water.

I had an inkling that the events about to unfold would change my current outlook and my life, and yet I would have to pretend as if they had never happened. I had a fleeting thought that because of our failing finances my father might wish to drown me and be rid of me. As it turned out, that was not the case.

When my father returned he had three gentlemen with him, although gentlemen was clearly not the correct term. These three wore bowler hats and black coats, and one of them carried a cane. I dove to the bottom of the tank and wrapped my arms around myself to hide my nakedness. I was so mortified I thought I might pass out. I nearly forgot to take a gulp of air from the breathing tube and was close to fainting, but my father tapped on the glass and gestured for me to swim and pose. I told myself I was in a dream, and the men in the room were figments of my imagination. They began to cheer when I moved through the water, exposing myself, and soon enough they grew rowdy. I heard the echo of their delight, and I could see one of them make a rude motion to me. The men were drinking, and my father pulled up chairs so they could make themselves comfortable during their viewing. They were so close to the glass I imagined I could feel the heat of their cravings. I hadn't known it was possible to cry while underwater, but it was. Still, it was a dream. The men in the room weren't real to me.

When they had gone, my father rapped again on the glass to indicate that he was leaving the room as well. It was a signal that I would now have privacy so that I might exit the tank and cover myself once more. After such a violation, I did not know how to proceed with my modest life. I thought for a moment of not rising to the surface. It occurred to me that it might be best to leave my existence, and all the woes to come. But I learned it was not so easy to drown oneself. My spirit revealed its desire to live. I came up gasping, wanting air. I climbed out of the tank, my breathing ragged. I was still sopping as I pulled on my undergarments. I felt so alone that I went to the tortoise's enclosure and stepped over the low wall to sit in the sand beside my old friend. I was no different than this beast, a captive. I wondered if on cold nights in Brooklyn the tortoise wept and hungered for another world, if it didn't view its long life as a curse.

After the events of that night, I did not dare to look for the keys to my father's workroom again. I was afraid to know any more of his past or his intentions for the future. At every turn, I held my breath. I knew I was on a precipice, and sooner or later I would have to make a leap. I did not tell Maureen about the nights when the Professor brought in men, and I certainly never confided any of the disgusting things they did while they watched me, nor did I disclose that several of them offered my father cash for me. In the echo of the water I had overheard nasty snippets of conversation, and I was aware of what they wished to do to me, how they would like to take me by force if need be, dragging me onto the couch my father had recently brought in so that they might be even more comfortable during their viewing.

None of what they did or said mattered; their boasts and vile notions turned to air, for these men did not exist. I always entered a dream when I was submerged in the tank. My dream was blue and I was alone in it. Still I did as my father said on those nights. When he left me a list of how he wished me to behave underwater, touching myself so that the men might become even more excited, acting in a variety of coarse, immodest ways, I did this as well. I continued to follow his directions.

Soon after, he hatched his new plan and I began to swim in the Hudson. It was there that I had the freedom to be truly alone. I fell in love with the Hudson; because of the nights I swam there, I no longer was forced to perform, and so I began to think of the river as my savior. I longed for it, as I soon longed for the man I had spied in the woods. I thought of him as a sort of savior as well, someone to whom I might reveal my truest self. I had felt the first pangs of love, and because of this I found my faith in the world, despite my current situation.

This changed after my last swim in the Hudson. The river that had always offered me solace had brought me grief in the form of the drowned girl. As we traveled back across the bridge to the museum, I thought again of the madwoman in the attic in Jane Eyre. The imprisoned Mrs. Rochester had burned to death before she could manage to flee. Wait too long, and you might be tethered forever, leaping when it was too late. On the night we

returned to Brooklyn with the body of the young woman in the carriage, I was told to go directly to my room, and I did so. I looked out the window into the yard. I was shivering in my sodden clothes, my damp hair hanging down my back. But inside, my blood felt hot. I was burning up. It wasn't fever but a slow-burning hatred. I saw my father and the liveryman carry the body down the cellar steps. In the morning the floor would still be wet with pools of dank river water that I would mop up without a word of complaint. All the same, on that night I was able to see the truth about my future and my fate.

I was born to disobey him.

APRIL 1911

THE QUIET of the off-season persisted, despite the emerging bloom of lilacs and the haze of green in the gardens of Brooklyn. Small leaves had begun to unfold on the plane trees, but the truest sign of spring was the mud seeping in between the slats of the wooden sidewalks. Even the wild area known as the Gut was quieter than usual, for all racetracks on the island had been closed down and gambling had been outlawed in the hope of lessening crime and vice, though certainly there were still illegal races along Ocean Parkway, often held by lantern light.

Fleets of fishing ships filled Gravesend and Sheepshead Bay, and before long wooden docks were strewn with catches of mussels from Coney Island Creek, along with bass and clams from the bays. The air was blue enough to glimpse the approach of warmer weather, yet the Museum of Extraordinary Things remained closed. A heron circled and considered nesting in the chimney, but when the wind blew cold from the sea, the ungainly creature was frightened off by the slap of a loose shutter banging against a window frame, and it heaved itself into the air. In any other year, carpenters would have been hired to unclasp the shutters, nailed closed in the winter to protect the exhibitions from light. They would have been at work repairing the broken stairs, and begun installing the wooden signs that invited customers to step inside. This spring the Professor had no time to order renovations. He locked himself in the cellar as soon as he awoke and rarely emerged. He refused proper meals and hadn't bothered to change his clothes in days, though the fabric reeked of chemicals. When the stench was impossible to ignore, Maureen presented him with a clean, starched white shirt, which he grudgingly pulled on. He was distracted, and his gaze was fiery, as though he saw something beyond the confines of their house.

"He's up to something," Maureen worried. Though she knew nothing of her employer's plans, she recognized the fever that marked an obsession. Clearly, some dark dream had taken hold of him. "The next thing you know we'll have a bear sitting at the dining room table or a giant in one of our best chairs. I only hope there won't be a snake in the kitchen sink."

While Maureen went to hang laundry on the line, Coralie crept on her hands and knees, pressing her ear to the wide planks of pine flooring in an attempt to eavesdrop. Her thoughts were consumed by the drowned girl, but there were no telltale sounds rising from the cellar. Still, she knew her father's urgency to present a monster to the world. He'd insisted this was the only way he could turn their fortunes around. "Do you think I'd have you swim for those fools if we weren't desperate for the money?" he'd said to her, as if that explained the dreadful things he'd had her do. "We need a real success!"

Coralie would have preferred to live like a mouse, on crumbs and crusts, rather than be subjected to those evenings. "Is there nothing else we might do to change our fortune?" she pleaded.

"There's worse," he said darkly, and left it at that.

They had grown poorer, left with only soup and bread for their meals. Maureen complained she could hardly buy groceries with her slim allowance. Coralie wished she could tell the housekeeper about her father's intentions, but it was as if those wicked evenings in the museum had left her bewitched and mute. She made certain to dispose of liquor bottles and cigar stubs in the mornings that followed her humiliations, tossing bits of evidence into the trash pile. Once a week, it was set on fire. Maureen always encouraged Coralie to come inside on these occasions, for bright cinders snapped up into the branches of the pear tree and smoke swooped above them. But Coralie sat on the porch steps, unmoving. She watched it all burn.

IN TIME, Coralie had come to wonder if the housekeeper had just as many secrets as she did. A house of secrets is like a house of cards, falling in on itself. The more you knew, the more you had to know, and Maureen's private life nagged at Coralie. The housekeeper had never spoken of where she came from, nor had she mentioned a family.

One day Coralie blundered upon a hint that her suspicions had been correct. She spied Maureen on Neptune Avenue, on the other side of the trolley tracks. It was Sunday, the housekeeper's day off. The air was bracing due to the spring fog that hadn't yet lifted. The haze turned the world into a mist, and within that mist Maureen appeared beautiful, her long auburn hair wound up with tortoiseshell combs. Shrouded in the hazy air, her damaged face seemed perfect, as it must have been before she'd been assaulted by her jealous lover. She had no photographs of herself in her earlier years; she insisted that photographs were for the rich. *But trust me,* she was always quick to say with a grin, *I made heads turn.*

On this quiet Sunday, Coralie followed the housekeeper to a building where many seasonal workers boarded. She trailed her inside, up to the third floor. When Maureen turned, as if she'd heard footfalls, Coralie darted into the stairwell. At last she dared to glance out, only to find she'd lost sight of Maureen. She went along the hallway, listening in at the doors, her ear pressed close. At one set of rooms she thought she heard the rise of Maureen's voice, but she couldn't be sure.

Nearby, a door opened and an old woman peered into the corridor. Coralie had no choice but to pass by on her way back to the stairwell. The hallway was poorly lit, but Coralie could tell the woman gazing out had worked at a carnival or a sideshow, for she was covered with tattoos. Living wonders looked down upon those whose attributes weren't natural, and the old woman may have felt she was an outcast. Her expression was coarse and bitter. She wore a heavy wool cloak, a hood over her head. When Coralie drew near, it was possible for her to see a mask of flowers and vines on the woman's aging face, a scrim of blue and red inked around her narrowed eyes.

"What are you doing here?" the tattooed woman wanted to know.

Coralie said she was looking for a Mr. Morris.

"Who are you?" the older woman asked. "His whore?"

Coralie felt the sting of outrage. "Of course not!" She calmed herself and went on. "But I think there is a woman who stays with him. As for him, you'd recognize him—he's quite covered with hair."

"Every beast can find a woman. It's so unfair, for what man would have a woman like me? You can barely bring yourself to look me in the eye, but if you'd like, you can come inside my room. I'll show you everything, if you have the nerve to look. These pictures cover every bit of me, even the most private parts that were sweet once upon a time." The old woman gestured for her to come in. "One whore knows another, darling. It's written all over our faces."

It was a wretched thing to say. Stunned, Coralie ran down the stairs, her heart pounding, the callous comment still cutting her as she fled. She couldn't help but wonder if the old woman had a talent as a mind reader, if she'd somehow intuited what had happened on those wicked nights at the museum. Coralie ran home, unaware of the world around her. Once safely in her room, she bolted the door and stood before the mirror. She was a plain girl, nothing more. There were no flowers, no ink, no signs of her true nature. Then she looked down and saw that in her hurry to follow Maureen she had forgotten her gloves. Her deformity had been there for the old woman to see, her own dyed skin, the webbing between her fingers, the mark of who she truly was.

Coralie threw herself across her bed. As she dreamed on this hazy afternoon she found herself lost in the woods. She spied the young man once again and followed him to a cliff. She could view the river from where she stood and hear the birds in the sycamore trees. The young man seemed to know her, and he stepped near. Coralie hoped he would embrace her, but instead he urged her to jump into the river. *It's the only way,* he said to her. The danger seemed so apparent, only a fool would make such a leap. Coralie was torn between her wish to win him over and her dread. *It's much easier than you could have ever imagined,* the young man told her. She took one step and began to fall through the air, not breathing until she hit the water. There, in the river, she became her deepest self, a monster, to be sure, but one with iridescent scales, a fierce and fearless wonder of the world.

Restless, Coralie went out walking regardless of the weather, often stopping to watch the workers at Dreamland. There were hundreds of men swarming over the park, painting and reconstructing the buildings to ensure that Dreamland would be ready for the last weekend of May. She'd hoped to see Mr. Morris among the crowd of newly hired performers, for many had reported in early so they might practice their acts throughout April and May, but he was nowhere to be seen. Still, the park drew her to its gates. She was fascinated with the land of Lilliputia, where everything had been built to scale, so that a tall man might easily lean his elbow on the roofs of the houses and a full-grown woman could stare down the chimneys to watch the miniature lives that would be led inside for the entertainment of Dreamland's patrons. Coralie wondered if these small people were grateful to be protected in their separate world, if they would light candles in the evenings and sit comfortably at their dining room tables, curtains drawn, so they might lead ordinary lives.

When she grew tired of watching the little village, Coralie peered through the wire fencing to gaze at the shell of the enormous ride Hell Gate. It was impossible to see inside, but she found herself frightened by the artwork that surrounded it, devils with their beards and magic wands. What she loved most was to view the animals in their pens. The great animal trainer Bonavita spied her watching and invited her in through the employees' gate. She immediately recognized him from posters that were hung all over Coney Island. Bonavita had been well known in Europe, and now, in Brooklyn, he was a star. He was a handsome, graceful man, despite having lost one arm to a maddened lion called Baltimore. The animals were kept year round in a lot beside the park, surrounded by tall fences spiked with nails and glass to ensure that neighborhood boys searching for thrills wouldn't climb over and find themselves in a cage of tigers or discover they had come face-to-face with Bonavita's beloved black-maned lion, Black Prince.

The animal workers lived in nicely furnished apartments above the animal arena. Bonavita invited Coralie to his apartment for tea; his wife and daughter were visiting friends in Manhattan. Coralie hesitated, wondering if he read the same thing in her face that the tattooed lady had divined. Did he see her as a whore, expecting more than the kiss the night watchman had begged for? And yet Bonavita seemed a perfect gentleman, even though he was so attractive movie stars wrote him love notes. When Coralie sat at the table, he served orange pekoe tea, asking if she would like lemon or cream. His disability did not seem to affect him or his thoughts about himself, and this alone amazed Coralie. Soon enough, she learned that he possessed the kindness of a truly great animal trainer. He confided that animals never responded to cruelty; trainers who used that method would one day find that their charges turned upon them and be maimed by the beasts they had beaten into a false docility. Bonavita proclaimed that human beings were not the only species that cried or formed deep attachments. He made reference to a Captain Andre, the trainer of Little Hip, the elephant who was the mascot of the park, leading the opening day parade every year. In Bonavita's estimation, Andre was a genius of a trainer, and in return his elephant was so resolute in his loyalty he would bellow all night if not allowed to sleep in Andre's room.

Coralie felt comforted by these stories of men's devotion to their charges. If a beast could be treated with kindness and respect, perhaps there was hope for her as well. Bonavita's animals were treasured companions, rather than possessions to be shown off and displayed. Bonavita took her to see Black Prince, his pride and joy, the lion he had raised as a cub. Prince was sleeping on a cushion. When his trainer called his name, he looked up lazily and yawned. Before Coralie knew what was happening, Bonavita had opened the cage and slipped inside. The lion rose to his feet when he spied his trainer. When they met in the center of the cage, the creature let out a sound that sent chills down Coralie's spine. He then leapt up to an enormous height, a black mane framing his ferocious face, his huge paws balanced on his trainer's shoulders. Certainly the trainer's deformity did not make him any less than any other man. He was, by far, the most courageous individual Coralie had ever seen.

Still, she imagined she would see his death before her very eyes.

The cage was open, and Coralie wondered if she would rush to the trainer's defense if tragedy struck, or if she would watch, paralyzed, as he was eaten alive. But the lion only rubbed his head against his trainer and seemed to embrace him. "That's a good fellow," Bonavita said. He pushed the lion off and afterward scratched at his mane with the palm of his hand, which the beast greatly appreciated. A deep rumbling came from Prince's throat and chest.

"Come inside," Bonavita urged his audience of one.

Coralie's heart dropped. But she thought of her dream, how she had feared to make the leap from the ledge in the woods, and then, when she had expected to crash to the ground below, she fell into the blue water and knew she had been made for another element entirely.

She stepped inside the cage.

"Don't scream or shout," Bonavita said softly. "Ignore him."

Coralie was still as the lion studied her. She dared not take a breath as the beast approached.

"I knew it." Bonavita was pleased with himself and how good a judge of character he was. "You have a form of bravery inside you."

The lion's scent was of straw and an earthy wildness. He rubbed his head against Coralie, and as he did, Coralie felt her own wildness. She sensed that all her waking life had been a dream, and that it was only in this moment that she had at last opened her eyes.

When Bonavita called to Prince and clapped his hands, the lion went trotting back to his cushion. Coralie left the cage so that Bonavita might bring the lion his breakfast, the half-frozen carcass of a cow, which the lion attacked with studied intensity. Coralie noticed there were several coarse hairs on her skirt, some golden and some black. Her heart was still pounding, yet she felt overjoyed at having been so close to such a fierce creature, and one as great as Prince.

She asked Bonavita what allowed him to be so fearless in the presence of his lion, especially having been attacked earlier in his life.

"Oh, I fear him," Bonavita assured her. "He could kill me if he wished. He and I both know that. But the lion that attacked me was misused and ill treated before I had him. I raised Prince from the time he was first born. There is a connection in that sort of companionship, a trust that goes beyond his nature, and mine as well I suppose."

Coralie asked if Bonavita's wife wasn't afraid at each one of his performances, some of which included a dozen tigers and leopards surrounding him in a ring.

"I am good to my wife and to my daughter, but they understand me. In my experience you can only have one great love, and I have chosen mine."

Coralie was certain that real love was nothing like the life she'd known, the lust of the exhibition room, the shadows lingering on the wall, the rasping sound of the tortoise in its pen, so calm and patient in its confinement, the men who had stalked her on the other side of the tank, then been ushered away as if they were mere figments, rather than flesh and blood.

The animal trainer had thought she was brave, but in her daily life Coralie remained a mouse. Her anger became self-directed, her wounds self-directed as well. When she was angry she stuck pins into her own flesh, but unlike the Human Pincushion, who had been with them for several years and who drank an elixir of nettle, blackberry, and lotus to stanch his wounds, Coralie bled. She felt the pain. In the evenings, she served her father large mugs of rum, so that he would close his eyes and dream and there would be peace inside their house. She shocked herself by considering how easy it would be to lace his drink with arsenic, which was stored in the garden shed and used to keep the rats away. She fled the house, frightened by the sheer wickedness of her thoughts.

The evenings were still damp and chilly even though spring had arrived, and the dusk fell in sheets that were mottled and fish colored. Coralie went to the shoreline where she had first learned to swim. The water's pull was difficult to resist; she could feel it in her blood, stinging like salt. It was here the whole world opened to her, as it always had, in a grid of sand and sea. She had come to believe that if her father had wanted a docile daughter, he should never have allowed her access to the ocean. It was here she found a strength that often surprised her. Perhaps she was not a spineless creature, but a wonder after all. Recently when she gazed into the mirror she believed she spied a series of lines at the base of her throat. Surely they were not the gills she had dreamed of but merely a pattern of throbbing blue veins. Still, she wondered.

The deepening night was soon strewn with stars. The beach, so crowded in summer months it was impossible to walk along without bumping into another beachgoer, was empty, save for the clam diggers, who called to each other from the beds of shellfish as they worked by lantern light. It was low tide, and the air was perfumed with seaweed. As the dark sifted down, Coralie undressed to her undergarments, unlacing her boots so she might leave them behind. She loved the feel of damp sand in the tide, how it tugged at her, pulling her into a world she could sink into. The waves rolled in, and soon enough she was waist deep in water. There was a film of phosphorescence in the water, an illumination caused by tiny fish that were invisible to the human eye, unnoticed in the daylight hours. This was the virtue of the dark: you were who you had always been, only no one could see you.

She was sopping wet, deep in thought. She had stood beside a lion.

Perhaps she had more courage than she'd imagined. She dressed and made the walk back home. When she reached the house, she sneaked inside, then left her sandy boots in the hallway and hung her cloak on a brass hook. Water had taught her how to move lightly, and she floated down the hall. The Professor had come up from his workshop and was asleep in the library, exhausted from the trials of his work, sprawled out in a chair. Coralie studied him from the doorway. How deeply he slept, how completely at ease he seemed, as if the world belonged to him and him alone. She drew closer to his sleeping form and leaned down, making no noise as she took the keys from his pocket. She had often sat beside the tortoise and had matched her breathing to echo that of the sea creature's. She practiced this technique now, slowing her breath and heart and blood.

In the kitchen, the white enameled stove gleamed. A supper Maureen had left for them earlier remained untouched in the cooking pot. Coralie took the cellar stairs in her bare feet. The floor was nothing more than raked dirt, and there were often mice in the corners. An earthy odor of roots mixed with the tang of chemicals. Coralie fitted the two keys into their locks simultaneously and turned them. There were two soft clicks. She let her eyes adjust to the dark before crossing the threshold. Once she was inside the workshop, the scent of formaldehyde was stronger, nearly overpowering. There were rows of teeth in jars set on a shelf alongside dozens of yellowing books. Nearby was the rack of tools, hammers and awls and saws in varying sizes, from one so tiny it could fit in the palm of a child's hand to an enormous wood saw. Because it was a humid night the cellar was especially damp, the air sweetened with turpentine and wild gum. There was a dark concoction on the desk as well, a sticky tar-like stuff kept in bottles that Professor Sardie rolled into beads to smoke in a pipe that let off a pungent stink.

A wooden crate more than five feet long took up most of the tabletop. As Coralie approached she found herself counting, as if that task would keep her fear at bay. She pushed on the cover so that it slipped forward. Inside, the crate was packed with solid carbon dioxide that appeared as snow. Curls of moisture rose up, which she waved away so she might peer inside. Coralie spied a shimmer of pale hair, the glimmer of flesh. The girl from the river, her blood replaced by formaldehyde, her world reduced to ice. This was her resting place, a box that would have been better used on the docks to pack bluefish or mackerel for delivery to the markets.

Coralie shoved the cover back in place and stood facing away from the coffin, shivering, as if she were the one dressed in chemicals, bloodless and pale. Without another thought, she went to search for the handbook, driven to discover what her father's plan might be. The room was dark and the items in the drawer were mere shadows to her eyes, but she grasped around until she found what she wanted, her hands fitting over the cover of smooth Moroccan leather. She had wanted to read her father's diary in its entirety, but there was no time for that. She swiftly thumbed through, finding the last page he'd written upon. The date was this very day, the ink fresh, an indigo blue he favored, the color of water.

Many of the Professor's notes were in French, and Coralie understood several phrases. *Je vais créer ce que je n'ai pas. De chair et le sang. De coeur de l'imagination.* But even without written explanations, the ink-stained sketches made his intentions quite clear. He planned to give the city of New York a variation of the trick for which he had been famous, half a woman. This creature, however, would be as monstrous as she was beautiful, a woman joined with a fish, stitched scale to flesh to become a real mermaid, the Hudson Mystery, a far better invention than Barnum's Feejee Mermaid.

Coralie thought of Maureen's warning: if you saw the dead twice you were doomed to be haunted. Indeed, the two young women seemed joined by strands of invisible thread, a single being, though one breathed and one was forever still. As Coralie turned to leave, she observed a jumble of belongings on the countertop. A comb, hairpins, a gold locket. She couldn't bear to see how carelessly these mementos had been tossed into a pile beside surgical tools and bits of bone. She scooped them up, hoping the tokens were so small and unimportant in her father's eyes he wouldn't notice their absence.

She left, tugging the door closed behind her, then quickly turning the locks. The cold had seeped into her blood and her eyes stung with tears. She knew that a monster should not feel anything, not sorrow or regret. She should not weep, or shiver, or sob. To do so would only cause her to give herself away and make herself a target. Better to slink through the dark as she did now. Through the kitchen, down the porch steps, into the yard. In the dark the newly greening leaves appeared black. Out at sea there was a foghorn, for the fog that often arose on spring nights had begun to roll in from the shore, blanketing the neighborhood. It was nearly impossible to see two feet in any direction. Still, Coralie could smell an acrid scent and she spied a flash of red sparks. In the corner of the yard wisps of smoke rose from the trash pile, though it was not trash-burning day. Earlier in the evening, while Coralie was at the shore, the Professor had hurriedly disposed of evidence. But he hadn't done a thorough enough job. Coralie recognized the blue coat. She grabbed for it, though bright embers burned her fingers. She carried the singed coat to the well in the yard and hurried to work the pump, forcing a stream of water out. The fabric sizzled as the flame was extinguished, with a gasp resembling a human sigh.

Coralie brought her find up to her bedroom. She folded it beneath her featherbed mattress, then lay there with her eyes open, her pulse pounding. She was exactly what she had pretended to be on those nights when she waded into the Hudson, a monster and a monster's daughter. If the man in the woods could see her now, distraught and lonely, weeping in her bed, he would think she had a heart. But a heart was not enough. She understood that now. What a monster needed most was a plan.

Coralie hurried to the locksmith in the morning, so nervous as she waited she thought she might faint. But in the end luck was with her. Upon returning home, she found her father's jacket on the hook. She could replace the keys she'd taken before he was aware they'd been gone. She had her own keys now, and a way to unlock her fate.

SIX

THE BIRDMAN

****

AFTER ALL these years I could still remember sleeping in the forest in Russia, there beside my father in the grass. Sometimes when I woke I was surprised by my current surroundings, the light of New York City that streamed in through the window, my dog on the floor, the chimes of the tubular church bells ringing in the Chapel of the Good Shepherd from inside the walls of the General Seminary. For a very long time I believed that when we left our home, we left my mother as well. Where our village had stood the burned fields would again become green and her flesh would be in every blade of grass. When we fled we abandoned the past, or so I then believed. My mother was called Anna, a name I still cannot say aloud.

I wept when we ran away from our home, because I was young, and because the forest was dark and I was afraid. There were so many birds in the forest at night, and I imagined they would carry me away. Night birds are predators, and we were easy prey. A man and a boy in black coats and hats, shoes worn, shirts frayed and unwashed, both lost and uncertain of what lay ahead. I held my father's hand and led him through

*the trees because my vision was better, my step steadier. When darkness
fell, he told me to close my eyes and dream, for in my dreams I would find
another world, and in my waking life I would soon enough find such a
world as well, far from the forests we knew, far from the fields of grass
where my mother bloomed again. My father was a realist, I see that now,
and a fatalist as well. He believed we were in the hands of God, and that
it was best to accept our fate, and not to battle impossible odds.*

*I often saw that quality in him when I worked beside him in the fac-
tory. He was a good worker and didn't complain, and I faulted him for
that as well. The meeker he appeared to be, the more rebellious I became.
I wished to be the opposite of all that he was, and hated every trait of
his that I found in myself. He was raised under the rule of the Cossacks,
the mad horsemen who burned our village and murdered our people and
turned us to smoke. Because of this he had learned to keep himself small,
like the mice that ran across the table, catching whatever crumbs they
could. The conditions of factory workers in New York were so deplorable
even a boy my age could tell this should not be the order of the world, that
we should suffer so for the sake of our bosses, who lived in town houses and
rode in polished walnut carriages and bought the first automobiles, which
they treated like fine horses, caring for them tenderly while the children
in their factories worked twelve hours a day for pennies and went to sleep
hungry.*

*Perhaps my father saw a new order when he closed his eyes and
dreamed, for in his dreams surely his fingers did not bleed from stitching
all day, and his tired eyes were renewed. He went to labor meetings, but
he stayed on the fringes, not wishing to cause trouble. A mouse. Nothing
more. I was excited by the idea that men could take their fates in their
own hands and could choose to strike. "We'll see," my father said with caution, and in fact new workers were quickly hired to replace our striking
group, brought in one early morning in horse-drawn carts as if they were*

cattle. We were beaten back with bully clubs by policemen from the Tenth Precinct when we tried to get at the men who had taken our rightful jobs. I remember that my father had a bruise on his face. He didn't even mention the pain it must have caused him. At home, I noticed he was spitting blood. A tooth had been knocked out, and he tucked a tea bag into his cheek so that the tannic acid would stop the bleeding.

At the next factory where we were employed the entire floor of workers was fired when there was a mild rumble of discontent; the bosses struck before we could, and newer, green men were brought in. That was when my father went to the docks, that patient, good man I had so little respect for, though we were of the same flesh and blood and he had saved my life more than a dozen times when we traveled over continents, finding us bread and shelter. He was a mouse who feared the forest, yet he had managed to take us into France and on to Le Havre, where he worked shoveling coal in a mill until we could afford steerage on a boat to New York, the only dream we ever shared.

In New York, my father allowed strangers to stay with us; anyone from the Ukraine was welcome to sleep on our floor. At shul he gave to the poor, though I couldn't imagine who could be poorer than we. He was a good man, but what was goodness in a world where men who were slaving in close quarters fell to tuberculosis and were all but worked to death? I looked upon the long-suffering immigrants with contempt. They were sheep to me, creatures who dared not raise their eyes to the bosses, let alone raise their voices.

On the night our village burned, when my father and I lay together in the grass, with owls swooping above us, our stomachs rumbling with hunger, I was not more than five or six. And yet this was when I began to view him as a coward. Side by side we were, a coward and a coward's son.

How could we leave my mother behind? Whether she was ash, or grass, or air, in my mind she was in our village still. We abandoned her,

and began our new life. I was certain that if I ever loved someone, which
seemed impossible to me even then, I would never let her go.

⌒

I saw a kindred defiance in Mr. Weiss when he came to me. I have often
wondered why I agreed to help him, and maybe this defiance was the
reason. Weiss was unwilling to allow his daughter to vanish; he refused
to consider her lost, a hail of ashes on the city streets. I had become the sort
of man who stood on the edge of things, as my father was, but I liked to
think it was my insolence that kept me separate, not any sort of timidity.
I was a rat perhaps, but never a mouse.

I should have remained aloof from someone else's misery as I was on
most occasions, yet I was drawn in. Weiss was an older man, dressed in
the black clothing of the Orthodox, but he was hardly timid. He had gone
to all of the authorities, stationed himself in the corridors of Tammany
Hall, where he was ill treated and berated. He had brought his story to
reporters at the Yiddish newspaper, the Forward, on East Broadway, as
well as to the English-language daily the Sun, but they had failed to look
into his daughter's disappearance. Only when all other efforts had been
unsuccessful had he come to me, the finder of what was lost. He believed I
had abilities granted by God.

I agreed to do as he asked because he was a man so unlike my father.

And perhaps I did have a gift, as Hochman always said, for I knew
how men's minds worked. When I imagined myself in their circumstances
I could think the way they did, no matter how different their lives might
be from my own. I became a criminal, a forger, a philanderer. I played out
my desires in these various guises, and therefore came up with a map of
where I might hide if I were such a person, how I would occupy my time,
and on which vices I would spend my money. This turn of my imagina-
tion had helped me as a boy in my ability to find men who thought they

had escaped detection. But now, in my search for Hannah Weiss, I found myself lacking in skill and soon enough came to an impasse. My usual ability to uncover a person's innermost self failed me. Even when Hannah's sister took me to their haunts—Miss Weber's hat shop on Twenty-second Street; the shul where they worshiped; Madison Square Park, where they fed pigeons on Sundays—I found no clue. Hannah seemed a sweet, pretty girl, hardworking and loyal. But in my background, I had no practice with such people. Good, trustworthy individuals were strangers to me, mysterious in their small desires.

I spoke with several survivors, girls who had known Hannah, in the hope they would help me uncover who she was. I took notes in a small leather-bound book where I kept my appointments jotted down. Her friends spoke with hushed voices when they talked of the fire that had moved through the workroom. It came upon them like a swarm, one survivor told me, red bees bursting through the wall. Many of the girls who had escaped thought Hannah, too, had survived, but it turned out it was Ella they had seen, for the sisters looked so alike it was nearly impossible to tell them apart, especially on that smoky afternoon.

As far as I could tell there was nothing unusual about Hannah—no secrets, no flaws. But perhaps everyone has a secret life, and on the last day of my interviews, I discovered someone who knew more about Hannah than the others. This survivor asked me to refer to her in my notes only as R, the first letter of her name. She didn't wish to be in the public eye, and feared the fierce determination of the press. The building where her family lived had been circled by reporters after the tragedy. She had been hysterical for over a week, unable to speak or understand what was said to her. Still reporters called out her name from the street when her parents refused to have her interviewed. R was too distraught to be in our world, a place where she had seen her two younger sisters perch like doves upon the ledge of the ninth floor. She had told her sisters to go on without her, and she went back for her new coat, cranberry-colored wool. By then the smoke was everywhere and the elevators were no longer running; she had managed to grab hold of the burning ropes in the elevator shaft by throwing her coat around the sizzling twine so her hands wouldn't burn as she lowered herself down.

She ran outside, and she saw her sisters on the ledge when she looked up. She thought that they saw her as well, for one tossed down her ring, as a gift and a keepsake. Unfortunately, the speed that carried it had embedded the ring in the sidewalk; the silver had been flattened, becoming a part of the concrete. R blamed herself for not catching the memento, though it would have likely burned her hand, perhaps even broken the small bones of her fingers.

R's parents only allowed me to speak to their remaining child because Mr. Weiss had contacted them and vouched for me, and because they knew of his predicament. When I agreed not to use their daughter's name in any way, and swore I would not upset her, I was at last invited to their home. Time was passing, and I knew from my work with Hochman that after twenty-four hours a missing person was half as likely to be found, and after a week, the chances were slimmer still. We were now passing the two-week mark, a very bad portent for recovery. Hochman always said that in two weeks a man could completely refashion his history; he could walk all the way to Ohio or Iowa, change his name and his accent, disappear into another life. In the woods, footprints faded, the wind rose up to disperse shreds of clothing, flesh became grass.

I sat in an unfamiliar parlor on East Thirteenth Street. The room was close, and there were rollaway cots that had been covered with white sheets, the beds where R's sisters had slept. A sheet also covered the mirror on the wall, as was always the case during mourning periods. R was nineteen and had been burned on her arms and legs. The skin was red and mottled now, coated with a healing gel of aloe and fish oil. She had been a pretty girl, but now she seemed ravaged, not just by the effects of the fire on her body but by the memory of all she had seen. She told me she had no wish to be awake. There were days when she slept for eighteen hours or more, doing her best to bypass time completely.

"Did I deserve this?" R asked me. Her voice was so young and plaintive I felt only a fool would dare to respond. Who was I to remark upon her life? All the same I made a comment I thought might ease our conversation. I told her no, she did not deserve her fate, and if there was a God, something I myself doubted, then he had made a terrible mistake.

She laughed hoarsely and said, "God has nothing to do with this. It's men's greed that made this happen."

Her mother was watching from the hallway, to ensure I didn't tire R or upset her by dredging up memories of March 25. I recounted what I had so far learned of Hannah Weiss. R's eyes were lowered as I spoke. When I finished she lifted her gaze to meet mine.

"They didn't know her completely," R said. "I was her closest friend."

I signaled to the mother then, and asked if she would bring us tea. She had been suspicious of me from the start and had insisted I leave my camera in the front hall. Now she looked at R with an uneasy expression, but R merely said, "I'll be fine with him. We could use the tea for our parched throats."

When her mother went down the corridor, I asked R what she meant.

"Hannah went to labor meetings and didn't tell her father. Mr. Weiss was strict. She knew he would fear for her safety. He would have never allowed her to risk going to prison. I saw her once with several strikers outside another factory on Great Jones Street. She ran after me and made me promise not to tell. So I gave her my promise. She hugged me to thank me. She said, I'll remember this."

"Even if her father wouldn't approve, there's nothing so unusual in any of that," I countered.

"She wasn't alone. She was with a man. She started going to union meetings with him. I think she was in love with him."

I leaned forward, interested. "And you knew this because?"

R laughed at me. I think she definitely took me for a fool. "From the look on her face."

That was all R could tell me—she did not know the man's name or address—but it was enough to make me wonder if the image of Hannah I'd been carrying had been distorted by the tide of her father's love. Perhaps I hadn't been able find a map of who she was because I'd been misled. She was more independent than I'd thought. More willing to take a risk.

I walked for a long time after leaving R. Without thinking, I found myself outside the building where the Weisses lived. I went upstairs and knocked on the door. I went by nearly every day, though I had little to report. It had become a ritual I felt I needed to complete, even on those occasions when I stayed only a few moments, embarrassed by how little I'd discovered. And yet Weiss never faulted me. He was still hopeful.

"Did you find anything?" he asked after he'd let me in. "The gold necklace? Her shoes? Anyone who saw her?"

I said no. I couldn't tell Weiss that his daughter had loved some man he'd never heard of or met and that she'd had a rebel's soul.

"You'll find her," he said, sure of himself, sure of me, perhaps desperate to be so.

I stayed for dinner, reciting the evening prayers along with him out of respect. I still remembered them. Hannah's sister made us a meal of barley soup, stuffed cabbage, then a roast chicken, along with bread, butter, and pavel, a plumlike butter. For dessert there was an apple strudel with sugar sprinkled on top. To me, it was a feast. I was reminded of my mother's cooking, the way she sang to herself as she went about her chores, her use of herbs to make the meal more appealing. I thanked Ella and said, in return for including me in their dinner, I would help her clean *up. The truth was, I wanted to stand beside her out of the old man's hearing, so we might have some privacy.*

"Your sister was in love?" I said.

Ella shot me a look. "What difference does it make?"

"Maybe nothing, maybe everything."

"If so, she didn't tell me."

"She told you everything," I reminded her.

"He was just a boy. Nothing serious. She'd only just met him. That's all she said. All I know is that his name was Samuel. She said I would meet him, but that day didn't come."

The plates were chipped and the dishwater was tepid. I didn't blame Ella for leading me astray by not mentioning this Samuel, nor did I berate her for the time I'd wasted searching for a vision that was untrue. I would now have to begin all over again, and think of Hannah as a different sort of person. I was about to let the topic drop when Ella surprised me by gripping my hand.

"I dreamt again that Hannah was in water. She was whirling in a circle, dressed in blue. When I woke up I heard her voice. She told me she couldn't come back to me. That she'd tried, but it was no longer possible."

She grasped my hand tightly, and I comforted her as Hochman might have, assuring her this wasn't an unusual reaction to great loss. I hoped I didn't sound as pompous as he always had. "It's normal to have such dreams."

I didn't tell Ella that I sometimes heard my own mother's voice after all these years, when I could barely remember her face and couldn't bring myself to say her name. Nor did I mention that I often dreamed of my father. Though he was alive, he was lost to me as well. In my dreams, he stood in silence, knee deep in the grass.

"You're saying this is normal? That I see her clear as day?"

"It is when you love someone," I said. I didn't know what I was talk-

ing about, but I'd heard Hochman express similar sentiments and I parroted his words. My next statement, however, I knew to be true. "You imagine what you wish for."

"My pillow was wet," Ella insisted. "She was there."

I shook my head. "You wept. It was you."

On the way home, I stopped across the street from my father's home. I had to pass nearby. It was dark, and the night was unusually warm. I wondered how it was that we could have slept side by side in the forest at one time in our lives and be complete strangers to each other now. Would he know me if he passed me by on the street, without my black hat and coat, my hair shorn close to my head, or would I just be another citizen of New York? I thought of my younger self, the child who did not understand how a person could be on earth one instant and gone the next. How was it possible that my mother, who had been so alive, had become nothing more than ashes? Surely she must be somewhere. I became a finder because I needed an answer to this question. So perhaps this was my gift.

I did not know Hannah Weiss and, if her sister was correct, I never would, but that didn't matter.

I could not let her go.

PATHS ALONG the river were rife with swamp cabbage, and sweet peas, and meadow grass. Even the city work crews, most of them ill-paid Irish immigrants, who had arrived at dawn to shore up the banks with huge boulders, could not disturb the larks floating from tree to tree. The clouds in the sky reflected in the river, as if they were stepping-stones that might allow a man to walk across the water, all the way to New Jersey. Eddie fished every Saturday near the same spot. Each time he wished that he would come upon the trout he'd set free. People were said to revisit the scene of a crime, and dogs had been known to find their homes after traveling hundreds of miles, wasn't it possible for a fish to be driven by memory?

As Eddie trekked through the unfolding ferns, the undergrowth gave off the scent of cinnamon when it was crushed underfoot. He felt the watch inside his vest pocket, beating, as if he had a second heart. He'd brought along another bottle of rye, in case Beck gave him any trouble for again coming onto what he considered to be his land. He found a quiet place and hunkered down. Though it was early in the season, crickets were calling, and there was the hum of mosquitoes as they drifted over the shallows. Eddie had brought along his rod, but today he merely watched the stream, looking for a flash of silver. After an hour, and then two, he still saw only the shimmering water. Clearly, trout were smarter than men, choosing not to return to the site of their previous sorrows.

He went to the shoreline and began to photograph the river, hoping to capture some of the beauty of the place. The air was soft, as it often was in this lovely month, and Eddie inhaled its sweetness. He found himself uplifted as he worked, caught up in something outside himself and his petty wants and needs. The clouds drifted like ice in a tumbler. Through his lens the river seemed made of light, there was the shimmer, and for a moment the world seemed whole to him. As the afternoon lengthened, the light began to fade. The river darkened and shadows cut through the woods. There was a shuffle in the bushes, most likely a covey of quail or a raccoon. Mitts, who had been so well mannered all day, now reverted to his exuberant ways. The dog didn't wait to find out what his quarry was, or whether it was larger and more dangerous than he, before he leapt into the brush and disappeared. Eddie went crashing after him, calling out and whistling. Once darkness fell it would be all but impossible to find him, and there were said to be coyotes that stalked their prey in these valleys.

Mitts's bark echoed from the woods. Eddie did his best to catch up, but he was soon hindered by thick mud as he crossed several small rivulets. The land was a cattail marsh, and blue herons had begun nesting, with dozens of enormous nests set into the top branches of the tall, half-dead sycamores circling the wetland. Eddie finally reached firmer ground. The last of the day's sunlight was a pale yellow drifting through the branches. Mitts was making a serious racket, growling low in his throat. The last time the dog had taken off Eddie had raced to find him in a clearing. Grabbing Mitts by the collar, he'd been struck by an unnerving sense that he wasn't alone. For an instant he'd thought he spied the figure of a woman. A white shirt, masses of black hair, a slim beautiful form. But there was no one in sight, only the wavering branches.

Now as he made his way over a grassy valley where Queen Anne's lace and red clover grew wild, Eddie sighted a tar-paper shack. There was Mitts in the clearing, barking like mad. The dog, and now his master, had discovered Beck's abode. On the porch, a wolflike creature had been tied to a post with a chain. The beast lunged at Mitts, but the chain snapped him backward. Mitts darted closer, enjoying the freedom of taunting the fierce creature. When Eddie ran to grab Mitts, the hermit's monstrous pet did his best to reach the both of them, but got no farther than the first steps before he was pulled back. Eddie noticed the beast had yellow eyes. He wondered if Beck wasn't a liar after all. No dog had eyes like that.

There was enough of a racket to wake the dead, but apparently Beck had slept through most of the clamor. Now Eddie's shouts had awoken him. He came out his door in a black mood, dressed in long underwear, holding a rifle. His unkempt hair was tied back, and he squinted through the falling dusk. He didn't appear to recognize Eddie, for he aimed straight at his intruder.

Eddie quickly threw his hands up to show he had no weapon, only his camera and equipment. "You know me," he called. "The photographer."

When he held up his camera, he managed to pierce the hermit's fog of sleep and drink. Beck nodded. "I know you're around these parts far too often. You and the rabbit that pretends to be a dog."

"I presume that's your dog." Eddie eyed the snarling creature beside Beck.

Beck snorted. "He's a wolf." He roughly patted the wolf's head, and the beast quieted. All the same, the creature showed a glimmer of his teeth to Mitts, who submissively lay down in the ferns.

The dark was settling in, and Eddie would have liked to take his leave and start for home; it was later than he'd hoped, and the journey was long, at least three hours. Still, he didn't wish to offend the hermit. Not when the old man carried a gun and knew these woods better than the squirrels that ran through the brambles.

"It's one thing to have you steal my fish, but I sure as hell didn't invite you here. It's my home, you understand. No one else's," Beck said darkly.

"This was the dog's idea, not mine," Eddie assured Beck. "He took off on me."

"Ah, Mr. Friendly." Beck came down the steps. He fitted his rifle over his shoulder and nodded for Eddie to follow toward his camp-fire. "Now you've stayed so late you're likely to drown if you try to make it out of here on your own."

Eddie shadowed the hermit to a ring of stones placed a few feet away from the shack, to ensure sparks from the fire wouldn't fly onto the tar-paper roof.

"Did you ever hear of the fish that climbed out of the Hudson?" Beck asked, as he took hold of the bottle of rye Eddie handed over, a peace offering quickly accepted.

"I didn't expect you to believe in fairy tales."

Beck grinned. "I believe in dogs with tails."

"In this world, a fish can't walk," Eddie ventured to say. "That much I know."

"It can if it has two legs."

There was a metal grill fitted over the campfire, used for cooking fish and game. Beck kept the sparks hot, and he quickly got the fire going by tossing on some tinder wood. Between this spot and the river was a series of freshwater bogs, some so deep the water reached a man's waist, where there might easily be snapping turtles nesting. The hermit was right. In the dark it would be difficult going. Eddie had no choice but to placate Beck if he wanted to be led through the marshland.

"Let's just say I've never heard of a fish with legs," he allowed.

"You think you've heard of everything?" the hermit asked. "I've seen a fox change from red to white right before my eyes. One minute he was scarlet, the next it was as if snow had fallen down on him. You ever hear of that?" He gave Eddie a look. "No. I venture not."

Beck had reached for a battered kettle, into which he spilled some water from his rain barrel; he added ground coffee beans and soon enough signaled to Eddie, offering a cup of what appeared to be mud.

"I think we've got the same thing in mind on this subject," Beck said. "The fish with legs."

"Fishing will have to wait for another time."

Beck narrowed one eye. "You really do think I'm stupid. You're too dumb to go night fishing. You'd wind up drowned."

They were sitting together on a log. Set up against the cabin was Beck's canoe, a beautifully made hand-built boat fashioned of birch and poplar. Eddie hadn't imagined the hermit capable of such fine work. People on the hill said that in the winter Beck carried his skiff along the ice until he located a current running through, for it was a rare season when the Hudson froze solid. A good fisherman knew where his catch could be found, regardless of the weather.

"I don't believe you're stupid," Eddie insisted. "Far from it."

"Do you believe in mermaids, then?"

Eddie treaded carefully. He gave the hermit a swift sidelong glance as the old man began to pour rye into his coffee. "Do you?"

"There you go. That proves you think I'm stupid. She wasn't no mermaid. There's no such thing. Just a flesh-and-blood woman once upon a time."

Eddie's pulse shifted. When he'd worked for Hochman the process of finding someone always began this way. A single sentence could create the beginnings of a map.

"Dead?"

Beck gulped the last of his coffee and rye. "The dead are with us even as we walk. That much I know."

"We're talking about a woman in the river?"

"Now you've got it." Beck clapped him on the back, pleased. At last Eddie was grasping his meaning.

Eddie brought out the photograph from his vest pocket. "Did the fish on two legs look anything like her?"

Beck peered at the photograph in the firelight, then handed it back. "Nope, didn't look a thing like her. But the dead one did."

Eddie felt his pulse quicken. "There were two of them?"

The hermit rose to his feet so he could douse the fire. For an instant, the world grew dark. "You want more information, you have to give me something in return," he declared as he headed back to his porch, leaving his guest at the campfire to consider his offer. Eddie tried to figure out what the old man could possibly want of him while Beck pulled on a pair of old trousers. He wore high fishing boots that were caked with mud. The Dutchman grabbed a walking stick, then returned to the smoky fire pit. "We should get going, if you want to make it back tonight."

"What kind of deal did you have in mind?" Eddie hoped the price would not be too high; after having given his father his savings, he'd have to sell some of his belongings in order to have any ready cash.

Beck nodded to his wolfish pet, sprawled out on the porch, head on his paws, watching their every move carefully. "You make sure he's cared for if anything happens to me. Set him free."

"And where will you be while I manage to accomplish this without him ripping me to pieces?"

"I'll be dead. Otherwise I wouldn't need you. I don't want to be in my grave unable to rest because I'm fretting that the wolf is starving to death up in my cabin."

"Does he have a name?" Eddie eyed the beast, which eyed him in return.

"You think a name means something? You are who you are, whatever you're called. Call him No-name. Call him Mr. President. They're the same to me. Just let me know where you stand. It's a deal or it isn't. Your choice."

The wolf was nothing Eddie wanted, but he took it on faith that the hermit would live a long and miserable life. Therefore, he nodded and they shook hands on the bargain.

"And burn this place to the ground," Beck said. "It's good for nothing once I'm gone."

Eddie agreed to this as well. He wished to hear more about the mermaid, but Beck signaled that it was best for them to move on.

Eddie tied fishing line through Mitts's collar to ensure that the rambunctious pit bull would stay close. The hermit's black boots stomped over ferns and low berry bushes as they headed for the river. Sparrows flitted by, dropping into the brambles to nest for the night. They went on for some time in silence, but when they reached a ridge, the hermit stopped. The moon was rising, already casting a white light across the long, sweeping view to the river.

"You know how I knew she wasn't no mermaid? Because her feet were bare. I was always told mermaids have no feet." Beck pointed to a hollow. "That's where I first spied them."

There was a bog to cross, and the earthy scent of mud rose up. Every step meant navigating the muck, which already reached their knees.

"You want to go on?" Beck said, poking fun at Eddie's obvious discomfort as he batted away gnats. "All sorts of creatures get stuck in there. I found the bones of a baby elephant a trader told me was a woolly mammoth. I'll probably die in there myself one of these days."

Eddie gestured for his guide to go on. He hoisted Mitts and carried him through the deepest mud. The clay would dry up in the summer months, but during a damp spring, mud as thick as this could easily pull a man or a dog down as if it were quicksand.

"Walk steady," the hermit called over his shoulder. "Stop moving and you'll sink into the land of the mammoths, my friend. I saw a man here at the end of March, stuck in right good, calling for his mother before he pulled himself out with a stick."

Clouds of gnats circled Eddie as he slogged along. On the other side of the bog there ran an old Indian trail followed by letter carriers before trains were used for mail delivery. Though mostly deserted now, recent wheel marks had been deeply driven into the mud by a horse-drawn cart.

"I came down from the cliff because I'd seen the mermaid pull the other girl out of the water."

Eddie found himself spooked in this hollow. He wasn't alone in that. Mitts set to whining, and Eddie ran a hand over the dog's shivering flank to quiet him.

"She ran away, that's how I knew she wasn't a mermaid. I saw she had legs. But she swims in this river the way something human never could. I'd seen her before. When she'd gone, I climbed down to the hollow to watch over the drowned girl. If I hadn't stayed, the raccoons would have been at her. They would have torn her apart.

"When I heard a carriage come near I took off. I figured the mermaid had gone to get help. But it wasn't help she brought, just two men. One of them called the dead girl a treasure, so I knew he was a bad one. Death's no one's treasure, except for ghouls. The other fellow spoke up that they should leave her in peace, but the first one spat at that idea. Told him no, that wasn't what they were about to do. So the one who drove loaded her onto the wagon. I should have shot them both before they took her."

The hermit looked at Eddie closely. "Too much for you to hear?" The old man reached into his jacket to bring forth the bottle of rye, which he offered companionably.

Eddie gulped a bitter mouthful of the liquor. "Do you think they killed her?"

"She was already gone before they got here. I checked. No breath. No heart. But somebody killed her for certain." The hermit brought something out of his pocket. A strand of blue thread. "Her mouth was sewn shut. I couldn't let her stay that way, so I told myself it would be like untangling fishing wire, otherwise it would have been too terrible a deed to undertake."

He gestured for his companion to take the thread, but Eddie recoiled.

"I figured this would happen," Beck grumbled. "You're scared by a thread."

Eddie's expression was dark; there was only so much insult he could take. "Thread doesn't scare me. I used to be a tailor."

"Well, I used to be a baby," the hermit responded. "Doesn't make me one now."

Eddie reached out, and Beck deposited the thread in his outstretched hand.

"The carriage men were there to steal the body," the hermit said with a sober expression. "The one in charge seemed happy to do so. Not your mermaid, though. She was crying."

"My mermaid?"

"You almost crashed right into her one night. She and I were both watching you and your rabbit." He patted Mitts, who panted happily at the attention, tongue lolling. "I wanted to make sure you didn't burn down my land, so I stayed up on the ridge. She was hidden in the trees. She's a good swimmer, and she's got good eyes. But you weren't much good at seeing what was right in front of you. That's why I'm leading you out now."

Eddie felt a burst of heat run through him. He must have glimpsed the girl. That was why he couldn't rid her from his dreams.

"Who is she?"

Beck shrugged. "A girl that thinks she's a fish. Maybe your trout brought her round. I told you that fish would lead you someplace."

"I don't suppose you recognized the men." An impossible, hopeless question Eddie didn't so much ask as think aloud.

"The first fella who almost drowned in the mud?"

"No," Eddie said. "The two with the body."

"Oh, I knew one of them, all right."

This was the way it happened, a single question that could crack open the world, letting in a shaft of light that might allow him to glimpse the truth.

"I saw his picture in the paper years ago. He was a criminal."

It was dark where they'd stopped, but through the trees the water shone a silvered, glittering gray.

"Do you remember his name?"

"Can't read. I just use the paper to wrap my fish to soak in cold water. But I read his face just fine, and I remembered it. It was the same man I saw with your mermaid. He put the body under the seat. Then he stood behind the carriage and fed the blackbirds crumbs from his hand. Never seen anything like it."

Eddie felt a chill along his neck and back. Beck was describing a scene Eddie knew well. The first thing he heard every morning was the sound of the horses breathing in the stalls below him and the liveryman crooning to his pigeons as he sang their praises. *Birds are smarter than you think. They never forget a kind word or a face.* He'd often witnessed the liveryman feeding the blackbirds out in the alleyway as they perched along his arms, each one waiting its turn, as if entranced.

"Now I've told you everything," the hermit said, "and all that I have belongs to you when I'm gone." They had reached the riverbank, the end of Beck's territory and his world. "Don't forget my wolf."

The city was quiet, but Eddie's mind was racing. On his way downtown, he found a grassy place and lay down to rest, his dog beside him. A mouth was sewn shut when there were secrets that might escape or when a punishment was delivered to an individual who talked too much. The thread was nothing special, not silk or mohair, just machine grade. Eddie closed his eyes, and sleep overtook him. When he dreamed he saw his father at his sewing machine. The thread he used was made of glass. It splintered in his hands and drew blood, but his father went on working as if this was an everyday occurrence. *This is what happens,* his father said in his dream. *This is what every man faces in his life.*

Dawn was approaching when Eddie woke. He stretched his legs, cramped from sleeping on the grass. He whistled for Mitts, and they headed back to Chelsea, trotting part of the way. Eddie's breath was hot and he could feel sweat stinging his body. The dog was joyous to have his master run along with him, and they ran until Eddie was doubled over, a stitch in his side. The last moments of night were drifting in between the wooden piers in bursts of blackened clouds. At the mouth of the harbor, the first rays of light broke through in glints of gold and red, and the dark night turned a wild, shivering blue.

The horses in the stable were just waking, ready for their breakfast, restless in their stalls. Their keeper was there and had already piled up hay with a pitchfork. Several of his prized pigeons perched along the old wooden beams. The liveryman sang to them as he brought out their breakfast of seed. With great trust and familiarity, his pigeons came to eat from his wide, callused hands. He turned, wary when he heard the door slide open, suspicious of who might arrive at such an ungodly hour, but broke into a grin when he spied Eddie and the dog. They'd been good neighbors over the years.

"Out early I see," the carriage man greeted Eddie. "Up before the birds."

"Long before the birds," Eddie said grimly. He thought of black-birds and the silver river. He thought how little he knew about this neighbor of his.

The liveryman finished feeding the pigeons. He then leaned to pet Mitts under the chin. "Here's a good boy who stays away from my birds, isn't that right?" The dog, exhausted from his walk, flopped down at the liveryman's feet. "I expect you'll both be looking for a few hours of sleep."

"It's not sleep I'm after." Eddie closed the door behind him. At the sound of the heavy doors shutting, the pigeons scattered to the rafters above. "It's you I'm looking for."

THEY CROSSED the Williamsburg Bridge early the next day, at a time when a steady stream of crowds were headed in the opposite direction, toward Manhattan and the working world. Eddie sat beside the sullen carriage man on the driver's high bench seat. He wanted to keep an eye on his companion, and for good reason. When confronted, the stableman had professed to know nothing of the matter of a missing girl. But when Eddie hadn't backed off, and had described the exact location where the body had been found in the muddy hollow, the liveryman had been stunned.

"You can't know that," he blurted. "No one knows where we've been and what we've done excepting my horse, and he wouldn't tell you if he could."

The stableman seemed under the influence; perhaps he was a drinker. Certainly, he was not reasoning clearly. He ran his mouth before he could think better of it, eyeing Eddie as if he possessed the psychic powers of a demon. "I told him I wanted nothing to do with it. I said it was bad luck, but he wouldn't listen and he was the one paying, so what was I to do?"

The liveryman swore he'd committed no offenses, for the girl was dead when they'd come upon her. All he did was help move the body to Brooklyn, and then only as an employee who had no choice but to obey the demands placed upon him.

"In the eyes of the law, that's an offense," Eddie assured him. "You'll be in the Tombs if the authorities find out. Maybe even Sing Sing prison."

"The eyes of the law are blind. You know it as well as I. Let's settle this as men, for men is what we are. I could kill you here and now," the liveryman boasted, "and never hear a word of this again."

Eddie laughed. "You?"

"Would you feel differently about holding a threat over my head if you knew I already served five years in Sing Sing?"

Eddie had assumed something about his companion's station in life from his scars, tattoos, and gold-capped teeth. But time in Sing Sing meant a serious criminal background.

"You know nothing about me, so don't pretend you do." The liveryman shook his head, for life in that infamous prison upstate was too harsh for anyone who hadn't served time to grasp. It was pure cruelty to lock men away and give them a view of the Hudson, keeping them always in sight of the beauty of the world while caging them like beasts. Many prisoners had tried to escape; some had drowned in the river, still more had wished they had when they were hauled out like fish and beaten with ropes and chains. "You have no idea what the world is like in that place or what men are willing to do in order to live another day. I'm including myself. I take responsibility for the man I used to be, for I carry him with me. As strong as I am, he's a heavy burden."

The liveryman's story tumbled out. This quiet, stocky fellow had run one of the toughest gangs in the Five Points section of the Lower East Side. His wild boys, the Allen Street Cadets, rode like madmen on their bicycles, perched upon their handlebars so they might attack a victim with a club before leaping down to finish a robbery. He'd risen through the ranks, from a bouncer at the New Irving Hall, a saloon on Broome Street, to a gang boss. The houses of prostitution and opium lairs under his control were overlooked by the officials at Tammany Hall, for those who were meant to govern for the good of the people were happy enough, once paid off, to ignore unlawful acts. In those days, this humble carriage man had often sauntered into the Tenth Precinct, where he let himself into the captain's office with ease, bringing gifts of whiskey and cigars. He'd considered himself untouchable, and for a while he was, but his long sentence in Sing Sing prison had left him without allies or connections.

When he was released, early, for good behavior, he'd had no choice but to hire himself out for petty crimes, including his work for a professor in Brooklyn. He was now thirty-four, and in the streets where he'd ruled, younger, more brutal men had taken his place. He'd found himself running a livery, mucking out stables, hiring himself out on a daily basis.

"So you lost your power and came to body snatching?"

"I was brought low by a certain passion I have," the liveryman admitted.

Eddie recalled the times he'd seen this fellow crouched in the alleyway behind the stable, all but hidden in the falling dusk. He'd often had a pipe with him. There had been times when Eddie had observed him fast asleep beside his horses, dead to the world or only half-awake, his eyes hazed over from the effects of smoking poppy. There were opium houses across lower Manhattan, in the cellars of bordellos and taverns. Eddie had been to many such places while working for Hochman. His young age hadn't mattered to anyone in this world where a man's craving was paramount. All that was necessary for him to gain admittance was to pay a dime to the sheriff who guarded the door; he was then allowed to search through the warren of cubby-holes. In these dim and filthy cubicles a man could smoke himself into a stupor, most often lying on one hip so he could get to his pipe even as he slipped into a dream. It was a dream from which he'd never have to wake, as long as he had money enough, and wasn't murdered in his sleep.

"The Professor concocts his own opium in his workshop," the liveryman informed Eddie. "He takes the raw stuff that looks like amber flakes and mixes it into a paste with those chemicals of his. He's a wizard, I'll grant him that. He vowed I'd never go without as long as I keep my mouth shut."

"But you're talking now," Eddie reminded him.

"So I am. I've had enough of being lorded over by the likes of some so-called scientist who has me dragging around the dead. I may take his money, but he hasn't got my loyalty. You keep me out of it, and I'll talk all right."

"You'll do more than that. You'll take me there."

Eddie then brought out the dime-store photograph of Hannah. After a single glance, the liveryman looked away, pained. Even a man such as he had a soul, one he worried over more as each year went by.

"That's her," he admitted. "God forgive me."

To Eddie's great shock, the carriage man then began the initial phrases of the Kaddish, the mourning prayer of the Jews. *Yit'gadal v'yit kadash sh'mei raba.* May His great Name grow exalted and sanctified. *B'al'ma di v'ra khir'utei.* In the world that He created as He willed. *V'yam'likh mal'khutei b'chayeikhon uv'yomeikhon.* May He give reign to His kingship in your lifetimes and in your days. *Uv'chayei d'khol beit yis'ra'eil.* And in the lifetimes of the entire family of Israel.

The prayer was so ingrained, Eddie found himself murmuring the words in unison, though the liveryman seemed less a Jew than a heathen, a criminal with no allegiance, however he might call upon God.

"There you have it," the carriage man told his confused companion when the prayer had been completed. "I'm one of your brethren."

"I've left my faith," Eddie was quick to inform him. "So we can hardly be brothers in any way, shape, or form."

"You think so? I did the same as you, covered up who I was. We're not so different. It was easier for a man like me to make my way without carrying the weight of our people. I suspect the same held true for you. I became whatever and whoever suited the times. I changed my name when need be, and who says that's a crime? I've been Bill and Jack, and half a dozen other people. Joe Marvin, Joe Morris, William Murray—there's an entire list of who I've been, and none of them have been too pleasing. But where do I go when there's no one else to turn to? Adonai, our God."

"If you think I'll let you off easy because of this, you're wrong. You'll take me to her."

The carriage man shook his head sadly. "You'll likely regret it. I say this in all respect and as a brother."

"Likely I will," Eddie agreed. "But I'll be in Brooklyn when I do."

A frayed red cushion covered the seat of the carriage, to ease the pounding a person's rear end took as the wooden wheels hit against the ruts in the roads. Eddie noticed the liveryman didn't use a whip on the horse, yet the gelding trotted easily, as if he knew his master's intended destination.

"You're good with animals," Eddie granted.

"I don't need you to tell me so. I owned a pet shop on Broome Street when I was young. I was bird crazy. Still am. Honest creatures, aren't they? Wild little things."

The weather was warm and the sky had opened into a clear cerulean blue. The liveryman stopped the carriage on the flatlands, where there were still farms. Rows of cauliflower and beets grew for nearly a mile. The road was dusty, and it seemed no one was around. Eddie's hackles were immediately raised as he speculated that some foul play was under way. It was possible that his companion would try to do him in on this empty stretch of highway; it might be that one of the liveryman's old cohorts was nearby, ready with a club or a gun. Then Eddie realized their journey had been halted because they'd come to a well. The carriage man had already leapt down to retrieve a bucket from beneath the rear seat, which he filled so that his horse might drink. Eddie jumped down as well, in order to stretch his long legs.

"What do you want me to call you?" he asked, feeling more good-natured in this rural landscape. The air itself was intoxicating. "You said you've been known as Joe?"

"Go right ahead. I'll answer to anything."

By habit Eddie had grabbed his camera before leaving the stable, and he was now moved to capture the scene before him. The carriage man, called Joe for lack of anything better, held the water bucket so that the gelding could drink. His free arm was draped tenderly over the horse's neck.

"All my other portraits were taken at the police precinct," the fellow Joe said with a grin, showing off his gold-capped smile. "Make sure my beautiful teeth show."

"Don't think so highly of yourself. It's the horse's portrait I'm interested in."

"I told you we were alike," the liveryman insisted. When he finished his chore, he climbed back into the seat and lifted the reins. "We both trust beasts more than we do men."

"If you mean would I rather stare at the horse's ass than look at you," Eddie remarked as he took his place beside his companion, "I can't disagree."

They both had a chuckle over that remark. Their defenses were down due to the utter beauty of the day. Terns wheeled across the sky and swirls of bees rumbled through clumps of tall grass.

"You thought I was about to murder you back there." Joe looked pleased with himself. "Admit it."

"It crossed my mind. Then I thought of your allegiance to God, and found relief." Eddie's edge of cynicism caused a smile to play at his lips. "You'd have to pay when you came before him."

"I'm before him now," the liveryman said solemnly. "I've come to understand I'm before him each and every minute."

The marshland sprawled to the south in patches of gold and green.

There was a slight haze as they crossed the wooden bridge that forded a watery fen and a rivulet known as Coney Island Creek. The original bridges over the creek had been constructed of wood, but the first roads were made of shells. Shells were still tossed down as seabirds dropped clams so they might smash open on the bridges and the roads. Several migrating ospreys nested in the branches of tall trees. Sun dashed onto Eddie's face and made his eyes tear. The salt in the air stung their faces and refreshed their spirits. The light was paler here than in Manhattan, tempered by soft clouds. It was the sort of light Moses Levy would have delighted in, for while it obscured the larger horizon, it allowed the camera's lens to pinpoint the smallest detail even as they entered the streets of Coney Island with their crowds of shoppers. All of Brooklyn seemed bathed in a glow. The gleam of the trolley tracks on Neptune Avenue, the carousels with their painted wooden lions and horses, all glinted with intense color. Even the market awnings shone with bright stripes of crimson and yellow and blue.

The liveryman stopped the carriage on Surf Avenue. The renovation at Dreamland was in its final stages. Huge piles of sandy earth had been dug up, then dumped in the street. Each time the breeze arose, sand whipped into little dirt devils that burst into the air.

"This is as far as I can take you. Otherwise he'll know it's me that brought you here." Down the avenue the roof and gables of the Museum of Extraordinary Things could be spied. "I'd like to kill him, and don't think I haven't had the chance. But he's got access to what I need, God forgive me, so I'll go no farther."

Eddie leapt down from the carriage, camera in hand. "Wait for me then. I'll need a ride back."

"What do you mean? I've done my part, haven't I? Do you think I'm your lackey meant to do your bidding?"

"I thought you were my brother," Eddie mocked.

"Half brother."

"Stay put. And hope that I come back."

The liveryman turned the carriage despite Eddie's order, and let out a whistle that caused his horse to break into a trot. "Hope that for yourself," he called over his shoulder. "Good luck making your own way back."

THERE WAS so much noise and commotion at Dreamland that it was a relief to turn onto the slate path that led to the museum. A wash of quiet settled over Eddie, and the air was cooler than it had been on the crowded avenue. The institution Eddie approached appeared to be more of a house than museum; it was still off-season, if only for a few days more, and the place was surprisingly run-down. At the end of the path, Eddie found the entryway door locked. The wooden signs that announced the spectacular marvels to be seen within had not yet been hung but were instead tossed upon the grass, the paint dewy and fading. Two lilac trees were lavishly in bloom, surrounded by a cloud of bees. By now Eddie had begun to hear voices. He followed the sound of conversation around the perimeter of the exhibition hall, finding himself on the outskirts of a large yard. There were new leaves on a towering pear tree. Eddie had to peer through the branches so that he might view the gathering on the porch. Another man might have been stunned by what he saw, but Eddie was delighted by the wonders he observed. For a moment he forgot why he had come and was content to simply gaze upon the miraculous forms that had appeared before him.

The museum began its season early, before Dreamland and Luna Park opened their gates. In this way they could hope to attract weekend visitors who might otherwise overlook such a small establishment in favor of the other parks. The billowing white sheets had already been removed from the cases of specimens, glass canisters and displays of bones had been dusted, and birdcages and fish tanks freshened. On this morning the living wonders had reported in to greet each other after a long winter, signing their names or, for those who hadn't the skill of writing, making their marks with Xes in a ledger book that charted the acts that would begin performing at the end of the week. Every year some alumnus went missing, and this season was no different. Gianni, for instance, an elderly man from Rome who ate fire and walked barefoot over a bed of hot coals, had simply disappeared. He had been ill at the end of last summer, coughing up bits of cinders and blood, and now people mourned his absence. Those who had returned embraced, gladdened to find they were not the only ones to survive another winter. Some had worked odd jobs, others had traveled with exhibitions or circuses in the South, still others merely waited for the season to begin again, like Malia, the Butterfly Girl, who bided her time in a boardinghouse where her mother took in mending to sustain their meager needs. This reunion was a day of celebration, especially as the Professor had been drinking late into the night and was still in bed. Eventually they would all have to meet with him and discuss their contracts, but for now it was far easier to enjoy themselves when his piercing glance was not evaluating everything that was said and done.

They were gathered around a table, drinking tea, delighting in Maureen's apple fritters, excellent as always, even better than usual on this day, pastries concocted of sweetened dough that had been boiled in a vat on the huge coal-burning stove before being sprinkled with brown and white sugar.

Eddie stood just inside the garden, inflamed and astonished. There was Jeremiah, a sword swallower who made sure to coat his throat with a thick syrup made in the Indies before each performance and liked his tea especially hot. Two young brothers from the Bronx, the Durantes, ate from the same plate. The Butterfly Girl used her bare feet to partake of her breakfast as another might use her hands, and the Jungle Boy, whom people around the table called Horace, could not speak, yet made himself clear enough when he wished to have three cubes of sugar to his tea. There was a new wonder this season, a spritely man named William Reeves, who kept an alligator the size of a hunting dog on a chain. In Reeves's act he removed the cap he wore, then held the beast's jaws open to fit his head inside its gaping mouth, an orifice that was currently tied with string, to ensure the safety of those nearby should the beast mistake a thumb or forefinger for one of the chicken bits he was fed each night.

Eddie hoisted up his camera so that he might catch an image of this wondrous breakfast gathering. The garden itself seemed enchanted. Bands of light streamed over the table in shades of lemon and gold, and there was the scent of mint, and of damp earth, and of fragrant black currant tea. Malia threw back her head and laughed at a joke the Durantes told in tandem—the older brother always announced the punch line—and the new man, William Reeves, gazed at her joyfully, fully appreciating the Butterfly Girl's beauty, while the sword swallower drank from his steaming cup of tea, his blade with its brass handle leaning against one bony knee. Though Eddie's camera was so very quiet, the hollow click was enough to make the group on the porch freeze. Perhaps their senses were attuned in ways an average person's were not. They turned en masse, wary, as though expecting to find a snake stretched along the length of a branch. They seemed startled to see such an ordinary individual there beside the pear tree, a tall young man with short-cropped hair and dark eyes, carelessly dressed in a blue jacket, light wool trousers, and laced boots.

As for Eddie, he approached humbly, knowing full well he was disturbing an intimate gathering. "I hope you don't mind me stopping. I was passing by and it was such a perfect scene. I'm a photographer."

Fearing his very presence would spook them, he held out his camera, evidence of his good intentions. Rather than shrink from him, the natural wonders were intrigued.

"I take portraits." Eddie came closer, encouraged by their reactions. "And I'd be so happy to take any of yours."

"Would you now?" the character named William Reeves replied with an edge of suspicion. "At what price?"

"Oh, there's no fee," Eddie assured him.

"Then you've got a deal."

Reeves was the first to pose, and once he'd agreed, the ice was broken. The others gathered round to watch the slight, wiry man lift the alligator over his lap, placing one hand on its gray-green scales. "I always wanted a picture of Arthur," he said, for he called his creature by this name. "Do you want me to look solemn?"

"Whatever suits you," Eddie recommended.

Upon hearing this, Reeves broke into a grin. "This is me, buddy. Happy go lucky. Arthur's the one who's glum."

From the kitchen where she was helping Maureen with the fried dough, Coralie overheard a murmur of conversation, then bright laughter. When there was a round of applause, she was compelled to go to the back door to peer through the screen. She could hardly believe the sight before her. There was Malia, perched on the porch railing as if ready for flight, a beautiful half butterfly. And, far more distracting, there he was, the man from the woods, right in Coralie's own yard, as if he'd been magicked to Brooklyn. He had beautiful hands, long and pale, like a musician's. When his jacket constricted his movements, he shrugged it off and continued working in his white shirt and suspenders. He had a brooding expression, so concentrated on his subject he seemed not to take in a single breath of air.

Coralie gazed through the meshing of the door, entranced as she watched him adjust the lens of his camera.

"Stay exactly as you are," the photographer called to Malia. "This is perfect."

The next batch of fritters sizzled in a pot on the stove, ready to be scooped out of the bubbling hot oil, but Coralie ignored her kitchen duties. This was the hand of fate. She was certain of it.

The photographer thanked Malia, then quickly began to set up his camera for another shot, removing one plate and inserting the next. The Durante brothers readied themselves for their turn, bending around each other in a fluid circle so perfectly round it seemed to defy the capabilities of the human spine.

Maureen had been pulled into the kitchen by the scent of fritters burning. She gasped when she saw the pot of oil, singed and turning black. "Here's a waste," she said mournfully as she quickly lifted the pot from the flame. She noticed Coralie at the door, a strange expression crossing her face. "I'd like to know what all the ruckus is about." Maureen approached the back door, narrowing her eyes when she took note of the man with the camera. The brothers were cheerfully posing for him. "What does he think he's doing? He'll get a thrashing if he's caught. We'll all be in the shit."

Maureen pushed open the door before Coralie could prevent her. "Stop what you're doing this minute," the housekeeper called sharply to Eddie. "This yard is private property and there are private lives being lived here."

Eddie gazed up to see a beautiful red-haired woman whose extreme disfigurement was evident even across the distance between them. He felt humbled by the strength and authority in her tone. "Miss," he said earnestly. "Forgive me for not asking your permission."

Hidden behind Maureen, Coralie again felt the hook of her attraction to him. The pulse at the base of her throat was pounding. As for Eddie, he spied a shadow and nothing more. Though he placed one hand over his eyes to block out the streaming sunlight, he could see no farther than the threshold of the kitchen.

"I have no permission to grant," Maureen told him, "so you'd better hightail it out of here, before the owner finds you trespassing. Then you'll see what trouble is."

"He's only a photographer," William Reeves explained to the housekeeper. "There's no harm done."

"I don't care if he's the King of Brooklyn," Maureen said smartly to Reeves, before turning her attention back to Eddie. "Sir, I'm asking you to leave. Take my advice if you've got half a brain in your head."

Eddie put a hand over his heart and pleaded, "Don't send me away before I take your portrait."

Maureen laughed dismissively, though she clearly found something charming in his actions. He appeared as a scarecrow might, with his baggy pants and long arms and legs and dark, handsome features. "Like that will happen," she called to him.

"Let him do it," Coralie urged the housekeeper from the shadows. "You've never had one taken before, and it will cause no harm."

Maureen was puzzled, but when she turned to see Coralie's look of fierce insistence, she understood the fellow in the yard was the very man her charge had spoken of, the one she couldn't forget.

"If that's him, he doesn't look like much," Maureen said thoughtfully. "Too skinny by far."

"Go on." Coralie gave the housekeeper a little push. "Go!"

"Are you mad? What if your father sees?"

"I don't care," Coralie told Maureen. The kindness with which Eddie had treated his subjects in the yard had uplifted her. Here was an ordinary man who did not flee from what he could not explain but rather was drawn to what was different, not lewdly out of some sinister inquisitiveness, but due to sheer wonder. "I trust him," Coralie said.

"Really?" Maureen murmured. "Shall I tell you what I think about trusting a man you hardly know? I'm proof of where that leads."

"It's only a portrait," Coralie reminded her.

"Might I ask what anyone in their right mind would do with a portrait of me?"

Coralie took Maureen's hand in her own. "Please. Do it for me."

The photographer gestured for Maureen to enter the vegetable garden. The sky was without a cloud now, causing the shadows to be especially deep, black ribbons running through the grass. As Eddie worked to ready the camera's plate, he thought about the apple trees in Chelsea, and the huge elms in upper Manhattan. He thought of the forest in Russia and the salty yellow wetlands he had crossed that very morning. The beauty of the world had been apparent to him through the lens of his camera, but he hadn't known a human being could be as marvelous as a marsh or a tree or a field of grass. Maureen stood between the rows of lettuce and peas, staring straight at him, hiding nothing. She hadn't even thought to take off her apron. Her face was beautiful and ruined and utterly devoid of artifice. When Eddie had finished her portrait, he went to her and got down on one knee. "My gratitude," he said.

He knew he had taken his best photograph. Nothing he'd done before or ever would do again would compare to this one image. He wished Moses Levy were alive to observe the print when it was developed. Maybe he hadn't been such a failure of a student after all.

"Don't be an ass," Maureen chided. There was the scent of cooking oil on her clothes. "As long as I never have to see that picture. I don't even look in mirrors."

Eddie rose to his feet, embarrassed by his show of emotion. Since the day of the fire, when he had photographed the dead, first on the street and then in their makeshift coffins, he'd been overly affected by his own passions. His eyes blazed with the fervor of a true believer, for though he claimed to have lost his faith, there was a jittery spark of it inside him. He clapped the soil from his trousers. Gazing up, he spied Coralie on the porch steps. Perhaps what happened next was influenced by the passionate state he was in, perhaps it was the intensity of her gaze. He fell in love with her in that instant. He had no idea what was happening, he only felt as if he were drowning, though he stood with his feet firmly on the ground. Coralie's long black hair was gathered in a ribbon. She wore a simple black dress and a pair of old-fashioned cotton gloves, the sort most young women would have cast away on such a warm, seasonable day. The more he looked at her, the more beautiful she became. Eddie experienced an ache he hadn't expected, immediate and undeniable, a rush of desire that might easily consume him.

"There you go." Maureen nodded when she saw his reaction. "Now you've seen the treasure of the house." She elbowed him to make herself clear. "Do her wrong and you'll answer to me."

Coralie came toward him, eyes shining. They greeted each other, then, after their introduction, they shifted into the rear of the yard without thinking, both wishing for privacy. The pear tree's bark smelled sharp and fragrant. The tendrils of the green peas grew beyond the pickets of the fence in wild profusion.

"I saw you and your dog in the woods once, near the river," Coralie confided, ignoring her shy heart. "I never thought it was possible that we would meet here in Brooklyn."

The light was fading in the section of the yard where they'd paused, near enough to the trash pile for the ground to be ashy.

"I imagined you," Eddie responded. "Or it might be that I saw you as well." Coralie's eyes were bright; a flush of color was rising on her throat. She hoped he might say *The world is waiting for us, all we have to do is run away*, but instead he murmured, "I'm here for the drowned girl."

She came to her senses then. So this was his mission. Another girl entirely.

"You can be truthful with me," Eddie went on. "To be honest, I know that she's here."

"And how is that?" Coralie wondered what the drowned girl meant to him. "Are you a mind reader of some sort?"

"Not exactly." Although he had always prided himself on evaluating people's thoughts and desires, this young woman seemed beyond his reach. He dropped his voice. "We share a liveryman it seems. The one who prefers birds to human beings."

When Eddie spoke so intimately, Coralie's attraction sliced through her. Still she remembered Maureen's words of caution. "Is it your wife you're looking for?"

"I'm hired to find her by her father, who longs to have her back, no matter her condition. I assume the body was taken for some vile purpose?"

Coralie lowered her eyes. "So vile you could not begin to comprehend."

"I might. I've worked with criminals for the newspapers. I think I would understand."

She yearned to tell him, but because of where such intimacies might lead, she felt a rising fear. She had entered a country she'd never visited before, though she stood in the ashy earth of the yard she'd known all of her life.

Up on the porch, William Reeves was sitting back in his chair so that he might recite a list of the massive amounts of food his alligator needed each morning: two chickens, three bunches of lettuce, a large haddock, bones and all. That, he announced, was just for breakfast. He intended to inform Professor Sardie that a larger salary was to be expected if he was to join their troupe for the season, for though he'd inked his name on the roster, he'd yet to sign a contract. The very idea of asking for more incited the museum's employees, and a lively discussion began concerning the possibility of a fair wage, something no one had dared to imagine before. Eddie and Coralie paid no attention to this debate. They didn't hear the clatter as plates and cups were carried off, marking the end of tea, nor did they recognize the passing of time.

"It's dangerous to look into things you don't understand," Coralie advised. "You haven't seen the half of what there is in this world."

"Perhaps you're one of the extraordinary things I don't understand. I've heard you're something of a mermaid."

"Have you?" The very word sent a shiver down Coralie's spine. It called up images of nighttime performances, mortifying scenes of flesh and wanton desire. "Whoever told you that knows nothing."

Eddie felt a chill directed toward him. "I don't mean to offend you. There's a hermit camped out in the woods who's spied upon us both. He said you're a grand swimmer, and that you did your best to rescue Hannah. That's her name. Hannah Weiss."

Coralie now understood why the body she'd left sprawled in the weeds had been discovered with her hands folded on her chest, her head placed carefully upon a grassy pillow.

"Can you take me to her?" Eddie asked.

"She's locked away, and my father is present so I cannot. But even if I could, she's no longer among the living. Should we not simply forget her?"

"Can you forget what's lost?" Eddie furrowed his brow, a sort of outrage passing across his features. "If it's such a simple thing to do, you must teach me, for my mother died when I was a child, yet I mourn her still." His words clearly touched Coralie, so he went on. "Should I go back to Manhattan and tell an old man to forget his daughter? Not to dig a grave or have blessings recited for her soul?" Eddie's glance held hers, and he dared to speak his innermost thoughts. "And should I forget you when I leave here on this day?"

"You should," Coralie insisted, for they had gone too far in words, and words, Maureen had always warned her, were soon enough followed by deeds. "Absolutely."

"*Should* is what you don't want to do, but do anyway. That isn't me."

A smile played at Coralie's lips. "No. I'm sure it isn't."

"Nor is it you, I'd wager."

Coralie shaded her eyes and gazed up into his. They were a deep brown, flecked with gold and black.

"I can get you her belongings." She did her best to keep her voice even. "Would that help?"

Maureen had come outside to wave at them, gesturing in no uncertain terms for Coralie to send the tall young man away. Coralie had been so caught up in their conversation she'd failed to notice the living wonders had already gone inside one by one to greet her father and sign their binding contracts for the season to come. The porch had emptied, with only Reeves and the alligator remaining.

"It would help greatly." Eddie's back was to Maureen. Most likely he would not or could not gaze away from Coralie.

"Wait for me. I'll be as fast as I can."

Coralie hurried to the porch, where Maureen was waiting to usher her inside, nearly faint with relief. "Thank goodness you've come to your senses," the housekeeper remarked. "Have you not seen me signaling for you to be rid of him?"

"Don't let my father find him," Coralie instructed her.

"You don't know where this will lead," the housekeeper warned.

All the same, Coralie could not be dissuaded. She could see Eddie through the screen door, out in the yard, whistling to himself, as he had in the woods. She didn't intend to deny or disappoint him. Whitman's poetry had been her schoolroom, and most of what she knew of life she'd taken from its pages. *Why should you not speak to me / And why should I not speak to you?*

She shrugged off Maureen's pleas and went swiftly through the hall, taking the stairs two at a time. As she slipped into her room, Coralie heard her father call out William Reeves's name so that he might be interviewed for his season's contract. She shifted the heavy horsehair mattress so that she could remove the blue coat she'd hidden. Clutching it, she went to her dresser. There, stored beneath her undergarments, were the tokens stolen from her father's workroom table. Some hairpins, a small tortoiseshell comb, the gold locket on a chain, the black buttons that had fallen from Hannah's closed hand. She swept these items into a handkerchief that she tied with a knot.

She prayed her case of nerves would not grow worse until her task was completed. It was then she heard her father's raised voice. He was shouting at William Reeves, and Coralie feared if she had to pass him, his rage would be directed at whoever blundered by. She went to the window and signaled to Eddie, who looked up confused. *Leave,* she urged him. *Run away.* He grinned at her and shook his head, and made it clear he intended to stand his ground. Coralie knew he was not the sort to run, and that he would not forget her, though it would be best if he did. Mr. William Reeves was shouting at the Professor, balking at the deal he'd been offered and suggesting the Professor rot in hell for paying his workers such a pittance, before he slammed out the back door, his alligator under one arm as if it were a suitcase. Apparently, Reeves's impudence and his demand for a more fitting wage had so infuriated the Professor, he followed the rascal out of the house and, in doing so, came face-to-face with the photographer in his yard.

SEVEN

THE WOLF'S

HOUSE

****

I F THE WOLFMAN *had not disappeared from my life I would have made certain to question him further about Jane Eyre, the book he held so dear to his heart. I suppose I was studying love, and in my studies of this subject I could never understand the brutal love of Rochester. I did grasp why Rochester revealed his humanity only after he had been blinded and disfigured; like the beasts around us who reveal their natures because they have no access to artifice, he at last had no choice but to be truly himself. I wondered why he didn't then realize how cruelly he'd treated the first Mrs. Rochester. Surely if he comprehended all he'd done to her, he would have locked himself in a tower to repent for the rest of his days rather than taking the sweet Jane as his wife.*

As for Jane, I considered her to be a fool, but what young woman has not been a fool under certain circumstances? The blind aspect of love was of great fascination to me. Could a person not see what was readily before her? Did the heat of passion have the power to change one's vision, so that what was false became true, and truth itself was nowhere to be seen?

I wondered how many women had come under my father's spell, and if he had ongoing affairs of the heart that he kept secret from me. He came in late in the evenings. I often heard him groan as he climbed the stairs, and sometimes he carried the scent of a woman's perfume on his clothes, along with the odor of the peculiar mix of tobacco he smoked, a black tarry substance. Perhaps if he'd been blinded as Rochester was, the best of my father might have surfaced and the future would have been written differently. Or perhaps there is evil in certain people, a streak of meanness that cannot be erased by circumstance or fashioned into something brand new by love.

Now that I was eighteen and thought so frequently of what drew one person to another, I pondered more often over my mother's character. I imagined her to be a naïve girl who could not resist my father. Or it was quite possible that she was the opposite, a wild creature that needed taming. I wondered, too, if she knew about my father's past, and if she'd learned, as I had from reading his handbook, about the half woman in his show who had accused him of mistreatment. Was it possible that, like Jane, she'd forgiven him his transgressions? Perhaps, like so many women, she thought she would be the one to change him.

I hadn't found the nerve to go back to the cellar, though I often carried the keys I'd had made in my pocket. Instead, I looked around the house for further clues about my heritage. My parents seemed the greatest mystery of all to me. I longed to go backward in time, to catch a glimpse of them, if only for a moment or two, so that I might discover not just the character of the people I had sprung from but who I myself might become. The Professor's bedroom was on the second floor, as mine was, but it was down a long narrow hallway, set off by itself. He valued his privacy, yet he was forced to survey the crowds of Coney Island. Whereas my room overlooked the garden, his had a view of the peaks of Dreamland's towers.

The electric lights must have infuriated him. He slept with heavy damask curtains drawn and a sleeping mask over his eyes. He kept his door closed at all times, for he was a reserved and meticulous person. But he liked his room clean and detested dust, which he said inflamed the lungs. And so, one day I suggested to Maureen that I tidy his room. She was busy with the ironing, a hot and thankless task made all the worse by the heavy black metal iron that produced sprays of steam turning her face sweaty and red. Without thinking, she nodded for me to go ahead.

Though it was my own house, and though I had permission granted to me, I felt like a thief as I made my way upstairs. My intentions were not pure, but they drove me on. I pushed open the door to my father's room, which was at least double the size of my own small chamber. I first took note of the dressing table, where he kept cigars and pipes and tinctures, along with a decanter of rum. There were pots of the tar-like oily stuff that he often preferred to his pipe tobacco. Strewn about were books of tabulations and reams of bills. My father's predilection for the rare had cost him dearly, and the creatures and artifacts on exhibit had not come cheap. Though I lacked accounting skills, I saw that the Museum of Extraordinary Things owed more than it earned. There were marks in blue, and more in red, all adding up to the steely truth of my father's statement that I must be able to earn my keep.

I tugged open the drapes. The view from the window was quite lovely in my opinion, all sky and then the outline of the white and silver towers of Dreamland. From here it was possible to make out the edge of the sea, and the fishing boats and ferries. I saw to the linens on the bed and dusted the woodwork. When I reached the feather duster to the highest window sash, I spied a sword, a glossy silver thing, embossed with designs of stars and moons. It was the very same sword he'd used in France to cut a woman in half, for I'd seen sketches of it in his handbook. When I took it down, it was heavy in my hands, an enormous, ornate piece of cutlery.

I noticed the blade was still sharp, but not before I unintentionally cut myself.

I gasped with pain, and it was my bad fortune that at that moment Maureen came bustling in, wondering why my task was taking so long. Surely, she immediately regretted allowing me entrance to my father's bedroom. Blood was pooling in my hand. She grabbed the sword from me, a look of despair on her face. If only I had nicked the webbing of my fingers, but the cut was in the center of my palm.

"This is not a toy or some amusement," she informed me. "I thought I taught you far better than this."

She returned the sword to its rightful place, drew the curtains, and ushered me from the room. In the hallway she held me by my shoulders and shook me. "I had no idea I was raising such a fool" was what she whispered to me. I was stung by her words, surprised by the depth of her anger. Then I saw tears in her eyes and I understood. She feared for my welfare. I knew she would not have sat idly by if she had been aware of my father's punishments, or of the way I earned my keep. I felt an apology upon my lips and longed to explain with a full confession of what my life had become. I wished to tell her how I ached to run away, as the Wolfman had done. I dreamed of climbing out my window to feel the rain upon my skin, and walk, if I must do so, all the way to Manhattan, where I could sift among the crowds unnoticed, and find the one man who might see me as more than a curiosity and connect to the soul I carried inside of me.

I yearned to tell Maureen all this and more, but I did not say a word. I could not bring myself to worry her or cause her any more pain than she'd already known. A few days earlier I had come upon her washing up after her day of work. She was at the sink with a pitcher of water and a washcloth, partially unclothed. I realized I had never seen her naked, for we were modest people. Now her muslin blouse was open as she rid herself of dust and grime. I saw that she had been burned not merely on her face but across her body as well. The splattering on her mottled skin convinced me that when acid had been thrown at her it had splattered, and had burned right through her clothes, for the blotches were everywhere.

On the afternoon Maureen scolded me in the corridor outside my father's room, I told her nothing of my own distress. Instead I simply promised I would not touch the sword again. I took her hand and kissed it, and I think she believed me, for she brought me down to the kitchen and had me scrub out pots while she made us a lunch of toast and fried eggs with mushrooms she had unearthed in the garden, a special treat she knew was a favorite of mine.

NOW AND THEN, on afternoons when I dashed off to the market to run errands at the end of the day, I caught sight of the Wolfman waiting for Maureen. I myself had not spoken with him since the day he disappeared. He usually positioned himself in the shadows of two large cypress trees that framed either side of the fenced entranceway to a funeral parlor. He rightly assumed that people would rush by that cold address, not wishing to see what was eventually in store for them and their loved ones. He wore a hooded cloak and made himself all but invisible, but despite the distance and his disguise, I could see his aspect brighten whenever he spied Maureen leaving our establishment and heading toward him. Each time I saw them together I understood love a little more.

I was on my way home from the fish market with a freshly caught haddock, one I chose for its bright pink flesh and silver skin, now wrapped by the fishmonger in a damp, wrinkled page torn from The Times. Black newsprint had seeped onto my white gloves, and I was thinking I was lucky that Maureen could wash away the ink with bleach and lye before my father discovered the mess. Before I knew it I had stumbled upon Mr.

Morris, only steps away. He was very still, like a heron in the bay that waits for the shadows of fish to appear. He most likely would have let me pass without a greeting if I hadn't spied him first.

He was thinner than I'd remembered him, and I admit that his countenance gave me pause. I had grown unused to seeing him close up, and the ease with which I was accustomed to greeting his fierce appearance had dissipated. I may even have taken a step back, so like a wolf did he appear. Then I looked into his eyes and remembered who he was. He said hello in that kind voice of his, as he had when we first met. Years had passed since that time. I was no longer a little girl and he was no longer a believer that the city of New York would embrace a man such as himself.

"It's a good thing I heard you had been hired by Dreamland, otherwise I might have fainted to see a man who'd vanished so completely from my life. I mourned you," I said bitterly. "For no good purpose it seems."

"We thought it best if you knew nothing of my presence," he told me. He seemed bashful now that I was a grown woman; perhaps he had seen me recoil when I first spied him.

"I wouldn't have said a word to my father." I was still quite hurt that the secret of his presence in Brooklyn had been kept from me. Since I'd known he and Maureen were still together, I hadn't made a single slip of this confidence.

"Your father is a man who can figure things out without any words being said. We did it to protect you as well. That was our concern."

"And now he knows you're here and will be working for our competitor."

Mr. Morris shrugged. "All men must work."

I noticed he had a bouquet of spring flowers, white tulips mixed with red anemones. I gathered they were for Maureen, but Mr. Morris took me by surprise when he mentioned they were meant for Malia, the Butterfly Girl. Just then Maureen left our house, hurriedly making her way down *the street, so I could not question Mr. Morris any further, though my face was hot with anger. Maureen was wearing her best dress, a green muslin with black silk trimming, along with a hat I hadn't seen before, gray felt decorated with pale blue feathers.*

When she saw me there with Mr. Morris, her expression darkened.

"I see your friend has returned," I said to her. "But of course I've known that for some time." I did not let on that I had often followed Maureen, but I suppose she knew, for she shook her head sadly, as if I was the one who had disappointed her.

"He was gone for two years, back to Virginia. He wrote letters, but of course I never received them, for they wound up on the trash pile as soon as they were delivered. Your father saw to that. When Mr. Morris realized he could not stay away, he came back to Brooklyn and we renewed our friendship. I thought it best that you not know that he'd returned."

"You made that decision for me?" I responded bitterly. "Even when there were rumors he would be at Dreamland you said nothing to me. Less than nothing, for you lied."

"Is the truth always the best remedy?" Maureen wondered. Perhaps it was a question she asked herself. As she thought this over, she saw that I had been to the market, and had tarried when I spied Mr. Morris. "You should be at home, miss. The fish must be put on ice immediately or it will go bad and I shan't be able to make supper tomorrow. You wouldn't want to be poisoned by a piece of bad fish, would you?"

"It's stinking already," I said. "Unlike the flowers for Malia," I continued, with a meaningful nod to the bouquet in the Wolfman's hands.

I didn't wish to hurt Maureen but rather to protect her, for I worried that Raymond Morris might not be as trustworthy as he appeared. For his part, Mr. Morris stammered and said a few words about the splendor of flowers, quoting from Whitman, "A morning-glory at my window satisfies me more than the metaphysics of books." This may well have been

the great Whitman's opinion, but I knew for a fact that Mr. Morris val-
ued books above all other things. If he might misrepresent his high regard
for books, he might be willing to lie about other issues. I wondered if I'd
caught him in a clandestine relationship with Malia. Maureen, how-
ever, did not share my suspicions. Instead she turned on me, rapping her
knuckles on my head, as she used to when I was a little girl and she found
me misbehaving.

"Do you think I don't know who these flowers were meant for?" she
said to me. "Are you trying to embarrass Mr. Morris?"

She then hotly announced they were on their way to a wedding, even
though Mr. Morris tried his best to hush her. The bride in question, she
went on, before her companion could stop her, was none other than Malia.

"That's what you get for snooping around, miss," she said to me. "The
truth and nothing but."

"But why wasn't I invited?" I had tried to befriend Malia from the
start, when we were only girls. Despite my attempts, she had always been
shy and somewhat standoffish. Still, I was surprised not to be invited to
such an important event.

"Don't you understand? Your father can't know—he doesn't believe in
such unions. The groom is a regular fellow. Your father would waste no
time in letting Malia go. If you had known, there might be a situation."

I was hurt and mortified that I'd been kept in the dark. "A situation?
Do you mean to say I would tell him and betray her?"

Who were we to each other, after all this time? Did she not know where
my loyalties lay? I glared at Maureen and briskly moved away from her,
as though she were a stranger, for at that moment I thought perhaps she
was. Now she was the one to look at me with a hurt expression.

"You weren't told out of concern for your welfare," Mr. Morris stepped
in to say. "What you don't know can't hurt you."

"Really?" I said, blinking back tears. "When you didn't know the

world, when you'd never spoken to a woman or walked down a street or stood in the rain, that didn't hurt you?"

Maureen approached and tried to make amends. "Please understand," she said, but I did not. I was deeply wounded by yet another deception, having been treated as if I were a child who couldn't be trusted. When Maureen attempted to embrace me, I shrugged from beneath her touch. I wouldn't say good-bye, and watched sullenly as they went on their way.

I hated to be thought of as my father's daughter and nothing more. I might have flounced off, but curiosity had always been my downfall, and now it bloomed inside my breast. I left behind the fish I'd bought for some street cats, then followed Maureen and Mr. Morris down Neptune Avenue to Ocean Parkway. It was a long walk. Their destination was the Church of the Guardian Angel, an imposing Gothic stone building. I had never been to a Catholic church before, and this one had rows of beautiful pine pews and carved fittings. It was a space that could accommodate more than three hundred worshipers. Today there were perhaps fifteen attendees, half of them people I recognized from the museum. The Durante brothers, wearing stylish black suits, stood up in place of Malia's father, a man she'd never known, and walked her down the aisle. There was the moody scent of incense, and dozens of candles were aglow. If an angel were ever to come to earth, I thought this would surely be the place he would choose for his arrival.

I ducked behind a column so that I might remain hidden from view during the service, not that anyone would notice me. All eyes were on Malia and her betrothed, both of whom stood like wondrous statues at the altar while the priest recited prayers in Latin. The prayers were like music, a river of words I didn't understand, though I recognized them as a blessing. From where I was concealed, Malia looked nothing like the

Butterfly Girl, that marvelous creature who perched on a wooden swing in the Museum of Extraordinary Things, resplendent in her orange and black costume, wings fashioned of silk and wire strapped in place of the arms she would have had if she'd been another girl. Now she wore a white taffeta dress, and a stunning veil of Portuguese-made lace tumbling down her back. Her groom stood beside her, a man of average height and appearance, love-struck, unable to take his eyes from his bride. He was a completely ordinary individual, not handsome or tall, and from bits of murmured conversation I overheard, I learned he was a streetcar driver. That was how they'd met, on a streetcar Malia and her mother had taken on an outing to Brighton Beach.

Many people cried during the ceremony, Maureen among them. She downright wept, and I was surprised to see her so emotionally wrought. Afterward, the guests rushed to congratulate both bride and groom before heading off to a small celebration at the groom's family's house. By then, I was halfway home. Because I couldn't bear to go back to my father's house, I went to the shore instead. I sat on a bench and breathed in the salt air. My gloved hands were folded on my lap, and the cotton fabric felt as if it had been spun from shards of glass. I knew what was inside of me: the green tendrils of jealousy. I wanted nothing more than to be an ordinary girl with the man I'd seen in the woods in love with me, though this seemed a more impossible occurrence than swimming out into Gravesend Bay, across the Atlantic Ocean to my father's homeland of France.

When Malia came to work the following day, I nodded a greeting. I did not offer my congratulations or ask why she appeared so radiant. I pretended I had never stood behind the column in the church to witness her joy. I noticed that she, too, went about her business as if nothing had changed. Because she could not wear a ring, her husband had given her a simple gold necklace, which was clasped around her throat. She acted as if she had always had this lovely ornament, and made no mention of it. She gracefully slipped on her costume and chatted with her mother in their pretty, birdlike language. If she felt my gaze upon her, I assume she was accustomed to being stared at, just as I was used to wanting what I could not have.

But all things changed, or so it was said. Maureen once told me she believed she was the last person in the world who might find happiness. She believed she didn't deserve it, she said, and had many times thought of throwing her life away, for it did not serve her well. Perhaps in the great scheme of things, another, more deserving person would be granted her time on earth. But each time she had considered ending her life, she'd had second thoughts. Who would have made your breakfast? she said to me. Who would have met the Wolfman when he first came into our yard, wearing his cloak, beaten by the world? Love happens in such a way, Maureen told me. It walks up to you, and when it does, you need to recognize it for what it is and, perhaps more important, for what it might become.

MAY 1911

THE OFFICERS had tramped through the garden, paying no attention to the runner beans, or the rows of lettuce, or to the huge bottle-green leaves of the squash plants, soon torn from their tendrils. The police in Coney Island could be hired as a personal squad for those willing to pay the price, and the Professor was among those who regularly made a donation on his own behalf so that he might run the museum as he pleased, unmolested by the authorities. It was a common enough practice, not just for reputable businessmen but for those with a more criminal intent, a world of con men and thieves. There were theater owners whose clientele had come to watch private shows of dancing naked women, only to be given knockout drops and robbed. Gambling houses where games of chance were rigged to ensure any and all players would lose. All of these establishments paid for the protection of the sheriff's men.

Upon seeing the photographer, the Professor sent one of the Durante brothers to fetch several officers. The lawmen arrived quickly, there to do the museum owner's bidding, for that was part of the bargain; they had their bully sticks at the ready, while the Professor and Eddie were still in the midst of a heated argument.

"If you've nothing to hide, why keep me out?" Eddie demanded.

"I won't be the one keeping you out," the Professor told him coldly. Though he was a liar, there was truth in his statement, for as soon as Eddie glanced over his shoulder, members of the sheriff's department were upon him. They wasted no time dragging him from the property.

He shouted that he had his rights, but in this garden clearly he did not, nor did he in all of Kings County. He cried out that he was being kept from his own property, for his camera and stand had fallen to the ground, but no one listened to his protestations. If he'd had ready cash for a payoff, he might have turned the situation around once they were out on Surf Avenue. But he had nothing to offer, and the officers did the job they had been paid to do, in which the goal was to dispose of him in such a way that he would never dare to return.

Coralie watched from her window, stunned. She had a wild urge to leap out and chase after them, and imagined grabbing the sword from the wall in her father's bedroom so she might fight off the officers. But when the Professor turned to gaze up into her window, a hand over his eyes to block out the sun, she ducked behind the muslin curtains, breathing hard, terrified he might spy her shadow. She was ashamed by her own lack of courage, yet she shivered there, immobilized, tears streaking her face. Where was the bravery the trainer Bonavita had insisted she possessed when she stood inside the lion's cage? Furious with herself, she tore off her gloves, then withdrew a needle from the sewing kit on her bedside table and stabbed it into the flesh between her fingers until there were drops of blood, each one a penance for her cowardice.

Later in the day, Coralie retrieved Eddie's camera, which had been pitched into the hydrangea bushes, along with the glass plates that had captured the images of the living wonders. One plate had cracked, but the others were safe enough, though wet with dew. Coralie stashed Eddie's belongings beneath the porch, then she went to her room and pulled down one of the curtains. She hurriedly returned to toss the curtain over the photography equipment to keep it from harm, weeping as she did so, as if it were a secret burial she was attending to.

That evening, Maureen called to her, suggesting they slip out to the porch, where they might be afforded some privacy. The Professor was in his study, still fuming, drinking too much rum. He had questioned Coralie after the incident. Had she ever met this young man who had dared to photograph the wonders? She vowed she had never before made his acquaintance, which was true enough. They had never formally been introduced.

"They took him over the bridge," Maureen confided, for she'd asked the Durante brothers to follow the police wagon and report back to her. "They treated him as you might expect. He did not come out as the winner of this encounter. The authorities made it clear that, should he dare to enter Brooklyn again, he'll find himself in the Raymond Street Jail, and that's a place no man deserves to see. Let this be the end of it, Cora, for it can only finish badly for one and all."

But it was not the end of it, not by far. The museum opened the following day. There were even fewer in attendance than anyone had expected, and several potential customers walked away rather than pay the price for a ticket, declaring forty cents to be an exorbitant fee. Still, it was the beginning of the season, with much to do to prepare for what they all hoped would be a more profitable summer, helped along by overflow crowds from Dreamland, which would reopen in all its glory on the last weekend of May.

The Professor made a special point to warn Coralie against strangers. He told her to report anyone who might be lurking about. They were in the parlor, beside the horrid cereus plant, its twisted brown form bare as sticks, its bitter scent dizzying. Coralie assured her father that she would do as he ordered, though she wished she dared ask what she was to make of the strangers who attended her private shows. She, indeed, looked out of sorts, her cheeks flushed and red, and the Professor insisted on testing her forehead for fever. The burning that consumed her, however, was not an illness, only the hatred she felt for him. All the same, his belief that she was afflicted suggested the beginnings of a plan. The following afternoon, she forced her fingers down her throat so that she might be sick and beg off her performance due to illness. She powdered her face so that she appeared infirm, and circled her eyes with coal so they seemed sunken and hot.

"Don't think this will be a regular occurrence," the Professor warned when he agreed to cancel the evening. "We need the income more than ever."

Coralie took the Professor's hand and kissed it, as if she were a dog willing to do his bidding. But dogs can bite no matter how well trained, and as soon as she went up to her room, Coralie brought out the keepsakes she had nabbed from the workshop desk. She did so every night, gazing at them, imagining how she might arrange a way to get them to those who were dearest to the drowned girl. Now she knew, her feigned illness would be the first step out the door.

The following morning, she said she was too ill to run errands, and was left in bed. It was Sunday, and the Professor had plans to visit one of the racetracks out on Long Island, where he often tried to double his money, or, at least, not lose it all. It was Maureen's one day off, and most likely she would spend the afternoon with Mr. Morris. Coralie quickly dressed. She peered down from her window to see that the liveryman had returned. This was luck indeed, for he was not merely a workman but also the means of her escape. The weather was warm, and the liveryman's shirt was off as he jumped down from the driver's bench to fasten his horse's lead to the fence post. Coralie could see what Maureen had whispered was indeed true—he had a great many wounds and scars, as well as a series of tattoos inked in deep reds and blues. On his back there was the image of a bird in flight, black wings stretched from one broad shoulder to the other.

He thought there was no one to spy him, and when men are alone they often present their truest selves. He whistled cheerfully as he set to his work, which consisted of bringing forth the carcass of a gigantic striped bass, one so large he could barely wrestle it out of his carriage. Surely it had been some fisherman's great prize and had cost a good price at market. A flock of birds had settled in the low-growing shrubbery. When they began their chirping, the liveryman took a moment from the work at hand to toss out a bit of his horse's feed.

"There you go, my dears," he said as the birds gathered round.

He had once informed Coralie that such birds were common starlings, black when resting in the shadows, but streaked a brilliant purple and blue and green when they wheeled across the sky. Two decades earlier, one hundred of their species had been brought from Europe, then released in Central Park. At first they were a novelty, with their lovely glittering feathers, but as their population grew, with thousands moving across the state and then the country, people came to despise them and consider them pests; there was even a call for starling potpie to be on the menu of every restaurant. The liveryman, however, believed they were equal to the sparrow and the robin, albeit misjudged and unappreciated.

When Coralie opened her window and called, the sound of her voice caught the liveryman by surprise. He turned and let out a soft shout.

Embarrassed when he spied her, he quickly reached for his jacket and pulled it on. "Miss, you shouldn't sneak up on a person. What if I'd been carrying a weapon and been taken off guard? I don't like to think what might have happened."

Coralie took hold of the cowhide bag she'd readied for this occasion. She opened her window wider and, before another word was said, climbed onto the roof, as she'd done so many times before to watch the crowds at Dreamland or to view the sunset. She was steady on her feet as she made her way to the porch overhang.

"Get back," the liveryman called, unnerved. He'd returned to work only grudgingly, for he despised his employer now.

Rather than listen, Coralie continued on toward the roof's edge, and there she grasped a branch of the pear tree. She shimmied down, and as she did the branches shook, driving the starlings into the sky.

"You should have listened to me when I said the river wasn't for swimming that night," the liveryman chided. "Will you at least listen to me now and stay where you belong?"

Coralie did no such thing but instead came to view the awesome form of the fish on the grass. "What's the use of this?"

A bass so large was frightening to see once it had been taken from its element. Yet this fish possessed an unearthly beauty. In the spray of sunlight that filtered through the leaves, the fish's scales shone a dazzling silver.

"This is nothing. Only a dead fish that stinks like any other." The liveryman took out a handkerchief to wipe his forehead.

"It appears to be something." Coralie had seen the Professor's tools, and the monsters he'd invented out of pieces. A chill went through her. "It seems my father wishes to create a sea creature that is half woman and half fish."

She waited in the garden while the liveryman dragged the fish down to the cellar, to be left outside the locked door. He'd brought along several bushels of ice, so the fish would stay cool in the dank corridor. He was merely following instructions, for the Professor had already sent out telegrams to the newspapers in which he promised to solve the Hudson Mystery. If he did not present a real mermaid on the last weekend in May, he would allow customers free access to his museum for the entire month of June, a bargain he never intended to honor, for such an arrangement would surely bankrupt him.

"You need to mind your business," the liveryman advised Coralie when he found she was still waiting for him. She had a defiant expression he recognized. Clearly she intended to do as she pleased.

"You need to take me where I want to go. To the man we have in common."

"Are you speaking of the Professor?" The liveryman tried a joke. "He's common enough."

"You know who I speak of. He told me you were the one who brought him here. That's a fact my father wouldn't care for, should he ever know your part in the photographer's finding his way to us."

Leaving the liveryman to think this over, Coralie retrieved Eddie's camera and plates, which she brought to the carriage.

"Fine, I'll take those to him," the liveryman allowed.

"No." Coralie stepped onto the carriage stair and drew herself up to the driver's seat. She sat calmly, with her hands folded. "I will."

The liveryman now entered into a frantic state. "Let's be reasonable. I've got the fish to deal with. As for you, this business will lead to ruin," he warned. "If I had a daughter, the last thing I'd want would be for her to know about the meanness in the world."

"If you had a daughter, you would likely want her to know what the world was like so that she might be able to live in it with open eyes."

The liveryman considered the girl's words. He had done terrible things in his life, most of which he strongly regretted. In Coralie's face, however, he saw an absolute faith in him. It was nothing he deserved, but it was most likely the reason he untied his horse, then climbed up beside his passenger.

"If I valued my life, I wouldn't consider this. You're lucky I don't believe myself worth saving."

Coralie could feel her heart pounding as the horse began to trot. Her plan had become a living thing, not air and thought, but flesh and blood. All at once she was in the center of her life, not hiding behind a curtain or eavesdropping with her ear pressed against a floorboard or a door. She ducked her head as they passed beneath the branches of the pear tree. The whole world smelled so fresh and new she gasped when inhaling the green-tinged scent. Sunlight filtered directly into her face, so that she had to blink in the light. Still she saw everything quite clearly as they headed along the road: the crush of afternoon shoppers, the streetcar barreling toward Coney Island Avenue, the shadow of the liveryman as he whistled at his horse, urging the old steed to quicken its pace, driving them out of Kings County with no idea that he'd already been saved.

EDDIE WAS half-asleep, slumped in the battered old chair in the corner, when there was a knock at the door. He did not move or respond in any way. He barely heard the rapping through the haze of drink. The dog, which hadn't been walked or given any attention, made a sad woofing response as he lay at his master's feet. Coralie waited in the dim stairwell, comforted by the chatter of birds echoing from the tack room in the stable. The day had grown unseasonably warm and she wasn't properly dressed for the weather in her black wool dress and heavy coat and the cotton gloves that made her fingers itch in weather such as this. She suffered from the heat, and with anxiety, but she pushed her nerves away. When there was no answer from inside the loft, she rapped on the door again. The future was spun from moments such as this. If she backed away, it might all unravel. She knocked again, more urgently. There was Eddie's voice at last, but his reply was far from pleasant. He shouted that whoever was bothering him should go the hell away and leave him in peace.

The door was unlocked, which seemed foolish in this area of Manhattan, where crime was rampant along the docks. But perhaps Eddie assumed that the worst had already happened to him, and had no fear of any further abuse. Coralie had been worried by figures lurking on Tenth Avenue, but she had been let out in the street with no recourse, for the liveryman insisted he would give her a ride back to Brooklyn only after dark, when he was sure the Professor wouldn't spy his carriage. She had no choice but to go forward, and so she pushed open the door to peer inside. It was afternoon, but the room was dark, the curtains drawn and no lantern lit. The only bit of brightness drifted down from the domed ceiling window, slashes of light that dashed across the horsehair plaster walls. Mitts rose upon seeing Coralie, trotting over to greet her. She recognized the dog who had followed her through the woods and who now yipped cheerfully, clearly glad for a visitor.

When Eddie looked up he thought he had conjured her or perhaps he was not truly awake. There she was, the woman from his dreams. He leaned forward, puzzled and grateful in equal measure, wondering if the gin he'd been drinking was the cause of his fantasy. Despite his drunken state, he realized she had brought his beloved camera, which he'd mourned, believing it to be lost forever. A grin broke through his somber expression.

As for Coralie, she now grasped what the police had done to him, for as Eddie shifted forward she saw that his face was blue with bruises. Far worse, one hand had bandages that covered a wooden splint. Eddie gazed down at himself, disgusted by his circumstances. "They broke it with a two-by-four."

In the corner were the empty bottles of booze he'd been nursing, as much for the ache of failure inside him as for the pain in his hand. Coralie blamed herself for his condition; she'd done nothing to protect him. She went to him and sat in his lap, her arms around his neck, face buried against his scruffy shirt, still stained with blood. She could feel the heat inside him, and the stirring of his desire. He was experienced with women, but certain she was an innocent he didn't act on his desire, not as he would have wished to. He had no idea how many books she'd read in her father's library, with graphic illustrations that she mimed when performing in the tank. It was pretense, meaningless to her. She knew how to excite her viewers, but every move she made was heartless and cold. The chill water, the icy glass, the way she touched herself, all of it was only to thrill her admirers. With Eddie she did not wish to disappear, to become another element, removed from herself. She slipped off her coat and her gloves, relieved it was too dark for him to glimpse her hands. Let him think she was an ordinary woman, and let her be so on this one afternoon. He had no idea that she was a monster and a monster's daughter.

He murmured she was too good for him; he was a man with a spotty past and a future that was likely going nowhere. Coralie told him the past was of no consequence, and that the future was unwritten. They curled up around each other, and time meant nothing to them. If Eddie could have broken his watch and stopped the movement of the hours, he would have. When he insisted she talk about herself, she avoided personal details and instead told him stories of the world she'd known: of a wonder who drank gin for breakfast and

slept with two wives; of the Queen of the Bees, whose poor, abandoned hive had pined for her; of a man who had no fear of lions,
though he'd lost his arm to one. She herself was ashamed of all she'd
seen and done, and of the many ways her audience had violated her
as they watched her in their drunken state of ardor. But for all the
wickedness she'd known, she'd never been kissed. Once they began,
she could not stop. How strange it was that Eddie, who'd been with so
many women, now seemed shy, while she burned with each kiss. She
urged him on, unbuttoning her blouse. He groaned with the delight
of having her in his arms, intoxicated and somewhat maddened. He
kissed her more and more deeply, then forced himself to back off.
He'd wanted her for so long, even before he knew she was real, but he
wouldn't allow himself to take advantage of the situation.

"You don't know me," Coralie insisted. "I'm not an angel. I sometimes doubt if I am even human."

Eddie laughed, not at all understanding her meaning, so she begged
him to light the lantern. If he wanted to know who she was, then she
would reveal herself, though she wept as she did. She showed him her
hands, what she considered her deformity, the flesh that separated
her and made her different, but also made her herself, the woman
he didn't want to let go of, not even after hours had passed with her
in his arms and the liveryman shouted up that it was time for her to
leave. She left behind the blue wool coat, neatly folded, on the chair,
and the handkerchief containing Hannah's belongings on the table.
He examined the tokens, holding them tenderly. Two black buttons, a
comb, hairpins, a golden locket on a chain, and two keys that he held
in the palm of his hand.

EIGHT

THE BLUE THREAD

* * * * * * * * *

I HAD ALWAYS been a good student. Even in the art of rebellion, I looked for those who might instruct me. I listened not to the rabbis but to my employer, Hochman, who seemed wiser in the ways of the world, an expert in the arena of human nature. Hochman suggested that each person had the option to remake the past as he or she remembered it. In this way, an individual who had betrayed someone dear to him could escape the pangs of guilt and remorse. One who had suffered great loss could manage to go on, despite the burdens of his life. He could forget certain details and focus on others, and in doing so could take strength from the past, despite the hardships he had encountered.

I saw that my father did not possess this capacity. He was caught in his love for my mother, a fish in a net. He could not remake the fire, or the ashes, or the cold dark night when we ran away from our village. The past clung to him, as it was and always would be, a shroud, a sorrow, a loss that was never-ending.

He had loved my mother, and the present and the future could not exist without her. I saw his struggle, but from a distance. I stood on the other *side of the riverbank, a fisherman with a cold, clear eye. I had witnessed what such emotions could do to a person, how they could rule his life, and ruin it by doing so. I learned my lesson in watching his grief.*

Love, for me, did not exist.

I'd had a series of encounters over the years. Lust was a story I knew. There were many women I took to bed for the night. I yearned for them in the moment, but in the morning, any lover I'd had was already claimed by the past, even if she was still calling my name.

I'd forgotten each woman before I left her room.

Now I thought of nothing but Coralie. I wondered what had filled my thoughts before. I dreamed of the trout I'd once caught. I begged him to tell me what I must do to win her. But my begging went unanswered, for even in my dreams he was a fish and I was a man, and all he knew remained a secret.

I had asked to take Coralie's portrait on the day she came to me, but she'd refused. You need to want the person that I am, she told me, not the one you capture. But I felt as though I was the one who had been captured. This was why I dreamed of the trout, imagining that he might hold the cure for what I felt, the piercing of my heart.

I hadn't grasped why my father always brought my mother's photograph to his workplace or why he propped it up on our table so that he might dine with her each night. Now I understood. She was his everything, and she was gone. This was the kind of love that overtook a man's daily life, wrapping him in knots.

Desire was too churlish and stupid a word for what I felt. I longed for Coralie. No wonder I had closed myself off. Love like this was all consuming. I found that I was jealous of the strangest things—sunlight, streets, curtains, even her clothing, anything that was close to her. The month of May was slipping away, and I didn't even notice it. Days and weeks meant nothing to me. I lived within my own hurt feelings, in a cave that was too dark to see the outline of the trees that filled with green leaves.

I took my dog and walked for miles. I thought that by doing so I might break the spell I was under. Walking had always been a tonic to me, steadying my spirit and my mind. But now as I went onward, I grew worse, as if I'd been enchanted. Somehow I had lost myself in my longings. Then I remembered what Hochman had told me when he read my palm. I had the river inside me. I followed alongside the river that was as much a part of me as anything in my life. In the grasp of my passion, I felt I was a madman, and perhaps I was looking for the same in a companion, for I began to think that the hermit might help me understand the intoxication that had befallen me. I'd heard that failed love had driven him into the woods, away from human company.

I didn't need a psychic talent to find him. He was at one of his favorite fishing spots.

"Did you come to see if I was dead yet?" He handed me the bottle of whiskey he carried with him, and I took a gulp. "You're the one that looks like hell. What happened to your hand?"

"Some fellows broke it."

I'd been to a doctor who'd set and bound it, warning that although I would regain some use of it, it might well be weakened and misshapen. I was fortunate that the police assumed every man was right-handed, which I was not. I readied my line with my left hand, and the hermit was impressed with my ability to get things done so neatly. Perhaps my art would not be completely undermined if one of my hands was functional. Still, I hadn't yet found the nerve to work my camera, just in case what little talent I had left had been broken along with my bones.

"Why'd they do that?" my companion asked. For all his alleged meanness he truly didn't understand the callousness and cruelty of others. "For the fun of it? Or did you betray someone or mess with the wrong sorts?"

"*I fell in love. That's my crime. With the mermaid.*"

"*You can't be blamed for that,*" the hermit said soberly.

"*You've been in love?*" I ventured to ask.

The hermit looked at me darkly.

"*Not that it's any of my business,*" I added.

"*Do you think I want to talk about my life?*" Beck asked in return. "*I came here to escape my existence. I couldn't stand the way people in the city treated each other, how they managed to ruin everything they touched. But now it seems the city is following me. Soon enough they'll pave beneath these trees we're standing under.*"

Beck's wife, Annetje, was also from an original Dutch family. She became ill with lung disease before she reached the age of twenty, and died in the bed they shared, one Beck's father had crafted as a wedding present from the wood of an enormous tulip tree that was said to have been planted on the day Henry Hudson first encountered the native Lenapes in 1609. It was their word for island that gave Manhattan its name, for it was the great island then, as it has remained. The Lenape people were accomplished archers and hunters who believed that the Milky Way, which they called the Starry Path, guided the souls of the departed on their journey to the world beyond ours, somewhere in the sky.

Beck abandoned his life soon after his wife's death, leaving his small farmhouse to fall into ruin. The neighbors helped themselves to his sheep and goats. The chickens became wild, and Beck occasionally found their descendants nesting in the woods. His wife had babied the chickens and let them stay inside during storms, yet they now lived hardily in what was wilderness, while she, who'd been so young and healthy, was gone after an illness of a mere two weeks.

"*I didn't know you had a wife,*" I said. "*I'm sorry for your loss.*"

"*What do you know?*" Beck muttered.

"*Apparently nothing. I'd be grateful for any instruction.*"

The hermit laughed out loud. "You're talking to the wrong man."

"Tell me this, do you regret it?"

"The lung disease? Are you an idiot?" he growled. "Of course I do. The weather was bad and our home poorly heated. Oh, I regret it, more than I can say. If I were a rich man, maybe the illness wouldn't have befallen her."

I shook my head, for that wasn't what I'd meant. I meant did he regret his marriage and the pain it caused him to have had a great love. When I explained, he glared at me. "Are you asking if I would have been better off if I'd never met my wife, or married her, or lost her? I'll tell you this, a day with her was better than a life without her."

I was stunned by the emotion in his voice. I had not expected so much from such a gruff fellow, and we both fell deep into our own thoughts. As we sat in silence, a covey of what I thought were quail flew up from the bushes, and we both turned, startled, as if a ghost were near. I voiced my initial notion, that spirits had been close by.

"I wouldn't mind being haunted. I'd be happy for it," Beck said as we watched the game birds trotting into the ferns.

When I left he offered me his congratulations.

"On what?" I asked, confused.

"Being human."

I made my way down to the river. I had the oddest feeling that just as we had become friends, we had also said our good-byes, and would never see one another again. Perhaps that was why he'd told me the intimate details of his life, so that someone would remember him. I noticed tracks in the mud and felt a shiver down my back. Possibly the birds had been startled not by a spirit but by a flesh-and-blood ghoul. Mitts charged off, following the trail all the way to the Old Post Road. As it turned out the game birds we'd spied weren't quail but wild chickens perching in the undergrowth. There were signs that someone had been past recently, for

I could see the fresh tracks of a horse whose rider had made his way down the old road. It seemed an odd coincidence. I wondered if I had been followed to this place, and, just as curious a thought, I wondered what reason anyone might have for doing so.

The following day, I still couldn't shake the odd feeling I'd had when I left Beck. I wondered if some of the talent I'd had as a boy had stayed with me, and I could still read the thoughts and fortunes of men. It was possible that my concern upon leaving him had been meaningful and he was in danger. I was too worried to let it be. I headed back to the woods, in such a hurry I didn't bother to bring Mitts along. I had a panicked feeling, as if I'd no understanding of the world or of being alive. I was fairly certain I'd wasted a good portion of my life. Only now did I realize what the hermit was telling me, that love was never a regret. I felt the need to thank him for speaking to me so frankly.

I'd let love take me like a river, and carry me forth, and I wouldn't fight it any longer.

Beck wasn't at any of his usual fishing spots. I shouted out for him, but heard nothing in response. When I went up into the woods I saw only charred wood in his fire pit. The air was scented with a sulfuric stink. There was a tin plate on the ground and a wash of silence in the clearing, except for the low calling of doves. Then I knew I was right, and that we had indeed said our last good-bye. I knew that men told you the truth for one of two reasons: when they wished to be rid of what they couldn't bear to carry, or when they wished to include you in what they knew so their stories wouldn't be lost. I would always know that his wife was so kindhearted she'd taken the chickens into their home during spells of bad weather. I would know that he was filled with emotion, as if he were still a young man in love.

I found him in the ferns, facedown, splattered with mud. He was wearing his long underwear. Nothing more. His feet were bare. Someone must have surprised him, possibly when he was sleeping, for I'd never seen him without his boots. There was blood on the ground, and in his hair, where a shovel or a club had split his skull open. When I turned him over, he was stiff, and I could tell he'd been gone for a while. Perhaps he had been murdered soon after I last saw him. I'd thought the trail I'd found was leading away, disappearing into the weeds. But it appeared I'd been wrong. It had led to him instead. The rider may have been waiting for me to pass him by so he might find his way to the hermit's shack under cover of the night.

I leaned down to close his eyes, already rheumy and paling. That was when I saw that his mouth had been sewn closed with blue thread. I wondered what Beck had seen or known that had brought him such a horrible fate. Someone did not want him to tell all he knew.

I had no choice but to do as he said he'd done. I removed the thread with a knife I found among his pots and pans, telling myself it was only fishing line I was unhooking. But I wept as I did so. Then and there I decided I'd give up fishing. The sport and hungers of men seemed wretched and insincere compared to the run of life in the river. I'd do no harm to any of its inhabitants from now on.

I buried Beck in a high meadow, where the land was not as marshy and there was a long, sweeping view of the river. I used an old shovel with a half-broken handle, and had only my one good hand, so the going was difficult. I didn't care. I was streaked with dirt when I was done and sweating through my clothes. My bad hand cramped, and my left shoulder was sore. I knew he wouldn't have wanted a coffin, he'd have wanted me to bury him in the earth, and I did so. That is the way of my people; we bury our own dead as a final and lasting gift. I said the prayers I'd been taught as a boy and tore my shirt, for this was the only way I knew how to mourn. Standing there, I felt I had lost something more than a man. It seemed a part of our city had been buried with him. The part I loved best.

Beck had told me to destroy his house when he was no longer in our world. He said that the Manhattan he knew would be gone when he was, and perhaps he was right in that. The villages that lined the highlands of upper Manhattan had already begun to drift into each other as the city moved northward. Soon there would be sidewalks in the last patches of the woods, and buildings to house families, and skyscrapers and highways. No one would know that deer had made their home here once, and that coyotes were spied in the dark, or that there had been wolves that had ventured down the river on those rare occasions when it froze solid in the most brutal winter months.

The wolf-dog was chained to the porch, frantic. I assumed he had seen the murder of his master, and because he was shackled he could do nothing to defend Beck. I thought he might attack me, but, when I set him off his chain, he merely darted into the woods. Good, I thought, for that was what the old man had wanted, for the beast to be set free.

I then burned the shack to the ground, as Beck had asked. I had the rain barrel readied to ensure the flames wouldn't get out of control. My bad hand was aching even more, and my heart was aching as well, but I set to my work with a vengeance. Beck's house was a flimsy edifice, and it went up easily. I'd seen enough of fire, and I hoped this one would be the last I ever saw. Afterward, I poured water on the remaining embers in case a flame or two should survive.

It was near dark, but I had no fear of these woods. I felt I had inherited them for whatever time there was left for them. It was then I saw Beck's wolf staring at me through the smoke. If there was anyone in the world who might understand who I'd been and how I'd lived my life it was this creature. We couldn't go back to the lives we were meant to live. Beck had wanted the wolf to be free, but there was no wild for him to return to and *no man to be his master, and he stood there uneasily, between worlds. I called him to me, and he came. I had said I would care for him, and I would do so. We walked downtown together, not quite companions, wary of each other, but together all the same. When we reached the more popu-lated avenues, I found a rope on the street and looped it around his neck so that he wouldn't startle when he saw carts and automobiles. He was sur-prisingly calm. Though the horses in the stable below my studio panicked at the sight of him, the wolf ignored them, as he ignored Mitts, choosing to slink beneath the table, where he made a sort of den for himself. I do not know if he had a name, but I called him North, an appellation I think Beck would have approved of, for it was the name the Dutch called the Hudson River when they first came here, when men set to changing the world in their image, and gave all the wild things their own names.*

MAY 1911

THEY WOULD come for the body in broad daylight, during the afternoon show, for they were less likely to be seen in the midst of a crowd. The Professor would be engaged at this time, his attention on the flow of customers. No one would expect thievery, if that was what it could be called, in the middle of the day.

"This is a task best done by ghouls," the liveryman said, for even he, with his criminal history, was queasy over the work that lay ahead.

"Then that's what we'll be," Eddie said grimly.

"And how will we get into the cellar, if you don't mind me asking?" When Eddie held up the keys Coralie had given him, the liveryman grinned. "I see I should give you a bit of credit. I won't ask where you got those, brother."

They had made a pact to work together, for this one day alone. They would never again speak of it, or speak of each other.

"What would make a person sew the mouth shut of a person who'd been murdered?" Eddie asked the liveryman as they traveled toward their destination.

"It's a message. Ask no questions."

"It was done to Hannah, the drowned girl."

"No. I saw her for myself."

"A person with a kind heart removed the thread. It may be he was killed for doing so."

"Perhaps he knew more than he should have. Or at least someone believed he did."

Eddie was now struck by the story of the man who'd been stuck in the mud; how the hermit had watched him struggle to break free. Someone had deposited Hannah in the river. Could this have been the man? "If that's true it doesn't serve to drive me away," Eddie told his companion.

"I wouldn't expect so. You're stubborn." The liveryman grinned. "It's part of our heritage. If our people weren't stubborn we would have disappeared by way of our enemies' hands long ago."

Eddie's obstinate nature surfaced in his refusal to accept the physician's verdict that his right hand might be useless in the future. At present, however, his disability was irrefutable. He had therefore stowed his camera in a cupboard, and he felt the loss of it even more deeply than he did the loss of his hand.

Eddie hadn't expected the liveryman to be so companionable, or so intelligent in his views. "You seem sure of yourself," he said. "I think we know each other well enough that I should call you by your right name."

"Eastman is right enough." The liveryman gave him a sly look. "As right as Eddie is at any rate. Names don't matter. Our God knows how to call us to him when he wants us, it's best to remember that."

They didn't speak much afterward; each man was lost in his own private thoughts. Eddie had worried about leaving Mitts alone with the hermit's wolf, so he'd locked the dog in a stall in the stable, and he couldn't help but think of the pathetic whining he'd heard when he left for the day. Once they'd entered Brooklyn, both men's imaginings couldn't help but turn to the horrors of the Raymond Street Jail, a turreted Victorian building that was damp and freezing cold, said to house the worst of criminal life, along with the largest, most vicious rats in New York.

"I've served my last term in jail," the liveryman mused. "I'll do myself in before I go back. Five years of my life gone to shit, watching the river and counting out the time, knowing I could never get it back. After this business today is done, I'm considering joining the military. It's a better life for a man such as myself."

"I thought you couldn't leave your pipe." Eddie tried his best to be civil in referring to the liveryman's weakness for opium.

"I don't wish to be a slave anymore. I'm switching to gin."

They both had a laugh over that.

"And you?" the liveryman asked. "What do you intend?"

"Once I've done what I promised, I'll go back for Coralie. If she'll have me." He noticed the liveryman's dour expression. "I take it you don't think she'll leave with me?"

"Do you think it's her choice?"

"It should be," Eddie remarked. "And it will."

"Then you'd best make sure you get rid of him," Eddie's companion told him. "I know him well, and what's his is his."

All that morning she could hardly keep away from the window. When she returned from Manhattan, she'd slipped back into the house before her father came home, but sooner or later a person breaking the Professor's rules was bound to be caught.

"You're a jittery one," Maureen said. They were making fritters to serve during the living wonders' tea break, but Coralie had dumped the dough in too quickly and the oil had splashed up, nearly burning them both.

"Spring fever," Coralie assured her.

Maureen gave her a sidelong glance. "Is that what it is?"

Coralie offered a compliment to deflect attention from her nervous state. "I'm not a cook, though you've tried your best to teach me."

Fortunately, there was much to be done, and Maureen was too busy to investigate any further. She was soon enough taking tickets at the entryway of the museum. Coralie had no one watching over her actions and was free to steal into the yard at the appointed hour. Eddie was already there, crouched beside the hydrangeas. Maureen had added vinegar to the ground to turn the blooms bluer, and they blurred against the color of the sky. As soon as she saw him, Coralie felt as she did when she was about to dive into the river; somewhere inside her there was a gasping, thrilling release of earth and air. She went to stand beside him in the grass. She smelled like salt to him, and some delicious variety of sweet, caramels. As for Coralie, she noticed everything about him in that instant, the cast on his hand, the shape of his head, the broad width of his shoulders, the way he gazed at her with his dark gold-flecked eyes, as if she had never been a monster possessing a monster's heart and history.

The liveryman had left his carriage down the street, and he now joined them in the garden. It would take two strong men to complete this task, both with steady hands and strong stomachs. Coralie felt a stab of fear. She imagined what might happen if her father discovered them, but she forced herself to push such thoughts aside. They went into the kitchen the way a dreamer enters into a dream, slowly at first, then all in a rush. The liveryman led Eddie down the plummeting stairs to the cellar. They had no idea of how much time they had, and when Maureen might return from the ticket booth, so every instant mattered. Eddie gazed over his shoulder and saw the darkness close in on them as Coralie shut the door, ensuring that anyone entering the kitchen wouldn't wonder if someone was in the cellar. Eddie quickly put the keys to work. Two turns of the locks and they were in.

"Don't look at anything," Eastman muttered. "Trust me, brother. You'll think you're in hell if you see where you are."

They went directly to the wooden box and lifted it from the table. Nearby, the enormous bass was being kept on ice, its fish blood drained into a bucket. The ice had melted and some water gushed out of the makeshift coffin. Eddie tried his best to pay no attention to the skulls of varying sizes set upon the shelf, or the unborn child with abnormalities in its face and limbs that floated in a jar of pale yellow formaldehyde.

"Work, don't look around," the liveryman reminded him.

And so, Eddie turned his attention solely to the task at hand as the two men carried the coffin through the narrow door of the workshop. They managed to climb the stairs with the liveryman leading the way, the weight of the coffin resting on Eddie's shoulder. Coralie guided them through the kitchen, and as she did Eddie took note of the plates and cups, the mops and brooms in a corner, napkins and tablecloths, sweets ready for tea, the stuff of everyday life. And yet amid these homely items Eddie's thoughts turned to darker things— blood, and sorrow, and men who had no aversion to sewing through flesh with coarse thread. Before he had time to gather his thoughts, they were in the garden, the light so bright it brought tears to his eyes. The hydrangeas were so blue it seemed the sky had fallen. Coralie kissed him quickly, then whispered that she had given him her heart. It was not possible to live without one's heart, yet she was smiling when she backed away. He thought about the first time he had seen her in this same place, as she came onto the porch, how it seemed as if he'd known her for a thousand years, and how it seemed that way still.

There were voices echoing, as customers on line for entry into the museum chattered to one another. They could hear the raucous calls of seagulls, those savage creatures, for birds circled above them. As they went on through the garden, the men inhaled the straw-like scent of lions from the cages of Dreamland across the street, and the sour, brackish odor of the sea, for it was low tide. They hurried from the yard, out to the street, where they stowed the box in the carriage. The plan was for Coralie to blame the liveryman. Eastman would then disappear. But now leaving her behind seemed all wrong. Eddie could see her gazing after them as Eastman shouted for him to get the hell onboard. The horse went full out when commanded to gallop, and still Eddie looked back, and still he saw her form, the swimmer from the river, the woman who had come to him the way a dream does, unbidden and uncalled for, impossible to let go of.

The horse was sweating when they crossed back over the bridge, racing to get out of Coney Island. They stopped beyond the marsh, to make certain the coffin was in place and the contents would arrive safely. It was broiling hot by then, and both men stood there hatless, sleeves rolled up, sweating through their clothes.

"Let me do it," Eastman said when it came to removing the cover and peering inside. "I've seen terrible things. One more won't do me any harm."

Eddie was grateful for the offer, but he said it was his duty. In the end, they lifted the cover together to survey Hannah's form. It was a shock to see the girl's pale, lifeless body. They said the mourning prayers together as well, as if they were indeed brothers, and then they set to leaving Brooklyn. Most men, Eddie had learned, were too complicated to judge. He would leave such things to heaven. He knew only that, if he were in battle, he would want the liveryman beside him. Moses Levy had told him that all men saw what they wished to see, and that was the purpose of a photograph, to show the irrefutable truth of the world as well as its beauty.

He leapt down from the seat when they reached the funeral home on Essex Street, and while the coffin was carried inside by the undertaker's sons, Eddie and the liveryman shook hands. The liveryman had sold his other horses that morning to another stable. He'd opened all the windows and watched his birds take flight. He had nothing left but the clothes he wore, his carriage, and this one horse, Jackson, an ancient bay no other stableman would want.

"It's not Eastman. The family name is Osterman," the carriage man said before he turned his old horse to trot along Essex to Grand Street, taking him as far as he could get from the life he'd led so far. "First name Edward. There's another thing we share."

"Between the two of us, the name is yours alone," Eddie admitted. "As for me, I was born Ezekiel Cohen."

THE TREES were in full leaf and the lilacs bloomed in great purple masses on the morning when those who had loved Hannah Weiss gathered at Mt. Zion Cemetery in Maspeth, Queens. Two black carriages had been hired, one to carry the coffin, the other to transport Mr. Weiss and his daughter, Ella. It was a lovely, bright day, but perhaps it would have been more fitting had the weather been gloomy. If that were so and sheets of rain had fallen, Mr. Weiss's wailing might not have sounded so loudly, bringing the other mourners to tears as he fell to his knees. There were nearly fifty people in attendance, many of them girls who had worked alongside Hannah and Ella, as well as several officers of the Hebrew Free Burial Association, the organization paying for the funeral, including the carriages and the horses draped with purple ribbons and black netting. A representative from the Workmen's Circle had been sent to deliver their membership's deepest sympathies and an envelope of cash that would help the family. From where Eddie stood, at the rear of the crowd, his battered hat in hand, he recognized the representative as Isaac Rosenfeld. He made certain to steer clear, but when Rosenfeld caught sight of him, the other man wound his way around the gathering so he might come to stand beside Eddie. As the rabbi offered up the mourning prayers, both men stared straight ahead.

"I heard you found her," Rosenfeld remarked.

Eddie shrugged, embarrassed. "A little late."

"Late or not, the Weisses needed to set her to rest."

Eddie wished he could erase the moment when he'd stood on the threshold of the Weisses' flat to hand the old man the gold locket. "I wish you'd never hired me," he'd confessed.

"It was the right thing." Weiss had turned the locket over in his palm. "You did what you were supposed to do. Now you'll find who did this to her."

"That's not what I do. I'm not a detective."

There was no point in going to the police, certainly not in Brooklyn. Eddie most likely would end up in jail if he offered the slightest complaint against Coralie's father. Even if he did, the worst the Professor might be accused of was possession of a body; a fine would be levied, little more. As for the men of the Tenth Precinct in Chelsea, they were not inclined to help those such as Hannah who might be associated with union activity. People disappeared and that was that. Once a corpse was discovered, there was no further inquiry. The matter was settled. But it wasn't, and Eddie knew it. He thought of the message of the blue thread, Beck in his mud-splattered long underwear, the flattened ferns around the hermit's body.

"You're better than a detective," Weiss insisted when Eddie had tried to beg off. "Your father said you would find out what happened to Hannah, and I won't rest in peace until you do." He gave Eddie a fierce look, eye to eye, man to man. "And you know as well as I, neither will you."

Eddie, always prone to insomnia, hadn't slept since they'd carried Hannah from that wretched workroom. He feared his dreams, filled with violent imaginings of what he might do should he ever come upon the cold-blooded killer who'd dared to take up a needle and thread to quiet the dead. He'd tried to pull himself together before attending the funeral, but his clothes were untidy and he hadn't shaved. His good hand seemed to have a tremor.

"You're in poor condition." Rosenfeld took note of his old companion's disheveled appearance, surprising Eddie with his concern. "Broke your hand?"

"It was broken for me."

Rosenfeld handed over a card that carried the address of the Workmen's Circle. "If you find out anything, contact me. Or if you need anything."

"You've got the wrong person. I'm the fellow you despise."

"Don't forget how long I've known you." Eddie had taken out his watch, which had continued to tell perfect time despite the broken face. Rosenfeld nodded, a smile at his lips. "Still have that, I see."

A flush of embarrassment crossed Eddie's face, for here was the one person who was well aware of how he'd come to possess the watch. The funeral was ending, and before Rosenfeld went to pay his respects to the family, he clapped his old companion on the back. "I've got the right person, brother."

Eddie watched as the mourners departed. A few people lingered: some of the girls who had worked in the Asch Building, along with a young man wearing a frayed jacket with a black mourning band wound around his arm. Eddie took the opportunity to follow a path leading to Moses Levy's grave, a site he hadn't visited since his mentor's death. Stalks of milkweed grew wild in the area, and Eddie pulled the weeds clustered around Levy's headstone. It was the least he could do for a man who had given him so much. He thought with gratitude about the night when he'd first encountered Levy, for he didn't like to imagine whom he might have become otherwise.

He left Mt. Zion and began the walk back toward the Second Avenue El, which would take him across the Queensboro Bridge, which had opened two years earlier to span the East River and cross into Manhattan. In the past, Eddie had journeyed to Queens County so that he might try his hand fishing in Jamaica Bay, but the varieties of fish once so common there, enormous schools of sheepshead and black drum, had all but disappeared. As he walked along now, he did his best to let the act of walking clear his mind. Yet he had a strange, spooked feeling. Perhaps he had been unnerved by visiting Moses's grave, for an odd brand of loneliness had settled upon him as he was leaving the cemetery.

He turned onto a nearly deserted road, the sun beating down on his black hat and coat. As he continued, he paid attention to his surroundings, as Hochman had taught him to do. *Listen, and you'll hear a story being told, one you may need to know.* Upon hearing a rustle behind him, Eddie stopped, as if to adjust the wrappings on his hand, taking the opportunity to peer behind him. He spied the young man who had lingered at the funeral, who now ducked behind a stable. He wondered if this was the man Beck had noticed in the muck near the river, and if he had found himself a murderer. Instead of continuing on, Eddie walked back toward the stable, going around the far side. He picked up a branch from a chestnut tree and approached his stalker, surprising him from behind, pushing him up against the shingled wall, the branch across his throat.

"Get off!" the younger man cried, choking out the words. He was only twenty-one or twenty-two, clearly unused to a fight. Eddie had no trouble keeping him in check, the branch pressed harder against his neck. "I've done nothing to you!" the young man managed to croak.

This man was a stranger to Eddie. "Why are you following me?"

"For Hannah. I think I know what happened to her."

Eddie dropped the branch away. The young man bent over, coughing, his hand clutching his neck.

"How would you know anything?" Eddie asked when the other man had begun to recover.

"We were in love. We planned to marry. She wasn't ready to tell her father, so we kept it to ourselves."

This was the fellow R had mentioned when Eddie interviewed her, the man Hannah had loved. His name was Aaron Samuels, and he'd been a tailor, but no more.

"I can't go back to my life. Not with what I know and what I let her do. We thought we could do what the unions couldn't. She was meeting with someone that morning, a representative for the owners. She had proof they were locking workers into the sewing rooms. I'd helped her, God forgive me. I removed one of the locked doorknobs from the tenth floor—it was on the door that led to the fire escape—and she had it with her. If they refused to change the conditions, she would do her best to go to the city representative for the Lower East Side, Alfred E. Smith, and beg for his help." Samuels broke down. He chided himself for his own idiocy and neglect. "I should have gone, but she thought she'd have a better chance of getting the boss's people to show up. They'd consider her less of a threat. Because she was young and pretty and a girl, I believed they'd think she was harmless."

"You know nothing about the person responsible?"

Samuels became agitated, and his dark eyes flashed. "If I did, don't you think I would have found him?"

They began to walk together toward the El train, both deep in thought. There were factories along the route, and some vacant areas in which crickets had begun to call.

"Her sister said she ran off to get something to eat before work," Eddie recalled.

"She was meeting him then. Before work. She didn't want Ella to know."

"So it was somewhere close by."

"The alley behind Greene Street."

Eddie's brow furrowed. "Why didn't you say so before?"

"I didn't think it mattered," Aaron Samuels said. "It was only an alley."

"Anything more?"

"She told me not to worry. She always carried a spool of blue thread with her for luck."

Eddie had returned the gold locket to Mr. Weiss but had asked to keep Hannah's other possessions. Hochman always said what a person carried revealed more about his soul than his affiliations with any philosophy or religion. When Eddie came home from the funeral, he arranged Hannah's belongings on his worktable. First the blue coat, then the hairpins and comb, and last the black buttons. He studied them, but he saw nothing unusual. Certainly, there was something beyond his vision and his understanding. He took out his camera, and though he struggled to work with his splint, he managed by tying his hand, splint and all, directly to the camera with a length of rope.

Each object looked ordinary enough through his lens. Once the plates had been developed and the prints readied, he tacked them to the wall to study them while they were still wet. The blue coat was in surprisingly good condition, girlish and hopeful, with its round collar and four gold buttons. The comb and pins made him recall that Ella had told him her sister combed her hair a hundred strokes each night. He turned his attention to the close-up photograph of the extra buttons, for they seemed an anomaly, too large and mannish for a young woman's clothing. Each had a star in the middle with holes at the points in which there were bits of frayed black thread. He looked more closely at these bits of uneven thread. Then, quite suddenly, he understood that Hannah had torn them from her attacker's coat.

He felt the swell of excitement he'd experienced as a runner for Hochman when he began to puzzle out the whereabouts of a missing husband or fiancé. He searched the cluttered tabletop for his magnifying glass, then set to work examining his photographs from the day of the fire. When the room became dim, he lit a lantern and several candles. He sifted through photographs he'd taken until he came upon a carriage pulled by two fine black horses. He brought the candle closer, though it dripped wax upon the print. He hadn't looked carefully enough when he first developed the image. He'd had so many from that day, and his eyes had burned with cinders. Now he recognized the dark-haired man gazing out from behind the velvet curtains of the carriage as Harry Block. He was the attorney for several owners of garment factories near Washington Square, so it was not out of the question for him to be in the area on the day of the fire. Upon closer inspection, Eddie saw that the man holding on to the rear of the carriage was carrying a thick bully stick, meant to do grave damage if anyone in the despairing mob rushed those making their escape.

The man holding the club was the one who'd chased Eddie from the scene on that day. The same man who had tried to rob him outside McSorley's. A man who might have used this same bully stick to pull himself out of the mud after he'd rid himself of a young girl's body, who might have been convinced an old hermit knew of his terrible deeds.

Eddie took his watch from his jacket and placed it on the table, running a thumb down the crack in the glass. He thought of the look on Block's face when he'd revealed the watch that had once belonged to him.

Eddie went to gather the prints from the library gala once more. A chill went through him when he came to the last photograph of the night. He studied the man who had attempted to rob him, the same individual who rode upon the carriage on the day of the fire, the one who was posted in the shadows of the front hall of the Blocks' town house, avoiding the gold-toned light the Tiffany chandelier threw onto the richly decorated walls. When Eddie leaned closer, he saw what he hadn't noticed before. Two black buttons were missing from his coat.

He should have gone back to Brooklyn, to address the matters of his own life and interests, returning for Coralie. Instead he took up his old post on the corner of Sixty-second Street. Something had taken hold of him, the urge to make things right. He barely knew himself or his desires. He had no obligations, and yet he was weighted down with a sense of responsibility. He felt naked without his camera, but he had come to this address for one reason alone. If he waited long enough, he was certain the fellow in the photographs who worked for Block would appear. It was morning, and the streets were busy, therefore Eddie didn't notice when a young woman came up behind him, having been out walking with her dogs, two large black poodles. The dogs alerted Eddie to the woman's presence, for they ambled up to him with a sort of haughty familiarity. The larger of the two nudged him.

"Go on now, big boy," Eddie said to the dog, giving it a pat and doing his best to send it on its way. He grinned to think of what Beck's wolf would make of such well-fed urban pets.

"He seems to know you," a woman's measured voice said.

Eddie turned to the young woman who had come to collect her dogs. She was dressed in an indigo silk and wool dress and wore a large fashionable felt hat, decorated with an assortment of blue feathers in a range from aqua to navy. She had dark blue eyes and a clear, pale face with fine features. "I know you as well," she said. "You were at the library gala."

Eddie realized he was in the presence of Harry Block's sister. He wished he hadn't the complication of being recognized.

"Perhaps you're thinking of someone else," he said politely, keeping his attention on the town house steps, so as not to lose sight of Block's thug if he appeared.

"No," Block's sister said with assurance. "I'm not. You were there."

"Only as a hired hand," Eddie granted.

"Except that no one hired you, I checked into it. And now it seems"—she paused to observe his splint—"you no longer have a free hand to hire. We've never been introduced. I'm Juliet Block, and you're the man who has my brother's watch."

Eddie searched her face and saw the intelligence there. She gazed back at him critically, but not without interest.

"Were you never taught not to speak to strange men on the street?" he asked.

Miss Block laughed. "I was taught all manner of things concerning what a woman should and should not do, and how the world should be run. Unlike the members of my family, I believe that all people have the right to speak, including women and workers." The poodles were standing beside Eddie, nosing around. Miss Block clipped on their leashes. "They seem to fancy you. I, however, don't know how I feel about you." She had quite a serious expression as she recalled their initial meeting as children. "I was terrified you'd steal my coat on the day you found us playing in the office. My father had just given it to me."

Eddie smiled. Pretense wouldn't work with this outspoken young woman. "I thought of it. But I didn't want to make you cry."

"Well, I cried all the same as soon as you left. I cried because my coat cost more than most children my age had to live on for a month. I was embarrassed even before you shamed us. I took a pair of scissors to the horrid coat myself. Made quite a mess. Still, I managed to cut it to shreds."

Eddie found he was at a loss for words. They stared at each other, each surprised at who the other had become. When Miss Block began to speak of her activities, it became clear she was an ardent feminist, involved in securing rights for workers and demonstrating for the women's vote. Her family, she revealed, was not pleased with what they referred to as her "antics," and had taken away her yearly stipend of twenty thousand dollars as punishment when she had protested at the Opera House and outside City Hall and had briefly been interned in the workhouse on Blackwell's Island. That was when her funds were cut off. Her brother was set to inherit everything from their father, since Miss Block was not deemed responsible by her father and his attorneys. Harry was the one who insisted that she take the dogs for protection when she went out walking. He'd chosen them for her, and had them trained by an expert. Perhaps the dogs knew Juliet would have preferred to have left them at home. Indeed, she thought of them as an extension of her brother, more or less employees meant to keep her in check.

"That's why they prefer you, sir," she told Eddie. "Not that I share their sentiments. If you don't mind, I'd like to know why you're here."

"I'm not sure you'd really like that, miss." Eddie had felt a certain compassion for her on the day he stole the watch. As it turned out, he felt an unexpected concern for her even now.

"Women shouldn't know too much? I take it that's your point. It might affect their brains or, worse, their reproductive organs? You spoke to me once as if I were an equal when you told me to shut up, please do me the same courtesy now. And call me Juliet."

Eddie was won over by her candor. Still, he hesitated. He had come for justice, and justice didn't always resolve as people wished. He'd brought along the photograph he'd taken at the gala, which he now withdrew from within his coat. "The man behind your brother. What do you know of him?"

"Frank Herbert?" Miss Block said. "He's my brother's employee."

"Does your family have anything to do with the Triangle Shirt-waist Company?"

"My brother is an attorney. He may have done some work for them. I believe he did." She gazed deeply at Eddie. "And the work was questionable, I presume."

"What if it was murder?"

Juliet suggested they walk around the corner, to the park, so they might find privacy and speak more freely. They did so, and the dogs were overjoyed to find they were not being dragged in the direction of home. They took a path that led to the reservoir. There were many starlings and sparrows on the branches of the trees. "Welcome to the petting zoo of the wealthy," Miss Block said bitterly. Once they had found a bench hidden by bushes, she took out a French cigarette and lit it, which surprised Eddie.

"Oh, stop looking at me that way." She laughed. "You can't be that easily shocked. I'll do my part to help you get Herbert, and in exchange you'll forget about my brother. In all honesty, Harry probably has no idea of his henchman's methods. He says make it so, and it's done."

"It was a young woman that was killed, if that makes a difference to your opinions regarding your brother's responsibility in the matter. She worked on the ninth floor at the factory, but it wasn't the fire that did her in. She never made it to work that day because somebody murdered her. They sewed up her mouth with blue thread, then tossed her into the river."

Juliet stared at him long and hard. "It matters to me very much, whether you believe me or not. But he's my brother. My offer stands. I'll give you Herbert, and in return, you'll leave Harry alone."

JULIET BLOCK was to inform Frank Herbert that her brother had given instructions for him to bring a file of information to a meeting in the alleyway behind Greene Street. Eddie would see to the rest. The hour was late, after workers in the nearby factories had gone home. Dusk was settling. It was murky enough so that Herbert could not see clearly when he turned off the street, yet he spied the slim figure of a young woman who found her way into the alley. He likely gritted his teeth, annoyed to see an interloper in the very place where he was to make a delivery of important papers to his employer. He didn't like taking orders from a woman, and had felt humiliated being told what to do by Miss Block, who, in his opinion, thought much too highly of herself, as if she was a man's equal. He had his bully stick with him, and he didn't mind issuing a threat or two to a stranger, then acting on those threats if need be. But before he could chase off the figure before him, Herbert took note of something odd. The girl in the alleyway looked familiar. Her pale hair plaited into braids, her girlish blue coat. It was the dimness surely, only a trick of the shadows, yet Frank Herbert hesitated, unsure. Quite possibly, the thing before him was not human in nature. Then, thinking himself ridiculous, he moved toward her. "Go on," he said with menace in his tone. "This is no place for ladies."

She looked at him fully. "Neither is the river." The young woman opened her hands. There were the buttons she'd pulled from his coat when she struggled with him.

"Get on with you," he said, confused. He took her now to be the girl he'd had to get rid of. Somehow she had returned from the river and found him. She had torn the blue thread from her lips to speak to him.

"I have your buttons," she told him. "From when you killed me."

He stepped forward, his club at the ready. "If you're a ghost, then you won't die again, though it was easy enough to kill you the first time."

It was then the wolf came from behind her, the one who'd been on the porch when he'd seen to the prying old hermit who'd been on the hill the day he dumped the girl's body. It seemed the wolf had died and returned as a ghost as well, and yet he was real enough that he had to be restrained with a chain, so intent was he on lunging at the man he recognized as his master's killer.

"Hold on to him," Herbert shouted. "He'll be after me!"

"Because you killed the old man?"

"I did him a service putting him out of the misery he lived in. Now go away, the both of you! Vanish from here! There's real business of the living to be going on in this place, and we don't need the likes of you."

Herbert did not hear the men from the Workmen's Circle as they circled him, then leapt upon him. They were indeed the living, who beat him down and shackled him with a length of rope, then slipped on iron cuffs. Isaac Rosenfeld got a black eye in the process, of which he was quite proud. There had been six witnesses to Herbert's confession; most Eddie had known as boys in the factories. Eddie took a photograph of the men who gathered around Frank Herbert, a memento they could show their mothers and girlfriends. Eddie had promised Juliet he would not pursue her brother, but that didn't mean others wouldn't take up the cause and do their best to connect him to the events that had led to Hannah's death.

Rosenfeld took the buttons as further proof against Herbert. Ella, who had so bravely consented to play the part of her sister's ghost, was asked if she would accompany them to the Tenth Precinct and make her statement as well.

"I need to go with them," Ella said when Eddie wanted to walk her home safely. "My father will understand. And it's you he'll want to hear from. You're the one he's trusted."

Mr. Weiss was waiting on the concrete steps outside his building, wearing a winter coat, though it would be summer in a matter of days. Eddie sat beside him, the wolf at their feet. When Eddie confirmed that the murderer had been caught, Weiss nodded. He didn't seem surprised. "I knew you'd find him."

"Yet I feel I've failed." Hannah was still dead. Harry Block was still in the mansion on Sixty-second Street.

"Every good man feels that he's failed."

Eddie grimaced. He shook his head. "That's not me. *Good* would never be a proper term."

"Your father told me that you were. That was why I came to you." Weiss seemed extremely sure of himself. "You know why I believed him?"

Eddie shrugged. "Because you pray with him each morning and a man you pray with is one you believe?"

"God is the only one I pray with," Weiss corrected him.

"So maybe you trust my father because you grew up in the same town and you worked together."

"Those things are true, but they have nothing to do with my faith in your father. In the town where we grew up, one boy slit his brother's throat and another stole from his own grandmother so that he could flee to Paris. Coming from the same town means nothing. I've worked with many men I wouldn't even speak to if I passed them on the street. Mules work together, so do men, it means nothing as well. I have faith in your father because he's a good man, and like every good man, he, too, has failed. But I can tell you this, he knows what it means to be a human being."

"To be a failure?"

Weiss sputtered out a laugh. His beard had turned white in a matter of months. He clapped Eddie on the back. "To forgive," he said. "As he's forgiven you."

NINE

THE GIRL WHO

COULD FLY

****

M Y FATHER *locked me in my room. When he discovered that the coffin had been stolen he informed me that he had never been as disappointed in his life, or as betrayed. He found me in the yard and confronted me, but I blamed the liveryman, as I was meant to do. Perhaps I wasn't convincing, for my father seemed to know I was no longer under his command. He may have noticed my expression of longing as I watched Eddie disappear with the liveryman. He tricked me into admitting I had gone to Manhattan without his permission by saying he'd had me followed. He was a liar, but he knew how to get the truth out of people. When I stumbled over my words, stating I had indeed traveled to Manhattan because I thought I needed to return the camera the photographer had left behind, my father shouted that I was a woman of deceit. He changed in a moment, before my eyes, his face filling with rage. Was this my thanks to him, for raising and caring for me? I promised him that nothing had happened, but he shook his head. Why should he believe me now? How could he know whether or not I'd been ruined by this man in Manhattan, and if I'd given myself freely to a worthless individual?*

He did not speak to me all the next day, but in the evening he told me to bathe in cold water, which I did, using the lye soap he left out for me. He put out my robe for me, which I slipped on. He waited in the corridor and had me follow him downstairs. In the parlor the cereus plant looked ghostly and green in the evening light. I'd always thought of it as a bundle of sticks, but now it seemed possessed with life, and I could have sworn it moved toward me, as if in warning. I had lived with it my whole life and had never once seen it bloom. I had thought the plant to be a burden, and yet I felt a certain connection to this wretched specimen, for I'd cared for it for so long. Perhaps plants knew gratitude, as humans did, and remembered kindness as well as cruelty.

My father led me through his library, into the museum. I thought of how I had so longed to enter it and know its secrets when I was a child. How intrigued I'd been when I'd been made to sit upon the stair where I could only peer through the dark to glimpse the many curiosities displayed inside. I had thought my father could make miracles, but I was wrong. He could only possess them.

My father gestured that I should go on without him. "We'll see if you're a liar or if you're still my daughter," he said in a cold tone.

When I went inside the exhibition hall, the Professor closed the door behind me. I heard the click of a lock. A man was waiting there. This was most unusual. I paled when I saw him. He rose from his chair to greet me.

"You needn't worry," he assured me. "I'm a physician." There was an urgency in his tone that caused me to worry. "Doctors are privy to all sorts of secrets hidden from other men."

He came forward, and there was that same urgency in his step. I hoped he didn't take note of the scent of my fear, for they say that terror makes a person weaker, and I did not wish to be at anyone's mercy.

"Your father has called upon me to judge your physical well-being."

"I'm quite well," I informed him. "I don't need a physician." There was the beat of my pulse at the base of my throat, the same throb of panic I'd felt when I stepped into the cage at Dreamland.

"I'm afraid that you do. Your father is worried. He reports that you've made the acquaintance of a man in an improper way."

I felt burning hot, even though the room was chilly. "There was nothing improper." I began to understand what my father had meant when he declared I was ruined. He believed I'd given myself to Eddie, and, in every sense but the physical act, I had.

"An examination is required. If you've been with a man, your father needs to know." The doctor came closer. When he reached to remove my robe, I stepped back. But he took hold of my arm and told me in no uncertain terms that my father had the legal right to ascertain whether I had cast away my virginity, and it would be his pleasure to assist in examining me.

He told me he had seen me swim in the tank on nights when I had performed, and this was how he had made my father's acquaintance. He had enjoyed himself immensely, and now he had an opportunity to see what I was made of without the tank between us. Immediately, I doubted the worth of his medical claims and wondered what sort of expert he was.

Now that my father had turned to him, the doctor hoped to do some research of his own interest, for I was such a rare specimen. He hoped to discover if I was a fish or a woman or both. His actions, he said, were purely motivated by research. In matters of my sex, would I be slippery and cold, as fish were known to be, or hot as a ruined woman? He took

out a black leather notebook and a fountain pen so that he might record
the details. He said he would like to examine every part of me, including
my bones, for a fish's bones are often hollow, like a bird's, and because of
this they are light in the water, as birds are weightless in air. His words
were like glass, cutting through me. I had never felt more wretched.

He went on to tell me that after the examination he could eliminate
my deformity if I wished him to do so. He brought forth a scalpel, which
he placed on a table, alongside his journal and fountain pen. The webbing
could easily be done away with, and no one would ever have to know who
I'd been. To all who saw me I would be a normal person, except to those
who knew me intimately, fortunate men, such as himself. I moved to hide
my hands behind me, fearing he might take it upon himself to begin an
operation. He was amused by my response.

"I, of course, prefer you the way you are," the doctor said. "But if you
ever wish to be normal, I'm always here for you as your surgeon."

I leapt away, thinking I would run from the room, and in doing so
knocked over the table on which he'd carefully laid out his equipment.

He grabbed me and held fast, and as I struggled he secured me by
wrapping fishing wire around my wrists. He was clearly practiced in
such matters, for, however much I tried, I couldn't slip out of the knots. I
cursed him, but he didn't care. He pushed me onto the floor.

Before I knew what was happening he swiftly moved a hand between
my legs. I tried my best to get away and scramble toward the door to the
street. The doctor, however, held fast. When he pawed at me he was real
enough, a demon perhaps, but not a dream. Perhaps that was a monster's
fate, and the fortune my father said I had brought onto myself.

The tortoise was scratching in the sand, and I felt embarrassed that
this ancient creature bore witness to my degradation.

"This is what I'm here for," the doctor murmured as he reached his fin-
gers inside my most private area. The man whom I wanted had refused to

take me when I offered myself to him. He believed I was an innocent, and now I realized that, until this very day, I had been.

I fought against my horrid inquisitor, but my actions seemed to arouse him more. The fishing wire was cutting into me and drew lines of blood at my wrists. Some pooled on the floor.

"It's red," the doctor said, delighted. "I thought you might have the clear blood of an icefish, or the blue blood of a horseshoe crab."

He brought out a glass tube and swiftly dashed some of my blood into it, so that he might study it, comparing it to the blood of bluefish and sturgeon, perhaps alongside the blood of his wife so that he might see which species I most resembled. I now understood how it was possible to stop thinking of a man as a human being, enough so that you might wish to take his life. Seeing the scalpel that had fallen to the floor nearby, I grasped for it, but he kicked it from my reach.

"We kill our fish, and slit them open," the doctor said. "You had better act like a woman if you want what's best."

He held me round the waist as he spoke these horrid sentiments. He acted as if he owned me, and I cried out, with shock and humiliation. The doctor held fast. He felt inside me and was pleased. "I can take you now and tell your father that I found you a ruined woman. He'd never know the difference."

The doctor wore a fine linen jacket that he tore off and left crumpled beside us, as well as tweed pants that he began to unbutton. I could feel his sex against me, and I knew what he intended. But I did not turn into rain or dew as I had during the nighttime shows. I was not an actress on a stage, and I did not disappear, leaving my body there for him to do with whatever he wished. I reached behind me, inching my clasped hands along until I grasped the scalpel. He might think I was only a woman or a fish, but I was nothing of the kind. I was a monster's daughter. I cut the fishing wire from my wrists, so quickly I nicked myself. I drew more blood, but I no longer cared. I pierced his forearm, admittedly with some pleasure, for the stab had immediate effects. He yowled and let go as if he had had fire in his embrace rather than flesh and blood.

"You little bitch," the doctor said as he rose to his feet. There was blood staining his shirt from the fresh wound. "Your father will punish you for this. I'll tell him what a demoness he has for a daughter."

I grabbed the shovel we used to clean the tortoise's pen. Before the doctor could walk away and find the Professor and tell him lies, I hit him squarely on the back. When he fell, he covered his face with his hands. Just as I suspected. A coward. He appeared related to the horseshoe crab as he hunched over, and between the two of us he was more likely to be the one with blue blood. I could not help but wonder if a well-placed shovel could break his spine, if it would then shatter like a black, hardened shell, bits flying everywhere. But I then imagined who he went home to—a wife, daughters, a faithful dog, a nurse who did his every bidding, a line of patients, each hoping for a cure. I did not strike again, though I kept the shovel in my hand.

I pushed the notebook and pen toward him.

"Write your review of me," I said. "Tell my father I am not ruined."

He did so as I stood over him. He did not dare look at me as he scrawled his testimony that I was indeed a virgin. He tore the page from his journal and left it for me.

I unlocked the door to the street that our customers came through. The doctor grabbed for his coat, but I stood upon it. I wanted the world to see the blood on him.

"Leave as you are," I told him.

When he'd gone, I locked the door. I folded his coat, which I would later throw on the trash pile in our yard. I still felt tainted by the doctor's intent and by his touch. I yearned for a cleansing, and so I went to my tank and climbed inside. I felt a sort of relief as soon as I was in the water, as if

I was destroying everything that had been done to me. I was still bleeding around my wrists, and a thread of crimson circled in the water. So that this evening would not claim me, I imagined the Hudson River, the woods at dusk. I was the rain, pouring down onto the streets of Brooklyn, into the yards where gardens grew, onto the cobblestone alleyways behind the fish markets. For a thousand nights I would not think of what had happened, nor would I remember the physician, a fool who thought it acceptable to defile a creature he wanted only for its rare qualities, like the shark is wanted for its skin, said to be the most beautiful in all the world.

When I climbed out of the tank, I put on my robe, then went to lie upon the floor beside the tortoise's pen. I had no idea whether or not the tortoise slept or dreamed or remembered. Sunlight streamed in beneath the closed curtains, causing patterns of dark and light on the floor. There was a rabbit, a hat, a bird in flight. I would not let this incident make me forget I knew what love was like. Outside the window, sparrows were singing in the milky light. On every branch of the pear tree in the yard there was a new leaf unfolding, a vivid green. Spring had truly arrived, a season that had always been my favorite but was so no more. Now I wanted winter, a time when snow covered everything, even though my hands would be cold in such weather, for I had decided I would never wear a pair of gloves again, not for warmth, not for protection, and never to hide who I was.

MAY 1911

LATE IN the afternoon, Maureen knocked at the door. By then the day was warm and Coralie's room was stifling. When there was no answer, the housekeeper cracked the door open and peered inside.

"Even if you're ill, you have no choice but to face the day," she called.

Maureen bustled into the room, convinced she had a cure for anything that might plague her ailing charge. Coralie wished that for once the housekeeper had left her alone. She was in no mood for human interaction, and in no condition to face anyone, least of all Maureen, who had a talent for reading her emotions. Coralie shrank beneath her blanket, mute and withdrawn, as a tray of tea and biscuits was placed on her bedside table. She sank down further when Maureen went to open the curtains.

"Don't," Coralie pleaded. When Maureen threw a worried look over her shoulder, Coralie said, "My eyes burn with the light."

She did not wish Maureen to spy the marks that had been left on her. There were two scarlet circles, fading in color but still quite evident on her wrists.

"Are your eyes the only problem?" Maureen knew her charge's temperament so well she quickly guessed there was more at hand. She sat at the edge of the bed, then pulled the quilt down and spied the bruises on Coralie's arms. She drew in a breath, then grasped Coralie's wrist and traced a finger over the red impression left by the fishing wire. "What happened to you?" she asked, distraught. "Some man, I'll wager. Don't tell me it's the photographer, for I told him I'd make him pay if he wronged you."

"No. Not him."

Maureen's expression was fierce. She rose to her feet, frantic, as if she intended to find justice. "If it wasn't him, then who? Where is this man who's treated you so badly?"

"Far from here, I hope."

Maureen and Coralie held hands and kept their voices low.

"Did he have his way with you?"

Coralie shook her head.

Maureen went to the kitchen and in a short time returned with a poultice of madder root and a thorny thistle, which she insisted would heal Coralie's bruises. The thistle was common enough, but it often caused the death of stray dogs when they carried off stalks growing wild in the fields. "Your father needs to know," Maureen put forth once the bruises had been treated.

"Do not speak to him of this! Do you hear me?"

Coralie was so firm in her assertion, and so grim, that Maureen grew ashen as a glimmer of understanding took hold. "Did he have a part in this?"

"It was a doctor he employed to see if I was still pure. The gentleman thought he might take it upon himself to ruin me." Coralie was so emotional, she held nothing back. It was a relief to be truthful with Maureen as she now admitted to the night viewings she had always kept secret. "It was to be mere theater. A show like any other. And yet it ruined me in some way, more so than what this horrid man tried to do to me."

Tears flooded the housekeeper's eyes. "I haven't allowed myself to believe it, but now I know you should never have grown up in this house. I wanted more for you," Maureen said with yearning. "And you'll have it." She appeared resolved, though her face was wet with tears. "You'll have a proper life, and when you do, you'll see that love has nothing to do with what you've found under your father's roof."

Coralie could not help but think of the tattooed woman who had thought her to be a whore. "I doubt that any man who really knew me would have me after all I've done."

"That's not true, Cora. Look at me! Would you think a man of any worth would ever want me? Would he travel from Virginia and wait outside my door even though I have been ruined a hundred times over? Mr. Morris doesn't see me from the outside. Men are men, with all their flaws, as we have ours, that's true, but the best among them manage to discover who we really are." The housekeeper lifted Coralie's chin so they might look into one another's eyes. "If we had no hurt and no sin to speak of, we'd be angels, and angels can't love the way men and women do."

"And what of monsters?" Coralie wished to know. By then her face was streaked with tears; her emotions were raw. "Can they love?"

Maureen tenderly ran a hand over her charge's dark hair. "We know quite well they can," she murmured. "For we know that they do."

THE MUSEUM OF EXTRAORDINARY THINGS failed to reopen. One or two customers rapped at the door, and, when their knocking went unanswered, they went away, puzzled but ready enough to find another entertainment. Professor Sardie's announcement that he would allow free entrance into the museum if he were unable to produce the Hudson Mystery was a promise he couldn't keep. At the present time he hadn't the ready cash to pay his players or his bills. He had been drinking heavily ever since finding his workshop door ajar, the coffin containing the body of his fabulous creature vanished.

He held the liveryman responsible; that unsavory character had never dared to return, and the Professor could be heard cursing his missing employee late into the night.

The last weekend in May was fast approaching, the beginning of the season marked by streets swelling with crowds, all searching for relief from the hot city and the brittle confines of their own lives. Soon enough Dreamland would reopen in all its revamped glory and beaches would be blanketed with visitors from Manhattan. All of the bathing pavilions, including Lentz's and Taunton's Baths, would be overflowing with customers. The New Iron Pier walk was busier each day, as all of the summer establishments prepared for the onslaught of visitors. The wooden horses at Johnson's carousel were freshly painted. The steel skeleton of the Giant Racer Roller Coaster, that heart-stopping ride, was readied as well, with the empty cars sent up on practice runs that rattled the street below.

No announcements were made concerning the closing of the museum. The door was simply barred and padlocked from the inside. The Professor was already humiliated among his peers, many of whom said they'd never trusted him or expected to see anything resembling the Hudson Mystery. He was a known con man who relied on the naïveté of the masses, those inexperienced customers who might be convinced to believe in such things as mermaids and butterfly girls, when they were in fact being offered freaks of nature, harmless individuals dressed up to resemble the inhabitants of their nightmares or dreams. But if there was no Hudson Mystery, there would be no reversal of their downward fortunes. That was not fantasy but fact. Already the tortoise was being fed weeds rather than lettuce and fresh greens. The caged birds were pecking at crumbs.

When the living wonders arrived in the yard on what they had thought was opening day, they were greeted by the stench of the rot-ten fish, for the giant striped bass had been lugged onto the trash pile and set on fire. Bits of scales rose into the air, and it seemed that silver wasps were soaring into the clear May sky. Maureen spoke to the employees through the screen door, too embarrassed to tell them face-to-face that they were no longer needed. She made her voice as stern as she could, for, given the circumstances, no one would benefit from sentiment. Malia, who had been a feature since the age of seven, wept in her mother's arms, and the others clustered together in disbelief, for they were suddenly without the means to support themselves. The season was about to begin, staff had been hired everywhere else, and it would be difficult to find work in even the lowliest museums and entertainment halls.

"Is this any way to treat us?" one of the Durante brothers called. "After so many years?"

"No," Maureen said. "But it's his way."

"Let him rot in hell," Malia's mother cried, surprising those who hadn't expected she knew any language other than her native Portuguese. "For hell is where he belongs."

Coralie wanted to apologize, but Maureen stopped her.

"This is your father's decision. Next season he may hire them back. The world is unpredictable."

"And when he no longer has any need of you, will he do the same?"

"He has already." Maureen dropped her voice to a hush. "I've been dismissed."

Coralie was confused. "And yet you're here."

The housekeeper admitted she was there only as long as it took for Coralie to pack her belongings. She insisted there was no way that Coralie could stay in this house, and suggested she take as little as possible, for haste was the most important aspect of their departure.

Coralie understood the danger and therefore rushed upstairs to fill her cowhide satchel with her most precious possessions, clothes and books, along with the strand of pearls left to her by her mother. She hurried downstairs, but once in the parlor she suffered pangs of regret for all she was leaving behind. She had the urge to take the cereus plant, whose woody stalks had suddenly turned a ripening green, to liberate the tortoise, whose shell she rubbed with oil in the winter months, to free the hummingbirds from their cages. Perhaps it was this moment when she tarried that allowed her father to discover Maureen lingering in the kitchen. She'd been told to vacate the premises, yet she had disobeyed him. His dreadful mood was intensified by a good portion of rum. Coralie heard her father's raised voice and then the murmur of Maureen's rational tone as the housekeeper did her best to assuage his anger. The Professor refused to listen to her excuses; he began thrashing her mercilessly. Coralie could hear the rising tide of their emotions as they struggled.

"I should have known I had a thief in my own kitchen," Sardie shouted. "How many times do I have to teach you the same lesson? How stupid can you actually be? I thought I taught you your rightful place long ago."

"You have no right to speak to me so anymore. I'm no longer your employee."

Coralie came to stand outside the kitchen door. When she peered inside she saw that Maureen held a frying pan up for protection as the Professor beat her. He'd cornered her beside the stove and now grabbed the frying pan to use it against her. Maureen could do nothing more than bury her face in her hands. Coralie ran and threw herself against the Professor. He nearly turned on her, the cast-iron pan raised high, before realizing it was his daughter who grasped his arm. "Please," she begged. "It was my idea to leave. Maureen has nothing to do with it."

"Are you conspiring to leave?" His anger had been entirely directed at the housekeeper; now he realized Coralie's intentions. "What other conspiracies have you been a party to? Why would I believe anything about you? Was the report about your physical condition a lie as well?"

"You need to go," Coralie urged the housekeeper, doing her best to hold Maureen's gaze with her own, all but pleading with her to run off before the Professor did any more damage.

The housekeeper's complexion was so chalk white that the random burns stood out in bunches, as if rose petals had been scattered across her skin. There was a fresh gash in her scalp, and dark butterfly-shaped bruises were forming on her chin and cheek. Still, she stood her ground until the Professor grabbed her, pulling her to the door. He locked it after he'd cast her out, pleased with himself. The housekeeper didn't give up but came to bang upon the window glass, calling for Coralie to be set free. Their eyes locked, and in their glance was an attachment that could not be broken, even though the Professor was already guiding his daughter down the cellar stairs.

"I had no plan to leave," Coralie protested. "I misspoke."

"That's what every liar says," the Professor told her. "I no longer have faith in you."

Coralie looked at him coldly. "Nor I in you."

"Silence will be the best teacher." Sardie opened his workshop door. Once Coralie was inside, he closed the door in one swift move. The room was dark, but Coralie found candles and a lantern, along with a box of wooden matches. She searched and found water in a jug; though it smelled rusty, she washed her face and cupped her hands so she might drink. She felt a shiver of pleasure knowing Maureen had gotten away, and that she had helped in her escape.

That night Coralie slept on the floor. The boards set over the windows made the room exceptionally dark, but she could hear the crowds on the pier. A shimmer of excitement was rising, for the new and improved Dreamland was set to open on Saturday. In the morning Coralie's eyes adjusted to the pale light that filtered around the planks of wood nailed across the windows. She found some dried fruit and seeds to eat, and relieved herself in an enamel pot. Then she gathered tools that might prove useful—a small shovel, an awl, and a hammer. At last, she opened the drawer where her father kept his journal. She grasped the book with a sense of rebellion, then sat upon the earthen floor with the book in hand.

She read for some time, coming to a section in which he listed all of his purchases, where he had discovered them, what their cost had been. The Professor mixed English and French in his writings and created a sort of code, reversing letters of the alphabet and often utilizing numbers in their place to ensure that his secrets would not be divined. Magicians did not share, and Sardie was particularly mistrustful, perhaps because he judged all other men by the measure of his own character.

He kept a list of obituary notices. If the deceased individual was a scientist or an explorer, he went to that person's home address at the time of the funeral, letting himself in by breaking open any locked doors, sifting through belongings, taking any interesting finds. In surgeries at hospitals throughout the city he was well known as a collector, and, in his younger days, he had traveled to Mexico and Brazil. It was there he had found Malia's mother begging on the street in a town where her daughter was thought to be cursed. The Durante brothers had been discovered in an orphanage in New Jersey, where they entertained the matrons with their acrobatics in the hope of a decent dinner. He'd paid twenty dollars for the two of them, and they'd begun their performances at the age of twelve, for there were no laws to protect children from theatrical exhibitions in the city of New York, and anyone could place them on display.

The tortoise was brought to him in the year Coralie was born. A very old sailor from the Canary Islands had owned the creature for eighty years, which meant the tortoise was now nearly a hundred. Its enclosure was above the workshop, and, as she read, Coralie could hear it moving slowly from one section of its confinement to the other. Grains of sand fell down between the floorboards. That was when Coralie wept, when she thought of a century of capture. She read on.

Sword, Hat, Mouse, Snake, Two of a Kind, Three Faces, Half a Woman, Fire in the Palm of My Hand, Cards, Aces, Deuces, Scarves, Doves.

The elements of each illusion were written in code, which Coralie had not yet completely deciphered. But there were other secrets as well. She came to one notation that was puzzling. *Baby in a Cradle.* The notation was set off by itself, and there was a blue image of a fish sketched below the letters. Coralie hurriedly turned the pages until she found another small fish inked in the margin. Before she could begin to read, however, she heard a disturbance above her, a pounding at the door and a man calling out. Coralie recognized the voice as Eddie's. She could hear her father's response soon enough, and the tone of the men rising into shouts. There was a clattering, as if pots and pans were falling. She could hear her father yelling that Eddie would never find Coralie. She had run off, the Professor said, leaving behind a note for the photographer, so he might know the truth. She wanted nothing to do with him.

Coralie pushed hard against the locked door. She called out until she was hoarse, but it did no good. Eddie had already slammed out of the house, and she could feel her future with him disappearing. By now Eddie would have crossed the yard and slipped into the crowded street, too hurt and disappointed to stay a moment longer. He could not know that, although Coralie was an avid reader, she had never learned to write. Her father had said her hands were too clumsy. She was better at household chores.

When it was too dark to see, Coralie lit the lantern, though there was precious little oil to waste. She found a blanket to wrap around her shoulders. The night was chill, and her spirits were cold as well. The paper of her father's journal was of a fine grade but delicate, tearing along the edges. Coralie came to the sign of the fish, and there she began to read again. The entry was made in the month of March, eighteen years earlier. A clear blue ending to the winter, Sardie wrote. Brooklyn was still dusted with snow even though the leaves of the lilacs had begun to unfold. He had been in New York for two years and practiced his English late into the night. He wished to be considered a New Yorker, and his accent was all that stood in his way. He heated the house with a single coal stove and ate simple meals of bread and fish and wine. He had bought the house in Brooklyn with money he'd earned from a concoction he made, an opium-like substance consisting more of acidic chemicals than of pricey raw poppy, using a stolen recipe from another magician in France, a man so addicted to his own mixture he hadn't noticed Sardie riffling through his papers.

The Professor used the winter months to travel and search for specimens. Animal, mineral, human. He wrote that he was a savior to many; he lifted them from lives of poverty and horror, though they didn't always appreciate his efforts on their behalf. His first stars, the conjoined twins Helen and Helena, pretty young women, were with the museum for the first season. They lived as servants to earn their keep, and were forced to sleep in his bed each night, but soon enough they ran away, leaving the Professor with no household help and no major attraction. Still, he intended to stay and would find other entertainments. He was in his early forties by then. He had seen a great deal of the world and was ready to settle down in Brooklyn. He'd had enough of magic in France. In New York he turned to science with a cold eye. But even a man of science could not control circumstance, and, as Coralie read on, she learned the unexpected had occurred in that same month of March.

On a Tuesday, after I made my way home from New Jersey, where I bought the jaw of a mastodon discovered in a swamp, I took note of something moving beneath the porch stairs. I thought it was a skunk, for there are many in Brooklyn. I myself had seen an albino specimen some weeks earlier, which I wished to capture, for I had taught myself the skills of taxidermy and was eager to put them to use. I left the bones I'd carried from New Jersey on the grass and went to see what fate had brought me. Surely it was fate that had driven me from France, and brought me to New York, and now made me cross the lawn on this day.

The creature made a wailing sound, and carried the odor of sour milk. Rather than discovering a skunk, I came upon a baby, a tiny pitiful creature. I left it where it was, tucked beneath the stair, thinking someone would soon come to retrieve it, for a kindly person had wrapped it in a clean woolen blanket and left it with some care. I saw to the mastodon jaw, and washed it off at the well. The baby wailed until it grew exhausted, then, at last, fell quiet. I had assumed the wretched mother would return for it, but when the dark fell, it was still there. I brought the baby inside and examined it on the kitchen table. It was an uninteresting female, and I thought it good for nothing until I unwrapped its bunting. To my joy I discovered it had a deformity, as if it had been created by the mating of a fish and a human being, its hands like flippers, its little body perfect in all other aspects. In order to test its aptitude, I filled a bucket and held it under the water to see if it could exist in this element. The child flailed and fought and came up sputtering, wailing even more piti-fully. If worse came to worse, I saw that I could drown it and be rid of it.

While I considered what I might do with the creature, I had one of my wonders take it home, a fat woman known as Darling, who lived with a normal fellow in Brighton Beach. She brought it back in two days complaining it had howled so piteously her husband had told her to take it and not return till she was rid of it. That was when I came to understand that freaks of nature and ordinary people had no business being together. Normal individuals would never be true to someone they considered beneath them. I fired Darling before the next season started. Soon after I came up with a list of instructions for those I employed. No marriages, that was the first rule. No chil-dren was the next. Brief alliances and love affairs would have to do, for commitments made for bad employees.

I sat on the porch and set the baby in a cradle that had been used by a wonder who had a monkey "child" that had escaped and disap-peared into the woods of Queens, ruining his master's livelihood. I tried to decide if I should sell the thing or, if there were no buyers, bring it to an orphanage, though I doubted any would take on an abnormal child. There was a hospital where I sometimes looked for specimens that kept such oddities under lock and key. I could most assuredly deposit the child there. Because the March air was chill, the baby had begun to cough. There was an old pear tree in the yard under which I buried animals and specimens. I thought that might be the final resting place for this thin, wailing creature. Certainly the fruit from this tree was sweet and the ground beneath it easy enough to excavate.

I gazed up to spy a pretty red-haired woman watching from beyond the yard. My blood raced at the sight of her.

"Your baby's crying," she said, the poor dumb thing.

Indeed it was. "Perhaps you can comfort it," I suggested. "Lord knows I have no business with children."

The lovely girl came forward and, after looking around a bit, lifted up the baby and hushed her.

"Be careful," I said. "It's a monster."

The woman laughed. "This beautiful girl? Don't be silly."

I pointed out the child's hands. "Look at the webbing. It may be a seal for all I know."

The red-haired girl shook her head. She seemed quite sure of herself. "That's God's mark of how special she is."

If I believed in God I would have thought this woman had been sent to me, for the baby seemed to wish to suckle at her breast and I got an eyeful that pleased me.

"I had a child but lost her," the woman said simply as a way of explanation.

"Perhaps you'd like to take care of this one, and take care of me as well."

She looked at me with a steady, even gaze, and I saw she wasn't so dim. She knew I was referring to my bed.

I told her I would take no nonsense from any employee.

I won't disappoint you, the girl told me.

Don't, I told her, or you'll live to regret it.

The mother from France who dressed in black, who always wore gloves and was so beautiful and gracious and had left Coralie her pearls, had never existed. She was nothing more than an orphan abandoned on the porch. Had Maureen not come along, she would have been given over to a hospital ward, or perhaps been drowned in a bucket, then buried beneath the pear tree. People say some facts are best left unknown, but those people have never had their own histories kept from them. As Coralie read on, it was as if she was moving backward through time. Everything that had ever happened shifted from the realm of black and white and was infused with color, the gray turning to red and indigo and a wavering spring green seen only in the month of March. All that she'd known and all she had ever been had turned to ashes. From those ashes, emerging through the earthen floor that the roots of the pear tree twisted through, she saw the truth. It was 1893, the year in which a serious man took in a baby and a red-haired woman and claimed them as his own.

TEN

THE RULES

OF LOVE

****

I CAME *upon the Wizard of the Lower East Side exactly as I had the morning I first met him. As I turned the corner onto Ludlow Street suddenly there he was, in the very same spot where I'd first spied him all those years ago, when I was just a boy. Perhaps he could tell the future, as people said, and therefore knew where he might find me, or perhaps it was the way New York City worked—it was a huge teeming place of strangers, until you stumbled into what seemed to be a village made up of people you'd known in your youth whom you couldn't seem to avoid. Hochman wore fashionable clothing, perfect for the season, a white linen waistcoat, a straw hat, white trousers, and cream-colored leather boots. He was on his way to a luncheon, he told me, given in his honor by the Workmen's Circle. He had recently helped them find a boy of twelve who had come to New York from the Ukraine on his own, only to be trapped into near slavery by a sly, unscrupulous businessman who made a practice of selling the services of young immigrants to farms in New Jersey, where*

*they labored in the fields with nothing more than a roof over their heads
in return.*

"You're a union man?" I said, surprised.

*"I'm a man of my people," he said. "Wherever that brings me. If the
Workmen's Circle wants to recognize my good deeds and call me a hero,
who am I to disagree? They may honor you one day as well. You're quite
famous at the moment. I heard about the girl you found."*

"As of today, I'm not in that business anymore."

*Hochman studied me. "No," he agreed. "It was never for you. There
was only one thing you were searching for."*

*I admit I was curious as to his psychic powers, in which I'd never had
any real faith. Now I tested him. "And what was that?"*

*I imagined he would say love, as I'd recently found the woman of my
dreams and could think of little other than Coralie. Unfortunately, the
feeling was not mutual, as she had fled and disappeared. Could I have
found her? Probably. But if she had no wish to be found, I saw little point
in doing so.*

*Hochman motioned me to follow him, and I surprised myself by
accompanying him. I wished to hear what he had to say. We went in the
direction of Essex Street, not far from the funeral home, to a saloon frequented by men of our faith. We went inside and sat at a rear table where
we might be afforded some privacy. After ordering our drinks, Hochman
continued.*

*"You were looking for the truth about your father, something I happen
to have. But maybe so much time has passed, you don't want to know. The
truth frightens people because it isn't stable. It shifts every day. If you'd
prefer to remain in the dark, I would understand."*

*Our drinks were delivered, and I gulped mine down. Perhaps that
gave me the courage to say, "Go ahead. Tell me your great secret. Let's
have it."*

"You've resented your father all this time for running away and attempting to drown himself. You judged him as a coward. Am I correct?"

I shrugged, but my answer was clear.

"That day on the dock, there were other men who'd been let go from the factory. They had arranged to meet to plan what action they should take. A member of the Workmen's Circle had been sent to meet with them."

I laughed and thought the Wizard's report preposterous. How could Hochman know this information when he wasn't there? "And you divined these facts out of thin air?"

"The man presenting me with my honor today at the luncheon was the representative from the Workmen's Circle. When your name came up in regard to Hannah Weiss, he told me your father's story. The bosses sent some thugs after your father and his friends. If you hadn't been there with him, your father would have stayed and fought; instead he saw that you had disobeyed when he told you to run. He went after you to ensure your safety and bring you home, but one of the henchmen sent to disrupt the union meeting came after him. Your back was to him when he was pushed into the river."

I had always been convinced of my father's weakness because he was in mourning for my mother, because he had cried in the forest in Russia. I couldn't stand to hear him weep. I'd covered my ears every evening. I had assumed he had leapt, a lost and helpless man. Never had I thought he'd meant to rescue me.

"You can say I don't have the power to see the future," Hochman went on, "but when you stopped me all those years ago on the same corner where we ran into each other today, I saw that we would meet again, and that the river would run through your life. I knew I'd be the one to tell you the truth about your father, although I didn't know what that was until just a few days ago, when your name came up in conversation."

I called for another drink. Without my resentment toward my father,

the hatred I'd been carrying around was now directed at myself. The terrified boy in the forest who thought the owls could carry him away. The
boy who believed there were ghosts in the grass. I was the coward who
had cried in the forest. I was the one who could not stop mourning my
mother.

Because I could not endure who I was, I had changed my name so that
I might be someone brand new. I had placed upon my father's shoulders
my many flaws and faults.

"Maybe you'll understand why he would risk everything for you now
that you've known love," Hochman said. He laughed when I gazed at
him with surprise. "There's no need of psychic powers to see that. I can spot
desire after all these years."

"Unfortunately she doesn't feel as I do." I had the letter I'd been given
in my jacket, which I'd read over and over again, a wound I couldn't help
but revisit. "She's sent me away."

"Don't walk away too fast," the Wizard said. "She may change her
mind." Hochman toasted my health and wished me good fortune. "Love
is the one thing that's not easy to find. It's an achievement, Eddie, to feel
such a glorious emotion, whether it's returned or not. Some men never do.
Though I'm not surprised to hear you have a passion. I saw it inside you,
even when you didn't know it was there. Why do you think I hired you?
I saw exactly who you were."

THE NEXT DAY, I went looking for my father. I knew I owed him an
apology. If I were to be honest, I owed him more than that. I had brought
Mitts and North with me, knowing they needed the walk, and they were
quiet, tempered by my mood. Once I'd climbed the steps, however, I found
I couldn't knock on the door. I stood there in the hallway where I had been
a hundred times before, and yet I was not the same person who had lived

here. *The corridor appeared smaller and more narrow than I had remembered. There was the scent of cooking from other flats, onions and chicken, and the dim lighting that turned shadows blue. I imagined my father on the other side of the door, his prayer book open as he said the evening prayers, the photograph of my mother on the table propped up beside an empty soup bowl. I had looked to find what I was missing in Moses Levy, in the hermit, in Hochman, in Mr. Weiss, but all along it had been here, at the end of this corridor.*

Still, I could not go farther. I couldn't imagine asking for his forgiveness. My throat had closed up. Could words burn you? Could they tear you to pieces? I stood with my back against the wall that was streaked with cheap green paint. Mitts and North were beside me, on edge. Did I bring them for protection or merely for company? Or was there another reason? I had met an old woman on the dock the day I rescued Mitts, and she'd told me that it was easy enough to judge a man by the way he treated his dogs. Perhaps I wanted my father to see that I was not a wretched, thankless person, the sort of man who would walk away without a look back, a son who would judge his father and fail to rescue him when he was drowning. I had a heart after all, not straw inside me, but blood and bone and flesh.

I did the only thing I knew how to do. I had the rest of my savings with me, all I had. I slipped the envelope of money under the door. I thought I spied a shadow. I thought I felt him near. I bowed my head and said the evening prayers. I was grateful for the teachers I'd had, though I now recognized myself to be a slow and unexceptional student. I finally understood what Mr. Weiss had given me in return for finding his daughter, for, like the angels who are said to follow men's lives on earth, he'd sent me a message. I was my father's son, no matter what my name was.

Soon after, I returned to the mansion on Sixty-second Street. It was the day when all New York pulsed with excitement, for President Taft had come to preside at the dedication ceremony of the New York Public Library on Fifth Avenue. The building had cost more than nine million dollars and boasted a collection of over a million volumes. The huge lions that fronted the staircase to Fifth Avenue, sculpted by Edward Clark Potter, were nicknamed Leo Astor and Leo Lenox, for the library's founders, John Jacob Astor and James Lenox. I avoided the crowds and slipped into a tavern, where I took my time over some warm gin till evening closed in. Then I went on to my destination. I stood in the dark, a shadow from my own past yet again. I looked up into the window I knew to be Juliet's bedroom, but it was dark. I wished to thank her for her help. She was so bright, I thought she could help me grasp why the one woman I wanted would run from me. Juliet was an advocate for women's rights. I, too, believed each woman had the right to follow her own destiny, but I hadn't paid attention to the personal liberties women were lacking. Perhaps there was much more I hadn't understood.

I saw a fellow bring a carriage round. He was a liveryman I'd heard his employers call Marcus. I walked over casually and paid attention to the horse.

"Keep away then," the fellow said to me. "This horse is worth more than you are."

The wondrous specimen was an Andalusian, sent from Spain, one of the finest carriage horses in New York. He was so spirited Marcus said he had to be ridden at a full gallop along the bridle path in Central Park on Sundays to ensure he burned off steam and therefore would be less likely to spook and run off with the carriage.

"Is Miss Block at home?" I asked.

At first he refused to answer, but I wouldn't let it go, and finally, most likely to be rid of me, he said, "We've been told not to bring up her name."

"Who gave you those instructions?"

Marcus shrugged. "We are to act as if she was never a member of the family."

It was a curious pronouncement, but I could not bring him to say any more. I decided to wait until the maids went out, hoping to have better luck with them. I'd watched the town house often enough to know they went out walking each day, and I recognized them right away. Sarah and Agnes had Juliet's poodles with them. The dogs saw me and strained to get to me, leaping up as if I were a long-lost friend.

"I never knew Jasper to be so friendly," Agnes said of the larger poodle's reaction to me. "He's a snobby thing."

"I'm a friend of Miss Block's," I said, which was not so far from the truth. "I'm here to visit her." The maids exchanged a look. "I take it she's not at home?"

"We have to walk the dogs," Sarah said, wanting to get away. She grabbed Agnes by the sleeve, steering her toward the park.

I followed along. I was still the same stubborn fellow I'd been from the start, unwilling to give in. "Will she be home later?" I focused on Agnes, the maid who seemed more willing to engage.

She shook her head sadly. "They were going to send her to a hospital in Massachusetts. I myself told her of the plan because I'd overheard them discussing her with the doctor. She was always kind to me, and I thought it evil that they were planning behind her back. I saw the jacket they planned to tie her into if she fought their demands—it was a horrible thing made of leather and canvas. When I saw what they intended, I knew I couldn't keep quiet."

"Let's walk on," the other maid said, troubled by the turn in the conversation. "Talk is cheap and it makes you seem so."

But Agnes clearly wished to tell the story of her mistress, and she went on. "It was all for Miss Juliet's political work and the demonstrations.

She'd been arrested again. When I told her what they meant to do, she said they'd never lock her up. She ran away, God bless her."

"That's enough," her companion told her. "It's nobody's business, and it'll be our jobs if they know you've talked about her. Don't say any more!"

"Oh, hush up yourself," Agnes said. "They don't give a damn about us, and Miss Juliet always did."

Sarah was chalk white. I realized that she was truly frightened, for she looked over her shoulder, anxious that they might be spied by a member of the Block family. "I won't be party to this," she declared. She turned and left us there in the park.

"Don't worry about her. Sarah won't say anything," Agnes assured me. "She's afraid of her own shadow."

We sat on a bench. It was a warm night and the park was crowded. The people here were different from the throngs downtown. We were far enough uptown for the social classes to be separated. And yet, against the wishes of the creators of this great green place that was meant to remain pristine, it was changing. The meadows had been turned into playing fields by groups of young men from downtown who traveled here to play stickball on hot nights.

As Agnes and I sat together, the dogs were very quiet, though clearly happy to see me. They sat at my feet as if they were my own.

"Would you think of taking them?" Agnes asked. "No one gives a damn about them either, and, forgive me for saying so, Miss Block hated them."

The dogs gazed at me beseechingly. They looked like fools in their clipped haircuts. I wanted nothing less than these silly beasts.

"They're Jasper and Antoinette," Agnes went on. "Poor things. They're ignored in the house, and I suspect that in time they'll be ill treated. If you have anything like a heart, you'll take them."

To placate her I said that at some point I might consider it; perhaps I would take them away once my own life was more settled. I most likely *did not mean this, but I had reason to strike a bargain, for I needed something in return: to see Harry. I asked Agnes if she would let me into the town house, and to my surprise she agreed most readily.*

"For Miss Juliet's sake," she told me. "Since you were her friend and she was mine."

Agnes was a young, cheerful girl from Ireland, and she resented the way the household help were treated; the saving grace of working for the family had been Miss Block, who regarded the maid as she might have a younger sister. We walked back together and went round the rear of the building. It was paved with cobblestones, and there was a large metal case for the milkman to deposit cream and cheese in the mornings. Agnes unlocked the door that allowed me into the house. She would wait for me on the corner of Sixty-third Street with the poodles until my business was done so she would not be thought to be associated with me in any way. I went through the empty kitchen—larger by ten times than the room my father and I had lived in—and found my way along the corridors, tiled with dark marble that was veined with pink and gold. There was a small sitting room, decorated for ladies, in tones of green and rose.

I continued on to the main hallway, which was shaped like a teardrop, and stood beneath the Tiffany chandelier, steadying myself. Agnes had informed me that the elder Mr. Block was ill and rarely left his bed. Mrs. Block had gone out to a party. Mr. Harry Block would likely be found in the study, for he'd slipped into a state of melancholy ever since his sister had run away. That was where I found him, practicing his chess game with an imaginary partner. I came into the study and closed the sliding walnut doors behind me. Block raised his eyes, and there was a flicker of fear. Perhaps he thought he was about to be robbed, as he had been all those years ago.

"Did Frank Herbert play chess with you?" I asked. "Because he'll be unavailable to do so for the next twenty years."

My enemy recognized me and nodded, as if we were old friends.

"Herbert was too much of an imbecile to understand the intricacies of chess. It was Juliet who played a good match."

I sat down in one of the green velvet chairs. "And yet you were willing to send her off to a hospital for her political views."

Block glared at me, confused as to how I would gain access to such information. "I would never have brought any harm to my sister if that's what you're insinuating. She was placing herself in danger by her choice of companions and activities. She would have soon found herself in jail. I wished to protect her."

"Now she's run away from your protection. For her sake I hope she's found some freedom in doing so."

"What business is my family to you?"

I was not the man to explain to him how deeply all of the workers had been influenced by the families that had employed them. Nearly every aspect of our daily lives had been affected by people who never knew our names. I picked up one of the chess pieces. It was the queen. "I never had time for games," I said. "Never learned chess. I was working from the moment I was able."

"You played the thief quite well."

"And it seems you played the murderer."

Block flushed with anger. "That had nothing to do with me. I didn't tell Herbert to kill her. I never would have. I simply said to scare her off. He didn't know when enough was enough and took it upon himself."

"I think the Workmen's Circle will take it upon themselves to watch you carefully. If you have business dealings that are questionable, if you cover up practices that place workers in danger, it's likely they'll know. I think you'll find yourself spending a good deal of time in court from now on. Good thing you're an attorney."

I reached into my waistcoat pocket for the watch. I had not realized the weight of it until that moment. My future had nothing to do with the time it told, nor did it define who I'd been in the past. I placed it on the game table.

"Do you think you returning my own property to me makes you an honest man?" Block asked.

"I think it makes me a man. I'm not sure you can say the same."

Before I left my old enemy, I took a last look at the watch I had carried for so long. It had never seemed like mine. Whether I was honest or not, I was free from its burden. I went out of the town house and met Agnes on the corner. We walked together speaking of Juliet, who was at that very moment on her way to California. We took the dogs into the park. Mr. Block kept them locked up in the kitchen; because he'd bought them for Juliet he despised them now. I let them off their leashes for once. As it turned out, broken or not, it appeared I had a heart.

MAY 1911

THE STABLE was empty, although several of the liveryman's pigeons managed to find their way in through gaps in the wooden siding to take shelter for the night. Eddie had taken to spending time in this gloomy place with both Mitts and North, breathing in the scent of hay, remembering how he had come here as a boy and slept beside the horses. After one tiff, when Mitts approached the wolf in an overly friendly fashion, the two got on well enough, if ignoring one another meant there was an uneasy peace. Eddie's hand was still wrapped, but the pain had eased. He supposed the bones were mending. His heart, however, was not in a similar condition, precisely the problem with having such an organ, for it caused pangs of desire and regret, reminding an individual that he was indeed human, prone to human sorrows and desires.

Eddie had reverted to his old insomniac's habits, avoiding sleep for as long as possible, existing on a diet of coffee and gin. When he did close his eyes, whether dozing in a chair or resting his head against the stable wall, Coralie came to him in his dreams. She was in the river, in his bed, out of reach and leaving him in a fevered and dejected state. He'd memorized several lines from the note she'd written him. *I do not love you and cannot pretend to. I am promised to a man in France, a family friend, and it is to him I now go. Please do not follow me. Forget me if you can.*

He wished to do exactly that, but had discovered it wasn't possible. He'd taken to drinking with serious intent, not for pleasure but for sheer inebriation. He missed the presence of the liveryman, and now held a deeper understanding of why a person might turn to opium, as he, himself, had embraced gin, for it was gin alone that allowed him a deep, black brand of sleep. Eddie tried not to dwell on the fact that he would soon be homeless. In a matter of days, the stable would be rented out to a tenant who had put in an offer to let the entire building. The new renter was an ironmonger who wished to set up a furnace in the alleyway and use Moses Levy's studio for storage. Eddie was to vacate by the first of June. It was already the end of May, and deciding where to go next loomed as an impossible task, for it was difficult enough to find loft space possessing good light, all the more challenging given his financial situation and the presence of two large canines, one of which was indistinguishable in form and temperament from a wolf. When Eddie was drinking heavily enough, he had half a mind to move onto Beck's property and build himself a shack. There he would take the hermit's place, equally embittered and alone, avoiding humankind, but close to the river, comforted by that proximity. Then he thought better of the notion, for what the old man had predicted would surely come true before very long. The woods would disappear, replaced by concrete and bricks. There would be no room for wild creatures, just as there'd be no room for men who wished to escape the concerns of city life.

Eddie soon unwrapped his hand from its splint. It had healed well enough in his opinion; he didn't need a doctor to tell him so. He was mulling over where he might go, perhaps to Queens County or even out to the potato farms of Long Island, when Beck's wolf-dog began to growl, the hair rising along his back. Mitts also fixed his gaze on the back door that opened into the alley. Eddie grabbed a pitchfork from a stall and told the ever-friendly Mitts to stay, while North accompanied him. A light rain was falling when he opened the door and stepped onto the pavement that led to the dirt alleyway. There was the stench of outhouses and of rotting garbage. North's growl deepened as they walked along, and although Eddie spied nothing beyond the dark, the wolf-dog suddenly lunged forward. A man's deep resonant voice rang out. "Hold him back, please! I beg you!"

Eddie grabbed North, pulling him off his quarry. The night was dark, starry, but in this narrow alleyway there was only a small slice of sky to be seen. As summer approached, a dense heat collected between buildings so that every inch was a tinderbox. Perhaps it was that heat, or perhaps it was the tension of a possible confrontation, that caused Eddie to break into a sweat. By now, his eyes had adjusted well enough to spy the hazy figure of a man. The stranger's head was bowed as he examined a rip North's sharp teeth had torn in the fine woolen cape he wore. "Please understand, I'm here for your benefit," the man said without gazing up. "I don't wish to frighten you."

Eddie laughed. He had the pitchfork as his weapon and the hermit's fierce companion beside him. "And how would you do that?"

The fellow stepped forward and North lunged again. Eddie kept his grip on the wolf-dog's collar and held fast, all the while mesmerized by what he saw. Before him was a man entirely covered by hair, growing down his face so that his features were difficult to discern. He had a feral, wild countenance, yet he wore a well-tailored suit under his fine woolen cape.

"I'm a man, though you might think otherwise," the stranger announced, obviously accustomed to a puzzled, often hostile response to his presence.

Eddie was bewildered. He gazed at the individual in the alleyway with unabashed curiosity. Though functioning through the haze of drink, he was still a photographer to the core, and he cursed himself for not having his camera at the ready so that he might record this visitation. "The world is more varied and wondrous than most men understand," Eddie said to his visitor. "No one is what he seems."

"I'd agree with that. And in that same vein, I'd say that beast is no dog." The stranger eyed North cautiously. "Dogs usually prefer me to ordinary men." Dogs, it was true, often had an uncanny sense of what a person was made of, while wild creatures did not take the time to discern such distinctions, for it was equally true that men mattered little in their world. Yet, it seemed that North recognized the stranger as an equal of a sort, for after he had assumed the stance of the dominant of the two, he seemed more accepting of the hairy man. The stranger appeared relieved. "We may need a wolf where we're going."

Eddie laughed at the notion. "Sir, it's late in the evening and I plan on going nowhere."

The stranger, however, seemed convinced otherwise. He had a rented carriage waiting on Tenth Avenue. He introduced himself as Raymond Morris, a resident of Brooklyn and a concerned friend of Coralie's.

Upon hearing his beloved's name, Eddie felt instantly sobered. "You'd best not include me in Miss Sardie's concerns. She wrote me a note plainly stating she never wished to see me again."

"Sir, you are mistaken. Coralie has not the ability to compose a note. She was never taught to write."

Eddie was startled to hear this, for Coralie had spoken of her love of reading. "Say what you will, but I received her note," he protested. Indeed he had the sheet of paper in the drawer of his bedside table, though he'd thought a hundred times of burning it.

"You received what the Professor wished you to have. The museum is closed and every employee has been let go. He has her trapped, for that is the only way he can keep her. The best course of action is for you to come with me, as I would never get a foot in that house. We may do well to let the wolf lead the way."

Mr. Morris slipped on his hood, then gestured for Eddie to follow. Like a dreamer who asks not for reason, needing only a single mission to move him forward in his dream, Eddie accompanied his new companion to the street. North, for his part, was wary, but willing to follow the stranger.

The driver of the waiting hansom seemed a nervous man. He had on a cap and a formal suit, for he worked full-time for a wealthy patron, and took odd jobs in his off hours. He'd known Mr. Morris for some time and had become used to his appearance, but he didn't care for the way the horse startled when it picked up North's scent. "You didn't say nothing about a wolf, Ray," he said to Mr. Morris.

Mr. Morris handed over an extra ten dollars, an enormous amount considering the streetcar crosstown was a dime, but one had to take into account the distance to Coney Island, the secrecy of their journey, and the wolflike creature now leaping into the rear of the carriage. In his haste, Eddie had left the stable door ajar, and Mitts, who could never tolerate being left behind, managed to push his way out. The pit bull galumphed his way to the waiting carriage and made a beeline for the driver, cheerfully ingratiating himself, licking the driver's hand and wagging his stump of a tail. Perhaps it was this genial, merry behavior that allowed them to gain their transit to Brooklyn that night, for the driver said he'd had a dog like Mitts in his youth and he firmly announced there was no finer or braver companion.

It was late when they reached their destination, after one in the morning. The sky was a bowl of stars in Kings County. The streets of Coney Island were deserted, but as the carriage passed by Dreamland they could see brilliant banks of lights and a boisterous crush of carpenters and workmen. A fiendish amount of last-minute construction was at hand, with hundreds of employees and day workers doing their best to finish before morning, when the park would open its gates for the season, with thousands arriving by excursion steamboat and ferry and railroad. In only hours, the first customers would be invited into the new and improved playground that had cost a true fortune to refashion. Great care had been taken to assure it would outshine all other entertainments, not simply on Coney Island but in the world.

Dreamland was illuminated by thousands of lightbulbs; the scene was so bright Eddie needed to blink to see within the gates as they passed by. He could spy the outlines of the grand entertainment Hell Gate, with its leering forty-foot-tall demons holding court at the entranceway to the ride's covered tunnel. Every light in the park had been turned on for the workers, but the strain was too much. All at once, as their carriage approached, there was a short circuit, with many of the bulbs shattering from the burst of energy that surged before everything went black. Mr. Morris's driver whistled for his horse to increase his pace, for he feared the creature would be spooked by the rising sound of the roars of lions and tigers pacing their cages, all startled and invigorated by the sudden dark.

Inside Hell Gate a team of workers who were mending fissures in the tunnel with hot, sticky tar that would shore up any leaks were suddenly engulfed in utter blackness. In the confusion that followed, with men panicking and rushing to escape the falling glass shards of the bulbs, a pail of burning hot tar was kicked over. It flowed much like lava, the black goo sparking with crimson flashes of heat.

"It seems we have good fortune on our side," Mr. Morris murmured as they passed the chaos in the park. "The dark is good for deeds such as ours."

Whereas Surf Avenue had only moments ago seemed as vivid as a theater's stage, there abruptly fell a cover of pitch. If a kidnapping of sorts was what they would attempt, then fate was indeed favoring their actions. The carriage halted on the corner, where the driver was paid another exorbitant fee and told to wait with Mitts, until their return.

The two men drew near the museum, one cloaked, the other still shaking off the haze of his heavy drinking. The wolf followed at their heels. Eddie half-imagined he was still inside a dream. Men did things such as this in dreams: approached a dark house filled with treasure, sank into a sea of true love, traveled with wolves and wonders on a warm night. The air smelled acrid from the tar across the road, and there was a tinge of sulfur to it as well, for inside the tunnel at the Hell Gate a flame had broken out. The workmen quickly scattered away, due to the rising smoke. A rush of air followed them through the tunnel, flinging sparks in every direction, as if the stars themselves had been replaced by embers.

Once in the garden, Eddie and Raymond Morris took shelter beneath the pear tree. There Mr. Morris revealed he had a key to the kitchen door in his possession. "A friend was kind enough to give this to me. She was to meet us here, but perhaps she's been held up by the ruckus on the street." He looked over his shoulder, worried, scanning the empty garden. At last he turned back to Eddie. "We have little choice but to go forward without her."

"Did your friend say where we might find Coralie?" Eddie assumed Morris referred to the red-haired woman he had photographed in the garden, for there was a softening in Mr. Morris's tone when he spoke of her.

"The cellar. A room you surely remember."

Eddie nodded. "I remember more than I'd like to." He still had nightmares of that room and of the box that contained the cold form of Hannah Weiss.

Eddie brought forth the two small keys he kept as a talisman. He hadn't known why he'd hung on to them, but perhaps it was due to a remnant of the abilities Hochman insisted he possessed. His thoughts were tangled in the puzzle of where fate had led him, to this house on this night. Through the din inside his head, a very real siren sounded. It was two minutes before two in the morning. The usual stillness of the hour had been broken by fire alarms at Dreamland. Sparks from the spilled tar had traveled with astounding speed. Canvas and fabric caught first, then the papier-mâché statues and rides went up, and finally there was a terrible leap of flame to wooden structures and rooftops. Already the firehouse at West Eighth Street, a hundred yards away, and the station at Fifteenth, near Surf Avenue, had sent out horse-drawn carriages, as well as their new hook and ladder trucks. The police had been called in, and scores of men in uniform advanced toward the New Iron Pier, some still pulling on their boots and buttoning their coats as they ran toward the disaster.

On the porch where they stood, Eddie and Mr. Morris could feel Surf Avenue vibrating as the first buildings at Dreamland began to fall. A scream barreled down the avenue, for fire has a voice. Eddie closed his eyes against the flashes of light in the sky. For a moment he was on the outskirts of his village, running through the forest while fire took everything that had been left behind; he was on the sidewalk of Greene Street watching beautiful young girls fall through the air, their hair and clothes aflame, in the woods watching the hermit's shack burn, embers floating upward like fireflies. He knew the language of fire, and recognized its destroying call. There was little time to waste, for time itself would soon be devoured by the flames that were increasing at a ferocious pace, racing faster than a man could think.

Mr. Morris hurriedly unlocked the back door. It was their good fortune to enter a quiet house. Sardie was nowhere in sight. All the same, North was left behind to guard the entryway as the men hastened to the cellar. The stairs creaked under their tread, and the darkness doubled until Eddie found and lit a lantern. He thought of the moment when he'd stood in the garden of this house and gazed up to see Coralie staring back at him. He wondered if the river had carried him here, and if perhaps he was again the person he'd been before he walked away from his name and his fate.

The workers and the paid performers who lived at Dreamland were already being evacuated, rushing down Neptune Avenue, which was hardly far enough. The Lilliputians had their own fire department, with small fire trucks and hoses. Once the women and children of their community had been evacuated, the men set to work pumping streams of water on the flames that were ready to engulf the baby incubator house. Nurses in the infant house had taken six premature babies from their incubators, making sure to wrap them in damp blankets to protect them from falling sparks. Under cover of the spray of water, they raced away from the park, with each child saved.

All through the neighborhood the cries of the animals could be heard as more than eighty beasts, all of which had been located in cages only yards away from Hell Gate, were rushed into the arena. Ferrari and Bonavita and eight other trainers did their best to keep order, which was all but impossible. Mortal enemies were let in together, bears with antelopes, leopards and hyenas alongside the high-strung Shetland ponies, which had to be blindfolded so they would not panic. Only the beloved elephant, Little Hip, who nightly slept beside his trainer, Captain Andre, now at a party in Manhattan, refused to be moved to the arena, despite a chain and whip.

Flames had spread along Surf Avenue, and the enormity of the disaster was just beginning to be understood by residents and bystanders. The heat was nearly unbearable, the black sky turning bright in fits and starts, with garish shadows falling everywhere. Mr. Morris's hired driver had taken off the moment he spied the inferno. He dared not tarry, for the rush of firemen and policemen would soon enough cordon off the area and the officials might decide to appropriate his horse and carriage to cart away survivors. The driver, who felt the need to save his own skin, apologized to the pit bull as he let Mitts out to fend for himself, certain that the stalwart nature of the breed would help the dog to survive.

The dog moved through the frantic crowds, making his way to the yard of the museum. In a desperate search for his master, Mitts managed to push open the back door. He quickly made a mess of things in the kitchen, leaping atop the table so that pots and pans scattered across the floor. Upon hearing Eddie's voice echo from the cellar, Mitts raced down the stairs, whimpering and panting, at last settling uneasily when he spied Eddie, now working feverishly on the locks.

The heat being thrown off by the fire could be felt even in the cellar, and the effects were dizzying. Hard to think, hard to breathe. In a dream you must go forward, Eddie told himself, otherwise the dreamworld will disappear with you still inside of it. Paint was melting off the walls and the knob on the workshop door was hot to the touch. Eddie groaned as he fiddled with the brass lock, finally unclasping it. He immediately set to work on the lock fashioned out of iron.

"We have time to get her out," Mr. Morris said through the billows of smoke that were filling up the corridor.

Eddie continued on, though blisters were rising on his fingers.

Mitts was huddled beside his master. When the dog heard footfalls in the kitchen above them, his cutoff nubs of ears pricked forward as he began to growl.

Mr. Morris cocked his head, upset, certain that Sardie had found them out. Eddie paused for a moment, and they steeled themselves for a confrontation, but no one came down the cellar stairs. Instead, the back door opened, then clattered shut as the footsteps withdrew. Eddie felt himself pulled back into real life, for this was no dream. His hands were sweating, but he managed to open the second lock, and at last threw open the door. A rush of dust, and heat, and darkness greeted him and then Coralie was with him, the scent of sulfur in her hair. She'd heard the cries of the wild beasts and the shouts of men. She'd dampened a cloth and tamped out any stray sparks that flew between the boards set across the windows. When clouds of smoke began filtering through the cracks in the stone foundation, she'd believed her life was about to end. She'd knelt on the dirt floor and said good-bye to the beautiful world. She'd held in her mind a vision of all she would miss: Brooklyn, the tortoise in its sandy enclosure, spring, the pear tree in the yard, Maureen's steady advice, the man who stood beside her now.

The fire alarms continued to ring so loudly that Coralie could hardly hear Eddie's words as he embraced her. She thought he said *The world is ours,* and she believed him, though it was tumbling down around them. By now the Dreamland tower had been set ablaze and could be seen for more than fifteen miles. Debris was picked up by the wind; all manner of burning belongings were flung into the air, only to set fire to other entertainments. Fire Chief Kenlon had ordered a double-nine alarm, a desperate plea that called upon all thirty-three fire departments in Kings County. Fireboats and tugboats approached from Gravesend Bay, using seawater to hose down the piers in an attempt to stop the fire from destroying the entire length of Coney Island. Huge crowds had begun to gather, but soon they were stopped a mile away from the sight. Anyone who passed the police stop point was entering into hell's gate itself—no ride, no trick, no loop-de-loop, but the scarlet portal of hell, with all its fire and agony.

To Coralie, being alive seemed a wondrous trick of fate, or perhaps it was a true miracle at last. She felt the least she could do was act on behalf of the creatures that had depended upon her. She thanked Mr. Morris for his kindness and his care, and told him to hurry and find Maureen, then began toward the exhibition hall. Eddie followed, Mitts at his heels, as he urged Coralie to come away. But she had already begun unclasping the doors of the birdcages, letting loose hummingbirds and cockatiels, along with a stray blackbird the Professor touted as Poe's pet raven when it was nothing more than a fledging that had fallen from its nest. When Coralie threw open the windows, smoke drifted inside, but the birds were able to make their escape. She turned then to glass containers of monarch butterflies, spotted beetles, and blue dragonflies, releasing them all in a swirl of color. At last she went to the tortoise's pen, and sat there weeping. This being that looked so monstrous to some had been a dear friend to her, defined by its patience and silence.

Eddie came to crouch beside her, concerned. "We can't save him."

"I can't leave him behind."

Eddie realized it simply was not in her nature to abandon even the lowliest creature. He felt overtaken by his love for her. Love like this wasn't what he'd planned or wanted or expected, surely it was indeed a trap, for even when you tried to run away, it followed you through the grass and lay down beside you, it overtook common sense and will-power. Though the fire was approaching, Eddie did as Coralie wished. He quickly struck down the low wooden wall of the flimsy pen with a few well-aimed kicks, then collected one of the velvet curtains at the doorway so they could push the tortoise onto it. He dragged the tortoise into the kitchen, with Coralie then making sure to hold the old beast steady as Eddie hauled it onto the porch, then hurriedly down the stairs. Already, the hedges were burning, the leaves turning to soot. The tortoise's shell clattered on the wood, the thud resounding so loudly Coralie feared they might mortally damage the very creature they intended to save. There was a last loud thump and the tortoise was free. It had been a hundred years since this had been so, and the poor thing seemed stunned, pulling in its limbs and head instinctively.

By now the air was billowing with smoke. Mr. Morris had searched the avenue for Maureen and had returned, having failed to discover her. He was beside himself with worry. "She should have been here hours ago. She's never late or thoughtless, especially when it comes to Cora."

It was then they spied her on the roof. The vision seemed like a dream, as all the night had been. In fact, Maureen had arrived too early, for she abhorred lateness, and the Professor had discovered her in the garden before Mr. Morris's rented carriage arrived. He'd grabbed her so that he might berate her, pulling her into the house to question her, demanding to know if she'd stolen the keys to his workshop and assisted the liveryman in his thievery. When flames broke out, he insisted she help him douse the roof with water. He did this every summer when lightning crossed the sky. Then and now his main concern was to ensure that all of his treasures would escape the fire. He was on the roof, at work with a hose that had been connected to the old well, shouting at Maureen, who'd been forced to fill buckets and pour them out inches away from the flames.

"He's going to finish the job," Mr. Morris said. "He'll have her burn to death."

Morris dashed inside, maddened, making his way upstairs so that he might gain access to the roof. He stepped out the window, as he had on the day he left his home, only on that occasion there was pouring rain and now the sky was pouring fire. Maureen went to him as soon as she saw him, forgetting that she was afraid of heights, and of fire, and of the Professor. She followed him through the window and then, at the last moment, thought to close and latch it.

In the kitchen, Maureen and Coralie embraced.

"I do not wish to leave you," Maureen told her charge, though Mr. Morris insisted they must do so immediately. She was streaked with soot, and her clothes were drenched. She clung to Coralie before stepping away. "But what we wish we cannot always have."

Coralie watched her dear friends go. They disappeared into the garden, then onto the avenue, where they would most likely seem like ordinary people, compared to what now roamed the streets. It was three in the morning, and there was a sudden shooting blaze above Dreamland. The tower that had burned for half an hour was now completely in flames. It crashed and hung on cables just above the animal arena. The keepers had no choice but to shoot as the animals attacked each other or leapt over the fences. In the yard Coralie and Eddie could hear screaming on the wind, and the horrible death song of Little Hip, whose keeper had returned to see his elephant burning alive. Dreamland was no longer an entertainment, and Brooklyn was no longer Kings County, but a wild country where the beasts ran down Surf Avenue.

The wind had shifted and the fire moved inland. In a matter of minutes sheets of it raced along the streets. The crowds on Surf Avenue panicked and ran, trampling one another, when a creature all in flames leapt through the Dreamland entrance. It was Black Prince they saw, the beloved lion, who raced through the crowd and across the street into the entrance of an entertainment called Rocky Road to Dublin, a scenic railroad ride to an outdoor pinnacle. The crowd backed away in terror, more so when the police began to fire at the lion despite the mass of human life. The creature climbed the ride until he reached the top and stood there in flames. It was his trainer, Bonavita, who had raised him as a cub and was more devoted to Black Prince than to his wife, who gave the order to shoot him. It took twenty-four bullets before he fell, and it was said the police were so terrified of him they split his head open with an ax to make sure he didn't somehow spring back to life. The crowd attacked the poor dead beast, vying for his tail and mane and teeth as souvenirs of this terrible night.

Sparks had been flung upon the roof of the Museum of Extraordinary Things, and the flames that raced along the eaves were impossible to douse. It was the only building on the north side of Surf Avenue to catch fire. Sardie had no choice but to give up his mission. He dropped the hose, which slithered across the roof and fell into the yard, water bursting upward in a rush, dousing the old pear tree. He went to the window, but the latch was down, and as he rattled it, trying to open it, he spied the wolf on the roof. The Professor had had contact with such creatures before, but only after they had been in the hands of a taxidermist. He had a dozen wolf's teeth in his collection, bought in Canada for a small sum, which he had attached to the mouths of certain specimens to make them appear more vicious. He'd been the master of creature after creature, but not when they were alive and on an equal footing. He ran from the beast, but there was no escape in the air, and he tumbled from the peak of the roof with no net to catch him, and no one who could reach out and break his fall.

By then, the police began to shoot every animal they saw. Bears and their cubs, horses gone mad, trained birds that could speak in a dozen languages, several tigers, along with a yellow-eyed wolf perched atop the roof of a small museum entirely set aflame, a loyal creature who plunged into the dark garden, lifeless before he landed beside the house.

The tar on the streets was melting and a streetcar burned, letting off oily black clouds. Police went door to door, alerting those who lived nearby to flee. People ran north and east; they climbed into storm cellars and jumped into boats so they might head out to sea. By now the Dreamland Pier was smoldering. The Atlantic had turned dark with cinders and the seaweed washing onto the shore was sparked with embers, giving off the scent of hellfire and salt. Eddie stood in the grass that had already begun to burn. He thought of his mother, and how she had remained a part of him, how he'd carried her with him, just as his father had. He kissed Coralie, believing this to be their good-bye, but she pulled away and said "You know the world is ours," even though the roof had caught, a line of flames flaring along the gables and the eaves where the Professor had fallen. Eddie wondered if Coralie would suggest they try to make it to the shore, though clearly that was impossible. Every inch between the museum and the beach was burning. By morning little would be standing, with more than four million dollars in property burned, and Dreamland completely destroyed. Johnson's carousel, the Whirlwind Ride, Taunton's Bathing Pavilion, Balmer's Baths, nearly everything along the New Iron Pier would be ashes.

But rather than flee, Coralie pulled Eddie back into the house. Surely she knew it was a death trap, and that every extraordinary thing contained within would burn in a matter of minutes. Still, she insisted. They went through the kitchen, into the parlor, the pit bull following at his master's heels. There was the cereus plant embellished with two enormous white blooms. This was the plant's one extraordinary night, but already the flowers were closing, dying so rapidly it was possible for the human eye to see the life sifting out of it. The petals were folding up more and more with every instant, no longer brilliant white, but a pale dove gray.

Coralie led Eddie to the exhibition hall, emptied now of all living creatures. The only things remaining were bones and minerals and the preserved bodies of creatures that would never again be seen: the white alligator, the cat with five legs, the conjoined monkey twins that held each other's hands. Coralie bid them all good-bye. They were already melting. The heat caused the chemicals inside the glass canisters to rise to a boil and the glass to crack. All at once, there was a wash of clear liquid upon the floor, as there had been in Coralie's dreams when she was a little girl, when there was so little difference between night and day she expected her dreams and nightmares to greet her at the breakfast table.

They went to the tank where she had been displayed. In her confinement she had always felt a sort of safety, cut off from the outside world of men and their cruelty. Eddie hesitated, confused, possessing the panicked notion that they were entering into their coffin, a place from which there was no escape. He thought of his father at the dock, how his coat floated out around him when he hit the water. They could hear the fire consuming the house with a whoosh of living breath. It swept through the upstairs bedrooms and was racing down the stairs, devouring carpets and beds, wooden banisters and the umber-colored Oriental rug in the Professor's library. The books caught all at once, the paper flaming into red ash, the leather bindings curling up and flickering into flame. The fire caught the withering cereus plant in its grasp. The twiggy stems caught first, becoming embers in an instant. The fading flowers turned rose-red and soared up to the ceiling before fluttering down to the floor. They carried a fragrant mix of perfume and salt water and cinders.

Coralie dove into the tank, keeping her head above water. "Now," she told him, for the walls were moving, bending in toward them. Eddie thought he was imagining it, but the plaster was curling up, inching away from the fire. Mitts looked at his master beseechingly, trusting as always. Eddie lifted the dog, dumping him into the tank before splashing in after him. Coralie took his hand, pulling him down, like a mermaid who had captured a sailor, and, like a sailor who desperately wanted that capture, he sank down beside her. She had the breathing tube, which she passed to him, for she herself seemed to have no need for air at all. Perhaps she was more fish than even she had imagined. Eddie gratefully took in air, then grabbed Mitts and pulled the dog to the bottom of the tank, placing the tube in the dog's mouth.

A sheet of fire passed over them. It was only seconds, but they could feel the burst of heat as the world turned bright and red. If the air they breathed through the tube hadn't been cooled by murky water, surely they would have burned their lungs. As it was, they huddled together while the water turned black until the roar of the fire moved farther away. Chunks of plaster fell from the charred wooden beams, walls caved in, windows stood alone in empty space. When Eddie climbed from the tank, the half-drowned pit bull under his arm, he found himself standing in a boiling soup, a mixture of spiders and crystals and shards of glass. Luckily he and Coralie had not had time to remove their shoes.

They found the wolf, shot, sprawled out in the blackened grass. They buried him beneath the pear tree, for it was the one thing in the garden to survive the blaze. Though the earth was hot with cinders, Eddie took a shovel from beside the trash heap. He dug until his hands were burning, and each breath burned as well, until Coralie stopped him, assuring him the grave was deep enough. Eddie set the wolf into the earth, knowing he was not made for the streets men built or for the cities they constructed. The hermit had been correct in his assessment. A city as great as New York grew without regard to men and beasts, and where it resided, certain creatures were no longer welcome. As they left, Coralie spied the tortoise. It had crawled under the porch to dig into the cooler earth, where green weeds were matted down. That was where they left the ancient beast, to enjoy its freedom.

On Surf Avenue people were sitting on the stoops of burned-out buildings and weeping. There were children who had seen wild animals on the rooftops, and women who had lost their husbands, and families who had been burned out of their homes and owned nothing, not a scrap of cloth or a cooking pot. There was a scrim of black clouds above them and the sidewalks were hot beneath their shoes. Coralie and Eddie had nothing but the soaking wet clothes they wore, which dried later in the day as they navigated through the marshes, for the sun was bright by then. Eddie knew the way. He and the liveryman had followed this very route, and had stopped nearby to view the body of Hannah Weiss, a young girl who had been robbed of her life.

Nothing was fair in this beautiful world. There were blackbirds settled on stalks of tall plumy grass, and the sky was blue and gold. Mitts walked soberly beside his master. The dog would never be as free-spirited again, and from that time forward he shied away from water, even when they moved outside the city and could see the Hudson from their porch. Eddie, on the other hand, was drawn to water after that night. He drank eight glasses every day, which he had come to believe was a tonic, good for the long life Hochman had promised he'd have. Each time he embraced the woman he loved, he thought of water, for he knew she longed for it, and, because of this, she had saved his life.

At night, when the window was open and his arms were around Coralie, he often dreamed he was fishing. As he slept he prayed that no one would wake him, for it was in dreams that a man found his truest desires. At last he came upon the trout he had been searching for, a slice of living light, darting through the shallows. He walked into the water after it, unafraid, still wearing his shoes, his black coat flowing out around him. It was there he found his father, waiting for him on the shoreline, as if they'd never been apart.

THE WORLD BEGINS AGAIN

****

Dear Maureen,

I hope that you are finding Richmond, Virginia, a pleasant
place to be. I was delighted to hear that Mr. Morris inherited
all that his family owned, and I was so happy to receive the
photograph of you standing beside him in your wedding dress
outside the house where he grew up. With all its flourishes and
the many balconies surrounded by white wrought iron, the house
reminded me of a wedding cake.

I myself am married now, and happily so. Our service was
small and I did not understand many of the customs, but I
understood my husband's love for me, and mine for him. For
us, that is enough. Sometimes I dream I am back in the museum
and there are flames and I can hear the tortoise crying, but
I know it's only a dream. I know a tortoise doesn't have the
capacity to weep, or so the scientists say. But I am less of a
believer in what people say these days. I want to see the proof.
Now I judge the world through my own eyes.

There are still rumors about a creature in the Hudson. They
say it was caught, and for a little while it was kept in a tank in

*Brooklyn, before that world ended in fire. While the fires burned,
the creature dragged itself over the low dunes, searching for
water. But others say that water was not the element it needed,
and that it was searching for love, for love changes everything,
and forces us into lives we never imagined we might lead.*

*In the village where we now reside, in a valley beside the
Hudson, there are rumors as well. People whisper about a
woman who swims in the deepest channels, one who can hold
her breath for so long she seems to disappear. Where we are,
the river runs silver and it is wider than I would have ever
imagined. It seems to go on forever; the current travels only
one way, to the south and the harbor of New York City. When
darkness falls, and the sky sifts down into the river, the woman
who swims in its depths holds on to the side of a canoe that drifts
toward her. She pulls herself into the boat, where a tall man
is waiting in the fading light, for he is an expert in matters
of light and darkness, a master of seeing through shadows.
He spies her every time, even when the sky is murky and she
is invisible to all other men's eyes. The water here in the north
Hudson is so cold that it's common knowledge no human can
withstand it, only creatures of the deep, miraculous things that
cannot be categorized or kept under glass.*

*I dream about the wondrous people that I knew, and the
shelves that were laden with butterflies and bones. Most often,
I dream of that extraordinary night flower I had the privilege
to watch bloom. In my dreams the flower is alive, with a bloody,
beating heart, all of its life lived intensely and with great
beauty, over in mere moments, as I now believe ours is as well.*

A lifetime is a lifetime whether it lasts one night or a hundred years.

I know we lived among extraordinary things but, perhaps more importantly, in extraordinary times. People may or may not remember the heroes and the villains of our day, but all that the brave among us did, and all that they were, remains with us still. We had a year in which everything changed, when the world shifted and became something new. We no longer expected cruelty or mistreatment. We expected more.

I give thanks that the Professor's manuscript burned on our last day in Brooklyn. I often look up into the night sky and imagine that every spark that flew upward from the burning paper became another star, for the nights seem far brighter to me now and the sky is dashed with heavenly light. I know what he did to you. I will never mention it again, for it seems unthinkable that a human being could be so sinister in his actions and so evil in his intentions. It happened in the years of cruelty, when we didn't know there was a better life. You were only a young woman when you met the Professor, and he had a side that could convince someone his approval was worth any price. I, more than anyone, can understand that. Perhaps this was his greatest trick, to be two people at the same time, the cruel person who betrayed those who came close, and the man who presented another world, one filled with miracles and books. Professor Sardie surely charmed you when you first encountered him; he made you believe in him, he was a conjurer, after all. You were ambushed by how brightly his attentions burned. When a star reaches for you, it is difficult to look away.

I cannot imagine the moment when you came through the door late one evening, detained by crowds on the streets, or by a slow shopkeeper, and saw him on the threshold with the vial filled with acid. I can't imagine the words he said to you, or how you might have pleaded with him. He wanted to teach you a lesson for crimes you didn't commit. He was jealous and he wanted to possess you, but you had never loved him. I know that. But I also know why you stayed. You resolved to have faith in the future, and to watch over me, and to teach me what the world was like. You taught me well. I know how to make preserves from ripe pears, how to plant a garden, how to love someone.

I will not write down all the Professor did to me, but suffice it to say he controlled me for a time, and I seemed unable to fight him. But then there came a day when I could. Perhaps I had been practicing to do exactly that for my entire life. In our time it was not difficult to make a woman feel she was not worth much, to convince her to be quiet and not cause a ruckus and insist she keep her thoughts to herself. But my father made one mistake when he raised me. In the past I thought his error was that he allowed me to be a swimmer, and that my abilities in the water gave me the resolve to defy him. But I was wrong in my estimation of how I managed to break away from him. The mistake he made was you. He should have kept us apart. He should have dismissed you before I could walk or speak or think. Every day that we spent together was a day I treasure. You taught me who I was.

I lived among miracles, but the greatest miracle of all was that you stayed for me. I would have drowned without you to watch over me. I think you knew that. I now understand there are a thousand ways to drown, and a thousand ways to rescue

*someone. I never properly thanked you for saving my life.
From reading the Professor's notes, I know you arrived to ask
for work the day after he found me in the yard. Whether that
was pure luck or a well-drawn plan no longer matters. Whether
you were the one who placed me on the porch steps when you
were unable to care for me, or whether it was a woman I will
never meet in this lifetime, matters even less. I remember how
you stood outside the back door when my father made you leave.
The light was fading, and I was soon enough locked away, but
for one vivid instant I saw you and you saw me in return. I will
always think of you as you were that day, for it is an image no
other can replace. I believe we saw the edges of one another's
souls.*

*In the charred remains of the museum I found a burned
letter you asked Mr. Morris to write to me, because you hadn't
been taught how to write out your thoughts. You had intended
to present the letter to me someday, but that day didn't come
before our world ended. I hadn't the ability to write either,
although I have learned, and my handwriting is surprisingly
fluid. Clearly a reader can become a writer, and for as long as I
can remember I could read as well as anyone. If my father gave
me anything, he gave me that. There were only a few words
left in the remains of the letter, but I think I made out the word
daughter. Whether or not I did, I see that word in blue ink. I
hear it said by you.*

*In my memories I have set my life in Brooklyn between
pieces of glass, separate from my current existence, and this has
enabled me to move forward. The past cannot tie me in knots,
nor can it reach for me and cause me to drown. And yet what
is stored in glass belongs to me still. Each piece is a part of me:*

the hummingbirds, the locked doors, Mr. Morris in the yard, the pear tree, the woman covered by bees, and you. Especially you.

We have made our home in a small village. People here know our names and our business, as we know theirs. There is a market and a dairy, and we have a large garden in which we grow beans and squash. I have two sheep, Matilda and Mary, funny creatures who follow me as I do my chores.

I spin in the evenings, and I often dye the yarn with madder root, the very herb you used to heal me when I was in need of help. All of the yarn I sell is red and I do quite well. I have even garnered a small amount of fame. People say my yarn is the color of roses. As it turned out, I have a talent for knitting. My hands, hidden for so long, are more agile than most. I have never worn gloves again. Even in the depths of winter I prefer to have my hands free. The sweaters and scarves I stitch are sold in Manhattan, at shops on Fifth Avenue. I wait for my husband on the days he brings my work into the city, the knit work wrapped in brown paper and string. I stand at the crossroads of our village where there is an elm growing that is said to be one of the oldest trees in New York. The Lenape people met here as dusk bloomed, so they might climb as far as they could into the sky and in doing so be closer to the Milky Way, the path to heaven and to those they had loved and lost. Some evenings there are dozens of starlings perched on the branches of the elm tree. When I see them, I think of our liveryman, who had more troubles with the law, but has now gone off to fight in the war overseas and is said to be a hero. I think that people can surprise you in so many ways, both with cruelty and with kindness.

I stand at the crossroads until the dark sifts down between the leaves. My husband often brings back the most unusual

items from the city. A present from the milliner's shop on
Twenty-third Street, where you bought your green felt hat.
A book of his photographs, published in a beautiful edition.
A wedding gift to us from his father, a fragile, old quilt that
carries the scent of grass. Once, most surprisingly of all, he
arrived from the city with two black dogs, haughty-looking
beasts with matching haircuts that now love to roll in mud and
run through the meadows with Mitts.

Every time I meet my husband beneath that tree, I insist we
walk home slowly. It's my way of making each day last a little
longer.

It was an ordinary life I wished for, and that is what I
have. Each time I swim in the river I am driven forward when
I imagine my front door, the windows facing east and north, the
dogs on the porch, my husband at his work, recording the beauty
of the trees in the woods so that no one will forget them. I still
have the portrait he made of you in our garden. It is the only
thing I saved from that time.

I pray that one day we meet again so that I can properly
thank you, for no one could have asked for a kinder, more
devoted friend. I hope you know I was always loyal to you. I
am loyal to you still. I do not know, and I may never know, if
you are my mother, but, as I could wish for no better woman
to have brought me into the world, I will consider you to be so.
You are the one who taught me that love was never what we
expected it to be and that it was all we needed. For that, and for
a thousand other things, I send my gratitude.

Acknowledgments

T HERE ARE some years when everything seems to change all at once. 1911 is such a year. I have tried to do justice to this time and to New York City. Although I grew up on Long Island, I spent a great deal of my childhood in Brooklyn and in Chelsea and have lived in Chelsea on and off for most of my adult life. I have lived elsewhere, but at all times I have seen New York for what it is, a wonder of the world.

This book is dedicated to my grandfathers, Michael Hoffman and Chaim Klurfeld. One began his working life in a pie factory at the age of twelve, then became one of the first electricians to light up Brooklyn, before going on to help bring modern Chelsea to life during and after the Depression. The other was a union man, a member of the ILGWU and the Workmen's Circle who was dedicated to the rights of working men and women. His writings, some of which were published in the newspaper the *Forward*, focused on the labor movement and on his childhood in Poland. Much like my character Eddie, my grandfather's political conversion began in a single afternoon when he heard the factory owner's children playing—in his case, swimming in a lake on a hot summer day beside the factory where he worked twelve-hour days at the age of eight.

I have tried to present the two fires that frame this book—the Triangle Shirtwaist Factory Fire and the Dreamland Fire—as best I could within a historical context while using imaginary lives and fates. Characters who are based on real people, including Monk Eastman, the gangster, and Abraham Hochman, the Jewish mystic, are real enough, and therefore their characters mirror the facts as closely as possible, but they, too, have been viewed through the glass of my imaginings.

A special thanks to Rob Linne from the Adelphi University School of Education, who first suggested I write an article commemorating the anniversary of the Triangle Fire. In doing the research for the piece, published in the *Los Angeles Times*, I was also beginning this novel and reconnecting with my own personal history as a New Yorker.

Although any historical errors are my own, I extend my deepest gratitude to the experts who were kind enough to read the manuscript and offer their comments. Many thanks to Suzanne Wasserman, historian, filmmaker, and director of the Gotham Center at the City College of New York for her support, her insights, and her knowledge about the Lower East Side. My gratitude to Annelise Orleck, author and professor of history at Dartmouth College, who took the time to carefully read the novel and offer suggestions and whose specialties in women's history, political history, Jewish history, and the history of American radicalism made her comments invaluable. Last, my heartfelt thanks to Charles Denson, author and executive director of the Coney Island History Project for his thoughtful reading of the manuscript. As a great fan of his writings and the work he has done on behalf of Coney Island, I was honored to count him among my early readers.

To Nan Graham, my brilliant editor, and to Susan Moldow, my beloved publisher, who have both changed my writing and my life. I could not be more fortunate or more grateful.

Gratitude to Carolyn Reidy for her continuing support, which means so much to me.

Many thanks to Roz Lippel for helping me feel at home at Scribner.

To Suzanne Baboneau, publisher of Simon & Schuster UK, deep gratitude for championing my books in the UK, and for so much support, then and now.

Thank you to Whitney Frick for her sharp eye, attention to detail, and care taken in her reading of this novel. Thanks to Kara Watson for her kind help in readying the manuscript for publication.

Thank you to Susan Brown for her copyediting knowledge and insight.

Many thanks to Katherine Monaghan for her invaluable assistance before, after, and during publication. To Camille McDuffie, who has helped bring many of my books into the world, many thanks for her grace and good advice.

To Maggie Stern, for years of invaluable friendship.

To Tom Martin, for always being my first reader and the first person I turn to.

A most special thank-you to Ron Bernstein, dear friend and agent from the beginning, and to Amanda Urban, for her generous friendship and wise counsel.

Thank you to the Lyceum Agency.

To everyone at the Elaine Markson Agency, especially Gary Johnson, many thanks for many years of working together.

And to Elaine Markson, I offer my deepest gratitude and love. Words cannot express my thanks or begin to list all you have given me, as an agent and a friend. I would never have been here without you.

—Alice Hoffman

F URTHER READING for those who wish to know more about the history explored in *The Museum of Extraordinary Things*.

Coney Island

Denson, Charles. *Coney Island Lost and Found.* Ten Speed Press, 2002.

Hartzman, Marc. *American Sideshow: An Encyclopedia of History's Most Wondrous and Curiously Strange Performers.* Tarcher Penguin, 2006.

Kasson, John E. *Amusing the Millions.* Hill and Wang, 1978.

McCullough, Edo. *Good Old Coney Island.* Fordham University Press, 2000.

Lower East Side and Triangle Fire and New York City

Argersinger, Jo Ann. *The Triangle Fire: A Brief History with Documents.* Bedford/ St. Martin's, 2009.

Ballon, Hillary, ed. *The Greatest Grid: The Master Plan of Manhattan, 1811–2011.* Museum of the City of New York, 2012.

Benin, Leigh, Rob Linne, Adrienne Sosin, Joel Sosinsky with the Workers United (ILGWU) and HBO Documentary Films. *Images of America: The New York City Triangle Factory Fire.* Arcadia Publishing, 2011.

Ellis, Edward Robb. *The Epic of New York City: A Narrative History.* Basic Books, 1996, 2005.

Gray, Christopher, ed. *Fifth Avenue: 1911 from Start to Finish in Historic Block-by-Block Photographs.* Dover Publications, 1994.

Homberger, Eric. *The Historical Atlas of New York City: A Visual Celebration of 400 Years of New York City's History.* Henry Holt, 1994; Holt Paperbacks, 2005.

Israelowitz, Oscar, and Brian Merlis. *Manhattan's Lower East Side in Vintage Photographs*. Israelowitz Publishing, 2011.

Jackson, Kenneth T., and David S. Dunbar. *Empire City: New York Through the Centuries*. Columbia University Press, 2002.

Sanders, Ronald. *The Lower East Side: A Guide to Its Jewish Past in 99 Photographs*. Dover Books, 1980.

von Drehle, David. *Triangle: The Fire That Changed America*. Grove Press, 2003.

Ziegelman, Jane. *97 Orchard: An Edible History of Five Immigrant Families in One New York Tenement*. HarperCollins, 2010.

Photography

Bann, Stephen, ed. *Art and the Early Photographic Album*. Yale University Press, 2011.

Burns, Ric, James Sanders, and Lisa Ades. *New York: An Illustrated History*. Knopf, 2011.

Gilman Paper Company Collection. *The Waking Dream: Photography's First Century*. Henry Abrams, 1993.

Lavedrine, Bertrand, et al. *Photographs of the Past: Process and Preservation*. Getty Conservation Institute, 2009.

Newhall, Beaumont. *The History of Photography from 1839 to the Present*. Museum of Modern Art, 2009.

Newhouse, Alana, ed. *A Living Lens: Photographs of the Jewish Life from the Pages of the Forward*. W. W. Norton, 2007.

For more, please visit AliceHoffman.com.

The Museum

of

Extraordinary

Things

Alice Hoffman

Coralie Sardie grows up in her father's "museum" on the Coney Island boardwalk where she appears as a living mermaid. Nightly swims in the Hudson River provide her only escape from her father's influence. One night, she encounters a handsome photographer named Eddie Cohen, a Russian immigrant who has turned his back on his Orthodox community. When Eddie photographs the devastating Triangle Shirtwaist Factory Fire, he is drawn into the mystery of a factory worker's disappearance, and back to the Lower East Side neighborhood he had abandoned. Set against the colorful, volatile world of early-twentieth-century New York City, Alice Hoffman's latest novel is a love story as strange and fantastic as anything The Museum of Extraordinary Things holds.

Topics and Questions for Discussion

1. The novel is framed by two spectacular fires. Why do you think the author chose to structure the novel this way? What effect does each fire have on the major characters and on the people of Manhattan and Brooklyn?

2. How does Raymond Morris, known as the Wolfman, change Coralie's perception of her father and their circumscribed world? What parallels does Coralie find between her own life and those of the characters in *Jane Eyre*?

3. Why does Coralie keep Maureen in the dark about her night swims and her father's sexual exploitation? Would Maureen have been able to protect Coralie if she had known?

4. Eddie says "the past was what we carried with us, threaded to the future, and we decided whether to keep it close or let it go" (139). Was Eddie able to let his past go? Did you sympathize with his decision to move away from his father?

5. Why does Eddie feel compelled to solve the mystery of Hannah Weiss's disappearance? What makes him a good "finder"?

6. When Coralie steps into the lion's cage, the trainer Bonavita tells her "you have a form of bravery inside you" (196). Do you agree? Does Coralie agree? In what instances does she defy her father, and when does she acquiesce to his demands?

7. Consider Coralie's claim that "curiosity had always been my downfall" (253). Did her curiosity about her father and the outside world worsen her situation or improve it? How naïve is Coralie?

8. What did you make of the living wonders at The Museum of Extraordinary Things? How did their treatment differ at Dreamland? What enables some of the wonders, such as the Butterfly Girl, to achieve a semblance of a normal life?

9. What sort of atmosphere does Alice Hoffman create by using dreams as a recurring motif? How do Coralie's and Eddie's dreams expose their inner lives and connect them to the past and future?

10. Professor Sardie and Abraham Hochman both present themselves as things they are not. How did you feel about their deception and self-aggrandizement? Do circumstances make one worse than the other? In what ways did the culture of early-twentieth-century New York City favor the corrupt and those who bent the rules?

11. Where, and to whom, did Eddie look "to find what [he] was missing" (327)? What did Moses Levy, Abraham Hochman, the hermit, and Mr. Weiss each have to teach him?

12. Why did Maureen choose to stay with the Professor and Coralie, in spite of his treatment of her? Of the lessons that Maureen taught Coralie, which were the most important?

13. Consider the role animals play in the novel. Why does Coralie save the tortoise? What is the symbolism of the trout that Eddie

cannot kill? In what other instances do animals reveal something about a character?

14. In thinking of her father, Coralie says "perhaps there is evil in certain people, a streak of meanness that cannot be erased by circumstance or fashioned into something brand new by love" (246). Do you think a person can be innately evil? Are the morally ambiguous actions of other characters, such as Eddie or the liveryman, redeemed?

15. Hoffman's portrait of New York City is of a rapidly evolving, volatile place. Which historical details stood out most vividly to you? If you've spent time in New York, was it hard to imagine the city as it was in the early twentieth century? What places are currently undergoing similar transformations or experiencing similar tensions?